FAVORITE MALADY

A DARK STALKER ROMANCE

JULIA SYKES

Cover Design: Jaqueline Kropmanns - Design

Editing: Rebecca Cartee

TRIGGER WARNINGS

This is a deeply personal book for me, and it's been a cathartic way to process trauma. However, I never want to upset someone who might find the themes disturbing. Please check my website for more information:

Julia-sykes.com

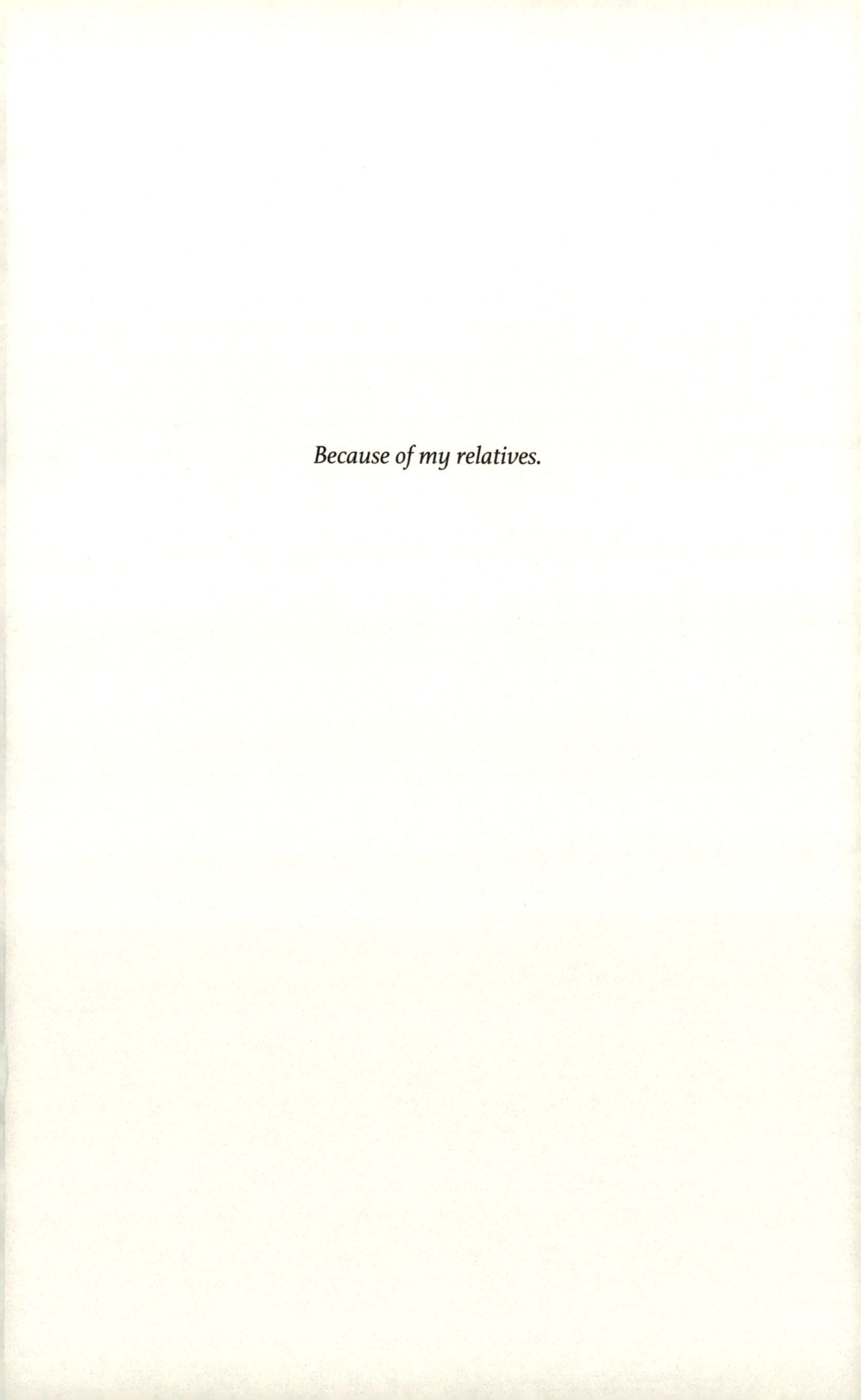

Because of my relatives.

PROLOGUE

ABBY

The masked man is waiting for me in the midnight shadows of my apartment.

I stumble slightly as I close the front door behind me and search blindly for the light switch. Before my palm brushes the hard plastic knob, strong fingers ensnare my wrist, and a broad body slams into mine. A gloved hand clamps over my mouth, muffling my shocked cry. My arm is wrenched behind me, and I'm forced to turn when my shoulder screams in protest. The intruder uses his grip on my arm as a lever to control my body, and I'm pinned in an instant, my cheek pressing against the inside of my front door.

The lingering, pleasant buzz of alcohol disappears from my mind like fog evaporating beneath harsh morning light, and my entire world sharpens in a burst of adrenaline.

I try to shove away from the door with my free hand, but my short nails scrabble uselessly against the peeling ivory paint. My other wrist is pinned behind my back, and my attacker's weight keeps me trapped between him and the door.

A low growl rumbles against my nape. The man's hand on my face slides upward, covering my nose and mouth. I can't breathe.

My entire body seizes with panic, and I writhe in his hold.

He releases my trapped wrist for a split second, but I don't have the time or space to fight him off before a sharp clicking noise is followed by a cold blade at my throat.

"Quiet." His voice is deep and rough, almost inhuman. "Don't fight me, and I won't hurt you."

It's a lie, but I have no choice: I comply.

My tears fall in silent streams as my world shatters, and my masked attacker breaks me down to reveal the most painful, darkest parts of my soul.

1

DANE

Three Months Earlier

The stunning woman at the bar has a quirky purple streak in her hair and a striking freckle on her right cheekbone. It's large enough that it's visible even at a distance. In my line of work, patients have asked me to remove smaller blemishes, but the longer I look at her, the more I think that it suits her. The mark makes her unique, and I admire the fact that she wears it with pride. She hasn't made an effort to conceal it with makeup.

Her posture is perfect, but her eyes stray to the floor even when she's speaking to her friends. The dichotomy intrigues me. She's shy, but her bearing indicates confidence.

A man approaches her where she's swaying her hips near the bar. She can't seem to fully stop dancing even while she's waiting in the queue to order her drink.

The man steps into her personal space without invitation and leans in close to speak in her ear, presumably under the guise of being heard over the Latin music.

She stops swaying in her gentle dance, and her willowy body goes stiff.

The bastard doesn't seem to notice her obvious discomfort.

I'm prowling toward him before I realize what I'm doing.

"Dane?" I hear my associate, Meadows, call after me, but I wave him off.

He's known me long enough that he won't be offended by the dismissal; he's never gotten in the way of a conquest before.

I'm with her in seconds, and the man is still far too close to her. My hand closes around his shoulder, and I drag him away from her. My grip is firm enough that the threat of violence is clear, but I don't toss him to the ground like I want to. I'm not sure how she would react to that, and I don't want to scare the woman who's captured my full attention.

And I don't want to get into a bar fight on my first night out in Charleston. That wouldn't reflect well on my new practice with Meadows. He has social connections in the area, and I can't afford for word to get out that I'm dangerous.

The man who was harassing her tenses in my grip and whirls to face me. His fists clench, but before he can raise them, his eyes meet mine.

I don't bother to hide the monster within. I let him see exactly how cold and unfeeling I am—hurting him means absolutely nothing to me. I could destroy him without a second thought.

One of the advantages of lacking the impulse for empathy.

"She doesn't want to talk to you," I say smoothly, looming over the smaller man. "You should go."

It's not a suggestion; it's a threat.

He's in between me and my pretty prey, and I won't tolerate his presence for another second.

He's smart enough to get the hell out of my way before I force him to move. He swallows hard, and his shoulders dip in submission as he slinks off onto the crowded dance floor.

"Thanks," she says, her voice so shy and soft that I barely hear her over the music. Her eyes drop to the sticky floor. "You didn't have to do that."

"He was harassing you," I reply smoothly. "I absolutely did have to do that."

I decide not to tell her that I simply wanted to do it. Because he was a nuisance, and I want to talk to her. And he was making her uncomfortable.

Over the years, I've found that women like to feel protected.

Her cautious eyes lift to meet mine, and I'm momentarily stunned at their clear, aquamarine hue.

"Thank you," she says again, and this time, she doesn't glance away.

It takes all of my willpower to stop myself from closing the short distance between us so that she'll tip her head back and offer those rosebud lips to me.

I'm not a single-minded fool like the idiot who invaded her personal space.

I'm a careful monster, the perfect predator.

And I always capture my prey.

Judging by the way her lovely eyes are studying my face, I already have her interest. Women have always found me attractive, so this part is easy enough.

"You don't have to thank me," I say smoothly. "But you can let me buy you a drink."

Her delicately arched brows draw together. "You want to buy me a drink?"

I allow an indulgent smile to tilt my lips, even though I'm slightly irked that she seems the tiniest bit hesitant to accept. "I do."

She presses those pretty lips together, considering me for a second. Her clear-eyed gaze pins me with discomfiting intensity, and I find myself looking to the bartender to catch his attention.

I choose to ignore the odd moment.

When the bartender meets my eye, I place our order. "Another whiskey and a cosmopolitan."

The whiskey here is cheap, but I can't stomach the thought of masking the acrid flavor with a soft drink. My lovely companion, on the other hand, has sipped two pink cocktails in the last hour. It's not difficult to guess that she wants something sugary.

"Oh," she says. "I was drinking the slushies." She gestures at the machine filled with an icy pink drink at the back of the bar. There's a sign advertising two for ten dollars. "I can pay for mine."

I suppress a frown at her resistance. Instead, I arrange my features into my most charming smile.

The cosmopolitan appears on the bar before me. "I'm not going to drink this. It'd be a shame for it to go to waste."

Proving my point, I take a sip of my whiskey, refusing to touch the sickly-sweet concoction.

She eyes me warily, and I choose to wait her out, quirking an expectant eyebrow.

"Okay." She sighs and reaches for the drink. "Thank you."

"What's your name?" I ask.

"Abigail. But everyone calls me Abby."

I don't want to be *everyone* to this woman. I want her to feel special. Desired.

She's strangely hesitant to succumb to my charms. My smile sharpens slightly. It's been a long time since I've been presented with a proper challenge.

"I'm Dane. Enjoy your drink, Abigail," I reply, savoring the flavor of her name on my tongue.

She lifts the frosted glass and takes a sip, as though she's complying without fully thinking through her actions.

Submissive.

Perfect.

As soon as she tastes the cocktail, her eyes practically roll back in bliss. They remain closed for a second, as though she's experiencing ecstasy at the sugar hit.

Hunger tightens my gut. She's definitely shy, but she's completely guileless. Her rapturous expression holds nothing back.

Her broad grin hits me square in the chest.

"This is *so good.*"

Fuck, the way she lingers over the words makes it sound like she could orgasm from her sensory response to nothing more than a sweet drink.

She'll sound beautiful when she screams my name in bed.

"I'm glad you like it," I say, half a heartbeat later than I should.

Something about this woman challenges my usual composure. I can't predict her actions, and she doesn't easily fall into my seductive games.

She almost refused my offer to buy her a drink, but then she submitted when I used a firmer tone with her.

I'm intrigued.

She's beautiful, but that's not what attracts me to her. As a plastic surgeon, I see beautiful women every day, and they come to me to make them even more physically perfect.

With her enchanting freckle and understated but lovely lips, Abigail isn't perfect.

But she might just be the most enticing woman I've ever met, and I've only spoken to her for a few minutes.

"Where are you from?" she asks. "I like your accent."

My chest warms at the first admission of her attraction to me, and my smile tilts into a smirk. Her gaze fixes on my mouth.

She's just as intrigued as I am.

"England," I reply. "But I've lived in the States for a while now. Are you from Charleston? I'm new here."

I like her accent too. There's a soft Southern drawl that makes her words almost breathy, but it's subtle enough to not be a distraction. I want to hear her panting and begging in my bed in that sultry voice.

She takes another sip of her drink, as though she can't resist sampling the sweetness on her tongue.

"I grew up around here," she says. "And I've lived in Charleston since college. It's such a beautiful city. I'm sure you'll love it here."

"Yes," I agree, allowing my gaze to flick over her face in obvious appreciation. "Beautiful."

A pretty shade of pink flushes her cheeks, and she takes a bigger gulp of her drink.

I'm starting to find her shyness charming. Will she blush when I lean in close and whisper all the filthy things I want to do to her?

Resolutely, I maintain a respectful distance between us.

My prey isn't ready to be cornered. She strikes me as a soft-spoken, sweet Southern belle. Judging by her perfect posture, she's probably a good girl, well-behaved. She'll be scandalized by my perverted plans for her, but I'm confident that I can bend her to my will.

"Have you been to Battery Park yet?" Her voice is a touch higher now as she struggles to make small talk when I'm practically burning her with my intense gaze.

I should probably soften that intensity, but I'm enjoying the edgy energy crackling between us too much to rein myself in. She sways toward me ever so slightly, drawn in by the threat lurking behind my cocky smirk.

"I haven't been to the park yet. I only arrived in town a few days ago. You can show me around."

I let my mask slip a bit further, and my smile sharpens. I keep her pinned in my steady, unwavering stare, and her lips part slightly on a panting intake of breath.

She drops her gaze and drains the last inch of her drink, as though she needs the cool liquid to soothe her flushed skin.

"What brought you to Charleston?" she counters instead of immediately agreeing to be my tour guide.

I smother a small frown at her renewed resistance. The chemistry we share is undeniable, electric. But perhaps it's potent enough to make her uncomfortable. I must be right about her: she's a good girl.

"I came here for work," I say simply.

I don't care to talk about my job; it doesn't define me. It's just a way to make money and afford the lifestyle I desire.

Before she can press for more information, I flag down the bartender and order her another cosmopolitan.

"I can get it," she says quickly, reaching into her purse.

I pay with my black card before she can fully pull out a wad of one-dollar bills.

Interesting. She's scraping money together to pay for her drinks, but she doesn't want me to take care of her.

Out of pride?

I shake off my curiosity. Her reasons don't matter; she won't pay for another drink tonight. She will have to accept that.

Women usually love being taken care of. This isn't the first time I've engaged in this little game where a woman reaches for her purse. But it is the first time that I truly believe she's uncomfortable with me paying. It's confounding, especially considering her meager funds.

I have plenty of money, and I want to spend it on her.

"I've got it." I deepen my tone again, brooking no resistance as I press the cocktail glass into her hand.

She accepts it without further protest.

Definitely submissive.

She takes another long draw of her drink, a sign of nervousness that I savor even as I worry that she might be drinking too fast. With her slender frame, I'd be surprised if she can handle much alcohol.

"You should check out Folly Beach sometime," she says, making more small talk to soothe her nerves. She's painstakingly polite, and she seems almost conditioned to continue the conversation.

Definitely a good Carolina girl.

I'll enjoy corrupting her later.

But for now, she won't drink more. I have no interest in taking a drunk woman home with me.

I want her fully aware of every moment we share, every drop of pleasure I wring from her delicate body.

"I'd love to go to the beach with you sometime," I say, maintaining my assertion that she'll show me around the area.

It's strange that I'm setting a date with a woman I barely know. Usually, a night or two is enough to sate my physical needs.

But I definitely wouldn't mind spending more time in Abigail's company. She's a puzzle I haven't quite figured out, and I won't let her go until I solve it.

I reach out and pluck the half-empty cocktail glass from her hand before setting it on the bar alongside my whiskey.

"Dance with me." It's a command, and she doesn't pull away when I take her hand in mine.

"But we haven't finished our drinks," she protests, even as she allows me to lead her away from the bar.

"I've had enough to drink," I counter smoothly, choosing not to chastise her for gulping her cocktails.

It seems to be an anxious response, and I don't want to rebuke her for being nervous around me. I like keeping her on edge.

"I'm not a very good dancer," she equivocates when we step onto the dance floor.

"Let me lead," I command. "Take my hands."

I grasp both of her smaller hands in mine before she can make the choice herself, caging her fingers in a careful but firm grip.

"Hold on to me."

I step toward her, and she eases back in perfect time. I'm not sure if she's following me in the dance or if she's edging away from my predatory energy.

I pull her into me, spinning her around so that she twirls before her back presses against my chest. Her shocked laugh is melodic, twining through the beat of the music. I keep her trapped against me with an arm around her waist for a few swaying steps. She moves with me beautifully, surrendering to my control despite her nerves.

I spin her away before she can get uncomfortable in my arms, and she laughs again. She tosses her glossy, sable hair, and the golden lights catch on the pretty purple curl that falls over her left shoulder. I crave to twine it around my fist and pull her in for a fierce kiss.

Instead, I spend the next two songs twirling her around the dance floor. Her cheeks are an even deeper shade of pink, and her lips part on little panting breaths as her body warms for me.

Desire pulses through my veins, and it's all I can do to keep my hands from straying to her pert ass instead of gripping her waist.

Hunger for this woman sets my teeth on edge, but I'm enjoying the new, slightly discomfiting sensation. I'm losing myself in the hunt: a more savage psychological dance as I lure her in with every step. Our bodies move in time, and I allow her to see my need for her burning through my eyes.

We'll be perfectly compatible when we fuck in a few short hours.

The music slows to something more sensual, and I tug her flush with my chest. My arm snakes around her lower back, pinning her to me as I methodically back her off the dance floor with each swaying step.

We reach a quieter, shadowy corner of the bar, and her eyes flare the moment she realizes that I have her trapped.

But she doesn't stiffen in distaste like she did when the uncouth idiot invaded her space at the bar earlier.

Her head tips back. Her pupils are dilated, and the lights flash over her eyes so that they shine like precious gemstones.

I finally indulge myself and twine her amethyst curl around my finger. Her hair is like silk, and I wonder how soft her skin will feel against mine.

I lean in slowly, and her head drops back farther. I allow her to simmer in anticipation, until she's practically trembling with need.

At the last moment, I tilt my face to the side so that my cheek skims over hers. My lips tease the shell of her ear when I whisper, "What does a good Carolina girl like you want me to do to her?"

I'm testing her, teasing her. I'll deny her the kiss she so clearly desires until she yields a bit. I want to know a sensual secret so that I can better manipulate her into accepting my twisted games.

"Who says I'm a good girl?" she breathes, and the words are hot against my skin.

My fine hairs stand on end, a strange prickling sensation on the back of my neck that I've never felt before.

I hum in consideration, and she shivers in response to the low rumble. I breathe in her sweet, slightly fruity scent and indulge myself, nuzzling her silken hair.

"What if I tell you to be a good girl for me?"

Her breath catches, but she shakes her head. "I'm not good."

Boldly, I shift my tender touch on her hair so that I can capture her nape in my hand. "I can make you be my good girl. Would you like that, Abigail?"

"Make me?" It's barely audible, a little puff of warm air on my cheek.

"You'll love being my good girl," I promise darkly, and she quivers in my hold. "I guarantee it."

I graze my teeth over her vulnerable artery. "Tell me what you want."

"I..." She trails off, so I give her a small bite to loosen her tongue with a little flare of warning pain. "I want you to make me," she whispers in a rush. "I want you to pin me down and use me."

Fuck. I swallow the curse and breathe through the pulse of lust that surges through my body. My cock stiffens, and I wrestle for control so that I don't get a hard-on in public.

"Will you struggle?" My voice is rougher now, crueler.

Her lips brush my cheek as she asks breathily, "Do you want me to?"

I bite back a groan. This woman is maddeningly perfect. I need to drive into her wet heat and fuck her hard until she weeps for mercy.

I've never unleashed my savage side before. I've always been careful to hide the cruelest parts of my nature behind cool control in the bedroom. I manipulate and seduce to get what I want, but I'm never fully myself.

The prospect of letting my mask drop entirely tempts me to the edge of sanity.

I grit my teeth and barely restrain myself from shoving her against the wall to claim her mouth with all the ruthlessness I'm capable of.

Not here.

I can't let anyone see me like that.

Expect maybe *her*.

The sensual promise of this darkest game makes my blood burn in my veins. My fingers tighten around her nape, and I drag her closer. I nip at the sensitive spot beneath her ear, and she releases the most erotic little whimper I've ever heard.

She wants this. She wants *me.*

The real, unmasked version of me that I've never shown anyone.

This is dangerous. Reckless.

I don't know Abigail at all, and I'm considering a rash act that's completely out of character for me.

"Abby!" A masculine voice calls out from behind me, tearing the moment I'm sharing with my pretty prey.

She jerks in my hold, and for a moment, I firm my grip on her slender neck. She draws in a sharp breath and softens against me, melting into the harsh touch.

So fucking perfect.

"Abby." The man says again. "I can't find Stacy. She's not answering my calls."

I round on him, fixing him with a glower like he's a fly I'll swat away without a second thought.

He pales slightly, and his mouth drops open on a gasp beneath his neat black moustache.

Fuck.

I struggle to summon up my civilized mask again. This person is clearly Abigail's friend, and he's concerned for another woman they know. I can't eviscerate him for daring to interrupt us.

"Franklin?" Her voice slurs slightly on his name when she returns to a normal speaking volume. I hadn't noticed the slower cadence to her speech when we'd been whispering forbidden secrets.

Is she drunk?

I recall the fact that she drank at least two slushies before I plied her with one and a half cosmopolitans. How much of a lightweight is she? Did she have even more slushies before I arrived at the bar?

I'd been concerned about allowing her to drink her second cocktail, but maybe she's already had too much.

I force myself to put distance between us so that her friend, Franklin, can talk to her.

She stumbles away from the wall as soon as I stop pinning her.

I rake a hand through my hair, strangely agitated.

"Where's Stacy?" she asks, and her eyes are slightly unfocused as she squints at the crowd of people swaying on the dance floor.

Franklin sighs and rolls his eyes. "Not you, too, Abby. Come on, I'll get you home before you stumble off with some hottie." He wraps a supportive arm around her shoulders and starts to steer her away.

She sways into him, and I barely manage to stop myself from tearing her friend away from her.

She clearly needs the support, and I'm a stranger to her.

The stranger who plied her with alcohol and then cornered her at the bar. I practically groped her in public.

No wonder her friend is considering me through narrowed eyes. I must seem like a predator to him.

I am a predator, but not in the way he thinks. The idea of claiming Abigail when she's inebriated leaves me cold. I want her fully aware of every moment we share. And I don't want her to experience an ounce of regret in the morning.

So, I fold my arms over my chest and remain rooted to the spot while I watch him steer her toward the exit.

"Is Stacy okay?" I hear her ask. She's speaking unnecessarily loudly; she's clearly lost her volume control.

"I don't know." Franklin is exasperated.

"We can't leave her," Abigail insists.

"She already left. We can call..." Their conversation is lost beneath the pulsing music, and I'm left standing in the corner like a granite statue.

My teeth are locked hard enough to make my jaw ache, but I have to remain resolutely still to prevent myself from going after her.

A mad idea sparks.

I can't let her slip away.

I need to know this woman, and I won't give up so easily.

My coiled muscles relax, and I saunter after her, keeping a dozen revelers between us to conceal the fact that I'm following her.

I didn't even get her number. I can't openly pursue her now without drawing negative attention from Franklin. He's clearly protective, and I don't want him to try to stop me from getting to my prey.

It would be unfortunate if I had to hurt her friend.

That would complicate my plans to seduce her.

I follow them out into the night, trailing her until she disappears into a dilapidated apartment building.

When I'm reassured that Franklin isn't in her apartment—I can see her clearly through her window that provides a view into her living room—I stroll away from her.

I know where she lives now. I can come back in the morning.

I'll find a way to conveniently meet her again. Charleston isn't a big city, and it won't seem too strange for us to see each other coincidentally.

She won't know that our second meeting will be by my design.

I'll have Abigail in my bed, and I'll learn her darkest secrets. She will surrender, and then this strange, clawing need that's assailing me will abate.

2

DANE

After I stalked Abigail home from the bar last night, I couldn't sleep. So, I return to her apartment building before six AM. Which is a good thing, because she leaves her building at six-thirty.

Judging by her black t-shirt and dark wash jeans, she's not going for a morning run. She's probably heading to work. Likely in the service industry, considering her simple outfit and the early hour.

I'm not usually one to ponder career choices, but I find myself wondering if she's content in her shabby little apartment with her low-paying job. A woman like Abigail should be dressed in silks and jewels, not practical cotton and jeans.

Once she's mine, I'll make sure to dress her up in a way that pleases me.

I shake off the strange thought and follow her down the street, keeping a careful distance so that she won't notice me.

I've never kept a woman before. It's never even crossed my mind. Not only do I get bored easily, but I know better than to risk forming a long-term relationship that might reveal my true nature over time.

A few nights with Abigail will surely be enough to sate my curiosity. And my lust.

My sleepless night wasn't only due to anticipation over seeing her again; I've wrestled with a raging hard-on ever since she trembled against me in the shadowy corner of the bar.

In another strange choice, I didn't slake my needs. Jerking off would have felt oddly like surrender. Defeat.

I will conquer Abigail, not the other way around. I won't allow anyone to make me feel weak. Certainly not a fragile, submissive woman.

I'm thoroughly in control of this seduction. She'll learn that soon enough.

We've only walked three blocks when she ducks into a small café. The lights are on, but the sign is still flipped to "closed". I check my watch. It's likely that the Sunny Side Café opens at seven. Possibly even later.

I harden my resolve. I'm not so desperate that I'll barge in the moment they open.

Abigail will need *me*, not the other way around. She'll beg and moan my name, and then I'll finally be satisfied.

She's disappeared into the back, so I can't even see her through the large windows that provide a clear view into the café.

I roll the odd tension from my shoulders and saunter off down the street.

I'll have to meet Meadows at our new premises by nine. Our practice officially starts operating next week, and we need to make sure everything is in order. We already have an impressive waitlist of patients, thanks to my partner's local connections and the shared reputation that we built in Baltimore.

Now that I'll have my own practice, I can be more discerning with my cases. And with my schedule.

I can make time for Abigail if I want to.

I smooth away my grimace at the errant thought. The woman is getting under my skin, and I've barely spent an hour with her.

Surely, a little more time in her company is all I need to prove to myself that she's nothing special. Beautiful and beguiling, but not special.

She'll be imperfectly human, just like every other person I've ever met: simple and easily manipulated.

I wander away from the café for a while before I stop in one of the only open shops, where I buy an insipid magazine about local interests. Then I find a park bench where I can sit to pass the time for an hour or so.

While I wait to approach my prey, I can at least learn a little more about my new home here in Charleston. My patients are gratified when I show interest in their small little lives. It's irksome, but it'll help grow the practice. I'll earn even more money, be even more secure.

I don't need my family's fortune to live a life of luxury. The first few years of university were hard, but nothing will ever make me go begging for a handout from my father.

You'll be back. My mother's final, spiteful words echo through my mind. *You can't make it on your own, Daniel. You can't embarrass the family like this. What will our friends say if you run away to America like a pathetic coward who can't face his duties?*

I shake off the memory and redirect my focus to the

article about an upcoming garden tour in Charleston's historic districts.

I haven't thought about that altercation with my mother in years.

It's possible that Abigail's obvious financial struggles are making me recall the years when I had to scrape by, too, before I earned my medical degree and established my reputation as a skilled surgeon.

I manage to read another article about a nearby plantation before I think about the wad of one dollar bills Abigail pulled out of her wallet when she tried to pay for her cocktail last night.

I used to be frugal with my money, too, when I had nothing more than a small stipend from my scholarship at Johns Hopkins.

Now, I'm more than wealthy enough to buy an expensive home in Harleston Village. I'll never be poor again.

And as long as I choose to keep Abigail with me, she will want for nothing. I won't be seen neglecting a woman who's on my arm. I can provide for her, and I won't allow anyone to think otherwise.

Clean up, Daniel. What will our friends think if they see you with bloody knuckles?

I hear my mother's voice again. Always so concerned with appearances, not with why her ten-year-old son might have blood on his hands.

I crumple the magazine in my fists.

I loathe pretentious people who perform for the sake of others, but I can't deny that I've been forced to live my life with my civilized mask firmly in place. I learned at a young age that I can't get what I want if I let people see the monster inside; charm works much better than fear.

I gnash my teeth and toss the magazine in a public rubbish bin. These irritating thoughts aren't something I often contemplate, and I don't know why they're troubling me now.

Must be the sleepless night messing with my usual composure.

I run a hand over my hair to smooth it into a neater style and stride toward the café. It's just past eight AM now. Surely, they'll be open.

The glass door isn't locked, so I'm able to stride into the Sunny Side Café with smooth confidence.

Abigail is almost entirely hidden behind the espresso machine that dominates the end of the counter; only the top of her brunette head and the barest hint of delicately arched brows are visible.

Is she shy even in her workplace? Last night, I surmised that she's a bit anxious in social situations. I'd enjoyed riding that edge, making her nervous while drawing out her forbidden lust.

"Good morning! How are you?"

I blink and redirect my attention to the pretty Black woman behind the register. Her name badge says *Stacy*. She must be Abigail's friend, the one they couldn't find at the bar last night when Franklin so rudely dragged my prey away from me.

I arrange my features into my usual charming smile and sharpen my focus. Abigail is within my sights once again. She won't escape this time.

"I'm well, thank you," I say in response to Stacy's inane question. This Carolina pretense at politeness will take some getting used to.

Although, looking into Stacy's large brown eyes, she does

seem more interested in me than rote niceties. I'm used to attention from women, but there's only one that I want to captivate now.

"What can I get for you?" Stacy's voice drops slightly deeper, an invitation rather than simply taking my order.

I keep my smile in place but don't allow it to tilt in anticipation of a flirtation. Usually, I'd enjoy toying with this woman. In a slew of social interactions that are so often mundane, making people flustered so that they'll trip over themselves to please me is mildly amusing.

"I'll have an Americano, please." My tone is warm and friendly, but nothing more.

Abigail probably wouldn't like it if I were rude to Stacy; they're friends, after all.

"What's your name?"

I pause for a moment and quirk a brow at Stacy. She's being quite forward, and I'm here for Abigail.

"For your cup," she explains when I don't answer right away.

I don't fully buy it, but I suppose it's probably common practice at their café to write names on cups to keep track of orders.

"Dane," I introduce myself.

I can't stop my gaze from cutting toward the espresso machine, but Abigail doesn't appear when I say my name.

"You don't sound like you're from around here," Stacy observes, leaning toward me slightly.

"I'm not." I suppress a sigh. My English accent often elicits this comment, and I'm getting impatient to speak to Abigail.

The sound of my voice doesn't seem to have attracted her attention. She liked my accent when we spoke last night. Why isn't she turning to greet me?

I anticipate her slight surprise at this "chance" second meeting: the way those pretty lips will part on a little intake of breath, and her remarkable aquamarine eyes will widen.

Maybe she's shyer than I thought. And she's sober now, so that might make her even more reluctant to approach me. Is she embarrassed at how inebriated she was?

Curiosity consumes me. I forget to continue my polite conversation with Stacy and prowl down the length of the bar.

Abigail appears in profile. Her lips are slightly pursed as she focuses so intently on pouring out latte art that she doesn't seem aware of my presence. Those lovely eyes are fixed on the steamed milk, but even from a side view, the light catches in the aqua pools, illuminating them like the Mediterranean Sea on a sunny day.

"Good morning," I greet, prompting her attention.

"Morning." She barely breathes the word, but her mouth quirks in a pleasant smile.

The perfectly polite, good Carolina girl is back.

But I know her secret now.

I'm not good. She whispered her forbidden truths last night when she tormented me with her responses to my dark questions.

She wears a mask, just like I do. Her genteel veneer hides a sensual woman with taboo desires: an inner darkness that complements my own.

Unlike me, she's not cold and calculated. She's guileless and soft.

The perfect match for my cruel needs.

But she's still not looking at me. She's finished her latte art, but she's moved on to grinding the espresso for my Americano.

She must be embarrassed about last night. I'll put her at ease by speaking in my practiced bedside manner tone. I won't allow any shame to get in the way of our connection.

"How are you feeling today?" I ask, noting the faint dark circles under her eyes.

I wonder if she has a headache from drinking too much. If so, I'll make sure she takes a break to drink water and eat something before taking ibuprofen. I'm sure I can charm Stacy into allowing her colleague a moment to collect herself.

Abigail's careful smile remains fixed in place, and she places a paper cup with my name on it beneath the espresso machine.

Irritation makes my own smile waver. I'm not sure how much longer I can tolerate this reticence.

"I'm fine, thanks," she replies softly. "How are you?"

The rote question doesn't hold the same depth of true interest that Stacy showed me. It's a bland social nicety, a requirement for her job.

I'm finding her shyness annoying this morning rather than intriguing. Maybe pursuing her was a mistake. If she can't bring herself to make eye contact unless her inhibitions are lowered by alcohol, she might be too tedious to hold my attention.

"I'm feeling good," I reply with forced nonchalance. "The whiskey at the dive bar last night wasn't good enough to tempt me to drink more than two."

"Oh," she says blandly. "I don't know much about whiskey unless it's mixed with Coke."

My smile quirks despite my irritation, and I indulge in one of her secrets. "You prefer sweeter drinks."

She blinks, and we finally make eye contact. Her pale cheeks flush a perfect shade of pink, and I think she's about to thank me for the cosmopolitans I bought her last night. Instead, her gaze is a bit wary.

"Yeah, I guess I'm a cliché. I do enjoy girly, pink drinks."

I don't understand her strange energy.

"Do you want milk in your Americano, Dane?"

She says my name, but it's not husky with remembered lust. There's no familiarity in the way she addresses me.

It takes me a full three seconds to realize that she doesn't recognize me. Apparently, she was so drunk last night that she blacked out our meeting.

I'm silent for too long, because she fills the awkward moment with a nervous laugh.

"I guess not. Black Americano, got it."

She puts a lid on the cup that has my name written on it and places it on the counter between us.

Something tightens my gut, a strange sensation that I've felt before, but never to this degree. The pang is harsh enough to make me grimace.

Anger.

I'm angry that she doesn't remember me. She doesn't remember *us*, the electric connection we share.

She drops her lovely eyes and quickly returns to her espresso machine. Her fingers tremble slightly as she reaches for the milk jug.

I realize that I'm scowling.

I never lose control of my facial expression.

"I'm sorry," I say as smoothly as I can manage. The last thing I want is to scare her off.

I'm more than just annoyed, but I'm finding the intensity of my response to her fascinating, even if it is unpleasant.

"I was short with you. I suppose I might've had more whiskey last night than I thought. A bit of a headache this morning." The lie comes easily. "The coffee will help. Thank you."

"No worries. Enjoy!" Her sunny smile is back, but she keeps her focus on her work.

Fuck.

I intimidated her.

How did this go so badly? I'd expected to sweep her off her feet. We should be exchanging numbers right now, and she's supposed to be sitting across from me at a sumptuous dinner in a few hours.

And she's meant to be screaming my name in my bed shortly thereafter.

Instead, she won't even look at me.

An odd feeling comes over me again, and I'm more reluctant to acknowledge this one.

Insecurity?

The ground feels like it's shifting under my feet, and the angry churning in my gut has been replaced by a disconcerting knotting sensation.

It's unpleasant and completely foreign to me.

Fascinating.

Suddenly, I'm eager to know what other new feelings this puzzle of a woman might elicit from me. I'm currently experiencing a spectrum of discomfiting emotions. But there's the other side of the coin, too.

What would it be like to experience more than cruel, fleeting pleasure?

What ecstatic high will I achieve when she murmurs my name like a prayer and begs me for an orgasm only I can give her?

"I'm new to the area," I say instead of leaving her side. "I'm sure I'll see you again."

Her nervous laugh fills the space between us. "We do have good coffee here," she allows. "And we always love getting new regulars."

"I'll see you tomorrow morning, then." It's a promise, and it comes out in a rougher, more intense tone than I intended.

A light shiver races over her fragile frame.

Arousal at the hint of danger? Or fear at my masculine attention?

Maybe both.

The impulse to grasp that alluring purple curl and tug her toward me makes my fingers furl at my side.

I force myself to relax. That would be far too frightening, and I'd probably end up in the back of a cop car.

I'm clinging to my control by my fingernails. It's horrifying and fascinating.

I have to leave before I say something else that I'll regret. Abigail will be here whenever I want to see her. I'll find a way to lure her into my bed.

"Have a great day!" she says in that falsely bright tone.

It's so practiced that I almost believe it.

I summon up my own familiar mask and barely suppress a grimace at the bitterness of the espresso on my tongue. Usually, I take my coffee with a splash of milk and one sugar, but Abigail thinks I like it black now. I can endure the bitterness to avoid further awkwardness.

I'll come back for her.

I recall her submissive responses to my firm commands last night. She must be pliable enough for me to seduce her without too much difficulty.

Then I can explore and master these strange new *feelings.*

I'll fuck her out of my system, and everything will go back to normal.

3

DANE

I've visited the café every morning for a week, and Abigail is simply polite to me, as though I'm like every other customer.

It's frustrating.

Infuriating.

So, I find myself strolling through her neighborhood after the sun sets. She won't even look at me when I'm at the café. I must've thoroughly intimidated her when I completely misjudged the situation.

I can't harass her while she's at work; that'll only raise more red flags.

But now that I'm a regular at the café, I can't approach her elsewhere without seeming like I'm stalking her. I'd only spook her even more.

I force my clenched jaw to loosen.

This woman is maddening, but the more difficult it is to pursue her, the more I crave to conquer her.

I've never been evaded by a woman before. No one has wanted to evade me.

But Abigail is a stubborn exception in so many ways.

I shouldn't be here. It's risky to follow her home.

And I never put myself at risk. I refuse to do anything foolish that might end with me behind bars. I'll never be caged.

I'm too smart for that.

I glance around the deserted street. This isn't the nicest neighborhood, but it's quiet.

Probably because no one seems to want to live in the dilapidated houses that surround her ramshackle apartment building. There's small, narrow house directly across the street. The powder blue paint on the exterior is peeling, and it's dark inside. No one's home.

The garden is overgrown, and that suits my desires. I duck beneath unruly foliage and push open the rusty gate. Within less than a minute, I settle into the shadows provided by the azalea and hydrangea bushes that haven't been pruned in years.

Abigail's window is a yellow rectangle shining through the night. At this distance, I can see her moving around her cramped living room. She's setting up an easel.

Curiosity nips at me, an insistent bite.

My pretty prey is an artist. I'm not surprised to learn that she has a creative streak. Her purple curl and the whimsical unicorn badge I've noted on her work apron indicate a playful energy that defies stricter social norms. Her quirkiness makes more sense now that I see her with a paintbrush in her delicate hand.

Despite her perfectly polite demeanor, Abigail isn't a

conformist. She marches to the beat of her own drum. Maybe that's why I'm having such a difficult time pinning her down.

Her hand moves in small, elegant strokes as she works with fluidity but precision. I can only see the back of her brunette head from this angle, but I have a clear view of her canvas.

She's too far away for me to make out the details of her painting. For a while, I'm content to simply watch her graceful, minute movements as she works. But the longer she continues, the more I crave to know what absorbs her attention so completely.

I retrieve my phone from my pocket and open the camera in an attempt to zoom in on her art. But the lighting is too imbalanced at this distance for me to make out more than a navy-blue blur on her canvas.

I frown and tuck my phone back in my pocket.

If I could learn more about her art, I might be able to capture her attention when we make small talk at the café.

I resolve that I have to know the subject of her painting. I'll learn Abigail's secrets, and she will submit to me.

No one seems to live in the powder blue house across the street from Abigail's apartment. I took some time to peer into the darkened windows before settling into the shadows of the overgrown garden. The house is devoid of furnishings, and the peeling wallpaper inside is in even worse condition than the exterior paint.

It's a convenient arrangement for me; I can watch her without concern about being interrupted.

After my frustration last night, I came prepared. I lean

back in the rickety garden chair and lift the binoculars I purchased this afternoon.

The back of Abigail's head appears in sharp relief, brunette waves shining in the golden light cast by her cheap standing lamps.

Her canvas is still propped up on the easel in the middle of her living room, but she's sitting on her couch now. Some maddened urge to keep my focus on her prevents me from shifting my attention to the painting for a full minute.

But she's on her laptop, probably browsing social media or something equally mundane. I'd much prefer to see her paint again, especially now that I'm equipped to view her art properly.

I blow out a sigh and focus on the unfinished painting instead. It's a stunning impressionist landscape, depicting a pristine beach before an incoming storm. The sand is captured in textured strokes of pale yellow, indicating a sunny day before the encroaching tempest. At the horizon, turbulent, dark navy waves surge, so at odds with the peaceful beach.

I wonder if this is a scene she's painting from memory, or if it's an embellishment.

I've never seen a storm like it.

But then again, I've never really paid much attention to the natural world. I prefer to spend my time amongst people rather than pondering my surroundings in solitude. I can control people, not the weather. So, nature doesn't interest me much. It's just a backdrop, scenery for the psychological games that keep me amused.

But there's something compelling about Abigail's art. I can't quite put my finger on why I'm still staring at the painting when I could be watching her instead.

I shake off the odd compulsion to continue studying the stormy sea and focus on her braided hair. The shade of dark purple is truly lovely against her brunette locks. I admire the way it weaves through her thick waves, how the heavy braid is loose enough to conceal most of her nape. I get the smallest glimpse of bare skin where her neck meets her shoulder, which is covered by her soft black work shirt.

She hasn't bothered to change after finishing her shift; she's gone straight to her laptop.

Why isn't she painting?

I'm scowling in the darkness, and I smooth away the unbidden expression of displeasure.

I'm losing control around her, and even if no one is here to see it, my cheeks still flush with a strange heat.

I definitely don't like the sensation, so I choose to ignore this particular new *feeling* she's eliciting.

I'll have her under my control soon enough.

What is she so absorbed with at her laptop?

I try to focus the binoculars on her screen, but whatever she's viewing is too bright and small for me to make out more than a white blur. Her fingers fly over the keyboard.

She's typing something, and the deft, rapid strokes of her delicate fingers fascinate me almost as much as the strokes of her paintbrush.

I'm not sure how long I indulge myself in watching her elegant hands before she puts her laptop away. When she stands up from where she was seated on the couch, she turns toward her bedroom rather than her canvas. I can see her in profile now, and her porcelain cheek is flushed a gorgeous shade of pink.

It reminds me of the alluring shade of her blush when we first met at the bar last week.

What was she writing that has her cheeks turning pink?

I'm burning for answers, but all I'm met with is darkness when she turns off the lights. She disappears into her bedroom. I can't see into it because this window only provides me a view into her living room.

I could prowl around her building to find out what she's doing now, but that would be even riskier than watching her from this shadowed garden. I'd be out in the open, and one of her neighbors might see me peering into her window.

I force my jaw to unclench and put the binoculars away. I'll come back tomorrow night. I have to know more.

SHE'S BACK at her easel, but the canvas is darker tonight. I had to stay at work later than I would've liked, so she's already deeply absorbed in her art by the time I finally settle into the rickety garden chair.

I'd anticipated watching her storm-tossed sea develop into a towering tempest, but she seems to have a different subject in mind tonight.

Heavy strokes of midnight black darken the edges of the canvas, and all of the light she captures with her paintbrush is focused on the center of her painting. Shadows cling to creamy flesh, as though they're drawing her subject deeper into their forbidden embrace. They curl around a slender neck like tendrils of smoke, and the distinctly feminine chin is tipped back as though to welcome the dark claim.

The knife at her subject's throat glints dully, a charcoal gray that's almost forged from the shadows that caress their victim.

Rosebud lips are parted on a gasp that's undeniably erotic.

And just at the bottom edge of the painting, two peaked, pink nipples beg for attention.

My teeth clench hard enough to make my jaw ache, and my cock stiffens to the point of discomfort in the confines of my jeans.

I was right to think that Abigail's desires are a perfect match for my own. She secretly fantasizes about being threatened and forced to experience transcendent pleasure.

I've never allowed myself to truly frighten a woman. There are certain parameters I have to operate within to fit social norms, even in more deviant subcultures. Those boundaries have irked me in the past, but now, they feel like the iron bars of a cage that's far too small to contain me.

What would it be like to throw off those invisible constraints and truly unleash myself upon her? Would she welcome the thrill of this darkest game?

I have no desire to harm Abigail; on the contrary, I'll do anything to shield her so that she'll welcome me back into her body again and again.

I know now that a few nights with this woman won't be enough.

The thought makes something slither down my spine.

Apprehension?

If I allow my mask to drop around her, my secrets will be exposed. I'll put myself at risk.

If I push her too far, she might scream in horror when I show her my true self. I could lose everything I've worked so hard for these last fifteen years: my wealth, my reputation, my freedom.

The temptation to indulge in this most forbidden connection is almost enough to drive me to madness, but I can't give in. I can't take on that risk.

Yet.

Until I know for sure that Abigail won't be repulsed by my crueler advances, I have to be patient. I can watch her. Study her.

And when it comes to my studies, I've always excelled. I have an eye for detail and an excellent memory.

I've never faced such a thrilling challenge in my life, and the prospect makes intense pleasure gather at the base of my spine. The temptation of her sensual painting is almost enough to make me come undone without her touch.

I take a breath and master the bizarre urge to surrender to the insistent pleasure. I'm not going to come in my pants when Abigail is out of my reach.

She's not in control of this seduction. I am.

She just doesn't know it yet.

4

DANE

Three Weeks Later

I straighten the painting on the freshly mounted hanger and then step back to check my work. The stormy sea is perfectly parallel with the top of the chest of drawers in my cramped little bedroom.

There's barely space in here for my king-size bed and a few basic furnishings, but I've made this ramshackle house comfortable enough. I finalized the cash sale three days ago, and I've spent the weekend setting up the bedroom. The rest of the house doesn't need to be furnished—it's best if it continues to appear uninhabited.

I don't want Abigail to get curious about her new neighbor. I plan to watch her from my garden across the street from her apartment building, and she'll never know I'm here.

My larger, grander house across town is much more comfortable than this aged home with its peeling, powder blue exterior. It's been vacant for some time, and the owners were all too eager to sell above market price without an inspection.

I still haven't decided how or when I'll approach her outside of our brief, daily meetings at the café. For now, I'm enjoying my clandestine study of my prey. Watching her is thrilling, fascinating like nothing I've ever experienced.

Earlier this afternoon, I acquired her painting—the first one I ever saw her paint. She has a modest stall at the market, and a clueless tourist bought the stormy beach scene.

They never would've appreciated the piece like I do.

So, I waited for them to leave the market and then purchased it from them. They didn't mind parting with the treasure for a measly hundred-dollar bill.

I sit back on my new bed and stare up at the painting. It deserves a far better display than the yellowing wallpaper in this dilapidated house, but for now, it will have to do.

In fact, if I acquire more of her art, I can conceal the cracks in the walls entirely.

I'll go back to the market next weekend and buy all of the paintings she sells to the appreciative tourists. They might enjoy her artistic style, but they're just looking for a pretty souvenir. I'm confident that my cash will be enough to convince them to hand over their purchases.

I love watching Abigail paint late into the night—especially her darker, erotic masterpieces—but the time she spends typing at her laptop is infuriating. I can't see what she's writing, and that's maddening.

Untenable.

I've formulated a plan to satisfy my burning curiosity. It's risky, but I can't deny that the risk is exhilarating.

I leave the bedroom and step out into the night. The street is quiet, and Abigail's window is dark. She's not home. I followed her to make sure of it almost an hour ago. It's half past nine, and she's at the dive bar where we first met.

The meeting she doesn't remember.

I force my tense jaw to relax. If I'd conquered Abigail in one night, I wouldn't experience this life-changing hunt. She frustrates me, but I can't deny that this is the most entertainment I've ever experienced when pursuing a beautiful woman. She doesn't know the game we're playing, but I'm enjoying it immensely.

When I take the first step across the empty street, all of my senses come alive in a way I've never known. I'm inside the ground floor breezeway of her building within seconds, tucked out of sight in the shadows.

My fingers shake slightly when I reach into my pocket, so I fist them around the lock picking kit I purchased online.

As a surgeon, I'm known for my steady hands. This anomaly is completely out of character, a novelty. Adrenaline hums through my veins, an almost giddy rush.

But there's no one around to witness my crime.

I won't be caught. I won't be caged.

Despite that knowledge, my body feels as though I might as well be skydiving rather than quietly breaking into her apartment.

My heart pounds against my ribcage when the lock disengages, and her front door swings open with a rusty squeak. I can navigate the cramped space by the streetlight that filters through the large living room window; it would be stupid to turn on the lights.

I often see her writing while she's curled up on her couch, but it only takes a few seconds for me to ascertain that her laptop isn't there. She usually carries it with her into her bedroom once she's finished with her feverish, mysterious typing.

I cross the living room, spanning the small space in four paces to reach her bedroom. It's barely big enough for a twin sized bed, which is tucked into a corner beside the only window. The view shows peeling yellow paint on the building next door, and nothing else.

Abigail's art showcases the natural world. Surely, she must feel stifled in this cramped, urban space?

A quick perusal through her drawers tells me that she either doesn't care much for fashion, or she can only afford a few basic items. I recognize the simple black t-shirts she wears for her barista job. There are a few more delicate tops mixed in: camisoles with paint stains.

I trace the shape of a particularly beautiful spray of azure on the neckline of a pale pink top. The colors are barely discernible in the dim lighting, but I imagine the blue hue is similar to the shade of her eyes.

My fist closes around the soft cotton, and before I can think better of it, I tuck the small shirt into my pocket. She might miss it, but I know she does her laundry in an aging machine that's shared by all six apartments in her building. If she can't find the top later, she'll assume she lost it there.

I try not to think too much about my rash act of possessiveness and turn my attention to the knickknacks on top of her dresser. There are three unicorn figurines in various poses—two of cheap plastic and one fashioned in clay with a pearlescent glaze. They're positioned around a neon sign in cursive script: *live deliciously*.

It suits her flair for whimsy.

I think about the pink and gold unicorn pin that's a constant presence on her apron. Otherwise, various anthropomorphic cartoon foodstuffs seem to be on regular rotation amongst her badges. I've noted a cupcake, an iced coffee, a donut, and even a frowning broccoli.

There are two similar food-related pieces on her dresser alongside the figurines and neon sign, but these smiling toys are plush and stuffed with cotton wool. I brush my fingers over a velvet-soft avocado and a little pod of happy peas.

They're mildly ridiculous, but I can't help finding them fascinating. They're childish toys for a woman in her mid-twenties, but Abigail seems to be an exception in so many ways. There's a fragility beneath her cheery smiles and shy glances, and although she doesn't know it, I've glimpsed an alluring darkness at her core that calls to my own.

A bizarre desire to shelter and covet that sunshine girl wars with my craving to shatter her cheerful façade and reveal her darkest secrets.

My hand is in my pocket, rubbing the soft fabric of her paint-splattered camisole.

I force my fingers to unfurl and turn my attention back to her bedroom.

There's a stack of books that can't be contained by her small nightstand. The bedroom isn't big enough for a proper bookshelf, but there must be at least three dozen titles in a haphazard array beside her bed.

I shake my head at the mess, but my disapproval of her disorganized nature doesn't stop me from thumbing through the books. I recognize some of the more popular titles, and I get a sense that she enjoys fantasy novels with heavy romantic elements.

On her nightstand, a copy of *The Invisible Life of Addie LaRue* is well-worn, as though she's read it several times. I check the book quickly, searching for any signs that she bought it secondhand.

No price stickers or penciled dollar amount on the interior.

It's likely that she's the one who damaged the binding while indulging in the story over and over again.

My touch lingers on the fine cracks that mar the spine, and I think about her long, elegant fingers caressing her beloved book.

Shaking my head, I set the book down and turn to the final space in her apartment that I have yet to explore: her closet.

I grasp the small knob and have to tug it sharply to open the ill-fitted, shuttered door. After a stuck moment, it snaps toward me. Something lightweight but rigid falls forward, colliding with my thigh.

I curse softly and catch the canvases before they fall to the floor.

There's a stack of them packed into the closet, and they're about to tip over into the bedroom. Carefully, I tilt them back so that they rest against the interior wall.

There are only a few extra dresses tucked away in here. The space is dominated by more paintings that are stacked on three shelves. There must be scores of them hidden in darkness.

I pick up three of the larger canvases and place them on her bed. No one will see me through the bedroom window if I use the light on my phone. The building next door is mere feet away, close enough to touch if I were to open the window. There aren't any vantage points to see into this room from outside.

My phone illuminates the first painting, and my breath catches.

Rough hemp rope digs into soft flesh. Her thigh cushions the bindings in creamy pillows, as though welcoming the painful bonds to sink deeper.

Another painting shows her delicate wrist, abraded from rope that's been recently removed. The ecstatic high of release after being cruelly bound is evident in the gentle furl of her long fingers: blissful relaxation in the wake of being utterly devastated.

The third depicts a gloved hand encircling her pale throat, the black leather in shocking contrast to her creamy skin. Thick fingers sink into her neck beneath the soft taper of her jaw, restricting the blood flow through her carotid arteries. Her rosebud lips are parted—a gasp for air and a plea for further torment.

Abigail is perfect for me. I know that I can fulfil her darkest desires. She's kept them secret from everyone, choosing to hide them away in her closet where no one can see her true artistic brilliance.

Does she hide them even from herself? Is that why she keeps her masterpieces shrouded in shadows?

I remind myself that risked this break-in for a single purpose, so I need to keep my focus on finding her laptop.

I put the paintings back in her closet and find the laptop on the floor beside a stack of books, tucked halfway under the bed. Was she looking at something online late at night? Maybe she has a particular, perverted website she likes to visit.

I'll make sure to check her browser history as well as any personal documents she's written.

Any further insight into her sexual preferences will help me seduce her. And if I'm right about her kinky predilections, I'll feel more secure showing her the darkest aspects of my cruel nature. There will be less risk involved if I know exactly what she wants me to do to her.

I set the laptop on the bed, which is an unmade tangle of sheets.

My lips twist with distaste. Abigail is untidy.

A bad habit I will have to break once she's mine.

I shake off the possessive thought and ignore the unease that stirs in my gut at how fiercely I want this woman.

The laptop instantly illuminates when I open it. A photo of the beach fills the screen, and a small icon with her face is framed in a circle at the center of the idyllic image. There's a text box just beneath it, the cursor flickering in a mocking rhythm.

Fuck.

It's password protected.

Her secrets are in my hands but hopelessly out of reach.

I narrow my eyes at the computer as though it's a particularly irksome enemy that I'm about to eviscerate. For a few long seconds, my fingers hover over the keyboard. I contemplate guessing her password.

But I have no idea if my attempts will be logged somehow. Even worse, I could end up locked out entirely. Abigail will definitely know someone has tampered with it if that happens.

She'll know someone was in her home while she was out.

She might call the police. There could be an investigation.

No, I can't try to guess her password. And I'm no hacker, even if I'm proficient with technology. It's a skill I've learned just like any other to progress my career, but I've never needed to learn how to break into a woman's private laptop.

My hands clench to fists just above the keyboard.

I'm going to have to leave unsatisfied.

The distinctive sound of a key scraping a lock grates down my spine. Her front door creaks open, and my stomach drops.

Abigail is home early.

She was supposed to stay at the bar for at least another two hours. She usually indulges with her friends until nearly midnight when she goes out.

Fuck!

I've only been watching her for a few weeks. I was a fool to think I could fully learn her habits in that time. Abigail is quirky, difficult to pin down. I should've known that I couldn't rely on her to stick to any sort of schedule.

I quickly close the laptop, and my eyes can't quite adjust to the darkness in the absence of artificial light from the screen. Her soft footsteps pad across the living room. In less than three seconds, she'll enter her bedroom and find me here. She'll scream for help.

And I'll end up in a cage.

I grit my teeth and dive under her bed.

I will not go to prison.

Even if the prospect of hiding from her is somewhat preposterous. It feels intrinsically wrong to be cowering in the shadows, as though this delicate woman could pose any threat to me.

But I don't have a choice. I'll have to remain quiet and hidden until I can slip out of her apartment without being noticed.

That might mean spending the entire night down here.

My fingernails dig into my palms, and I draw in a deep breath as quietly as I can manage.

Can she hear my heart hammering? My blood is pounding in my ears.

If I felt like I was skydiving before, now I'm in freefall without a parachute. The peril isn't just pretend anymore. If I'm caught...

I gnash my teeth and forcibly close off that line of thinking. Spiraling into anxiety won't help get me out of this farcical situation.

I can't do anything except remain still and draw in careful breaths. The adrenaline thrums through me, making my limbs shaky and my mind fizzy. It's terrifying and exhilarating.

I've never experienced anything this powerful, and even though I'm losing control, I revel in the intense new emotions. Ensconced in darkness, I allow myself to sink into the fear-soaked physical responses, marveling at the way my breath shudders in and out of my tight lungs.

Even this existential dread is a gift only she can give me.

I can hardly wait for the day I feel the opposite. How visceral will my pleasure be when I finally claim her?

The prospect causes my muscles to coil in carnal anticipation, and to my shock, my cock begins to stiffen.

Before I can fully process the fact that I'm getting a hard-on, she turns on the bedside lamp. Then her soft cotton, periwinkle blue dress drops onto the hardwood floor, and I can no longer deny my erection.

Her panties drop next: pale pink cotton briefs.

I bite my tongue to hold back a hungry growl. The small rumble that manages to escape is mercifully smothered by the creaking of her aged mattress springs when she gets into bed.

Naked.

Right above me.

Her hand appears, fumbling at the floor just to the right of my head. I crane my neck to the side, and her long fingers nearly brush my hair before she feels the familiar shape of her laptop.

She picks it up, and the computer disappears along with her hand.

Damn it.

This can't be happening. I'm going to have to listen to her typing whatever it is that absorbs her so completely, and I still won't have a clue what she's writing.

Within seconds, I hear the rapid tapping of her fingertips on the keyboard, but I remain completely ignorant. She's probably typing in her password, but there's no way to discern a pattern.

A few soft clicks. More tapping.

Faster now.

She blows out a long sigh, as though she's purging physical tension. The mattress shifts above me. She must be moving into a more comfortable position.

It shifts again.

The aged springs must be causing her discomfort, because she seems to be practically squirming in her sheets.

And still, she keeps typing.

Another sigh. Another shift.

A realization is dawning, but I don't want to acknowledge it.

My cock already seems to know exactly what's happening because it's painfully stiff in the confines of my jeans.

Then she stops typing, and her low moan flushes the humid air with erotic heat. The movement of the mattress is undulating now, a regular, rolling rhythm.

No.

This can't be happening. The woman I've been lusting after for weeks is masturbating directly above me while I hide under her bed.

For an insane moment, I consider joining her on the bed. I could pin her down and clamp my hand over her mouth to muffle her pretty scream. She'd fight, but my other hand around her throat would be enough to subdue her. Those remarkable, aquamarine eyes would shine with tears even as they soften at the edge of losing consciousness.

She doesn't breathe unless I allow it. She doesn't speak unless it's to moan my name.

"Dane..."

My entire body locks up tight.

My dark fantasy of our mutual, twisted pleasure is all too visceral. I can't give in to temptation. She's not ready to accept me like that yet.

"Dane..."

It takes me several racing heartbeats to process the fact that I didn't just imagine her moaning my name.

Jesus Christ.

She's thinking about me while she pleasures herself.

She'll barely look at me when I'm at the café, but some part of her must remember our intense connection.

Abigail wants me.

My fist unfurls, and my fingers fumble at my belt. It's as though some irresistible compulsion has taken hold of my body, and even as I know this is madness, I free my aching cock. My sharp intake of breath is masked by her rapid panting and the squeaking of her mattress springs.

Pleasure shudders down my spine, and I bite the inside of my cheek to hold in a primal snarl of frustration and desire.

I should be inside her right now. The tight sheath of her cunt should be squeezing my dick, not my own fist. She should be weeping and begging me for release.

"Dane!"

She cries out my name, and for the first time in my life, I lose control of my body entirely. Ecstasy overtakes me in a vicious wave, dragging me to completion against my will. Cum sears my hand, and my cheeks heat with pleasure and a hint of shame.

Unease twists my gut as I crash back down from my cruel high. The power this fragile woman holds over me isn't just thrilling; it's shaking my entire worldview.

I close my eyes and draw in a deep breath at the same time as she sighs in contentment.

Abigail will pay for this. She'll crawl to me on her hands and knees and apologize with her mouth. Only when I'm satisfied that she's thoroughly humbled and completely desperate for me, I'll finally allow her the mercy of an orgasm.

The savage thought is almost hot enough to stir my lust again, but for now, I'm spent.

The mattress dips, and her hand appears again as she returns her laptop to its place beneath her bed.

My mind whirs. I have to know what she was writing that got her so aroused.

Does she write about me? Is that why she moaned my name?

I formulate a daring plan to discover her secrets. I've risked breaking into her apartment once. I can do it again.

After I borrow her laptop for the day.

Someone in Charleston will know how to unlock it without her password. My money will ensure that any qualms about hacking will be alleviated.

Then I can return the infuriating device to her bedroom, and she'll never know it was missing.

Satisfied with my course of action, I finally allow myself to relax. As I listen to the sound of her deep, even breaths, I follow Abigail into sleep.

5

ABBY

Two Months Later

I feel his forest green eyes on me, even though I barely glimpsed him in my peripheral vision when he entered the café. Luckily, my coworker, Stacy, is on register today; I'm able to hide behind the espresso machine and lose my frazzled thoughts in the morning rush of thirsty caffeine addicts.

But as much as I'd like to remain cushioned in my mindless bubble of steaming milk and pouring out familiar latte art, I'm always aware when he comes in for his daily black Americano.

His name is Dane.

That's what it says on his cup every morning when he places his order like clockwork at eight-oh-five AM.

The name suits him: it's a hot name for an insanely gorgeous man.

He's so beautiful that I can barely look at him, much less hold eye contact.

Sometimes, I indulge myself when he's chatting with whoever is on register. He's charming, with a brilliant white smile that flashes in contrast with the dark, perfectly manicured stubble that covers his anvil-sharp jawline. Midnight-black hair is artfully swept back from his heartbreaking face, longer on top and cropped close at the sides. Heavy brows that might be too harsh on another man accent his boldly masculine features.

Except for that soft, sensual mouth. It would be almost feminine if it weren't for his otherwise rugged perfection.

Stacy heaves a dreamy sigh as soon as he greets her. His deep voice rolls through the small café, his English accent enhancing his refined aura.

He moves past the register to stand at the end of the bar, waiting expectantly for his Americano. I keep my eyes on the milk I'm currently steaming for a flat white and try my best to ignore the shivery sensation elicited by his attention on me.

"Good morning, Abigail."

His voice is shockingly intimate, and the smooth cadence caresses my name.

Dane is friendly with everyone. The accent and deep timbre are seductive enough to make any woman swoon; his allure has nothing to do with me personally.

"Hi." I manage a breezy greeting but fix my attention on the swan I'm attempting to pour onto the top of the flat white.

Through sheer force of will, I keep my lips curved in my usual affable smile despite the fact that my soul is shattered into jagged pieces that cut at my heart. I brush my fingers over the small unicorn badge that I keep pinned to my apron. The pink and gold enamel is smooth and familiar beneath my shaky touch. I take half a heartbeat to connect with my lavender cupcake and smiling iced coffee pins, too, until my falsely bright grin matches their whimsical demeanor.

My outward disposition is my customary pleasant smile once again, but I still can't bring myself to meet Dane's stunning eyes. His gaze is keen enough to cut through the façade I'm desperately working to maintain. I've crafted it through sheer determination and stubbornness over the last two years, and it's so solid now that I mostly believe it myself.

Until last night wrecked it, the traumatic experience exposing the darkness at my core that no number of bright smiles can dissipate.

"Sorry, it'll be about a five-minute wait for your Americano," I apologize. "We're really busy this morning."

Truthfully, it's a fairly typical morning for everyone in the Sunny Side Café.

Except for me.

Not after what happened to me.

Proprietary hands on my body. A terrifying, ferocious growl that barely sounds human. A macabre white skull standing out in sharp contrast to the black ski mask.

My stomach lurches, and I swallow quickly to quell the surge of nausea. I focus on the lingering bitter taste of the espresso I quickly downed a few minutes ago, when I'd been running late for my shift.

The scent of coffee fills my senses, the familiar smell permeating the air and reminding me of the drink orders that are piling up to my left.

I look at the swan that I created on the flat white. The stylized bird is bright white against the espresso-tinged foam that surrounds it.

A harsh but familiar noise starts up behind me. Stacy is griding a bag of coffee beans that a customer purchased at the register.

"Abigail?"

I suck in a shocked breath when my name in his lilting accent hits me like a gut punch.

My mind scrambles, and I struggle to continue practicing what I remember of the grounding technique I learned from the single therapy session I did in college.

Taste, smell, see, hear...

I'm forgetting one of my senses. There's something else I should focus on to complete the act of grounding myself.

But all I can think about is that stark white skull glowing through the darkness of my apartment in the middle of the night. The fear that tasted like copper on my tongue. The abject horror when my body—

"Are you all right?"

Gentle fingers graze the back of my hand, harnessing my full attention.

Touch.

Dane is touching me. I feel the softness of his skin brushing mine, lighting up my nerve endings with awareness.

After my ordeal, I should be repulsed by a man's proximity. But the sparks that dance over my strangely chilled skin are subversively alluring.

How many nights have I fantasized about this breathtaking man when I'm alone in my twin-sized bed?

The time spent pleasuring myself while thinking about his sexy accent must've warped my brain, because my core heats for him even as my stomach turns.

I jerk my hand away as though he's burned me; I'm horrified at my twisted reaction to his tender touch. The flat white goes flying, and hot, espresso-darkened milk splatters his crisp white shirt just before the mug smashes on the polished hardwood floor.

Even the curse word that drops from his lush lips sounds sensual in his cultured accent.

"I'm so sorry!" Mortification washes through me in a searing wave. Mercifully, it burns away my trauma response.

I grab a clean cloth, and before I realize what I'm doing, I've rounded the coffee bar. I'm standing in front of Dane. My frenzied focus is fixed on the ugly brown stain that mars his perfectly tailored shirt. I press the cloth against the mark, and it soaks up some of the coffee while leaving the brown splatter clearly visible.

"I'm so sorry," I repeat, dabbing at the stain as though it will make any difference.

Long fingers ensnare my wrists, halting my panicked blotting. My entire body goes rigid, and I freeze like a spooked doe.

"It's fine." His voice is soft and soothing, as though he senses my spike of fear at the masculine shackles around my wrists.

But he doesn't immediately release me. His forefingers rest directly on my pulse points, and I'm not sure if my blood is thrumming through my veins from panic or from the hit of intense arousal at his firm hold.

"It's okay. Breathe, Abigail."

A scent like salt-kissed cedarwood with a hint of peppery spice suffuses my senses. I must be imagining the slight tightening of strong, sure fingers on my wrists—my jittery mood is messing with my perception of reality.

"Oh my god, Dane!" Stacy appears beside us, her tone sharp with disapproval that's directed at me. "Are you all right?"

"It's just coffee," he reassures her. "I have time to change before work."

He's still touching me.

He shouldn't be touching me. This prolonged contact is making my stomach flip and my hands shake, even as my core heats with feminine awareness of the beautiful man who stars in my fantasies.

As though he senses my mounting distress, he slowly eases his fingers from my chilled skin, his fingers brushing my pulse points one final time.

My arms drop to my sides—a marionette with her strings cut.

It's all I can do to keep my knees from folding. A visceral sense of relief? Or loss?

"Look at me, Abigail." That same soft but compelling tone in his delicious accent.

My eyes snap to his, and I'm locked in his steady gaze. This close, I can see the striations of hunter green that deepen the verdant forest shade of his eyes. His irises darken at the edges with an almost black ring that makes the rich hues vibrant despite the more muted color palette. Thick, black lashes form ebony frames around his remarkable eyes, enhancing the intensity of his stare.

"It's all right," he says, a low, intimate promise meant just for me.

"But I might've burned you." The words drop from my numb lips. I'm so cold, despite the heat flashing beneath the surface of my frosted skin.

That lush mouth tilts in an arrogant smirk. "I've had worse than anything you could throw at me."

"But your shirt—"

"I have another one at work that I was going to wear after the gym." He cuts me off, still speaking to me in that slow, reassuring cadence. "If you want to make it up to me, you can agree to go to dinner with me."

It's not a question, and he's so cajoling that I almost say *yes* before I can think better of it.

But my chest is too tight to say anything, iron bands clamping around my lungs. The residual shock of his touch hits me like a north wind wave, and memories of the assault slam into me.

A gloved hand shackles my wrists, pinning me to the wall. The peeling paint in my aging apartment flakes beneath my cheek, and a hard, broad body cages me in from behind. His other hand is clamped over my nose and mouth. I can't scream. I can't breathe...

"Abby?" The frosty disapproval in Stacy's voice melts into honeyed concern. "You don't look so good. If you're sick, you need to go home."

"Come on," Dane says when I don't answer right away. "Let's get some fresh air."

His sure fingers touch my elbow, and I simply allow him to steer me away from the mess I made with the flat white.

Just like last night, I don't try to resist; my body softens and submits.

I let it happen.

Something must be broken in my brain, because I lack the fight-or-flight instinct—when threatened, my body does neither.

Not that Dane is a threat. The stunning man who frequents the café every morning is a suave gentleman. Even though he's still touching me, the contact isn't remotely violent. And it's not entirely unwanted.

I shouldn't be enjoying a man's nearness, but I can't help edging toward his powerful body as we step outside into the Carolina heat. A soft ocean breeze barely cuts through the thick, humid air, and sweat instantly beads on my chilled brow. I can't seem to regulate my body temperature.

Maybe I am going to be sick, after all.

The prospect of vomiting in front of him is far too mortifying. I can't bear the thought of coming completely unraveled around the man I've secretly lusted after for months.

I close my eyes for a moment and draw in a deep breath through my nose. I inhale the scent of Dane's expensive cologne again: spicy, salt-kissed cedarwood. He's close enough that it blots out the slightly briny smell of the harbor and the musky scent of the carriage horse clopping by on the cobbled street.

His fingers finally drop from my elbow, only to skim up my arm so that his hand rests on my shoulder.

I've often admired his hands when he grasps the coffee cups that I offer him every morning. More than once, those long, deft fingers and the thoroughly masculine, broad palms have shown up in my paintings. The secret paintings that I've never shown to anyone.

His hand is heavier than I imagined it might be, and his fingertips press into my shoulder ever so slightly, as though his firm but careful grip will somehow hold me together when I'm on the verge of shattering. My composure is already in tatters, my cheery mask cracked to reveal the anguish inside.

"Breathe, Abigail," he intones. "Just breathe."

I obey and inhale more of his intoxicating scent.

"Why do you call me that?" I ask on the exhale before I can think better of it.

His dark brows knit together. "It's your name, isn't it?"

I gesture at my name badge that's pinned to my black apron. "Everyone calls me Abby."

He flashes me a dazzling smile that knocks the precious oxygen from my lungs. "I suppose I'm still a bit more formal than the locals. Bad habit from back home."

I don't bother to tell him that my local family raised me to be highly formal as well.

I never talk about them. If I can avoid it, I try not to even think about them.

"You're from England, right?" I ask instead, happy for the distraction from the churning in my gut.

He nods. "From York originally. The old York."

"Oh," I say, somewhat inanely. "What brought you to South Carolina?"

His smile turns a touch rueful. "You don't have to make small talk with me, Abigail. How are you feeling?"

In this moment, I decide that I love the way he says my full name. I don't want him to call me Abby. Despite the formality, it feels intimate; something I share only with him.

My heart gives a weak flutter, and the giddy reaction is so much sweeter than the shredding sensation that's tormented me all morning. I try again to lift my lips at the corners, and this time, my facial muscles cooperate.

I smooth my apron and touch the unicorn pin like a talisman: a reminder of the whimsical, joyful energy I choose to embody in the new life I've established for myself in Charleston.

"Better, thanks," I reply truthfully.

"Good."

God, that smile. He's always been too painfully perfect to look directly at him, but now that I'm caught in the full force of that cocky grin, I can't tear my gaze away.

"Are you feeling well enough to go out to dinner with me tonight?"

"What?"

His hand is still on my shoulder, grounding me far more effectively than the therapeutic technique of focusing on my five senses. Despite the fact that I no longer feel like I'm going to be sick, my brain is still too scrambled to fully process the fact that he's asking me out.

For months, it's felt safe to fantasize about him because he's too gorgeous and refined to ever consider as a real possibility. He's an untouchable prince, but I've crafted my secret rakish villain to wear his face when I'm alone in my bed. This invitation for a date seems impossible.

Not to mention, he's a customer, and I shouldn't date customers.

"You heard me," he admonishes, but his voice lilts with arrogant amusement. "Have dinner with me."

His grip on my shoulder tightens ever so slightly.

Gloved hands on my body, roughly groping and exploring my curves as though he has every right. A cloying scent of cheap amber aftershave makes the air sickeningly thick, so that it clogs in my constricted throat. That awful skull leers at me as he takes what he wants...

I jerk away from Dane, wrenching free from his hold. My stomach hollows out at the loss even as I gasp in a breath of humid air.

His allure is messing with my head when I need to hold the shattered fragments of my soul together in the wake of the attack.

No one knows what happened to me last night. I barely speak to my family anymore, and my friends don't need to know my shame.

There's no point calling the cops when the masked invader made me orgasm. Some part of me got off on it. The dark pleasure had cut deeper than the knife that'd threatened me.

I'm too fucked up, too broken, to be with a charming man like Dane.

"I can't," I blurt out. "I'm sorry."

He calls after me, but I spin on my heel and duck back into the café to finish my shift.

I act as though this is a normal day, and I manage to lose myself in rote, mundane tasks. Tonight, I'll get drunk with Franklin so that I won't be tempted to paint.

Because if I pick up a brush, I know the erotic horror that will spill out onto my canvas.

6

DANE

She's not painting tonight. And if I wasn't fully aware that her male friend is dating someone else, I might be tempted to violence.

Franklin showed up at her apartment with a cheap bottle of red wine two hours ago. He lives upstairs from her, his own cramped one-bedroom just as shabby as hers, but slightly tidier.

I know because I checked in on his place when he was out one day, only to find a picture of him kissing a handsome man framed on his nightstand. That same man enters this building and spends the night every weekend.

They seem to be in a committed relationship. I don't have to worry about Franklin's hands on my Abigail when they're tucked away in her apartment.

Still, I don't like how they drink wine together for hours. I know they often watch cheesy animated musicals together. But does she share her secrets with him? How much does he know about this woman who is my obsession and my greatest mystery?

Something ugly sours my stomach.

Jealousy?

I shake off the odd sensation. If I'm going to experience a shadow of true emotion—a rarity that I've only known since first setting eyes on Abigail—it won't be jealousy over her platonic friend.

I lean back in the rickety garden chair, slipping deeper into shadows as I watch her through the thick foliage of my overgrown azalea bushes. I lower my binoculars for a moment so that I can take in a long draw of my whisky.

Abigail is elusive in a way that irks me.

Does she see the monster beneath the carefully crafted façade?

She did seem afraid this morning. She jerked away from me twice: first, when she spilled the coffee on me, and again when I escorted her outside.

But she willingly made contact with me when she tried to blot the coffee splatter on my shirt. Her hands had fluttered around my torso like frantic flaps of a caged bird's wings. And when I captured her wrists, her pulse jumped at the contact. I'd indulged myself, maintaining the domineering hold for longer than appropriate.

And when her wide, aqua eyes met mine, her pupils were huge and dark—dilated from either fear or desire.

Maybe both.

Thinking about that makes my arousal rise, so I push the memory away and take another sip of my drink.

If Abigail is afraid of men, I'll prove to her that I'm capable of protecting her. She has no idea the lengths I'll go to in order to keep her safely with me.

She rejected me.

That's unacceptable.

I'll find a way to woo her. She'll come to my bed willingly, and she'll offer her wrists for the shackle of my firm grip.

We'll start with my hands. They're more than strong enough to bind her fragile frame until she's ready for the darker games that I need to play with her.

I settle into the shadows, watch her mind-numbing movie through my binoculars, and formulate a plan to sweep her off her feet.

7

ABBY

"Don't scream." The harsh, inhuman growl threads through the haze of my oxygen-starved brain. His gloved hand is clamped over my nose and mouth, and my muffled cries sputter and die as my lungs begin to burn. Darkness creeps in at the edges of my vision, making the shadows in my apartment lengthen to obscure my limited view.

My cheek is pressed against the peeling ivory paint on the inside of my front door. His hard body cages mine from behind.

The shadows darken, and my lashes flutter. I'm going to float away. Only his firm grip is keeping me anchored to reality.

My knees fold, and his hard chest presses against my back as he releases a sharp curse. His massive body pins mine, preventing me from falling. His smothering hand drops from my face.

"Breathe."

I suck in a ragged, desperate breath, and my entire body convulses at the burn of oxygen flooding my deprived lungs.

Before I can find the air to release a cry for help, icy metal kisses my throat, and my chest seizes again; I don't dare to draw breath when the knife could pierce my skin at the smallest movement.

Spiky fear dances through my veins in sharp, sparkling snowflakes. The chill is thrilling even as it shreds me. A bizarre urge to release the unspent adrenaline on a maddened laugh bubbles up in my tight chest, but the knife at my throat renders me silent.

The gloved hand slides down the length of my arms, and my nerve endings jump at the perverse caress.

His leather-clad fingers slide over my hair before skating down my nape. I shiver at the gentle contact. It's so at odds with the violence of the scene that my mind spins into a surreal state. My eyes slide closed, trying hide from what's happening to me.

I hear him inhale deeply, as though he's savoring the scent of my abject terror. His chest rumbles at my back when he releases a low hum of primal, masculine satisfaction. The sound of his pleasure vibrates through me, making my heart stutter and my belly quake.

The gloved hand traces my side, exploring the dip at my waist and the soft curve of my hip. It splays possessively over my stomach, and he applies pressure to tuck me more tightly against his hard body.

Time blurs. As he touches me, exploring at his leisure, a strange heat blossoms beneath the surface of my skin. It makes my cheeks burn and my breath come in shallow pants.

"You're wet." The observation is as rough as his curse. With disapproval? Or desire?

Something slick coats his glove when he traces the shape of my lips: my own traitorous arousal.

"Look at me."

I keep my eyes resolutely shut, hiding from the darkest part of my soul.

His fist tangles in my hair, wrenching my head back. Little sparks of pain light up my scalp, and my eyes fly open on a gasp.

"Look at me."

Forest green eyes glow like some sort of demonic creature, bright points of light glowering from the darkened sockets of the skull. It stands out in macabre contrast to the black ski mask, fixing me with a perpetual, cruel grin.

"You're so beautiful, Abigail."

My name lilts on the last. That voice. That accent.

Those eyes...

I jolt awake in my bed, sitting bolt upright. My eyes dart around my darkened apartment, searching the shadows for signs of my attacker.

I hug my arms tightly to my chest and focus on my five senses.

My skin is clammy beneath my hot fingertips. I hear my own sawing breaths echoing in my ears. I taste copper on my tongue and realize that I bit the inside of my cheek during my nightmare. The peeling, pale blue wallpaper in my bedroom reminds me of the peeling paint on my front door. And the scent that surrounds me is musky with my unmistakable arousal.

I want to crawl out of my own skin. It feels filthy, and my fingers itch with the need to scrape the grime away.

I heave in ragged breaths and struggle to purge the nightmare.

The masked man never said my name during the attack. His voice had been low and gravelly, not smooth and cultured with an English accent. His eyes had been black pools in my shadowy apartment; there had been no green glow.

My emotions are a snarled mess. In the stillness of sleep, my subconscious melded my ordeal with the man I've fantasized about: Dane.

Because the awful truth is that both turn me on.

My fingernails bite into my upper arms, but I manage to resist the urge to scrape away the toxic sludge that seems to roll beneath the surface of my skin in nauseating waves.

I flex my fingers and force my vise grip to release so that I can reach for the ancient laptop I keep tucked beneath my nightstand. I prop my back against my pillows, and comfort blankets me when the familiar weight of the laptop settles onto my thighs.

My fingers shake as I open it and enter my password. The website where I've catalogued my secret shame under an anonymous pen name is bookmarked, so I access it with a single click. Instead of typing out a new erotic story that blurs the lines of consent, I navigate to the messenger service.

My heart sinks when I notice the gray check mark beside my pen pal's screenname. GentAnon is offline.

I glance at the time on the top right of my screen. One-seventeen AM.

It's not uncommon for my trusted stranger to be online at this time. I tap out a message and hold my breath.

CAGEDBIRD

Are you awake?

My heart hammers against my ribcage, and I flex my fingers in an attempt to dispel the residual shaking from my nightmare. A pang lances my stomach, and I almost double over at the sudden surge of nausea. I hug my arms to my chest and struggle to drag in painful breaths while I anxiously await his reply.

The check mark turns green, and three dots appear. He has an alert set up on his phone for our late-night conversations, just like I do.

GENTANON

For you? Always. What filthy things are on your mind, little dove?

My breath hitches on a soft sob at the visceral relief of his online presence.

We've been exchanging fantasies for two months now. My steamy pen pal found kinship in my dark erotica that I posted on the Eroticlit online forum, and he DMed me one day to tell me how much he admires my writing. What started as compliments slowly turned to questions about my disturbing, secret urges, and then the dirty messages started.

My fingers finally steady as calm settles over me. I'm safe with my anonymous admirer. In this secret space, I can purge my inner darkness in a way I've never known before. I've always had my painting as an outlet, but I've never been able to share my shameful fantasies with another person.

In the wake of the attack, I'm craving safety, even though our clandestine connection is fucked up. There's a perverse security in expressing my secret self with this stranger who shares my deepest fantasies.

Three dots appear. I've allowed too many seconds to pass before replying. His admonishment lights up my screen.

GENTANON

Don't keep me waiting. You know the consequences of denying me.

My pulse quickens, and my core heats. I sink into our game, hiding from the horrors of my real life by losing myself in the thrill of our anonymous correspondence.

CAGEDBIRD

Fuck your consequences.

GENTANON

Such a dirty mouth for a sweet girl. I'll tame that tongue of yours with my cock down your pretty throat.

A familiar thrill dances up my spine—sharp sparks that prickle their way over my scalp, as though he's pulling my hair while he forces his cock into my unwilling mouth.

GENTANON

I like a little fight in you. Clipping your wings is such a pleasure, my little dove.

My core turns molten, and I squirm beneath my duvet as my clit begins to pulse in response to his crass threats. They should terrify me, but the thrill that fizzes through my veins is subversively alluring. I'm addicted to this fear, drawn to it like a moth to a flame.

And I want him to burn me up until I don't have any thoughts left except for the desire to submit to his perverted will.

CAGEDBIRD

Tell me what you want to do to me.

GENTANON

Making demands? That's not how this works. Beg.

Arousal wets my labia, and my inner muscles clench.

"Please..." I whisper the plea aloud as I type it.

I allow my eyes to drift closed for a moment. Dane's gorgeous face fills my mind, and in the darkness of my fantasy, his dangerous frown is directed at me. His green eyes spark with displeasure, and I tense in anticipation of his retribution.

My messenger pings an alert, and my eyes snap open.

GENTANON

"Please" isn't good enough. Get on your knees and show me how sorry you are.

CAGEDBIRD

Make me.

GENTANON

Stubbornness is a distasteful trait in such a pretty toy. I'll break you of that.

My breaths come fast and shallow, and my hand skims down my belly.

GENTANON

Don't you dare touch yourself. Wait for my permission.

All of my muscles coil tight with the effort of restraining

myself, but I still on his command. It's unnerving that he knows me so well, but that disturbing fact only stokes my lust.

GENTANON

If you don't want to kneel for me, I'll bind your ankles to your thighs and force you onto your knees. Then you won't be capable of doing more than crawling for me. I think I'd like to have you as my needy pet. I'll slip a ring gag between your teeth so that you can't do anything but whimper and drool for my cock.

My inner thighs are slick with my desire, and I'm aching to touch myself.

But I won't. I'm enjoying our game too much to deny his control, even if he's not here to witness any disobedience.

CAGEDBIRD

You left my hands free. Your pet still has claws.

GENTANON

Claw at me all you want. It will make taming you all the more satisfying. I can feel your nails sinking into my forearm while I pin your throat. You writhe and whine, but you're so small and weak. So breakable. Your fingers soften as your vision tunnels. You can't breathe unless I allow it. You're trapped on your bound legs, and you melt into my arms. It's almost too easy to wrap the rope around your wrists. Do you hear me laughing, little dove? It's no effort at all to subdue you. You're my tame pet now, and there's nothing you can do about it. I'm your master. I own you.

Green eyes flash through my mind, and sensual lips curve in a cruel smirk. My core contracts, desperate to be filled.

CAGEDBIRD

Please. I need to come. I need to touch myself.

GENTANON

Naughty thing. Pets don't talk. You'll take my cock in your mouth and moan around my dick if you want to beg me for an orgasm.

CagedBird

I love how your cock tastes, Master. I love when you use me for your own pleasure.

GENTANON

Sweet little pet. You feel so good when I'm fucking your mouth. I know you're trembling for release. Your cunt must be aching, but you aren't allowed to come yet. This is your punishment. You earned it. Show me how sorry you are.

CAGEDBIRD

Deeper, please. I don't want to breathe unless you allow it. Make me suffer for you, Master.

My lungs are burning. I'm not breathing, my body bending to his will even though he's nothing more than words on a screen.

GENTANON

Swallow everything I give you, and come for me. Now, little dove.

I shatter at the barest brush of my fingers over my swollen clit. Ecstasy crashes through me in vicious waves, and I bite down on my other fist to hold back a scream.

In this moment of cruel bliss, I'm stripped down to my most primal, perverted self. Tears slip down my cheeks as I sob my release. Deep in my soul, I know that this is where I belong: alone in the dark with my shameful secrets.

What am I doing?

I came while I was violated last night, and now I'm seeking to relive the same thrill with my sexy pen pal.

This isn't a distraction. It's not catharsis.

It's a sick compulsion.

I've made myself a magnet for predatory men. They must

be able to sense that some part of me wants it. My filthy messages with GentAnon are proof of that.

I swallow against the burn at the back of my throat and snap my laptop closed. My phone immediately pings with an alert. GentAnon has sent me another message.

I scramble to my feet and stumble toward my beloved easel, moving through my small apartment in a drunken lurch. The soft glow of my lamps doesn't fully illuminate the space, but it's only right for me to paint this forbidden scene while cloaked in shadow.

My brush moves over the blank canvas in feverish strokes. A macabre white skull coalesces on my canvas, and striking green eyes blaze from its black sockets.

8

DANE

"You'll bail me out if I get caught?" The thief swipes sweat from his tanned brow, which is too youthful to show any signs of age. He can't be more than twenty, but he's already chosen a life of crime. I found him dealing drugs to a couple of kids younger than he is.

Even if I possessed a conscience, it would be at peace; manipulating this little shit doesn't bother me in the slightest.

"You won't get caught," I say, more of a threat than a reassurance. I've made it clear that there will be consequences if he goes blabbing to the cops. "And what I've already paid you is more than enough to cover any bail. You'll get the other half after."

His tongue darts out to lick his thin, chapped lips—a sign of nervousness or greed?

It doesn't matter. He's a means to an end.

"Remember," I add coolly. "You don't know me. You've never seen my face."

He swallows hard when I flip the knife in an idle threat and deftly catch the hilt. His shaved head bobs in a frantic nod.

"I remember," he agrees quickly, voice cracking slightly. "I just want my money."

I close the switchblade and tuck it out of sight with a sigh before flashing the wad of cash in my wallet. "This is yours. After you finish the job."

His brown eyes are huge, and I swear he's salivating at the sight of the hundred-dollar bills.

"I'll see you in the market at noon. Wait for my signal."

He nods again. "You got it, boss."

My lip curls in contempt at his obsequious reply. I command respect, but I've had enough bowing and scraping to last a lifetime.

I turn from the pathetic excuse for a man and stroll out of the alley between the two derelict brick buildings on Cooper Street. Despite my eagerness to get to Abigail, I keep a leisurely pace as I make my way across town to the market. With each step, anticipation coils my muscles, until my entire body thrums with the thrill of the hunt.

In a matter of hours, Abigail will be mine.

Then I can punish her for shutting me out last night. She's never been scared off by my perverse messages as GentAnon before; she thrives on the dark thrill of the fantasies we share online.

But she logged off and refused to respond to my demands for a reply.

An echo of the frustration that'd clawed at me all night rakes my insides with an aggravating sting.

She refused a date with me when I asked her out at the

café yesterday, and she denied me as GentAnon last night. We've been messaging for months, and I can't bear the wait to claim her in every way.

It's time for me to escalate my plans to possess Abigail.

9

ABBY

Franklin shoots me a broad grin from across the bustling market aisle. I force my lips into a semblance of a smile. They twitch at the corners, but long practice allows me to keep my appearance outwardly cheery. I learned at a young age to remain poised under the most stressful circumstances.

I feel my back going ramrod straight, adopting the perfect posture that was enforced at my mother's dining table. I'm determined to overcome my social anxiety so that I can sell my art.

No matter how shaken I am after my awful nightmare and sleepless hours at my canvas.

I straighten my bright pink t-shirt, reminding myself of the bold black words emblazoned on the front: *ON WEDNESDAYS WE SMASH THE PATRIARCHY.*

It's Saturday, but that doesn't bother me. It's the overall, confident vibe of the outfit that counts.

I offer Franklin a little dismissive wave, encouraging him

to focus on his sales. My friend's gaze turns back to the tourist who's admiring his sculptures. He's so much more skilled at selling his art than I am. Maybe if I were less socially awkward, I would earn enough to cover my rent.

As it is, I can't survive without my barista job.

Selling my work is stressful, but it's the only way to share my art. My landscapes will have to be enough to leave my mark on the world in some limited way.

In an attempt to be more personable, I gather my courage and step around to the front of my stall, just to the right of my paintings. I make deliberate, friendly eye contact with a potential customer. The elderly man returns my smile before his gaze skates over my work. He offers me a kind nod of acknowledgement but keeps walking through the market.

My heart sinks slightly, but my smile remains fixed in place. Franklin captures my attention again and gives me a thumbs-up.

Then his eyes slide past me and widen.

"Abby!" he exclaims, pointing to something behind me.

I whirl, and my heart leaps into my throat.

A man is behind my table. He's clutching my second-hand purse. The purse itself is too worn to be worth anything—the pale yellow, quilted fabric is wearing thin, and the bluebell pattern has faded over time. There's not a lot of cash inside. I've only made fifty dollars from selling one painting this morning, but I need that money to buy food this week.

"Hey!" I shout, instinctively lunging for my purse to save the precious funds.

The man's brown eyes meet mine, wide and a bit wild. His brow is creased with anxiety, and his shaved head is shiny with sweat.

"You don't have to do this," I say quickly. "Just leave it. Please."

His jaw firms, and his fist crushes my purse.

I'm blocking his way to the exit. Not out of bravery; the market is busy, and my stall is at the end of the row.

"Please," I repeat, more desperately this time. "I won't call the cops if you just—"

He surges toward me, and I stumble back. Rough hands shove my shoulders, forcing my falling body out of his way. Stinging pain scrapes my palms as I hit the concrete floor.

"Abby!" Franklin shouts my name, and I crane my head back to see that he's scrambling around his own stall to get to me. A throng of shocked tourists separate us, and he's pushing his way through the small crowd.

"Abigail." That deep, lilting cadence caresses my name. "Are you all right?"

"Dane?" I ask breathlessly, turning my face to search for the familiar voice.

Forest green eyes fill my world. They're tight with concern, fine lines drawing deep at the corners. His brow is furrowed, and those lush lips are pinched with worry.

The strong hands that I've painted so many times reach for me. Just like at the café yesterday, they encircle my wrists in gentle shackles. This time, he tugs my hands close to his face so that he can inspect them. He scowls at the shallow pink scratches that mar my palms. They're not deep enough to have drawn blood, even if they do sting a bit.

"I'm okay," I promise shakily. "I'm not hurt."

"I'll be the judge of that," he counters sternly. "Stay still. I'm a doctor."

My brain blanks for a few seconds, and I comply out of

shock more than intentional cooperation. Dane is touching me again. It's thrilling and surreal.

My heart hammers in my chest, and I'm not sure if the elevated beat is because of the encounter with the thief or because of the visceral physical reaction elicited by Dane's nearness.

"Can you stand?" he asks, his tone low and gentle.

"Yeah." My reply is still a touch shaky, but I try to summon up some semblance of dignity.

I tug my hands from his so that I can push myself onto my feet.

His scowl deepens, and he captures my upper arms, steadying me as I rise.

"I'll call the cops." Franklin is at my side, his ochre eyes flashing with anger on my behalf. He turns to the elderly man who smiled and nodded at me. "You're a witness, right?"

The man's nod is grim this time. "I saw everything."

"It's fine," I say quickly.

I don't want the cops involved. They'll ask for my full, legal name. There will be paperwork. Possibly a small story in the news.

I suppress a shudder at the prospect of public exposure, the risk that my family might find out about this incident. I've learned to find joy in the small, quiet life I've built for myself, and I can't bear the thought of their censure if they find out that I have a stall at the market rather than my own gallery.

"It wasn't a lot of money," I insist. "It's not worth calling the cops."

Franklin looks at me like I'm crazy. "That psycho hit you. I'm calling nine-one-one."

"I just stumbled," I counter quickly. "And I'm fine. Seriously, Franklin. Don't."

His eyes search mine, and his lips thin beneath his neat black moustache. He must see some of the panic churning inside me, because he nods after a tense moment.

"Okay. It's your call, Abby."

Dane's eyes turn stormy. "I was walking through the market and saw you, so I decided to come say hello. I should've been here five minutes earlier."

The protectiveness in that fierce statement makes something distinctly feminine swoon inside me, and I release a small sigh.

"How much did he take?" His voice rumbles with anger. On my behalf.

"I really am okay," I promise. "Thank you for coming to check on me."

His eyes remain fixed on mine, but he tilts his chin in the direction of my purse, which the thief discarded when he grabbed my cash and ran.

"How much did he take?" he repeats, and his deep tone demands an answer this time.

"Fifty dollars." I'm compelled to reply. "It's early. I'll sell another painting to make up for the loss by the end of the day."

His attention turns to my work. I'm seized by the sudden urge to step in front of him so that he can't see my art. For some reason, it feels too deeply personal; I squirm at the prospect that he might critique my paintings. Someone as suave as Dane probably has expensive taste in art, and even though painting is my passion, I'm far from gallery-worthy.

His head cants to the side, considering for a long, agonizing moment.

"I'll take all of them," he says with a sweep of his arm to encompass the entire table.

"What?" I ask on a puff of air.

His lips quirk in a devastatingly sexy smirk. "You heard me. I want to buy all of them. And then we can talk about meeting for drinks tonight."

An ingrained instinct to protect myself tenses my muscles, and I forget all notions about being charmed by his white-knight behavior. "I don't want your money."

His jaw firms in response to my swift defiance. "It's not charity, Abigail. I want to buy your art."

I've offended him, but I won't bend. "No, thank you."

I might be struggling to make ends meet, but I will not be indebted to anyone. I've learned the hard way how to stand on my own two feet, and I won't make myself vulnerable to financial manipulation ever again.

It would've been one thing if he'd simply asked me on a date. But the qualifier that he wants to buy the privilege makes my stomach churn. What more will he expect of me when he's bought and paid for my time and gratitude?

"Let me help you," he says, his tone heavy with something like admonishment, as though I'm being stubborn for no reason.

"No, thank you." My back goes ramrod straight once again.

His gaze flicks over my squared shoulders, noting my stiff posture. Then his eyes capture mine. They glitter with irritation and something a bit darker that I don't fully acknowledge. A shiver races through me, but I hold my ground.

Dane blinks, and the disapproving glint vanishes from his eyes. They're warm with concern again, and his handsome face is fixed in a rueful smile.

"I didn't mean to offend you," he says, his voice resuming his smooth, alluring cadence. "If you'll forgive me, I'd still like to meet for a drink tonight. I'll feel better if I can see that you're okay at the end of the day."

My mind reels. Did I imagine the darkness lurking behind his eyes when I refused him? He's so genial now, completely disarming. His six-foot-four frame even seems less imposing, as though he's making himself less intimidating in order to put me at ease.

I suppose it's a small mercy, considering how shaken up I am from the robbery. Dane said he's a doctor. He must have a good bedside manner to adjust his bearing in order to reassure me.

My reaction to his offer to buy my paintings was terse, and he was just trying to help me. I won't back down and allow him to purchase them, but I am grateful to him for checking on me when I fell.

And he's still the gorgeous man who comes into my café every morning and greets me with a warm smile.

"A drink sounds nice," I agree. "Where do you want to meet?"

His grin lights up my world, and I'm breathless for an enraptured moment.

"The Magnolia Hotel at eight. Have you been to their rooftop bar? The views are beautiful at sunset."

I return his grin, my own smile a bit punch-drunk and giddy. The last few minutes have been an emotional rollercoaster.

"That sounds great," I reply.

"I'll see you then," he says warmly. "I'll let you get back to your paintings."

The world around us slides back into focus. Somehow, everything had fallen out of existence during my intense exchange with Dane.

He shoots me one final crooked smile and turns. I watch him saunter away until he disappears into the crowd of tourists that fill the bustling market.

My mind is tumbling through the wild events that've unfolded over the last fifteen minutes. I'm so absorbed by excitement for my date with Dane that I don't pause to worry over the fact that I've agreed to go out with a customer from the café.

10

DANE

"Where's the rest?" the thief demands, holding out a grubby hand for the cash that's still tucked away in my wallet.

"You hurt her." The words are smooth and amiable as they leave my tongue.

He doesn't read the condemnation in my calm tone.

Keeping one hand outstretched for the money, he swipes at his sweaty brow with the other, leaving a smudge of dirt behind.

The man is filth, and I don't bother to hide the disdain in my sneer.

The plan had been for him to steal her wallet so that I could swoop in and save her. If she sees me as her protector, she'll start to depend on me. She'll welcome me into her life and be grateful for my help.

Instead, she'd seemed angry that I tried to help her recoup her lost funds. She refused to allow me to buy her paintings.

Something hot simmers in my veins, and my muscles flex with mounting aggression.

"She tried to block my exit," the thief insists, his frantic gaze searching my body as though X-raying me for my wallet. "I told you that I didn't want to get caught." His eyes narrow on mine when I don't hand over the cash immediately. "We had a deal. You owe me the other half."

"The deal was for you to steal her purse. I warned you not to damage anything. You damaged *her*."

The faint pink scratches on her palms flash through my thoughts, and a strange red haze descends over my vision.

My fist smashes into his jaw, and his head jerks back. He crumples to the dirty pavement, momentarily stunned from the blow. My designer leather boot kicks his soft belly, and his shocked cry dies as his diaphragm spasms. Another clinically placed kick to his kidneys ensures that he'll be pissing blood tomorrow.

He gasps, but he can't inhale the air he needs to groan in pain.

Something savage heats my chest, a visceral sensation I've never experienced before. I've known satisfaction in my life, but never anything like this. I imagine this must be what Roman gladiators felt in the arena: pure, primal bloodlust.

I haven't allowed myself true violence since I was a very young child, when my family first noticed my abnormality. I quickly learned to hide my disconcerting nature. My mother made sure I knew how important it was to conceal the monster within.

But as the thief's teeth rattle beneath the impact of my boot, I let the mask fall away entirely. I'm fully myself for the first time in my adult life: cruel, powerful, and vicious.

And it's all because of *her*.

The memory of her wide, aquamarine eyes fills my mind, and I fixate on the hint of trepidation that tightened the fine lines around them. Back in the market, I allowed my frustration to crack my charming façade, and she'd been observant enough to sense the danger lurking inside me.

Abigail desires me, but part of her also fears me.

I've never wanted her more than I do in this moment. My blood runs hot in my veins, and my cock stiffens at the thought of claiming her while she looks up at me with that intoxicating mix of trepidation and longing.

The thief moans when I drop the hundred-dollar bills on his shaking body. I barely notice him anymore. As I turn on my heel and stride out of the dank alley, all I can think about is Abigail.

She wouldn't let me buy her paintings. My grand gesture was completely ruined by her stubborn will. I'm still irritated, but now that I've purged the vicious feelings that'd overtaken me, I'm more fascinated than ever.

Clearly, she needs the money. But she wouldn't accept my help.

Out of pride? Or something deeper?

I recall the way her shoulders straightened as she stared me down like a defiant queen. That woman wasn't the same person as the cheerful barista who shyly greets me at the café every morning.

I'm more determined than ever to win her over so that I can learn all of her secrets.

11

ABBY

I smooth my dress, ensuring that it's wrinkle-free. I'm wearing one of my only designer outfits—a gem of a find from an upscale consignment shop off King Street. The silky, royal blue material skims my modest curves, and the high halter-neck design is demure enough to make the garment classy despite the thigh-high slit at the left side. The dress dips into a low V at the back, and the warm evening air caresses my bare skin.

I hesitate just inside the entrance to The Magnolia, the boutique hotel with a rooftop bar where I was supposed to meet Dane eight minutes ago.

This might be a mistake. Now that I'm faced with the reality of this meeting, I'm wracked with uncertainty. Dane is a customer, and I'll have to see him at the café even if this goes badly. I'm still troubled by the fact that I've spent hours fantasizing about a dark villain that wears his handsome face. He proved through his actions at the market that he's truly a white knight, and as much as I crave that version of him, I can't let go of my shameful imaginings. I'm not sure if I want him to rescue me or to ravage me.

My fingers tighten around my small black clutch as I struggle to master my rising anxiety. I only have a single twenty-dollar bill and a wad of ones inside the bag—just enough to cover two cocktails. If I choose to go up to the bar and see this through, I won't be able to rely on alcohol to soothe my nerves; I can't afford it.

Dane is waiting. I should've ridden the golden elevator up to the rooftop already, but I can't stop staring at the art that fills the hotel entry hall. This space has been set up as a small gallery featuring work by local artists. I love it here, and a stroll down the corridor always calms me. Even if I will never be talented enough to have my landscapes included in the collection.

A pang twinges my gut—something between envy and longing—as I stare at the abstract expressionist piece that dominates the wall beside the elevator. It's a breathtaking study in various shades of red: fiery rage, sultry seduction, and the blush of innocence corrupted. It evokes the full spectrum of passion, and I allow myself to become absorbed by the beauty of the painting to distract myself from my mounting anxiety.

The elevator dings, the sound jolting me out of my reverie like a reverberating gong. I startle, and the golden doors slide apart to reveal Dane.

He's stunning in a sharply fitted black jacket paired with dark wash jeans. His crisp white shirt is unbuttoned at the collar, revealing the tiniest peek at masculine chest hair.

My gaze snaps from that little hollow between his collarbones to his wrist as he tugs back his sleeve to check his Rolex. He quirks a dark brow at me, and his expression is enigmatic for a heartbeat while he fixes me in a steady green stare.

I shift my weight on my strappy, black high heels, and my cheeks flush a shade of pink that matches a swatch on the painting beside him.

"Sorry I'm late," I say, embarrassment softening my tone.

I hate being late. My mother is perpetually tardy, and the remembered shame of entering every social function over half an hour late heats my face. I never want to be like her.

Dane's dazzling smile hits me square in the chest. "It's my fault," he assures me. "I should've waited down here to meet you. I'll escort you upstairs."

He offers his arm like some sort of gentleman out of Regency England. I stare at it for a moment, taken aback by the formal gesture.

I've spent the last few years trying to forget the pretentious, genteel behavior that I was taught by my family from a young age. But Dane's suave bearing suits him, and I can't help being charmed; he's not putting on a performance to impress me. This is just who he is. He's chivalrous like one of the dashing princes out of my favorite movies.

My lips curve in a smile of my own, and I step into the elevator to join him. My arm slides through his, my fingers resting on his forearm.

For a moment, I flash back to the awful night of my debutante ball and the performative bullshit that masks the rot at the core of Southern "high society".

I take a breath and force those memories away. I won't allow them to taint this night with Dane.

Shock immobilizes me when he casually touches my hair, trailing his long fingers over the purple streak. It's curled in a loose wave, and I intentionally keep it swept in front of my shoulder as a matter of habit.

"I like this," he remarks, and his deep voice seems to rumble through me. "Why purple?"

"It's my favorite color," I reply.

"It suits you."

I flush at his compliment and speak before I can stop myself. "My dad used to say he would disown me if I ever colored my hair."

I'm babbling to dispel some of the overwhelming tension that's building between us in the cramped space of the elevator. I'm anxious in a way I've never experienced before—it's a fizzy sensation that makes my body feel strangely light even as my stomach flips with nervous energy.

"But I've wanted to do it since I was thirteen," I continue. As soon as I dropped out of college and started my new life two years ago, I made sure to dye in my amethyst streak. "So, I'm glad I did. My manager at the café doesn't mind. Another advantage of avoiding a corporate job."

"Beautiful." Dane isn't looking at my hair anymore, but he keeps the curl loosely curved around his forefinger. Those verdant eyes are fixed on my face, flicking over each of my features as though he's memorizing me.

My cheeks heat again, but not from embarrassment this time; I'm gratified at his intense attention.

"What's your favorite color?" I ask, even if the question is a bit inane.

"Blue." He's staring into my eyes now, as though he can peer straight into my soul.

My head tips back, and I sway toward him, drawn in by his hypnotic gaze.

The elevator dings, breaking the intimate moment. His

fingertip traces the shape of my purple curl almost regretfully, then he withdraws.

He steps out of the elevator and guides me onto the rooftop. The bar is to our left, the area covered with a black awning that shields our eyes from the setting sun. To our right, the golden syrup sunlight bathes the open rooftop with waning summer heat. The sky is turning a stunning shade of pink at the horizon, framing the historic church steeples that define the Charleston skyline.

The familiar artistic urge to drink in the vista tugs at my heart like a cord toward the railing that surrounds the rooftop, but my hand might as well be glued to Dane's arm. I can't bring myself to put distance between us, not after that magnetic interaction in the elevator.

A reckless, giddy thrill thrums through my system. The strange high should be slightly alarming, but it's too addictive for me to question it.

We reach the bar, and Dane summons the bartender with a single nod. The gesture is almost imperious, but the air of authority suits him.

I'm so caught up in his commanding bearing that I don't immediately protest when he orders an old fashioned and a glass of champagne. It's not until the crystal flute is placed in front of me that I realize he's ordered for me.

I shoot him a small frown.

"What's wrong?"

"I was going to order something different."

I can't afford champagne, but I'm too embarrassed to admit it. I intend to pay for my own drinks, but this means I can only have a single glass of bubbly on my meager budget.

A dark brow lifts. "Oh? Don't you like champagne?"

I shrug as nonchalantly as I can manage. “I had planned to order a strawberry daiquiri.”

He huffs a laugh, and the rich sound surrounds me like I’m being submersed in warm honey. “Why am I not surprised? I should have known you’d want something sugary.”

I tilt my chin at him, puzzled. “And how would you know something like that?”

His half-smile is a touch indulgent. “Those badges you wear on your apron,” he explains. “I particularly like the happy donut.”

I release a small laugh of my own—a shy, girlish giggle I’ve never heard issue from my own throat before.

“I didn’t realize you pay so much attention to my pins.”

“I want to know you.” He gestures at the glass of champagne. “Leave that. I’ll order a daiquiri for you instead.”

“That’s okay.” I say quickly. I definitely can’t afford to waste the precious bubbly. “I like champagne.”

His expression firms to something slightly stern. “I’ll get whatever you want, Abigail.”

I meet him with my own steady stare, standing my ground. “I want the champagne. You don’t have to order for me.”

“What if I like ordering for you?” he replies with a small smirk that makes my belly flip. “What if I want to take care of you?”

There’s a teasing edge to his questions, but his smoldering gaze is pure temptation.

I sway toward him for half a heartbeat, drawn in despite my independent sensibilities.

I find the willpower to pick up the champagne flute and tip my glass at him in a sardonic toast. My heart is fluttering, and my fingers tingle against the cool crystal. My entire body feels alive in a way I've never experienced before.

"Thank you, but I can take care of myself. I'm happy with the champagne."

His eyes spark, and his nostrils flare slightly—like a predator that's caught the scent of its prey.

A giddy high floods my veins, and my arm practically floats upward as I lift the flute with a teasing smile of my own.

"Cheers." I clink my glass against his.

His smirk sharpens to a grin that's almost feral, and he silently lifts his own drink. It's not a capitulation; he's indulging me. I'm not the only one caught up in this wild energy.

"Come on." His hand abruptly engulfs mine, and he tugs me away from the bar. "You'll want to watch the sun set."

I lift a brow at his imperious tone, but my insides are molten. I don't mind his highhanded manner one bit, and he's absolutely right: I would love to watch the sun set with him.

He rumbles another low chuckle. "I saw you glancing longingly at the horizon as soon as we got off the elevator. You're very easy to read."

A laugh bubbles from my chest. His intense focus on me goes straight to my head, and I'm in awe that this gorgeous man is so fixated on me.

We come to a stop at the railing, and I rest my elbows on it. I crave to be close to him in a way that defies all logic. After what happened to me only a few nights ago, I shouldn't want to be near any man.

Before memories of the attack can surface and drag me out of this perfect moment, I lean into Dane so that our forearms brush. Even the light contact makes my skin prickle with awareness of his powerful body so close to mine.

"How long have you lived in Charleston?" I ask, eager to learn more about the man who's starred in my fantasies.

"Only three months," he replies. "I came for work after finishing my residency at Johns Hopkins."

"You're a doctor?" He told me his job at the market when he checked my scraped palms, but I want to know everything about him now.

"Yes." He gives a dismissive little wave. "But that's work. I'd much rather talk about your art."

"Don't you like your job?"

He shrugs. "I like being good at what I do. I like being successful and self-sufficient. The details of my profession don't really matter. I find that Americans tend to be defined by their careers in a way I've never fully understood."

"What brought you over from England? Did you want to come to America for college?"

"Yes." He acknowledges my query, but he doesn't allow me to change the subject. "From what I saw at the market, I noticed that your preferred style is impressionism. Did you study Art at school?"

I fix him with a small pout. He's not being forthcoming, and I've spent too many long nights wondering about this gorgeous man to let it go so easily.

"Do I have to beg for more information?"

He releases a low hum, and his lips tug in a lopsided smirk. "I don't hear you begging yet."

My cheeks flame with a surge of lust and embarrassment, and I drop my gaze to hide from his intense attention. If I maintain eye contact, he might glimpse a shadow of my inner darkness.

Because the pulsing between my legs indicates that I would very much enjoy begging this man for satisfaction. I would eagerly debase myself and relish every deviant second of submitting to his cruel will.

I shove the perverted thoughts away. I have to stop thinking of him like he's the rakish villain from my forbidden fantasies. The real Dane is here with me: solid and imposing and almost painfully beautiful.

I try for a nonchalant shrug and choose to engage with his preferred topic: my art.

"I studied Art at College of Charleston, but I didn't finish my degree," I admit. "I just love painting. I decided that I don't need a degree to prove that."

I have my own reasons for dropping out of school, but that's too much to dump on him. I summon up an easy smile and skate over the moment of discomfort.

"My only regret is that I didn't get to study abroad before I quit," I continue. "I actually wanted to study in London for a semester. I'd love to visit England one day. You said you're from York, right? Is that close to London?"

He shoots me a half-smile. "By American standards, yes. By English standards, it's quite far. Yorkshiremen can get very prickly about differentiating themselves from Londoners."

My brows lift, interest piqued. "Oh? Are you a Yorkshireman, then?"

He barks a laugh, white teeth flashing in a perfect grin. "Let's just say I was born in Yorkshire, but I don't exactly fit in with the locals."

"Is that why you decided to come to America for college?" I press. "Don't you like where you're from?"

His gaze focuses on something beyond me, and the slight distance between us makes it feel as though he's shut off the sun.

"Yorkshire is beautiful," he rumbles. "But I wanted to forge my own path."

Maybe I have more in common with Dane than I would've guessed.

"I understand," I murmur, drawn to open up to him so that he'll focus on me again. Being the center of his attention is thrilling and addictive. I'll confess almost anything to get it back.

"My family wanted me to finish my undergraduate degree and then pursue a master's." I reveal one of my secrets. "They wanted my success to be their own."

His gaze cuts back to mine, sharp enough to pin me in place.

"They put a lot of pressure on you," he surmises.

I nod and continue my confession, the words tumbling from my lips as though I can't help myself.

"My parents never really cared about my art. They just wanted to be able to tell people that their daughter's a successful artist."

"My family had certain expectations for me too," Dane says, offering me a small confession of his own.

I latch onto it like a lifeline. A sense of intimacy blossoms between us, and the promise of this connection is as seductive as his heated gaze. I crave more, so I press, "And you defied them?"

He inclines his head. "I'm here, aren't I? An ocean separates us, and I prefer it that way."

I've only managed to move a few cities away from my family, but I'm determined to live my life separately from them. This shared, painful history with Dane takes my breath away.

He takes a sip of his old fashioned, and I mirror him, allowing the moment of kinship to settle between us.

He commands my full attention, and I'm hyperaware of him: his intoxicating scent swirling around me on the light breeze, the setting sun illuminating his green eyes, the subtle brush of his arm against mine.

He's being respectful of my space, allowing me to dictate the contact while staying close enough to maintain our simmering connection.

I want to trust Dane, despite everything I've been through at the hands of dangerous men.

He came to my rescue at the market. He's protective, even if he is imposing.

I decide to push for more information. "So, you came to Charleston to practice medicine? Didn't you like Baltimore?"

He takes another sip of his drink, as though he's considering his answer. I do the same because I'm feeling slightly jittery. I don't want to ruin this moment between us with inane chatter.

"I value the education I received there," he says. "My time in Baltimore gave me the skills I needed to pursue the life I want. One of my colleagues is from Charleston, so when he asked me to move here and form a private practice with him, I said yes." He fixes me with that wicked half-smile. "I'm still fairly new to the area. You can show me around."

He's charming enough that it doesn't sound like a command, even if it isn't exactly a question. Why would I argue with him about his imperious manner when I'm eagerly hanging on to his every word?

"What kind of medicine do you practice?" I ask, anticipating more intimate confessions from him. "You must really care about helping people if you chose to move to a strange city and start from scratch."

The slight shake of his head is a touch self-deprecating, and I think he's going to dismiss my enthusiastic description of his altruism.

"Like I said, it's just a job," he reiterates. "I chose plastic surgery because I'm good at it."

My heart sinks.

"Oh," I reply, and my voice is a touch cooler than I intend. "I didn't realize that's your area of expertise."

I'm not sure if I can stomach it if he's chosen a profession where he gives people fake masks to present false perfection to the world.

The image of my grandmother's strangely stretched features fills my mind. She'd never looked like herself after the facelift. And my mother's perpetually frozen expression haunts my most anxious nightmares—even when she's feeling especially cruel, her face remains disturbingly serene from years of Botox treatments.

We need to get that large freckle on your cheek removed, Abby. Imagine having the blemish in your wedding photos. You don't want that. And you'll find a husband more easily once it's cleared up.

The snide comments about my own physical flaws tease at the back of my mind, tainting the moment with Dane. The reality of him might not be as perfect as I've imagined in the months since he first walked into the café.

12

DANE

"Are you going to tell me why my career bothers you?" I ask, keeping my voice bland and nonconfrontational.

It takes considerable effort to prevent the strange tension that's coiling my muscles from showing on my face. The moment I told her I'm a plastic surgeon, something shifted between us. She's guarded now, and I don't like being denied access into her thoughts.

She keeps her gaze on the horizon rather than meeting my eye. "I would never change my appearance to be more pleasing to others."

I study her lovely profile: the gentle slope of her nose, the sharpness of her cheekbone with that fascinating freckle, and her slightly stubborn chin that offsets the soft definition of her jawline. Her petal-soft lips are understated—I have plenty of patients who might ask for fillers with that mouth to keep up with current trends. But Abigail's Cupid's bow is sharply defined and symmetrical. Her lips are perfectly in balance with her large eyes and the delicate taper of her jaw.

"You value authenticity," I surmise rather than extoling her beauty. I don't want her to retreat into herself if I compliment her physical attributes when I sense that she's talking about something much deeper.

Her gaze finally meets mine, as though she's surprised at my incisive remark. "I don't like fake people," she admits.

"I meant what I said before," I assert. "It's just a job. I do it because I'm good at it."

She presses her lips together, dissatisfied with my answer. "You don't care at all about what you do? You must've studied very hard for something you're not passionate about."

"Are you passionate about being a barista?" I challenge, my own lips pursing in irritation at her imbalanced assessment.

She blinks. "No. But it's how I pay my bills. It allows me the time and creative energy I need to paint."

"And my job affords me the lifestyle I desire," I counter.

She's quiet for a beat, and I struggle to maintain eye contact as she stares straight into me. This connection goes both ways, and the power of our intimacy unnerves me.

Something squeezes in the center of my chest, and I can't draw breath until she offers me absolution. I need her approval more than I need oxygen, and I'm bizarrely cold in the absence of her sunshine smile.

"You value your independence, too," she finally murmurs. "You said you left your family behind in England and chose a different path for yourself. I understand. And I'm sorry I judged you."

For a moment, I'm at a loss for words. I'm shocked at her easy apology. And her insight.

"I'm sure you'll love living in Charleston," she says before I can formulate a response. "If you want to explore the area, we have beautiful beaches around here. I spent all of my free time by the ocean when I was little. I grew up just an hour and a half south of here, so the South Carolina coast is home for me. Did you go to the beach much in England?"

I'm relieved at the conversational shift after the tense moment, so I'm happy that she's changing the subject.

"The North Sea is a bit colder than the southern Atlantic," I reply in traditional British understatement. "I never cared for it when I was a child."

"I'd love to see it one day." She sighs the words, and that dreamy expression softens her gaze again. "I'm fascinated by Whitby. Have you ever been?"

I blink at her in surprise. Whitby was a staple day out during my childhood, and just thinking about the dreary place fills my memories with scents of briny sea and newspaper-wrapped fish and chips. "Many times. How do you know about Whitby?"

She cocks a brow at me, as though the answer is obvious. "The ruined abbey was the inspiration for *Dracula*. All of the pictures I've seen online are breathtaking."

I shouldn't be surprised that she likes *Dracula*. I'm starting to sense a darker theme to the fiction she prefers. I'm quite familiar with the romantic fantasy titles that she keeps in a haphazard stack beside her bed. I memorized all of them when I broke into her place to learn more about her preferences.

I already know that she's perfect for me, and I'm relishing each new revelation about her forbidden desires.

"What do you like to read?" she asks. "For some reason, I

can picture you with some politician's autobiography in your hand."

I shake my head and don't bother to hide the slight twist of distaste that curls my lip. "You're right, I usually prefer nonfiction. But I'm not interested in other people's self-indulgent ramblings. I like theoretical physics, particularly astrophysics."

Her smile takes on a rueful tilt. "Science isn't my strong suit," she says, as though it's an admission of a personal failing. "I've always been more into the arts."

She sees the natural world in a way that I've never considered before, and she captures the darkest aspects of human nature in her private, erotic paintings. I'm in awe of her art, but she's not ready to hear that yet.

"I like understanding how things work," I explain instead. "Knowledge is power. But I'm starting to appreciate that the arts have their own power too."

Our gazes are locked, and her cheeks flush my favorite shade of pink. It's the ideal complement to the stunning aquatic blue shade of her eyes. The soft, rosy hue is enhanced by the cool purple tones of her amethyst curl. She's completely beguiling and utterly perfect.

It's all I can do to stop the impulse to touch her cheek and feel the warmth of her blush.

I don't bother to hold back the wolfish edge to my grin. "I could do with some instruction when it comes to art. Teach me your ways."

She shakes her head at me. "Why do I get the feeling that you're a difficult student?"

I fix my features in an expression of mock-disappointment. "I'll have you know that I was head boy at Eton."

Her brows lift. "Is that supposed to mean something in American English?"

She's not impressed by my posh upbringing, and I'm starting to realize that I like this about her. There's a reason I left all that bullshit behind and moved thousands of miles away from my family and their expectations of me.

I shrug. "No, it doesn't mean anything, really. Other than the fact that I'm a model student."

She takes the final sip of her champagne, and I gesture at the empty glass. "Another?"

"No, thank you." Her refusal is perfectly polite, but I'm not going to accept an end to our evening anytime soon.

"Ah, yes. Your strawberry daiquiri." I say it with warm indulgence, savoring yet another of her secrets. Her love of sweet treats is charming, if a bit superficial.

She will surrender all of her secrets to me eventually. I'm enjoying getting to know her on this date, but I crave so much more. She already belongs to me—body, heart, and soul.

She will accept the truth soon enough.

I grasp her hand and start leading her toward the bar. "I'm buying the drinks. Order whatever you want."

Her fingers tense around mine. "No, thank you."

"I want to pay," I insist, dismissing her resistance. "I want to take care of you, Abigail."

She allowed me to buy her cosmopolitans on the night we first met, despite her initial resistance. She will accept the fact that I will take care of her in every way, and there's no point in playing games about who will get the check.

I squeeze her hand in a pulse of reassurance and step into her personal space.

She flinches, and my chest tightens.

Fine lines have drawn deep around her eyes and mouth, a private anguish I don't fully understand.

My mind races through our past interactions about money. She was upset when I tried to buy her paintings at the market. And she's deeply uncomfortable with allowing me to pay for something as trivial as a cocktail.

She doesn't trust me to take care of her. She's afraid of relying on me financially for some reason.

I can't stop my muscles from flexing with unspent aggression at the revelation.

Some bastard hurt her in the past, and that's getting in my way of winning her trust.

Her abuser will face my retribution. It's only a matter of time before I get his name.

Then I can work out some of these unpleasant feelings of frustration and resentment. I'll extract my revenge in blood and soothe myself with his screams.

The memory of the wild rush that'd overtaken me when I beat the thief flashes through my mind. The power and savagery of the violent moment had been the most ecstatic high I've ever experienced.

"Who hurt you, Abigail?" The question is a rough demand.

She pales, unnerved rather than comforted.

Fuck.

She tugs her hand free from mine.

"I have an early shift tomorrow," she says instead of answering my intense query. "I really should go home."

I consider her for a long moment, wrestling down the impulse to compel her confession. If I just step a little closer to her and thread my fingers through her silken hair, I could capture her lips and kiss her into submission. She'll tell me anything on breathy little sighs and pleas if only I'll grant her more pleasure.

I force myself to take a step back instead. She's still disturbed by whatever dark memories she has associated with financial abuse, and I won't risk scaring her off by coming on too strong.

"If you don't want another drink, I'll walk you home," I declare, forcing my voice to gentle so I won't further provoke her.

"You don't have to do that," she protests. "Stay here and enjoy your old fashioned."

I can't suppress a deep frown. "I came here to see you. I have no intention of staying without your company."

"All right," she acquiesces after another tense moment.

We go to the bar, and she doesn't argue when I pay for our drinks.

One day, Abigail will eagerly accompany me on lavish dates where I provide her with everything she could possibly want—but for now, I'm irritated that I have to be cautious.

It takes considerable effort to keep my charming mask in place when all I can think about is punishing the bastard who inflicted the damage that's keeping her from me.

13

ABBY

I'm still raw from the masked man's attack, and Dane's domineering aura sets off primal, feminine alarm bells at the back of my mind.

Who hurt you, Abigail?

My heart twists. I was right about his protective instincts, but my recent trauma is warping my responses to that fierce protective streak.

I'm sensing danger when I should feel comforted.

I'm not ready for this. As much as I want Dane, I can't be with any man right now.

My resolve wavers when we step into the elevator. The moment the golden doors close, erotic tension fills the space. He stands beside me, just at the edge of my bubble of personal space. Desire builds between us, making my skin tingle with anticipation of his touch. He hasn't made physical contact since I pulled away from him on the rooftop, but in this private moment, he might as well be trailing his fingers along my spine.

The elevator comes to a merciful stop, and the doors open. Cool air conditioning floods the desire-heated space, like the shock of an icy shower after a long summer run.

We step out into the gallery space, and I'm so focused on evading his allure that I don't pause to glance at the art that's on display.

He has other ideas. With the barest brush of his fingers around my wrist, he gently urges me to turn away from the exit, so that I'm looking at the red abstract piece again.

"What do you like about it?" he asks, his voice dropping to that seductive register.

I can't resist the calm ring of command.

"I'm an impressionist, but abstract expressionism fascinates me," I reply.

My focus centers on the painting, but I'm still hyperaware of his hand on my wrist. His thumb slides along my palm, tracing my heartline in a shockingly intimate caress. My senses come alive, and the painting's varied shades of red become richer, as though someone has turned up the saturation.

He releases a low hum. "Explain it to me. I just see red."

I blink at him in surprise, and he shoots me a devastatingly sexy smirk. "I like science; you like art. I want to understand what you see when you look at it."

"You seem like you belong in spaces like this," I say, puzzled. Dane is almost painfully suave, and I've imagined him to be a man who enjoys the finer things in life. "I can easily picture you at a glitzy gallery opening with a glass of champagne in your hand. Or at some sort of charity gala."

It's the kind of world I walked away from two years ago, and I'm surprised to realize that I don't resent this impression

I have of him. He embodies effortless elegance rather than putting on a show for others.

Maybe it's just the sexy English accent throwing off my usual judgmental assessment of entitled rich people, but I can't see Dane in the same negative light as I view my family's social circle.

His eyes shutter for a second, and his smirk melts away. "I've attended my share of gallery openings and galas," he allows. "It's never meant much to me."

His hand fully engulfs mine, and a thrill rushes through me, blanking my mind for a moment.

"Tell me what you see."

Heat sinks from his hand into my flesh, warming me all the way to my core. He's not looking at the painting anymore, but I'm fixated on it as though it's the most breathtaking thing I've ever seen. His intense focus is centered on me again, and I bask in it like I'm soaking up the August sun on Folly Beach.

The power of his will compels me to respond.

"Passion," I breathe.

I gesture at a deep crimson splatter: "Rage." A brighter spray with an orange hue: "Joyful abandon." A swath that's a rich shade so dark it's almost purple: "Seduction."

"Stunning," he remarks. His other hand lifts to touch my hair, his finger twining in the amethyst curl again.

An echo of the giddy thrill at the beginning of our date tempts me to surrender. I recall the initial surge of desire for him in the elevator ride up to the rooftop—how excited I'd been to get to know him.

He's touching my nape, his sure fingers sliding into my hair. He cradles the back of my head in one hand and urges me to turn, so that I have no choice but to face him.

His touch is gentle, but I'm locked in his hold as surely as if he had my hair tangled in his fist. He binds me in place with no more than his gaze, his powerful bearing keeping me thoroughly under his spell.

Molten honey drips down my spine to pool in my belly, and an insistent pulse between my legs echoes the beat of my heart.

"Dane..." His name is a plea, and I'm not sure if I'm begging for him to release me or for him to grant me the mercy of his kiss.

His remarkable eyes flare when I say his name, and his jaw tightens with masculine hunger. I soften in his hold, allowing him to cradle my head in his broad palm.

"I never want to make you uncomfortable," he says, easily reading my tumultuous emotions. "But I've wanted you for far too long, and I fully intend to claim a kiss by the end of the night."

I blink up at him, shocked at his fierce declaration and undeniably wet from his confident bearing.

He offers me an arrogant smirk. "I'm glad we're in agreement."

"You're very self-assured." I manage a breathy remark.

"And you like that." His smile tilts into something a touch wicked. "We're a good match."

I resist the urge to squirm at his intense scrutiny. He's looking at me with carnal hunger, and I feel like I might as well be naked before him.

I'm almost trembling with sensual awareness, as though all of my nerves are hypersensitive. The barest flex of his fingers in my hair draws a soft gasp from my chest, and his sexy smirk tilts in response.

Dane is confident to the point of arrogance, but I can't deny that his cocky smile makes me melt inside. And that confidence is well-deserved, judging by the way I'm drinking him in like the most compelling work of art I've ever seen. He's utterly gorgeous and hypnotically alluring, and it's more than just his good looks. The air of easy authority I've sensed in him draws me in.

I could easily see myself falling to my knees for this man. Worshipping his perfection like he's my own personal god.

He lowers his face to mine slowly, his stunning eyes searching mine for silent invitation. When his lips are an inch from mine, he pauses, his heat teasing across my mouth. I'm not sure if he's allowing me to make the final move, or if he's relishing toying with me, but his motives don't matter. I can't resist the magnetic pull between us, and I arch up to meet him.

His lips are just as soft and sensual as I imagined, and he caresses me with a tender kiss, coaxing me to open for him. I soften on a sigh, melting into him. My arms twine around his shoulders for support, and I cling to him as he claims my mouth deeply enough to take my breath away.

My mind begins to spin, and I'm swept up in the delicious heat of his powerful body and the sure, seductive strokes of his tongue against mine.

One broad hand pins my lower back so that I'm pressed tightly against his hard abs. The confident hold makes me flower open for him on a low moan, and his answering growl of desire vibrates through my body.

The masked man's fierce growl rumbles through me, vibrating all the way to my core. My clit pulses, and my labia are wet with desire. My entire body softens and submits, preparing to accommodate my attacker so that he can slake his lust.

I freeze in Dane's arms. I'm still melded close to his body, caged by his strong hands.

Desire shudders through me at the sensation of being trapped and helpless.

My stomach lurches, and I jerk away from him. For a fleeting instant, his fingers contract, nipping into my flesh in a punishing hold.

I'm burning inside for Dane, but my skin is chilled. The air conditioning turns frosty, and ice sinks into my heated flesh. Nausea churns in my gut as my twisted desire rises, threatening to consume me.

I'm perverted, broken. Something is deeply wrong with me, and it's not just because of the masked man's attack.

My body only finds this thrilling pleasure in moments of violation. My instinctive fear response makes me wet when I should be screaming for mercy.

Consensual sex has always been a painful experience for me; I'm too tense to accept a man, and my inner muscles won't soften to accommodate a cock. But when I'm forced...

I shake my head, throwing off the terrible thoughts and disentangling my hair from Dane's grip.

He releases me so quickly that I think I must've imagined the tightening of his strong fingers as part of my perverted fantasy. He allows me to step away and gasp in a breath of cool air.

"What's wrong?" His low rumble is a touch gravelly this time, roughened by a dark emotion I don't fully understand. Frustration? Disapproval? Residual lust?

My gaze fixes on the red abstract painting again. He might see some of the sickness in my soul if I allow him to look into my eyes.

"Sorry," I murmur. "It's too public here."

I fumble over the almost-lie. It's not entirely untrue that I don't want to have a full panic attack in the gallery. But Dane will think I'm talking about disliking public displays of affection.

"What if I want people to see?" he counters, his voice dropping to the deep register that seems to thrum through me. "What if I want every man to know that you're with me?"

Anxiety tightens my muscles, even as my core pulses for him.

Dane clearly likes control, and that prospect intrigues me as much as it scares me. I could so easily melt for this man, but he's far too cultured and refined to understand the darkest parts of me.

Gathering my wits, I force my lips to curve at the corners.

He lifts my hand and brushes a featherlight kiss over my knuckles. The gesture is almost reverent, and my heart skips a beat. His intense attention is gratifying and more addictive than anything I've ever experienced, even though I'm still reeling from the awful flashback of the attack.

"More later," he promises.

Desire is still pulsing between my legs, and sweat beads on my brow. I crave more time with Dane, but I need space to breathe without his alluring scent threading through my senses. The horrific, cloying scent of amber cologne still seems to saturate the air, warring with his.

"I have to go," I announce. "You don't need to walk me home."

He frowns. "It's dark. I'll escort you."

"It's East Bay Street," I counter. "And my walk home is well-lit. I've never had a problem before."

"You were robbed this afternoon," he reminds me. "I'll feel better if I know you're safe."

My heart flutters even as my stomach turns. I want to be a good match for this protective, white knight of a man. I have to master my sick reaction to our kiss before I can spend more time with him.

"I really need to go. I have that early shift."

A muscle barely flutters in his jaw, but it smooths quickly.

"All right," he concedes, even though his eyes are still burning with dark green fire. "But I want you to text me when you get home."

My brow furrows. "Why?"

He blows out a soft sigh and offers me that indulgent smile. "Is it so difficult to accept that I want to know you're safe? I want to take care of you, Abigail. Let me."

My heart tugs with longing. No one has taken care of me in years. Possibly ever, if I examine the truth too closely. I've been on my own for so long, resolutely standing on my own two feet. The prospect of leaning on Dane for support is terribly tempting.

"I can take care of myself," I say, but the assertion isn't sharp with resentment. I'm touched by his concern, even if I can't allow myself the moment of weakness. "But thank you for caring about my safety."

"I never said you aren't capable of taking care of yourself," he replies smoothly. "But that doesn't change the fact that I want to. Trust me, Abigail. I will never hurt you."

I glance away from his x-ray gaze, hiding my secrets from him.

Instead of replying to his intense declaration, I focus my attention on my purse and find my phone. My fragile smile is back in place when I look up at him once again.

"What's your number?"

His smile is sharp with something like triumph when he takes my phone and enters his number. He connects a call, and his phone vibrates in his pocket.

He has my number now too.

His fingers brush mine as he places my phone back in my waiting hand. The slow slide of his withdrawal is a sensual caress, and my cheeks flush as though he's swept me up in another scorching kiss.

"I'll text you," I promise as my stomach flips. It's a slightly queasy sensation.

My fingers are itching for my paintbrush. Tumultuous emotions surge within me, making me seasick. I need to purge them at my canvas. Then, maybe I'll be capable of enduring Dane's kiss without my trauma ruining the moment.

He offers me a short nod of acknowledgement. "I'm looking forward to it."

The statement seals my promise; his firm tone brooks no resistance. He's expecting a message confirming that I'm safe.

His protective instincts soften any irritation I might feel in response to his highhanded manner. I could throw myself into his strong arms and allow him to shield me from all the bad things in the world—including the horrors of my past.

I offer him a quick, slightly awkward wave goodbye and force myself to walk away from him. As I put distance between us, I can practically feel the shadow of his imposing frame lengthening behind me, as reluctant to release me as I am to leave him. It makes my skin prickle with residual awareness of his touch.

I resolutely ignore the unreasonable, thrilling sensation that he's still with me, even though I know I left him behind in the gallery.

14

DANE

ABIGAIL

Home safe. Thanks for the champagne.

I stare at her perfunctory text and try to ignore the hot churning in my gut. I'm irritated. Frustrated.

Almost irrationally *angry*.

My fist tightens around the phone. I refuse to be ruled by these *feelings* she brings out in me, even if I do enjoy the novelty.

So, I relax my grip and tap out a reasonable reply.

DANE

Glad to hear it.

There's no reason for her to thank me for paying. I wanted to, and her resistance was grating.

That irritation pales in comparison to the feelings that are assailing me in the wake of that kiss.

She shuddered and pulled away from me when I'd been experiencing the greatest high of my life. It'd taken all of my considerable willpower to appear genial and understanding instead of acting on the savage instinct to cage her in my arms and claim her mouth until she softened and submitted.

I crave to unleash myself upon her, but I have to handle her with care. She'll run screaming if I allow her to see the full truth of what I am. I can be patient. Careful.

I know she secretly fantasizes about the dark things I need to do to her. It's simply a matter of time for me to earn her trust.

She's setting her phone down and picking up her paintbrush. But I'm not ready to let her elude me.

I lean farther back into the shadows of my azalea bushes and lower my binoculars so that I can type out another message.

DANE

I want to see you again.

The rounded end of the paintbrush touches her lips. She stares at her phone where it rests on the small side table that she keeps beside her easel for access to her pink water bottle. The brush slips between her lips, and I imagine my cock sinking into that lush mouth.

She doesn't touch her phone for several long seconds. She's looking at it like it's a feral animal that might bite her if she makes a sudden move. The paintbrush is tapping against her lower lip now as she twirls it between her deft fingers. A small furrow creases her brow.

I forget how to breathe while the seconds tick over into a full minute.

She's afraid of our connection for some reason. But she's also intrigued. Tempted.

The way she's toying with that damn brush is practically erotic, even if she has no idea how she's tormenting me.

Fuck, I need to see her lovely eyes up close, to watch them darken with that intoxicating mix of trepidation and desire.

My cock stiffens, but I ignore my mounting lust. I'm rooted to the spot, frozen in breathless anticipation as I wait for her to pick up her phone and answer me.

There's a slight tremor in her fingers when she finally bends to my will. She taps her screen, hesitates, then taps it again.

My phone chimes, and I suck in a deep breath.

ABIGAIL

> That sounds nice. Where do you want to meet?

I force myself to pause, determined to make *her* wait. It's only fair that she's tormented by the same maddening uncertainty that plagues me every time I'm near her.

My mind races through potential dates, and my thumb strays toward the internet browser icon on my phone. For the hundredth time, I consider looking her up online. If I know more about her, I can manipulate her more easily.

I crush the impulse, forcing my way through the moment of weakness. Social media is anathema to me, and even if I created a fake account to stalk her, the information I would glean would be superficial. I've seen into Abigail's soul, and I won't be satisfied with a falsely cheery public persona that she might present to her friends online.

I will learn her secrets in person. She will surrender each one to me, until I possess her completely.

I return to our messages instead of opening the browser.

DANE

I'd like to surprise you. I can pick you up at six-thirty.

I need her to share her address willingly. Then I can come see her whenever I want.

The paintbrush dips between her lips again, and she grazes the tip with her teeth.

I nearly growl as my lust surges, but I manage to cling to my iron control.

My phone buzzes, and her address appears on my screen.

Triumph heats my chest, and I don't have to hide the savage edge of my grin; I don't have to wear my mask for anyone in this moment. I'm fully myself in a way I can only be with Abigail.

She's not ready to see me like this yet, but one day, she'll moan my name and tremble for me while I hold her with cruel passion.

I type out a confirmation of our plan to meet and then set my phone down, allowing her the quiet time she needs to paint. I won't distract her again, not when I'm burning with curiosity to see what will coalesce on her canvas.

Time slips away as I watch her paint. It takes a while for the feverish brushstrokes to form a cityscape scene. For a short while, I'm mildly disappointed; I'd hoped for another dark fantasy tonight.

But then the Charleston skyline at sunset takes shape. The historic buildings are bathed in waning sunlight, syrupy and golden.

She's painting our date.

This is far more intimate than an erotic scene. Those

paintings reflect the dark desires she shares with GentAnon, but this view from the rooftop bar at The Magnolia is what she shares with *me.*

I forget all about sipping my whisky as she continues to work late into the night. My full attention is harnessed by her vision of what we shared on our date this evening.

The white railing that surrounds the rooftop is barely visible, a subtle frame at the bottom of the painting. Two hands are entwined atop it, and I recognize the familiar shape of her slender fingers beneath my own.

She might've run from our kiss, but Abigail is clearly still thinking about the allure of our physical connection.

By the time she sets her paintbrush down for the night, I'm buzzing with a strange high—it's definitely not from the alcohol I barely touched.

When she disappears into her tiny bedroom, I briefly consider relocating to my larger, more expensive house across town. But I'm craving to be close to her, so I choose to stay in the ramshackle property I bought just so I can watch over her.

I pass her landscapes as I walk through the entry hall and living room. There's nearly a score more in my bedroom—a cramped space that barely fits the high-quality king-size bed. This place might be rundown, but it doesn't mean I have to be uncomfortable.

I fall back onto the Egyptian cotton sheets and stare at my trophies: the precious paintings I've purchased from the tourists who bought them from her in the market. I keep her stormiest works in my bedroom. It's the only glimpse at her inner darkness that's evident in her otherwise lovely art depicting the natural world.

My cock is still hard from watching her toy with that damn paintbrush all night.

I should let her sleep, but I'm too selfish to hesitate. I want her, and she will meet my needs.

I pick up my phone and navigate to Eroticlit, immediately finding our months' long private messaging thread.

GENTANON

Wake up, little dove. I have need of my pretty pet.

The tick beside her screenname remains stubbornly gray.

I give her five minutes to see that I've messaged her.

My gut twists into knots, and my chest heats.

GENTANON

Answer me. Your silence is rude, and rudeness will be punished.

A green tick mark. Three bouncing dots.

They disappear, then appear again.

And again.

My fingers are tight enough that my knuckles are white around the phone.

CAGEDBIRD

I'm sorry. I can't tonight.

I taste copper on my tongue, and I realize I gnashed my teeth hard enough to cut the inside of my cheek.

I've been frustrated by her refusals and rejections over the last several days. Even though she clearly enjoyed our date this evening, she still ran away from me at the end.

I won't tolerate her evasiveness. When we're in this virtual space, sharing the darkest parts of ourselves, I don't have to wear my charming mask.

GENTANON

You can try to run, but I will chase. I will capture you, little dove. And then you'll be sorry that you tried to deny me.

Those fucking dots bounce on my screen again. My fist is a vise around the phone.

CAGEDBIRD

I mean it. I'm sorry, but I can't.

A low growl reverberates through my bedroom, a predator with its hackles raised.

GENTANON

Why not? I expect an explanation.

For several long seconds, I contemplate smashing my phone against the wall as those three dots dance in a mockery of my mounting rage.

CAGEDBIRD

I met someone. I can't do this anymore.

Something expands rapidly at the center of my chest to the point of pain, as though my ribcage can barely contain it.

She's not rejecting me; she's choosing me.

The real me, not my anonymous online persona.

And her message indicates that she's developing feelings for me. Why else would she stop exchanging dirty messages with her pen pal?

She wants to be loyal to me. To Dane, not GentAnon.

My cock is still painfully hard, but my lust holds a

covetous edge. I can deny my desire to share dark fantasies with her tonight if it means I'll have her in my bed for real.

Soon, she'll be snuggled up beside me in my much nicer house across town, a space that's worthy of her. She'll cuddle close to me, and I'll make her so safe and comfortable that she'll never want to leave. Her dilapidated little apartment will be a thing of the past, and no walls will separate us.

GENTANON

I understand. Be happy, little dove.

CAGEDBIRD

Thank you.

I log off the messenger service, and my phone doesn't light up with another notification. She's logged off too.

That era in our relationship is over now. Until she trusts me enough to share her body with me, I'm sure I'll face nights of sexual frustration. But the wait will be worth it.

I reach under my pillow and find the soft, paint splattered camisole that I stole when I broke into her apartment. Her scent is faint beneath the fading, sweet florals of her detergent, but I can still detect her delicate strawberry bodywash infused in the fabric.

I imagine burying my face in the crook of her slender neck and breathing her in as my teeth mark her shoulder. Her sharp cry is the sweetest music that I've never heard, but I've imagined it over a hundred times. I will make her weep with agonized pleasure, and she'll taste the salt of her own tears on my tongue when I claim a brutal kiss.

I snarl into her camisole, biting down on the soft fabric as I come undone for her.

15

ABBY

I'm in the shared laundry room for my building when the stranger approaches me.

At first, I don't notice him; I'm too busy grabbing my clothes out of the dryer. Dane is coming to pick me up any minute now for our surprise date, and I need to finish this chore first. One of my favorite painting camisoles went missing recently, so I'm not willing to leave my things in the dryer where they might get taken.

It's only when the stranger lets out a low whistle that I realize I'm not alone in the small, hot room.

I jerk upright from where I was bent over the dryer, my heart leaping into my throat. Instinctively, I recognize the unwanted attention of a predator.

A thrill shivers up my spine—a primal warning that all women possess.

I dread the shameful heat that might accompany the spike in my heartbeat, but mercifully, it doesn't come. Maybe letting go of my illicit connection with GentAnon last night truly will help me overcome my sickness. Maybe I can be worthy of Dane.

I just need to evade this creep so that I can go on my date with him.

"Well, hello, Peaches," the stranger says, his Southern twang more pronounced that the softer Carolina drawl I'm used to. His pale blue eyes wander down the length of my body, pausing at the curve of my hips.

I have an awful suspicion about why he chose to call me *Peaches*, even though my butt is now firmly pressed back against the washing machine.

I shake my head slightly and gather my clean laundry to my chest, holding it between us like a shield.

"My name is Abby," I say coolly. "And you shouldn't be in here."

He chuckles. "Don't be like that," he admonishes. "We must be neighbors. I'm moving in upstairs. Just checking out the rest of the building in between hauling boxes up to my new place. Too bad I'm not more presentable. I wasn't expecting to meet a beautiful woman."

He waves his hand in my general direction, and I notice the dull glint of a wedding ring.

"I don't think your wife would appreciate you flirting with me," I reply, speaking calmly and clearly despite my elevated heartrate.

I've dealt with skeevy men plenty of times before. But after the attack by the masked man, I'm flooded with adrenaline. Even though I'm not experiencing a disconcertingly erotic reaction, I still can't seem to tap into my fight or flight instinct. As always, I'm frozen.

He's blocking my way to the exit, and I have nowhere to

go. Nothing but my words to talk my way past him. If I can manage to unstick my feet from the concrete floor.

"Oh, this." He frowns at the ring, as though he forgot he's wearing it. "Damn thing's stuck. I'm separated. That's why I'm moving in here. Drove all the way up from Mississippi to get away from that bitch."

Charming.

I suppress a contemptuous grimace and keep my features schooled to a polite mask. Provoking him when we're alone in here would be stupid, especially if I'll have to see him around the building for the foreseeable future.

I note the small beer belly that strains against his too-tight white t-shirt. His finger bulges around the constraint of the too-small wedding ring. I suppose he's not in the same shape as he was when he first put it on.

"My name's Ron." His broad, bright white smile could be considered boyishly charming, and his tousled brown curls add to his *good ol' boy* vibe. They peek out at the sides of his oversized baseball cap, and I wonder if he's hiding a receding hairline. "Pleasure to meet you. I could really use a friend in the neighborhood."

My new neighbor has an entitled air about him that I recognize all too well.

"I'm sorry to hear about your troubles," I say, barely managing to soften my tone to something conciliatory. "I hope your move goes smoothly. But I need to get this laundry folded."

He steps toward me. "I can help with that."

I recoil from his grubby hands. "That's okay. I've got it."

He chuckles again and shakes his head. "I'm just being neighborly, Peaches. I'll help you, and then you can help me. I don't know the area yet. You can show me the best dive bar in the neighborhood." He winks at me. "We're gonna get real close. I can tell."

My stomach churns, and sweat beads on my brow. The intensity of my fear response is out of proportion with the perceived threat.

He takes another step toward me, and his dirty hand fists one of my black work shirts.

The air in my lungs turns to solid ice, and my entire body locks up tight.

I want to tell him to leave me alone, but I can't find the oxygen to speak. I'm so cold despite the heat of the running dryers in summer.

The door to the laundry room opens, revealing my white knight.

"Dane!" I say his name like a prayer, and his forest green eyes narrow on my creepy new neighbor.

Ron is in between us, my shirt still trapped in his fist. He turns his head to see who's interrupted us, and his throat bobs when he takes in Dane's thunderous expression.

Then his shoulders draw back, and his arms flex. He drags my shirt out of my arms and turns to face Dane.

"This your boyfriend, Peaches?" He asks, his twang heavy on the contemptuous question. He eyes Dane up and down, taking in his perfectly tailored, light blue shirt all the way down to his polished leather shoes.

Dane prowls toward us, every step a warning. Ron stiffens, but he holds his ground. His pathetic posturing would be almost laughable if it weren't for the fact that ice lingers on my skin. The sour tang of fear curls my tongue. The remembered terror from the night of the masked man's attack clings to my psyche, and I'm reeling as I try to focus on Dane's remarkable eyes.

His gaze is fixed on Ron, his forest irises darkening to a dangerous shade of hunter green.

He comes to a stop within punching distance, and I realize that Dane has at least three inches of height and considerable bulk on Ron.

"Her name is Abigail, not Peaches." Dane's voice is light and smooth, so at odds with his threatening stance. "And yes, I'm her boyfriend. So, if you ever think about harassing her again, you'll have to deal with me."

Shock renders me mute at his words. The genteel cadence of his voice dropped to something rougher on the last: a gravelly declaration of ownership and a promise of retribution.

Dane tips his chin at my shirt. Ron's knuckles have gone white against the soft black fabric.

"That doesn't belong to you."

For a moment, I think that he'll insist on giving it back to me.

Instead, he plucks my shirt from Ron's grip and claims it for himself.

Ron's jaw works. "Tough talk for a fancy man. I was just being neighborly and helping with her laundry."

Dane's eyes remain fixed on him like he's a bug he'd like to grind under the heel of his designer shoe, but he addresses me.

"Do you want his help, Abigail?"

"No," I manage to breathe.

With every passing second, the ice is melting from my bones, leaving me wrung out and shaky. Fear is giving way to shock at the unexpected events unfolding in the cramped space of the stifling laundry room. Dane radiates menace, but relief rushes through me at his protective presence.

"You heard her," Dane prompts darkly. "She doesn't want

you. Unless you have a good reason to be in here, I suggest you leave now."

Ron throws up his hands and shakes his head, as though Dane is making a big deal out of nothing. "Fine, buddy. I have boxes to move." He shoots a glower in my direction. "Ungrateful bitch."

Dane moves lightning fast, and suddenly, his chest is almost pressed against Ron's. His entire body swells with barely leashed aggression, but his face is completely devoid of emotion. The cold, clinically calculated way he's studying Ron is more terrifying than his warning scowl.

"Use that language with her again, and you'll end up with a broken jaw."

Ron seems to finally understand the gravity of the danger he's in, and he takes a hasty step away, edging toward the open door behind Dane.

"Fine," he says again, but his voice wavers this time. "She's your girl. I get it. Fucking psycho." He mutters the last as he ducks out the door to evade my fierce protector.

Dane's cold gaze glitters. He keeps his frigid focus fixed on Ron until the threat is gone. Ron's quickly retreating footsteps slap against the concrete floor of the entry hall as he makes a swift exit onto the street.

"How did you know I was in here?" My lips feel oddly numb, but my voice barely wavers on the question.

The dangerous glimmer melts from Dane's eyes when he turns his gaze on me. "I was knocking on your front door when I heard your voice," he explains. "You sounded scared."

"Did I?" I'd thought I was speaking in a calm, disarming tone.

I guess I was even more shaken up than I realized. My

body is still reeling from the spike of adrenaline, and my knees are strangely weak.

"I'm sorry." I offer a reflexive apology, and embarrassment flushes my cheeks. "I should've been able to handle him myself."

If I weren't still jumpy from the masked man's attack, I might've been capable of walking away from Ron on my own.

But I can't explain myself to Dane. He can never know what happened to me, my shameful reaction to being violated.

My white knight is touching me again, his careful fingers making light contact with my wrist to test my pulse. It's still racing from the burst of irrational fear.

"You shouldn't have to handle him by yourself," he rumbles, his jaw flexing with a shadow of his righteous anger. "I'll take care of you, Abigail. He won't bother you again."

I try to shrug. "It wasn't that serious. I would've been okay."

A shadow deepens in his cheek as his jaw ticks more with more force. "I'm not asking," he says firmly. "I want to keep you safe. Trust me."

His long fingers close around mine before I can respond. "You're shaking," he remarks. "Let's go somewhere quiet. You need to sit down and hydrate."

I attempt a dismissive laugh to alleviate his concern. "I'm just being silly. It really was nothing." I square my shoulders with considerable effort and summon up a smile. "I thought we were going out on a date?"

He fixes me with a disapproving frown, and my chest hollows out.

"Come on," he prompts, wrapping his strong arm around my shoulders. "Let's go into your place."

"You really don't have to take care of me." I try to protest as he steers me out of the laundry room. The humid summer air is oddly cold against my sweat-slicked skin after the heat of the running dryers. "I'm fine."

"I know I don't have to, but I'm going to," he counters. "And don't lie to me, Abigail. It's okay to be disturbed by what happened in there. That bastard shouldn't have cornered you. You were a woman alone in a small space with a much bigger man. You don't have to be proud around me and conceal your emotions." That shadow at his jaw flutters again. "Did he touch you?"

"No." I soften on a sigh and lean into Dane, allowing myself the moment of weakness.

I'm so tired of holding myself together, and he's refusing to allow me to pretend I'm fine. I don't want to lie to Dane, even if I can't tell him about the masked man's attack. I can at least be honest with my emotions. I can be vulnerable with him.

He opens my unlocked front door, and his frown deepens. But he ushers me inside without admonishment.

"Ron didn't touch me," I say. "He just tried to help me fold my laundry. I told him I didn't want his help, but he grabbed my shirt anyway. Thank you for getting it back from him."

My arms are still locked around the rest of my clean clothes, holding them like a shield.

But I don't need to shield myself from Dane.

When he steers me to the couch, I unlock my muscles and drop the laundry onto it. Then my knees finally fold, and I sink down onto the cushions beside my clothes.

He squeezes my shoulder, and my stomach flips. My fear responses are still on high alert, and I internally curse the warning flutter at the center of my chest.

I'm alone in my private space with Dane, but he's not a threat. I've conditioned my body to have this thrilling response to his touch because of my fucked-up fantasies about him.

I take a breath and try to calm my racing heart.

"I'll get you some water," he says, and again, it's not a question.

My place isn't exactly difficult to navigate, so he has no trouble walking three paces to enter the cramped kitchen space. He manages to find my water glasses on the first try—there aren't many cabinets to choose from—and makes quick work of filling one.

He returns to the couch and presses the cool glass into my colder hand before settling down beside me. The seat is so small that his hip brushes mine. I could move the laundry and scoot away from him, but I don't want to put any distance between us.

His body heat pulses over me, chasing away the last of the chill that lingers in my flesh. I melt, my tense muscles easing as calm finally settles over me like a soft blanket on my shoulders.

Allowing Dane to take care of me feels almost euphoric after years of stubbornly making my own way. A sense of lightness makes my bones feel almost hollow, as though I could soar like a bird. I lean into my fierce protector, tentatively pressing my shoulder against his corded arm. His hand comes up to cup the side of my head, and he gently urges me to tuck myself close to him. My breaths slow to match the steady rise and fall of his chest, and his deft fingers trail through my hair in a soothing motion.

A sense of intimacy blossoms between us, and for a few blissful moments, my mind is utterly quiet. I can simply languor in this safe space with Dane, and I don't have to feel guilty or weak for accepting his support.

He won't allow me to refuse it, so I'm able to give myself permission to surrender, sinking into his strength.

"Is that the first time he's harassed you?" he rumbles after I've taken a few sips of water.

"Who, Ron?" I ask on a sigh. I'm so comfortable and calm that an echo of my fear doesn't so much as tingle up my spine. "That's the first time I've met him. He said he's moving into one of the apartments upstairs."

He tucks a stray lock of hair behind my ear, and little sparks ping along my scalp in response to his tender touch.

"But it's not the first time a man has harassed you." He says it like a condemnation of all men, his voice dropping to a deep, disapproving register.

"No," I agree softly. "It's not the first time. I'm a woman." That's explanation enough, and he blows out a sigh so rough that it's almost a growl.

I'm not ready to open up to him about my past trauma; I'm still trying to get a handle on my own physical responses, and I don't want to scare him away with my baggage.

"But I can handle myself," I assure him.

I want to stay in this quiet, safe space with him for a while longer without emotional upheaval.

"You don't have to handle it alone," he says with the weight of an oath. "Not when I'm around."

My heart tugs with longing, but I know it's foolish to become too attached to him so quickly. I've never been good at guarding my emotions.

"You didn't have to tell Ron that you're my boyfriend," I murmur. "But thank you for coming to help me."

Two fingers curl beneath my chin, and he guides my face to his so that I'm caught in his intense green stare.

"You have a rather bad habit of telling me what I don't have to do," he remarks, and his thumb traces the line of my lower lip. He speaks over my soft gasp of arousal at the tender touch. "I make my own choices, Abigail. You don't need to protect me from them."

"Sorry," I breathe. "I don't want to be controlling."

I will never be like my mother. She controls everyone around her with cutting comments that she wields with the precision of a scalpel.

Dane releases a low chuckle, and his chest rumbles against my cheek. The sound vibrates into me and warms my flesh like a lover's caress.

"You can't control me, Abigail. No one does." His voice drops deeper on the last, a private declaration that he's spoken aloud.

An ocean separates us, and I prefer it that way.

I reach for him reflexively, drawn to connect with him on a deeper level as I recall what he said about his estrangement from his family. It's something we have in common, and I crave to know more about my dashing hero.

Our fingers entwine, and he gives me a gentle squeeze.

"I like the way we fit together," he remarks. "I particularly like the way you captured it in your painting."

I realize that my painting of our date scene is still propped on my easel, and an intense sense of vulnerability knots my stomach.

"I didn't think you'd see that," I say quietly.

His eyes are green pools, drawing me in deep. "It's stunning."

He traces the line of my cheekbone, and my breath catches.

"You said I don't have to tell people that I'm your boyfriend," he says. "Do you want me to be?"

"We hardly know each other," I try to protest, but the longing in my heart roughens the words.

His fingers slide into my hair in a gentle grip. "I don't want to see anyone else. I only want you, Abigail."

16

ABBY

Dane pins me in place with nothing more than a tender touch and his intense green gaze as he slowly dips his head toward mine. The instant his lush mouth brushes my lips, I melt for him. Warmth floods my chest and spreads all the way to my fingers and toes. It's a safe, gentle heat rather than passion that strikes like dangerous lightning.

I sink into the sweet moment, clinging to the sense of security. I won't allow my twisted desires to rise up and ruin this moment with my white knight.

"Don't be afraid," he murmurs against my lips. "I know someone's hurt you in the past." His fingers firm in my hair ever so slightly before he takes a breath and relaxes. "But you're safe with me."

"I know," I promise.

He's nothing like the men who have hurt me.

I melt into his muscular arms and allow myself to lean

into his strength. He's so much more powerful than I could ever hope to be.

The thought of my helplessness to resist him makes my core pulse with dark desire. My lips still beneath his caresses for a tense moment of pleasure and shame.

He must think I'm getting scared again, because he strokes my hair in response, petting me as though I'm a spooked animal. The tender care he's showing me draws a shudder from deep in my chest, and my eyes sting. I keep them resolutely shut and master the bizarre urge to cry. Instead, I focus on the softness of his full lips on mine, the hot flick of his tongue as he traces the shape of my mouth.

I sigh and open for him, welcoming him deeper.

He enters my mouth in a tentative stroke, testing me. When I don't recoil in fear, he kisses me more boldly, taking me with firm confidence.

I flower open for him, and to my surprise, my body responds to his careful, gentle treatment. Warmth pulses between my legs. It's not the painful throb of full arousal, but it's pleasant.

Safe.

"I only want you too," I pant against him. "Only you, Dane."

He seals my lips with his, and he plunders my mouth, as though he's savoring the taste of his name on my tongue. His hand cradles the back of my head, holding me like I'm made of porcelain as he ravages my mouth.

The dichotomy draws a shiver to the surface of my skin, and a fine tremor races over me. I'm protected, cherished. No one can hurt me while Dane is holding me in his strong arms.

I release a soft cry of loss when he tears his mouth from mine, but his lips are immediately on my heated flesh once again. He kisses his way down the column of my throat, featherlight brushes like a butterfly's wings. My fingers spear through his dark hair, tugging him closer, inviting him to mark me with his teeth.

But he remains achingly gentle with me.

I take a deep breath and inhale his spicy cedarwood scent. It reminds me that this is Dane. I can be good for him. His tender care touches something deep in my heart, even if it does little to incite arousal at my core.

Taking another calming breath, I force my fingers to loosen in his hair. This seduction will be slow and sweet, and I refuse to allow my perversions to darken the intimacy between us.

He keeps one hand cradling my nape as the other skims up my thigh, slowly pushing the hem of my dress up to expose my bare legs. He doesn't pause to ask for permission, but his movements are slow. I could stop him with nothing more than a word of refusal at any time.

And even though I'm barely aroused physically, I don't want to refuse this connection.

His fingertips brush over my pale pink, cotton panties, and I sigh into his mouth when he resumes our deeper kiss. I make little humming noises as he rubs my clit through my underwear in a confident but gentle rhythm, coaxing out my pleasure.

My inner muscles give a weak flutter because this is *Dane.*

But it's not enough to make me wet. I'm not throbbing for him, and the soft sounds I'm making are meant for his benefit rather than giving voice to my own passion.

I encourage him to continue with hungry flicks of my tongue against his, urging him on.

He releases a low hum that rumbles through me, and my clit pulses once in response to the primal sound.

More than anything, I want to please him. I want him to want me.

One thick finger slips past the band at the edge of my panties, finding my heated folds. He strokes my clit directly, and I gasp into his mouth at a soft burst of pleasure. It dances through me like dandelion seeds on the wind, gentle and calming rather than sweeping me up in a tempest of churning lust.

He slowly penetrates me, but I'm not wet enough to ease his entry. My inner walls close, clamping down on the intrusion of his finger and refusing to accommodate him. Pain lances my core, and I can't quite manage to swallow my whimper.

He breaks our kiss. His brows are drawn together, and his mouth is tight with restraint. "Did I hurt you?"

"Don't stop," I plead, crushing my lips to his so that he won't be able to see the fine lines of discomfort around my eyes.

He kisses me like he wants to consume me, and I manage to pass off my sounds of pain as desire while his tongue is deep in my mouth. The tension in my fingers can be interpreted as fierce passion, and my fingernails bite into his upper arms as I desperately hold him to me.

I can't bear for him to pull away and leave me alone.

I only want you, Abigail.

I cling to his promise, playing the words over in my mind like a mantra as I will my body to accept his finger. How will I be able to accommodate his cock if I can't even manage this smaller intrusion?

My fingers flex with determination, and I focus on the

gentle pleasure of his thumb on my clit while he crooks his finger inside me.

Sweat slicks my skin, and I'm panting as I attempt to breathe through the pain.

When I can't keep up the pretense any longer, I intentionally clench my inner muscles and sharply cry out into his mouth.

His lips firm around mine, a grim pinch before he recoils from me.

"Did you just fake an orgasm?" The angry shadow flutters at his strong jaw, and this time, the rage is directed at me.

My stomach drops to the floor. Cold rushes over me, and I suddenly feel awfully exposed. He's not touching me at all anymore.

I close my legs and quickly tug my dress down to cover myself.

"No!" I say, reaching for his hand.

He jerks back, and his lips curl as though he's tasted something disgusting.

"I warned you not to lie to me, Abigail."

A pang lances my heart, and my chest tightens around it in a protective cage. I barely find the breath to protest, "I want you, Dane."

He shakes his head as though he can toss my desperate words from his ears.

He surges to his feet, and for a terrifying, arousing moment, he towers over me like a vengeful god. My lips part, and I suck in a sharp gasp. His eyes darken as his gaze roves over my face, reading my carnal secrets in response to his threatening posture.

In the next second, he's striding away. I stare after him for a dumbstruck moment.

"Wait!" I beg. "I'm sorry."

I stumble after him and manage to grab hold of his forearm. "Please stay."

He shakes his head again, but he won't look at me. As though the sight of me is too disgusting to bear.

My stomach churns, and my head spins with rising nausea.

He wrenches his arm from my weaker grip. "Goodbye, Abigail."

My door slams shut between us, a resounding refusal to listen to my pleas. Dane walks out of my building, and I fear that he's walking out of my life entirely. I might never see him again.

17

DANE

CAGEDBIRD

Are you free to chat?

I'm sorry about what I said before.

Please, I need to talk to you.

I need you to use me. I need you to hurt me.

I stare at the string of messages on my lock screen. All to GentAnon. Nothing from Abigail to Dane.

I won't log on to answer her desperate pleas, no matter how hard my own unslaked lust is riding me.

I'd been so careful not to spook her. I'd been the perfect gentleman. And even though I usually prefer kinkier sexual games, I'm expert in manipulating women's bodies. I know exactly how and where to touch to wring pleasure from them.

But Abigail faked her orgasm.

I'd been right when I'd sensed that she was in pain. But

based on her hungry kisses and soft whimpers, I'd assumed she was enjoying a twinge of discomfort that accompanied penetration. She'd been so tight around my finger, and I'd almost lost my control at the thought of her cunt squeezing my dick.

But she hadn't softened and opened to accept me. She'd been rigid and tense when I'd expected her to melt for me.

Our chemistry has never been a problem. I don't understand what happened between us. All I know is that this particular *feeling* that's assailing me is familiar, and I don't like it.

My teeth are clenched as tightly as my fists, and my muscles are bunched as though I'm preparing to fight. Or I'm bracing to take a blow to my gut.

Fury.

I force my fingers to unfurl so that I can pick up my glass of whisky. When I lift it to my mouth, I catch the faint scent of her pussy that lingers on my hand.

My cock is painfully hard, despite my rage.

I'm tormented by thoughts of how I want to punish her for lying to me. For daring to fake her pleasure with me.

She treated me as though I'm some simple fool with a fragile ego that she has to placate.

The next time I have my hands on her, she'll shatter for me.

I saw the way her pupils dilated when I loomed over her, barely containing my wrath. She'd wanted me more in that moment of fear than in the entirely of the time I'd been kissing her so tenderly.

My darkness calls to hers.

Handling her with care had been a stupid fucking mistake.

When I allow her to come back to me, she'll come crawling on her hands and knees.

She will beg for my touch before I grant her the mercy of release.

So, I won't respond to her messages. She can stew in what she's done. I want her twisted up in knots that only I can loosen by the time I reach out to her again.

Only when I'm satisfied that she's thoroughly sorry and utterly desperate, I'll crook my finger, and she'll come running like my eager, obedient little pet. She'll offer her slender neck for my collar, and she'll worship at my feet.

I'll settle for nothing less than her absolute devotion and complete submission.

18

ABBY

I've barely slept in a week, and the desperation is starting to show on my face—in the dark circles under my eyes and dullness of my skin. Whenever exhaustion pulls me under, erotic nightmares of the masked man's attack torment me. He always peers at me with burning green eyes. Dane's eyes.

The man I want but can never have. I was a fool to ever think I might be capable of mastering my dark perversions so that I could be with my white knight.

Because Dane is nothing like the selfish, cruel stranger who took my body without my consent. He's patient and tender.

And my broken brain doesn't respond to that gentle treatment, no matter how hard I swoon for his protectiveness.

I've been making too many mistakes at work, and today, Stacy had to take me into the kitchen to have a private word about how many ruined drinks I've wasted.

Even worse, I haven't been able to paint. Every time I sit at my easel, my fist locks around my paintbrush, and nothing but uninspired daubs of paint appear on my canvas, refusing to coalesce into a coherent scene.

My only outlets for my pain are closed to me, and it's eating me up inside.

GentAnon won't answer my messages begging to reconnect.

And Dane hasn't shown his face in the café.

It should be a small mercy after how terribly things ended between us, but I find myself searching for him every morning at eight oh-five AM. I long to hear his melodic accent caressing my name, to see his cocky half-smile as he locks me in his gaze like I'm the center of his universe.

My exhaustion is so acute that little black dots float at the edge of my vision, and I completely zone out at the espresso bar.

Pain sears my fingers, and I drop the milk jug with a sharp cry. I steamed it for too long, and the hot, thick liquid bubbled over to burn my hand. The metal jug clangs on the tiled floor, and milk spills everywhere. Little white droplets spray the fridge, and it rapidly spreads to pool under the counter.

Despite the pain in my hand, I dart into the back to grab a mop without pausing to treat the burn. I whirl to return to the mess I made, but Stacy is blocking my way back into the café.

Her hands are on her hips, and her berry-painted lips are pressed into a thin line. "What is going on with you?"

My eyes burn hotter than the prickling sensation on my fingers. "I'm so sorry. It was an accident."

She shakes her head, and her voluminous, glossy black curls sway around her heart shaped face. "I know you didn't do it on purpose. And I'm not here to chew you out. I'm worried about you."

"I'm fine," I say quickly.

She blows out a sigh and takes the mop from me. "Run some cold water over your hand. I'll clean up the spill."

"I can do it," I protest. It's my mess, my responsibility.

Embarrassment heats my face. *I'm* the biggest mess here.

Stacy's eyes soften with concern. She's not just my manager; over the last two years, we've become friends.

"No, you need to go home." Her tone is firm but calm, not cruel. "For a few days, I thought maybe you'd been out drinking late, so I was pissed. But I texted Franklin, and he said y'all haven't been out. I'm not sure what you're going through, but I can tell you need a break."

My shoulders curve inward, and I'm too wrung out to maintain my straight posture. I feel like a clipped flower, slowly wilting after being cut off at the root.

"I haven't been out partying," I say. "I promise."

"I know, and that's why I'm telling you to go home and get some rest," she reassures me. "Whatever you're going through, we're here for you. And not just for karaoke and dancing. You can talk to me."

My heart twists painfully, and tears well in my eyes. I consider her a friend, but I realize in this moment that I've been keeping her at an emotional distance. We go out with the girls and Franklin, and we always have a good time.

But I haven't allowed any of them to truly know me. They don't know anything about my past, my family, my dreams.

Dane is the only person in years to glimpse the real me behind the sunny smiles and pretty paintings.

Stacy pulls me in for a quick hug. "Okay, we don't have to talk about it now," she allows. "Take care of yourself, Abby. When you're feeling better, we'll go out for tacos and salsa dancing. Everything will be okay. We're all here for you."

I dash the tear from my cheek as she releases me from her embrace. "Thank you. I really am sorry about the mess."

"Don't worry about it," she reassures me. "I've got it."

With that, she carries the mop out into the café to clean up the milk I spilled.

I move as though in a daze, following her instructions to put my hand in cold water for a minute. My skin is flushed an angry shade of red, but it won't blister. When the prickling sensation eases, I turn off the faucet and trudge to my locker to retrieve my purse.

My eyes are downcast when I slink back into the café. I'm mortified that I'm being sent home because I'm too tired to function, but I'm touched by Stacy's concern.

I try to curve my lips in a pleasant expression as I make my way around the counter and through the seating area. I'm almost at the door when I hear his voice: that deep, lilting rumble that makes my heart flutter.

"What happened to your hand?"

"It's nothing." I tuck my hand behind my back and fight the urge to cringe.

I'm barely keeping it together as it is. Seeing the disgust in Dane's eyes when he looks at me might break me in my current fragile state.

"You're hurt." He's using his low, bedside manner tone. It's gentle but authoritative. "Let me see."

Suddenly, his muscular frame is in front of me, blocking my path to the exit. His sharply tailored black shirt fills my vision; I can't bring myself to look directly at him.

"I'm fine," I say with a breezy wave of my uninjured hand. "I'm just going home."

"I'll be the judge of that." His broad palm appears

between us, facing up in clear expectation. "Show me your hand, Abigail."

I blow out a sigh, and my shoulders slump again. I'm too exhausted to fight him. If I just appease him quickly, I can make my escape.

Even if the prospect of enduring his touch makes my heart beat against my ribs almost painfully. I try to ignore the bruising tenderness at the center of my chest and place my hand in his waiting palm.

His clinician's fingers are featherlight on my stinging, bright red skin. They're blissfully smooth and cool on my enflamed flesh.

"How did this happen?"

I shrug. "I wasn't paying attention, and I burned the milk I was steaming. It was a silly mistake."

He releases a low hum and turns my hand, inspecting every inch of it.

"I'm taking you home," he announces. "I can treat this properly there."

My jaw drops, and my eyes finally snap to his.

"I didn't think I'd see you again," I say before I can fully consider my words. "You were so angry with me. Why are you helping me?"

"I came here to see you, Abigail. But I want to talk in private." He boldly cups my cheek as though he has every right, gently lifting my face to study the signs of exhaustion. "I should've come sooner. But you're right. I was angry."

"I'm sorry," I whisper, regret tightening my throat around the apology. "I didn't want to upset you. That's the last thing I wanted."

His jaw firms, but he nods. "I think I understand. Let's go somewhere we can talk. Come on."

He wraps his arm around my hunched shoulders and steers me out of the café. His other hand holds his phone, and he opens an app to call a car for us. We stand under the bright Carolina sun for a few quiet minutes, and I close my eyes. My lids are so heavy, and now that Dane is touching me again, I finally feel safe enough to rest.

A black sedan arrives, and he helps me into the backseat before getting in on the other side. His arm is around my shoulders again, and he applies gentle pressure to encourage me to lean on him.

"I've got you," he murmurs.

My eyes sting, so I close them again to hold in the flood of relief that wets my lashes with tears. I inhale his unique, heady scent and allow my body to fully relax for the first time since he stormed out of my apartment.

I'm not sure how many minutes pass, and I think I might've drifted off for a while because we're suddenly coming to a stop.

Shock renders me mute when Dane drops a quick kiss on my forehead. "Stay."

The world turns surreal, and everything is fuzzy at the edges. He's opening my car door for me. I take his waiting hand with my uninjured one, and he helps me to my feet. He's every inch the charming, chivalrous gentleman, and I can't help swooning for him all over again.

His presence is a miracle, a blessed mercy after days of self-loathing and regret.

His palm spans my lower back as he confidently directs me to the sidewalk. Our physical connection hits me like a lightning strike, and my heart throbs in a painful, heavy rhythm. I want to be with this man more than anything. I thought I'd ruined everything, but there might still be a chance for us.

He leads me to the hunter green door on a white house with matching green shutters. I blink and glance around to get my bearings. We're in Harleston Village, a nice neighborhood across town from my apartment.

"I thought you said you were taking me home."

His dazzling smile hits me square in the chest. "I am. This is my home."

He unlocks the door, and it swings open to reveal a large entry hall. My breath catches when I see the painting that dominates the white wall directly in front of us.

"Dane…" His name is little more than a tremor on my lips.

He closes the door behind us and ushers me forward, guiding me down the hall until the painting fills my vision.

It's the red abstract expressionist piece from the gallery at The Magnolia. The one we both admired on our first date.

His hard body looms behind me, and his hands frame my shoulders. "I couldn't stop thinking about it," he murmurs. "I couldn't stop thinking about *you.*"

One hand lifts to my hair, and he twines my purple curl around his finger. "I'm not good with emotions," he admits. "I think that must be why I've never really understood art. But you see the world in a way I've never contemplated before. You are remarkable, Abigail."

"I thought you hated me for what I did." My voice breaks, and the painting blurs behind a wash of fresh tears.

"You said this painting is passion," he says. "But I can barely see the difference between the shades of red without you to describe them so eloquently. You said that's rage." He gestures at a crimson spray. "And that's seduction." His finger hovers over the purplish smudge. "But to me, they aren't so different."

"What are you saying?" I ask, my heart in my throat. I crave his forgiveness, but something like fear dances down my spine in a primal warning. It floods my core with forbidden heat.

"You lied to me when you faked your orgasm," he says. "But I wasn't being myself, either. I think it's time for us to both be honest about what we want."

"And what is it that you want?"

"You. All of you."

19

ABBY

"You're exhausted," Dane says before I can formulate a reply, his voice deep with concern rather than judgment. "Let's sit down, and I'll treat your hand. We can talk more after."

I practically float as he guides me into an ultramodern, minimalist living room. I'm no longer certain if I'm conscious or if I've slipped into some sweet dream where my charming prince is focused on me like I'm the most important person in the world.

He urges me to sit on the plush cream couch and orders me to stay before disappearing into the next room. I take a moment to stare at my surroundings, taking in his private space.

All of the furnishings are sleek and clearly expensive, but there's something almost sterile about the pale color palette. It feels like a show home that someone has designed as a model of a house rather than a place someone actually lives in. Everything is too new, too perfectly polished and clean.

Even the glass coffee table doesn't have so much as an errant water mark marring the surface.

I remind myself that Dane only moved in a few months ago, and he's admitted that he doesn't have an eye for art. It's likely that he hired some high-end interior designer to furnish this place, and he simply hasn't lived here long enough to make the space his own.

He returns to me before I can puzzle over it further.

"Give me your hand."

I comply without hesitation, even though my cheeks flush with soft heat. I'm still embarrassed that I was so careless at work.

"It's really not bad," I assure him. "It doesn't hurt anymore. My skin just feels a little tight."

He frowns at the angry red splotch over the back of my fingers, but his touch is careful as he rubs a cool salve into the burn. I release a long, slow exhale. The relief from the lingering burn is almost euphoric; I hadn't realized that I was still experiencing pain until he soothed it away.

When he's satisfied that my injury has been treated, his green eyes meet mine, pinning me in place with that rapt focus that makes my stomach flip.

"I should've come for you sooner," he says, as though it's an admission of a grave sin against me. "But I needed to get the paperwork together first."

My brow furrows. "Paperwork?"

He sits down beside me and reaches for a leather folder that I hadn't noticed on the side table. His expression is blank, completely enigmatic as he hands it to me.

"I had my lawyer draw this up. I hope you're not offended, but I have to be careful."

I open the folder and glance over the official document.

"An NDA?" My gaze meets his again, and I still can't read him. It's like a wall has gone up between us, and I'm shivering in its cool, looming shadow. "What's this about?" I press. "You can trust me, Dane."

His jaw tightens ever so slightly, the barest sign of tension. "I think I've made it clear that I'm not exactly close with my family, and I want things to stay that way." The words are so formal in his accent that they almost sound rehearsed. "But if what I want to say to you ever got back to them, they wouldn't let me be. It took a good five years for them to accept that I wasn't coming back home. They're content with their spare now, and they leave me to live my own life in America. I don't want that to change if I cause a scandal."

"Their *spare*?" I ask, still not understanding. "What do you mean?"

His face remains a careful, stony blank, like a beautiful sculpture of male stoicism.

"My father is the Earl of Ripley. I am the firstborn son. But I rejected my birthright when I left England to study at Johns Hopkins. They've learned to make do with my little brother, James, as the new heir."

I place my hand over his closed fist, trying to get him to open up to me again. My heart tugs toward his as though we're tethered by an invisible cord.

"My family isn't royalty, but I understand the desire to avoid scandal," I assure him. "I don't want to draw my parents' attention, either."

"Nobility, not royalty," he corrects me in a bland, rote tone. "The British media aren't all that discerning when it comes to celebrity, though. If there's juicy gossip, they'll splash it all over the tabloids."

I want to earnestly promise him again that he can

trust me, but I get the sense that my words won't reach him at the moment. He's protecting himself; he's possibly even in survival mode. That's why he's shut down right now.

I'm not good with emotions. I recall his vulnerable confession.

He needs action, not words. I'll prove to him that he can trust me.

I'm burning to learn more about him now that he's shared a little more insight into his fraught relationship with his family. I'd been right to think that his estrangement mirrored my own.

"Do you have a pen?" I ask.

"You'll want to read it carefully," he admonishes. "There are some steep penalties involved if you break the terms of the NDA."

I hold out my hand, expectant. "I'm not worried about any consequences because I won't betray your trust. I need a pen, please."

His eyes remain shuttered, but his mouth softens as some of his tension eases. There's still something too formal about his bearing, and I realize that his stiff posture isn't so different from my own.

He picks up a pen from the side table and places it in my uninjured hand.

I don't bother to peruse the NDA further before signing at the bottom. I meant what I said: the consequences don't matter. I will never betray Dane.

I close the folder with a decisive snap and place it on the coffee table.

"There," I declare, capturing his eyes with mine again. "Now you can tell me anything."

He huffs out a breath and considers me for another long moment, as though he's choosing his next words carefully.

"I treated you gently because I thought you were scared of men," he says. "I only ever want you to feel safe with me."

I thread my fingers through his, and after a tight moment, he parts them to allow me to hold his hand.

"I do," I promise. "I haven't let myself lean on anyone in a long time. I was scared to let go and trust in your support, but I know now that you won't let me fall. I can be vulnerable with you."

A shadow flits at his jaw. "You're scared of more than that." It's a rough statement of fact. "You don't have to tell me what happened until you're ready, but I know someone hurt you. That will never happen again. I've got you now."

I lean into him, finding strength in the undeniable connection we share. This intimacy is almost painfully intense, and a thrill races through me. He could crush me with a word, but I'm held safely in his strong hands.

"I know you won't hurt me," I breathe, lacing my fingers more tightly through his.

His eyes rake over my face, reading every nuance of my expression.

"But you want me to."

My stomach drops to the floor.

I can't let him see that fucked-up part of me. He'll be disgusted, and he'll walk away from me forever this time.

I remember the way my lust surged when he stood over me after I faked my orgasm. I'd been afraid that he'd read my moment of dark desire in response to his dangerous aura, the power of his fury. That beautiful, terrible scowl directed at me had made me wet.

My heart shreds, pain lancing deep in my chest.

He knows.

And I can't bring myself to lie to him again.

Shame presses down on my shoulders, and my head dips in defeat. I drop my eyes to the cream rug, unable to bear the censure that I'll see in his handsome face.

Two fingers touch my chin, and my ravaged heart gives a weak flutter as he lifts my gaze back to him.

His eyes blaze with green fire: desire, not disgust.

"I want you, Abigail. I want all that you are, and that includes the dark parts of your heart. Because they match my own perfectly."

"I didn't think you'd understand," I confess. "You're a good man. You've proven that you want to protect me."

He cups my cheek, grounding me to him. "I will always protect you. And I will never violate your trust. But I suspect that I have your consent to indulge in my darker games."

Desire shudders through me, strong enough to make my fingers tremble.

He caresses my shaking hand. "Don't be afraid."

"I'm not afraid of you," I promise. "I'm scared you'll leave if you find out what I'm really like. I don't want to lose you."

"You have me, Abigail. I'm not going anywhere."

My tongue darts out to wet my suddenly dry lips. "I've never talked to anyone about this. I don't think I know how."

His thumb traces the shape of my mouth, and my sensitive lips tingle at the tender contact.

"This is new territory for me too," he admits. "I'm skilled at what I do, but I've never kept a submissive of my own before."

My pulse quickens. I've spent enough time reading erotica that I'm familiar with BDSM, even if my own fantasies have always blurred the lines of consent.

"Do you understand what I'm talking about?" he asks, his eyes searching mine.

I swallow hard and nod.

His jaw tightens. "Have you engaged in BDSM before?"

Is he...jealous?

My chest heats with feminine gratification, and my nerves finally start to settle. Dane truly does want me as fiercely as I want him. The dangerous flash over his eyes is pure possessiveness, and my core pulses in response.

"No," I reply. "But I've read about it."

The tension eases from his powerful frame, and he traces my cheekbone. I lean into his touch, proving my trust in him with my body language. He needs reassurance, too, no matter how strong he is. He's making himself vulnerable, and I'm drawn to support him.

"You're safe with me too," I promise. "You can be yourself with me."

His features sharpen with unmistakable hunger, and for a moment, I think he's going to crush his lips to mine in a savage kiss.

Instead, his hand drops from my face so that he can retrieve the leather folder from the coffee table. Cold air rushes over my heated cheek, and I quickly breathe through the knifing sense of loss at his withdrawal.

"I'm not going to change my mind," I reassure him. "I won't tell anyone your secrets."

"Yes, you signed the NDA, even if you didn't bother to read the ramifications." He shoots me a wicked smirk that makes my heart skip a beat. "You're mine now."

He flips the page over and sets the open folder on my lap.

"I have a different contract for you now, pet."

Desire shudders down my spine, quivering all the way to my core.

I think I'd like to have you as my needy pet. GentAnon's dirty message plays through my mind, but I quickly dismiss it. This is *Dane.* He's real and warm and solid, not an anonymous, faceless man on the internet.

"Is that a Yorkshire endearment? It's sweet." I can't keep the breathiness from my voice when I try for an offhand tone.

His low chuckle rumbles deep inside me. "You can't hide from me, Abigail. You're pressing your soft thighs together to suppress your lust. I see you. I see everything. You want to be my pretty pet." He taps the folder, an authoritative gesture that has me complying without thinking. "Read it."

Unlike the NDA, this contract has been written in slanted cursive rather than neatly typed. I know it's Dane's handwriting without having to ask. It's every bit as elegant as he is. The bold strokes of black ink indicate a fountain pen, and I can easily picture his long fingers deftly holding it as he wrote this illicit contract.

By signing below, my pet, Abigail Foster, gives herself to me, Dane Graham. She will abide by my rules and obey my commands. She will at all times endeavor to please me. Nothing is more important to her than my pleasure.

In return, my pet will be rewarded. When I am satisfied with her behavior, she will be allowed to come. When she disappoints me, she will be punished with a variety of implements of my *choosing. She will submit to her punishments and will thank me for correcting her.*

Sometimes, she will suffer because I will it, and for no other reason. She will find ecstasy in enduring this suffering and surrendering to my control.

In the unlikely instance that I ask too much of my pet, a safe word will be honored. "Red" will end our games, and I will ensure that she feels safe and comforted.

At all times, my pet will be cherished and cared for. She trusts in me to take responsibility for her. When it comes my decisions regarding her wellbeing, defiance will not be tolerated.

My pet is a valued individual, and she will speak her mind. She will deny me nothing, and that includes giving me full access to her thoughts and feelings. Dishonesty will be met with swift retribution.

With her signature, my pet gives herself to me, her Master.

I stare at the elegant script, struggling to process that this is reality. My body trembles with lust. I can feel my inner walls clenching, and my labia are almost painfully swollen.

The contract is concise but powerful. There isn't an endless list of rules and expectations. Dane's will *is* the expectation. He'll issue commands, and I will obey, no matter what he decides to ask of me.

Except for the clause that allows me to withdraw consent at any time. My safe word will make everything stop.

My mind spins at the deviant possibilities. I've never imagined having a safe outlet for my dark desires, but Dane is offering me exactly that: erotic abandon, but with a promise of security.

I read over the final paragraphs again.

He wants me to give myself to him, not as a mindless plaything, but as *me*.

This contract proves it.

My fingers shake when I pick up the pen, and I can't bring myself to look directly at him as I sign myself over to him.

In this moment, I'm choosing to trust that he means it when he says he'll take care of me. I'm surrendering to the darkest, weakest parts of me that want to be both hurt and cared for. I never dared to dream that I could be with someone who understands my needs but also values my consent.

He plucks the pen from my trembling fingers and places the signed contract on the table. I stare at his slanted handwriting as he adds a final line:

With my signature, I vow to cherish my sweet pet.

The pen indents the paper with the force of his signature.

I take a moment to imprint the scene in my memory. Later, I'll paint his dexterous hand firmly holding the pen, and I'll strive to capture the confident strokes as he boldly lays claim to everything that I am.

He turns to me, and his triumphant grin is wickedly sharp.

"You lied to me when you faked your orgasm," he says, his tone heavy with condemnation even as his eyes glitter with carnal anticipation. "What does our contract say about dishonesty?"

I swallow hard, and warning snakes down my spine. "I'm sorry. I only faked it because I wanted to please you. I wanted you to feel good about our connection."

He trails his fingers through my hair, the tender stroke belying the dangerous, hungry tension around his mouth.

"I know, but your apology won't spare you. You're going to suffer for me, and then you're going to come for me. We won't stop until you lose count of your orgasms. You will learn that there is exquisite pain in pleasure, and you will beg for mercy before I'm finished with you."

He stands, looming over me like my own personal dark god. My lips part for an enraptured moment, and I stare up at his masculine perfection with open awe.

"It's time for your punishment, Abigail."

20

ABIGAIL

I place my hand in Dane's outstretched palm, and his fingers close around mine in a firm cage. Apprehension flutters in my belly like the frantic beats of a trapped butterfly's wings. The disconcerting sensation sets my senses on high alert, and my entire focus centers on him.

His handsome face is etched with hungry lines, as though someone has enhanced the sharpness on the world. His eyes blaze with emerald flames, burning with dark fire that entrances me. Our connection is hypnotic, and I rise to my feet as though he's lifted my limbs on a puppet's strings.

With no more than a gentle tug at my hand, he pulls me in his wake. I float alongside him, my breaths coming faster as though I'm jogging in the summer heat rather than strolling through his house. He leads me up the stairs, and we enter his bedroom.

The color scheme is vastly different from the sterile, pale tones in the rest of the house. The walls are painted a deep green that's so dark it's almost velvety, and the furniture is built in sturdy mahogany. A massive four-poster bed with a black-draped canopy dominates one wall.

My steps falter as my anxiety rises, eating away at my lust.

What if my body won't relax to accommodate him? What if my inner muscles close so tightly that he can't penetrate me?

Now that I'm in his private sanctuary, only mere feet away from his bed, my insecurities nip at me with sharp teeth.

As always, he's attuned to my moods. He pauses and turns to me. Both hands settle on my waist, holding me so close that our bodies are almost touching.

"Tell me what you're worried about."

"It's nothing." I placate him automatically. I don't want to ruin this moment with my damage.

I straighten my shoulders, determined to master my own body so that I can be with Dane in every way.

His lips firm to a warning slash that makes my stomach dip like I'm on a rollercoaster. A familiar, giddy thrill fizzes through me. I'm riding the edge of danger, and yet, I'm completely safe with Dane.

I marvel at the dichotomy, the fact that I'm able to indulge in this space where I'm both threatened and protected.

"Have you forgotten our contract already?" he challenges. "Complete honesty, Abigail. I want all of you. That means you will tell me all of your thoughts and feelings. You're worried about something. Explain."

"Sometimes, my body gets so tight that I can't accept penetration," I admit. "I'm scared that will happen again."

His cocky smirk makes my clit pulse. "Trust me, pet. Your body will bend to my will. I fully intend to claim your sweet cunt. All you have to do is give yourself to me, and I'll make sure you experience more pleasure than you ever thought possible. No matter how long it takes, I will toy with you and torment you until you flower open for me."

"But what about you?" I ask breathily. The contract had been clear that my purpose is to please him, but he's talking all about me and taking nothing for himself.

He caresses my cheek. "Sweet pet. Don't worry. I'll use you for my pleasure once I'm satisfied that you've been thoroughly punished." His thumb rubs my sensitized lips. "I'll devote just as much time to training this pretty mouth as I do to conquering your tight pussy."

My breath stutters at his crass words. It's like something out of my darkest fantasies, but this time, I'm completely willing. I'm eager for him to fulfil his wicked promises. It's all I can do to keep my knees from folding so that I can worship his cruel perfection.

"I didn't know it could be like this," I confess.

His low laugh holds a mocking edge. "You don't know anything yet. I will teach you the meaning of suffering, and you will weep in gratitude."

This arrogant, domineering side of him should seem shockingly different from my dashing prince, but somehow, this feels right. It's as though I'm seeing him clearly for the first time, but this hidden facet of him doesn't diminish the goodness of the man I've started to know over the last few weeks.

I marvel at the prospect that I can have both: my white knight and my dark god, all in one gorgeous package.

I push up onto my tiptoes, seeking a kiss. His cruel smile pierces my chest like a knife, but my core pulses in response as he denies me. This seduction will be on his terms, not mine. I don't have to guess how to satisfy him; all I have to do is give myself over to his control.

My breath shudders between my parted lips, but he doesn't caress them with his. He shows no mercy.

Instead, he keeps me pinned in his stare as he slowly drags my black cotton shirt up my torso. His hands skim my sides, tracing my shape without stimulating my most sensitive areas. He hasn't so much as brushed my breasts, but my nipples are hard, aching buds against the inside of my purple bra.

He tugs my shirt over my head and tosses it away. Then he twines my amethyst curl around his finger and boldly cups my breast with his other hand.

It's the lightest flex of his strong fingers, but it sends a pulse of pure lust humming through my entire body.

"This is a beautiful color on you," he says. "You'll wear it for me more often."

It's not a request, and his casual authority makes me melt.

Before I can nod in agreement, he wraps my curl around his wrist and pulls me in for a vicious kiss. He claims me with tongue and teeth, alternating the softness of his full lips with punishing bites. My hair is an anchor in the chain of his hand, keeping me steady as I'm swept up in desire as strong as a storm-tossed sea. He's the only thing tethering me to reality, the only person in existence.

He doesn't break our kiss or release my hair as he deftly unbuttons my jeans with his free hand. I shimmy out of them without needing to be told. I'm eager to be naked with him, to finally feel his hard, glorious body against mine.

My fingers fly to his collar, fumbling at the small buttons.

He shackles my wrists, directing them away from his shirt.

"No," he murmurs against my lips. "I want you naked and vulnerable. This is your punishment, pet."

"But I want to touch you," I protest breathily. "I want to see you."

He nips at my lower lip. "You have to earn your rewards. It's time for you to suffer for me."

He releases me entirely and takes a step back. Cool air rushes over me, and my skin pebbles in the absence of his steady heat.

Before I can fold my arms over my chest to chase away the chill of vulnerability, he commands, "Take off your bra. I want to see what's mine."

I almost whimper at the wave of ruthless desire that rushes through me. My panties are wet with my arousal, and my clit pulses madly.

I'm his possession, his pet.

And he's going to punish me.

My fingers tremble, but I manage to unclasp my bra after two fumbling attempts. The straps slide down my arms, and the soft skimming sensation over each of my goosebumps sets my entire body alight with carnal sensation.

He takes another step back, and I can't help swaying toward him, as though I'm bound to him by invisible rope.

"Stay," he admonishes. "I'm admiring my pretty pet."

I manage to obey, but my hands are still shaking with the force of the adrenaline coursing through me. I want him so desperately that my swollen sex aches to be touched, but I'm compelled by his will.

A sense of lightness floods my mind, and my thoughts float away. There are no insecurities, no worries about whether or not my body will accept him. There's no room in my world for anything other than his control. He has claimed ownership of me, but I've never felt freer than I do in this moment.

He strolls around me, taking me in from every angle. I hardly breathe, determined to obey and remain still for him to admire at his leisure. I feel exposed but safe. No one will hurt me while I'm in Dane's care.

No one but him.

He's promised to make me suffer, and I eagerly await the absolution he will offer me.

I feel his heat recede further, and I barely resist the urge to turn so that I can see where he's going. My teeth worry my lower lip, and my fingernails bite into my palms in the long seconds that pass without his nearness.

Just when my anxiety begins to reach a fever pitch, his hand spans my lower back.

I jolt, and he shushes me gently.

His hard body is behind mine, and his corded arms encircle my waist. "Give me your wrists."

I lift my hands in offering, and he loops hemp rope around them. His movements are quick and efficient, and in less than a minute, my wrists are bound together. He holds the length of rope like a leash and uses the tension to force my body to turn. I spin in the cage of his arms, and suddenly, I'm trapped in his glittering emerald stare.

He's almost a foot taller than I am, but I feel even smaller in his imposing shadow—as fragile as a wren captured in his elegant hand.

He keeps me pinned with his imposing gaze as he tugs on the rope, pulling my arms upward. When they're fully extended above me, he loops the length over the wooden beam of the canopy. Another short tug forces me to stretch until I'm almost on my toes.

His chuckle rumbles with dark amusement at my predicament as he ties off his work, leaving me bound and naked except for my black cotton thong. He takes his time to study me, as though I'm not even a person. I'm a pretty thing for him to admire, a work of art that he possesses to view whenever it pleases him.

The sense of being objectified should be shameful, possibly even offensive. But I'm molten for him, my entire being burning for more of his cruel attention. As long as he's looking at me, I have value. Without his imperious gaze on me, I would be insignificant: a cheap replicated print not worthy of notice.

But he's looking at me as though I'm his coveted masterpiece, his most treasured possession.

"Exquisite," he praises, and I sigh in bliss.

I've been so enamored with him that I didn't notice what he placed on the bed before he bound me. He reaches past me to pick up the cane, and my stomach flips.

He touches the cool rod to my belly, using it to pin my bound body to his front. His erection presses into my ass, huge and insistent.

I writhe—equal parts need and fear.

"Are you scared yet, Abigail?" His dark question ruffles my hair as he practically coos into my ear.

"Yes," I admit on a tremulous whisper. I don't dare lie to him when I'm in this vulnerable position.

"Good. Pets should fear their master's retribution. And you've more than earned mine." He touches my inner thigh, and his fingers swirl in silken wetness. "You love the fear. You love being at my mercy, my pretty plaything."

"Yes." I release the affirmation on a shuddering sigh: a confession offered up from the deepest, darkest part of my soul.

He nuzzles my hair and inhales deeply, as though he's breathing in the scent of my wanton arousal.

"I'm going to hurt you now. Do you trust me?"

"I do." It's an oath, and I let my head fall to the side, further exposing my throat to his teeth. "I want you to."

They graze my artery as he commands, "Beg."

"Please hurt me." My plea is little more than a desperate whimper.

He presses a soft kiss to my forehead and pulls away. Cool air closes over my exposed body, and I shiver in anticipation. My heart flutters against my ribcage in rapid beats—a bruising promise of the pain that is to come.

He's behind me now, and my upraised arms are like blinkers on either side of my head. I can't see him without twisting my bound body, and I can barely maintain my balance as it is. So, I remain perfectly still, taut as a bowstring. Apprehension and desire coil my muscles tight, and sweat beads on my brow as though I'm enduring physical strain.

The first tap of the cane draws a yelp from my chest, and it takes me a second to process that the hit isn't painful. Another tap: a firm, bouncing pressure against my ass. Heat blooms beneath the surface of my skin, a prickling warmth that sinks deep into my tender flesh. The cane is a hard, unyielding rod against my soft body, but he's using it with deft precision. Each short strike sends a fresh wave of warmth thudding through me, rippling into my core.

He paints my upper thighs with carnal heat, until I'm simmering in lust.

I'm a being of pure sensation, and I lose myself in him. All that exists is his will and the light pain he inflicts, granting me the greatest high I've ever known. The pain sparkles like fireworks, crackling through my nervous system. My mind relaxes in a way I've never experienced, and all thoughts float away.

"Suffer for me, Abigail."

His dark command is my only warning. The cane lashes me in the first true, punitive blow. A line of fire blazes across my tender flesh, and I release a shocked cry.

"One," he intones, and I scramble to process that fact that he's counting. There will be more.

"Dane..." His name is a tremulous plea. My ass is smarting, and my tight muscles are beginning to strain from maintaining the stress position.

"You lied to me," he reminds me. "Don't you want your punishment?"

My eyes burn, and my head dips in shame. "Yes."

He hums his approval. "Four more."

My next breath hitches on a soft sob, but I nod. I'll accept whatever he wants to do to me. I want to be his more than I need oxygen, and I will offer myself to him in every way.

Fire lashes my skin, an inch beneath the first strike.

"Breathe," he reminds me.

I gasp for air, compelled by his will. Euphoria floods my mind as I fully surrender to the sweet rush of pain. A low moan sighs from my lips, and I sag against the restraints around my wrists. The rope bites into my skin, another blissful hit of pain. I'm helpless to resist Dane, but I'm completely safe in his cruel hands.

Another punitive stroke, another line of fire, another rush of white-hot bliss.

I'm no longer certain where pain ends and pleasure begins. The release is nothing short of ecstatic. Tears roll down my cheeks, siphoning my shame in steady streams.

I lied to Dane when I faked my orgasm, but there's no

dishonesty between us now. There's nowhere to hide when he has me stripped bare and bound in place for punishment.

"Are you sorry?" he asks, and the fourth blow lands.

"Yes!" I confess on a harsh cry.

"You don't have any secrets from me, Abigail. Never lie to me again."

"Never." It's a fervent promise.

He seals my vow with the final strike, pressing the cane deep into my thighs after the blow lands to imprint a bruise: a mark of forgiveness.

He kisses my cheeks, and when his soft lips finally caress mine, I taste the salt of my tears. His tongue plunders my mouth, laying claim to everything that I am. I relax into his harsh embrace, welcoming him to take all of me: body and soul.

His hands bracket my hips, and he guides me to turn on the spot. The rope above me twists, allowing me to turn but keeping me bound for his dark games.

When I'm facing him, he captures me in his fiery emerald stare. He's looking at me as though I'm his most precious possession, and the sense of being fully seen and valued draws fresh tears to my eyes. I'm more vulnerable than ever, but Dane will cherish me. He looks at me as though he doesn't see any flaws, and I'm desperate to keep his rapt attention fixed on me.

My jaw drops when he gets on his knees. His white teeth flash in a wicked grin before he leans in and nips at my black cotton panties. He traps them in a firm bite that grazes my clit, and a burst of pure pleasure wracks my body.

My knees go weak, and he catches me, cupping my ass to hold me steady as he drags my panties down my legs with his teeth.

He's kneeling before me, but I'm worshipping *him*. I'm offering myself as a carnal sacrifice to my dark god.

One hand remains braced beneath my ass while the other tests the wet heat that paints my inner thighs. His intense gaze fixes on my pussy like it's the most fascinating thing he's ever seen, and my cheeks heat with a mixture of gratification and embarrassment.

I've never had a man this close to my most intimate area before. My swollen labia are aching and hot. Each of his even breaths sends a wave of cool air over my sensitized flesh, teasing and tormenting me.

"Beautiful," he praises. His thumb carefully parts my folds, inspecting me like I'm a priceless treasure. "My cunt is so pretty and pink. And so wet for me."

He's talking about my body as though he owns it. I signed the contract and gave myself to him. Every part of me belongs to Dane now, and surrendering to him is the most erotic high I've ever experienced.

His forefinger dips between my labia, easing inside me in a slow slide. My inner muscles clamp down on the intrusion, but there's no pain.

My eyes sting with the force of my relief. I don't have to pretend with Dane. Being with him like this feels right, and my body finally makes sense to me for the first time in my adult life. This is fully consensual, and yet, I'm more than ready to open myself for his cock.

I've never experienced anything like it.

What we're doing is undeniably kinky, but I feel like a normal woman, not a perverted deviant who can only experience pleasure when forced.

Dane is the only one who can give me this gift, and I will grant him anything in return.

He eases a second finger into my tight channel, and I tense for a moment at the sensation of fullness. He shushes me gently and presses his lips directly to my clit.

Stars burst across my vision, and I blink hard so that I can remain fixated on his handsome face drawn in sharp, hungry lines. He flicks his tongue over my clit, and my knees buckle. He catches me with his arm braced beneath my ass, and his fingers press into the welts left by the cane. The flare of pain sends me flying even higher, and I'm oddly weightless. Only Dane's arm behind my thighs keeps me chained to reality.

"Open up for me, pretty pet," he urges between licking my clit. "I'll need to stretch your tight pussy wide enough to accept your master's cock."

He crooks two fingers inside me, finding a sweet spot I've never known before. My entire body convulses at the vicious pulse of pleasure, and I cry out as the orgasm rakes through me.

"Don't stop," he commands. "I want more. You will give me everything, Abigail."

"Yes!" I shout when he circles my clit with his tongue. "I'm yours. All yours."

Ecstasy crashes in relentless waves, pleasure churning through me like a riptide. I'm powerless against him, completely at his mercy. I experience bliss at his whim, and he intends to drown me in it.

My head drops back on a primal scream of release as all of my emotional walls crumble away beneath his onslaught. I don't have to hold myself together. I don't have to pretend to be something I'm not. Dane has stripped me bare to reveal the dark truth at my core, and he's still holding me as though I'm wanted. Valued. Worthy.

"That's it," he urges. "You're mine."

A third thick finger slides into me, and this time, the edge of pain is a sweet sharpness to my pleasure. He pumps into me in ruthless strokes, willing my body to accommodate him however he chooses. At the same time, his teeth graze my clit.

"Please..." I writhe in his grip, but there's nowhere for me to go. "It's too much... I can't..."

"You can take it," he says, a command rather than a reassurance. "I want another orgasm."

My eyes slide closed on a low moan. Pain flares on my inner thigh when he sinks his teeth into my soft flesh in rebuke.

"Look at me."

The deep green facets of his glittering eyes are sharp enough to cut into my soul.

"You belong to me, Abigail. Tell me."

A tear slides down my cheek and wets my lips as I murmur, "I'm yours."

He bites my thigh again, and I cry out at the shock of pain that layers over the waves of pleasure he's coaxing from that sensitive spot inside me.

"*Master*," he corrects me, his voice dark with warning.

"Master," I whisper it like a prayer. "I'm yours, Master."

He releases a savage sound, and he buries his face between my legs like he wants to devour me. My clit stings in sensitized protest after the multiple orgasms, but my master isn't finished with me.

My core contracts helplessly around his invasive fingers as he plays me like his favorite instrument, drawing pleasure from my overstimulated body until I'm babbling and weeping for mercy.

But he has none.

21

DANE

Mine.

It's like something out of one of my most feverish fantasies: Abigail is calling me *Master* while she cries and comes all over my face.

But this is real. Nothing has ever been more real in my life.

Until meeting her, I'd seen the world in cold, clinical terms. I assessed everything at a numb distance, and I was thoroughly in control because I wasn't hampered by the frivolous emotions that weaken other people.

Now, I feel *everything.* And I've never been more powerful.

These savage emotions Abigail evokes in me are almost debilitating at times, but my control over her makes me stronger than I've ever been.

This stunning, talented woman has chosen to give herself to me. She places her full trust in me.

It's the greatest high I've ever known, even though she's the one screaming out her orgasm right now.

Her pussy gives a weak flutter around my insistent fingers,

tempting my own lust to rise to a maddening pitch. My cock is painfully hard, and I've been aching to bury myself in her wet heat. Only my control over her has given me the strength to restrain my most primal urges. I won't rut into her like a beast when having her completely come undone is a far greater pleasure.

I want her on her knees, so that I can see those lovely aquamarine eyes staring up at me with devotion and awe.

Her cunt fully yielded to me three orgasms ago. She's tight, but her body surrendered to my will.

I lick my lips and taste her delicious arousal, all that wet desire just for me.

It's her turn now.

I keep one arm braced around her lower back to support her as I rise, then lift my free hand to undo the knot that keeps her wrists bound above her head. She sags against me, her muscles weak and shaking after the long period of erotic torment.

I ease her down, guiding her to her knees. She sways slightly, like she's drunk on the pleasure I've drawn from her lovely body.

I touch two fingers beneath her chin, and her perfect posture immediately straightens her shoulders. Her back arches slightly, putting her modest, pert breasts on display for me. Her pink nipples are pretty little buds, and I wonder how sensitive they are.

That exploration will have to wait for another time. I've barely begun to learn the secrets of her body, even if I already know her hidden, dark fantasies from our late-night messages.

Abigail is my perfect match.

And now, she's all mine.

She walked right into her cage when she signed the contract to be my submissive. There's no going back now.

I reach into my pocket and retrieve the collar I purchased for her weeks ago. One way or another, this was always going to end up locked around her pretty throat.

But my pet is proving to be sweetly docile. It's almost a shame she's not putting up more of a fight.

I blink once so that she can't see the dark thought in my eyes. She's staring up at me with that wide, guileless gaze, and I fear she might see straight into me if I don't keep my new, surging emotions in check.

I want Abigail to feel safe with me. The fact that she's willingly placing her trust in me makes something throb deep in the center of my chest. It's almost a painful sensation, but I decide that I like it. I want more of this.

"Lift your hair for me," I command.

I don't wait or ask for her permission to collar her. She's already agreed to this with her signature on the contract. Only a single word can stop what's happening between us, and I won't do anything that might push her to use it.

The black collar is a thin, midnight band of leather against her creamy skin. The rose gold ring at the front brings out the soft pink hues in her complexion. The matching buckle at her nape has a small ring that punches through the leather, and I deftly loop the delicate padlock through it. The soft click of the lock engaging draws the most delicious shiver from her, and her hair cascades from her fingers in sable waves.

I find the purple one and curve it around my finger. The gesture is calming in a way I've never known before. I smooth the vibrant locks into one perfect, loose curl that falls over her left breast, brushing her tight nipple. The rich amethyst shade against the pink bud is the most breathtaking thing I've ever seen.

Her lips are a deeper shade of pink, slightly glossy from her tears. I trace my thumb along them, memorizing their shape and pliant texture.

So many long nights, I've laid alone in bed and fantasized about these lips around my cock.

The time for fantasies is over.

Abigail is my collared pet now, and she will eagerly give me access to every part of her body.

"Open your mouth."

As I free my stiff cock from the confines of my trousers, those lovely lips part. Her hands brace at my hips, and her head dips forward to accept my length into her mouth.

My fingers anchor in her hair, stopping her short with a little warning tug. I tap my cock against her cheek in a light slap—a swift rebuke for trying to take control.

"What did I—?"

I slap her again, more firmly this time. "Open your mouth." I repeat the command, clipped and clear.

Her eyes shine with fresh tears, and they're so blue that they practically glow like a sunlit, azure sea. Her lower lip trembles when she parts her lips again, then waits for my next move. She barely breathes as she stares up at me, completely vulnerable and willing to be used for my pleasure.

"Stick out your tongue."

She complies, and I rest my cockhead on her waiting tongue. Desire courses through my veins, hot and insistent. But I'm strong enough to master my own lust; mastering *her* gives me that strength.

I watch in rapt fascination as a bead of my precum drops onto her tongue. It pools there, spilling deeper into her waiting mouth. A tear rolls down her rosy cheek. I capture it on my fingertips and rub the wetness over my cock. Pleasure lances me like a lightning strike down my spine, and I grit my teeth to hold back my orgasm.

I take a small step forward, wedging my shin between her thighs. She gasps, and the soft rush of air over my dick torments me. I bite back a growl and increase the pressure, so that her sensitive little clit is griding against my leg.

"Don't stop," I say. "You're going to come for me again."

A high whimper eases from her chest, but she obediently rotates her hips, stimulating herself even though I know she must be aroused to the point of pain.

"Good girl. You're such a good pet."

I finally, slowly, push my cock into her waiting mouth.

"Does that feel good, Abigail? Does it hurt?"

Broken moans hum around my dick, and I bury my fingers in her hair, clinging for my control.

A dark laugh fills the bedroom. "That's right," I praise. "Pets don't talk. All you can do is whimper and moan around Master's cock."

Her eyes roll back on a blissful whine, and I tug sharply at her hair to recapture her attention.

"Look at me."

Her lovely eyes are dark with lust, her huge pupils rendering the remarkable aqua shade a thin ring of blue. Her gaze is unnervingly focused despite her euphoric state, and again, I get the sense that she's peering straight into me.

And in this moment, I can't hold anything back. I let my civilized mask drop away entirely; I allow her to see my selfishness, my ruthlessness, my cruel hunger that only she can slake.

She moans around my cock, and I can't restrain myself in

any way. My length sinks deep into her throat, and she gags around me. I can't stop. I pull back slightly to allow her to breathe, but I come all over her tongue.

The rush of pleasure is strong enough to make my knees weak, and I grab the bedpost for support as I roar out my release.

I watch in awe as she greedily swallows everything that I offer her. She's frantically licking my shaft when she grinds hard against my leg and lets out a sharp cry, finding her own ecstasy in my pleasure with her.

I withdraw from her and scoop her up in my arms. She's completely limp in my hold, implicitly trusting me to take care of her in the aftermath of absolutely shattering her.

The painful pulsing at the center of my chest starts up again, an insistent, addictive throb.

I lay her lovely body out on my bed and tuck her close to me. I'm still mostly dressed while she's fully naked, but I just need to hold her now. I can worry about mundane things like clothing later.

"How are you feeling?" I ask, stroking her hair back from her sweat-slicked brow.

She's so still and quiet.

I barely breathe until she slurs, "Wonderful."

My entire body relaxes, and I marvel at this moment of unknown intimacy. Only a few hours ago, I'd feared that she wouldn't sign the NDA. Now, Abigail is naked in my bed, and she looks as peaceful as one of the sleeping princesses in her favorite animated musicals.

The last week without her has been deeply unpleasant. I was forcing her to live without me and to reflect on how she'd disappointed me by faking the orgasm.

But I'd tortured myself too.

Never again.

From now on, Abigail will sleep in my bed every night. I won't tolerate another arrangement.

I'm her Master, and she will learn what it means to be mine.

22

DANE

Abigail's face is upturned to catch the sun, as though she's a freshly bloomed flower soaking in the warm rays. In the bright light, her dark freckle stands out in fascinating contrast with her porcelain skin. Her cheek is flushed slightly from the summer heat, but I'm reassured that she's not getting burned. I helped her put on her sunscreen before we left her place, where we stopped off to pick up her clothes for this outing.

The memory of her soft body beneath my hands is enough to tempt my lust, so I do my best to suppress it. We're on a public beach, and I don't need an erection right now.

Her outfit is simple and inexpensive, but the style is classic. The bright blue bikini brings out the lovely hue of her eyes, and a pale pink sarong is wrapped loosely around her hips.

Abigail clearly has good taste, even if she doesn't have much money.

Very soon, I'll be able to dress her up in whatever pleases

me most. I anticipate some defiance when it comes to me spending money on her, but I already have a plan to subdue her.

She signed herself over to me. She belongs to me.

I don't want to change her—I covet everything that she is —but she will obey.

"What are you thinking about?" That clear, open gaze is fixed on me again, but her lips are curved in a small smile rather than a concerned frown.

She isn't scared of the darkness that lurks in me. When we were together last night, I allowed my civilized mask to fall away entirely, and she didn't run screaming; she came so hard that she passed out for twelve hours.

"I'm thinking how lucky I am to have you as my pretty pet." I don't bother to hide the wolfish edge to my grin.

I never realized how heavy my mask is until I allowed it to drop in her presence. I feel free in a way I've never experienced before, and it's all because of her.

Her cheeks flush a brighter shade of pink, and she quickly glances around to check if anyone overheard.

Even my chuckle comes with shocking ease—a sound of natural pleasure rather than a carefully constructed social response to appear charming. Normal.

"No one heard me," I reassure her.

The beach is crowded today, but everyone is too concerned with their own lives to listen in on our quiet conversation. The crashing waves and cawing gulls overhead provide a backdrop to the buzz of dozens of conversations. It's more than enough to grant us privacy, even if we are surrounded by people.

"And you were right," I drawl. "*Pet* is a Yorkshire endearment."

I pause, relishing the soft downturn of her lips and the small furrow in her brow. For a moment, she's disappointed. She wants our game to be real. She wants her new title to be more than a casual endearment.

Another low laugh rumbles from me. "But don't worry. We both know what it really means: you're mine."

Her breath catches, and her pupils dilate. Then she huffs and lightly slaps my chest.

"Don't mess with me like that," she admonishes, but her voice holds a sultry edge. She's turned on by my possessiveness.

My grin sharpens, and I grasp her hand, holding it so that her palm is pressed directly over the center of my chest. There's that steady thrum again, the beat slightly elevated.

"You love it when I toy with you."

She scoffs and tosses her hair, but she doesn't try to pull away.

"You can't hide from me," I taunt. "Complete honesty, remember? Unless you already want another punishment."

Her blush is delicious. She's wearing the sarong to cover the beautiful marks left by my cane. I caught her admiring them in the mirror this morning.

She's perfect for me.

Her rosebud lips press together, as though she's debating another retort. She wants to see how far she can push me.

"Go on." I dare her to try it. "Defy me, and see what happens."

She blows out an exasperated sigh, but she sways toward me, drawn in by my cruelty.

I lift her hand to my lips and brush a kiss over her knuckles. "Such a good girl."

I'm baiting her. I'd love a reason to hurt her again, to indulge in the darkest parts of our intense connection.

She practically squirms at the praise. She likes it, even if my patronizing tone makes her bristle.

I'll break her of those notions of pride and independence. She doesn't need them anymore. Not when she's mine to care for.

She shakes her head. "I'm not falling for that. Bait me all you want. I'm not going to give you a reason to punish me so easily."

I press another reverent kiss to the back of her hand. A strange, giddy thrill soars through me. I'm more pleased by her response than I could've imagined. She's not defying me, but she is trying to deny me. Abigail won't walk into my traps so easily. It makes our game more complex, and I'll never get bored.

"Are you forgetting the part where I can make you suffer at my whim?" I challenge. "I don't need a reason."

"Dane!" My name is a breathy admonishment. "We're in public. This is too much."

"I rather like seeing you blush and squirm for me in front of all these people. Do you think they know how wet you are right now?"

"Dane!" She's almost alarmed this time, but that flush deepens to the prettiest shade of pink, and she licks her perfect lips in open desire.

My arrogant laugh seems to affect her even more, because she tears her gaze from mine and stares out at the ocean. Her chest rises and falls more rapidly as she draws in little panting breaths. I shift my hold on her hand so that I can test her pulse at her wrist. It's racing for me, elevated with lust and an edge of fear at public exposure.

"I can be a merciful master," I allow, tucking a stray lock of hair behind her ear. "We'll discuss this more later."

She releases some of her tension on a relieved sigh. "Thank you."

I caress her cheek, lingering on her pretty freckle. "Such a sweet, grateful pet. How did I get so lucky?"

Her teasing smile is wide and brighter than the summer sun overhead. "You're welcome."

I hum my approval and wrap my hand around her nape to pull her closer. "I'll tame this sassy mouth later."

I press a quick kiss to her parted lips, relishing her little scandalized gasp.

"I am lucky to have you, Abigail," I say earnestly.

One way or another, she was always going to be mine. But I captured her with such ease. I didn't even have to remove a man from her life to gain access to her.

Although, there is still the irksome issue of the man who hurt her in the past. The one who made her thorny about financial control and skittish when I kissed her the first time. Someone has abused her, and I won't be satisfied until I make him suffer. His actions made it more difficult for me to win Abigail's trust. He'll pay for that.

"Tell me about your relationship history," I say. "How is it possible that such a stunning woman was single and waiting for me to come along?"

The question is meant to soften my intense inquiry, but she edges away from me slightly. I'm not sure if it's my compliment that's making her uncomfortable or the prospect of talking about her painful past, but I won't relent until I have answers. I want the name of her abuser.

"You don't want to hear about my past boyfriends," she says with a dismissive wave.

"I'll be the judge of what I want to hear," I admonish. "Tell me."

Her brows lift. "Is that an order?"

"Yes." I don't bother to hide the warning, cold edge to my tone.

She considers me for a moment, then shrugs. "There's not much to tell. I've only had one boyfriend, and it wasn't that serious. We dated for about six months during my freshman year at College of Charleston, but he transferred to a different school for sophomore year. The relationship was never significant enough to warrant trying long distance."

"Is he the one who hurt you?" I ask, my voice dropping even colder.

She blinks, as though caught off guard by my question. "No. He was a nice guy. We just didn't have much chemistry."

Some of the violent tension eases from my muscles. "So, he's the one who couldn't satisfy you."

I'm still annoyed that the fumbling fool is the one who made her think that her body isn't capable of experiencing pleasure. She was painfully tense when I was gentle with her that first time. He probably reinforced that stiffness with his inept attempts at seduction. I wonder how many times she forced herself to endure the pain to soothe the boy's ego, the way she'd tried to do with me when she faked her orgasm.

He might not be the one who hurt her, but he should suffer for that sin against her.

"What's his name?" I demand.

"Devin." Her brows are drawn together in a small, concerned frown. "What are you going to do, fly to Seattle and beat him up for being too nice?"

I force my body to relax with considerable effort. She can

see me so clearly. I don't want her to read the extent of my vicious intentions in my eyes. I'll take care of her, but she doesn't need to know my violent plans for the men in her past.

"How do you know he's in Seattle?" My tone is light, as though it's an offhand question. "Are you still in touch?"

She huffs an exasperated breath. "No. That's where he transferred for college. I don't know if he's still living there. Can we please change the subject? I'd rather spend time getting to know you than talking about my ex."

"I've never been in a serious relationship," I offer in order to placate her.

I'll have to return to this line of questioning later, when I've managed to get my new, surging emotions under control. I won't risk scaring her off if I reveal the extent of my violent nature. She craves my erotic cruelty, but I suspect she'd be upset if she saw it directed at others.

"I'd rather not hear about your womanizing," she says frostily.

Fuck.

Sometimes, I feel like a fumbling idiot when I'm around her. I never lose control of a conversation like this, but I'm saying all the wrong things.

I'd meant to reassure her that I've only engaged in casual flings to sate my needs. I'm skilled at BDSM because it's provided an outlet for my darker urges, even if I've never been fully satisfied. I've kept my mask firmly on, and the women I've been with never knew anything about my family or my past. I didn't put myself at risk for them. I didn't make myself vulnerable.

I can only be this way with Abigail.

"I've never wanted to be with anyone before I met you," I

say earnestly. "That's all you need to know. You make me feel things I didn't know I was capable of feeling."

That seems to be the right thing to say, because she softens, and her frown eases.

"Sorry, I'm being insecure." Incredibly, she's the one offering an apology.

That throbbing beat starts up in my chest again. I can hardly believe I've captured this sweet woman. She possesses her own inner darkness, but she's nothing like me. She doesn't have a cruel bone in her body.

Distant thunder rumbles, breaking the intense moment. I blink and tear my gaze from her x-ray eyes. Dark clouds are rolling at the horizon, the storm drawing closer to the beach.

"We should go," I say, but she pulls her phone out of her bag.

"Just a few more minutes," she requests, taking a picture of the encroaching storm. "This is my favorite weather."

"Ah, yes. I noticed your preference in your paintings."

She sets her phone down and focuses on me again, brows raised. "At the market that day?"

Fuck.

She thinks I've only seen her work one time: on the day I came to the market to save her from the thief.

She has no idea that I stare at scores of her paintings every day. And she doesn't know that I've seen her darker art that she keeps hidden.

I manage to keep my expression neutral and nod.

"Do you always paint landscapes?" I ask, pushing her to confess about her stunning, erotic work.

Her eyes cut away from mine, fixing on the horizon. "It's what always resonated with me most. And the tourists seem to like them."

She's not lying, but she is evading me.

"What do you like about them?" I press.

She blows out a sigh. "This will always be home," she admits, keeping her gaze fixed on the coming storm. "I have a complicated relationship with my family, and I sometimes feel resentment about my inability to leave them far behind. Like you did." Her clear eyes finally focus on me again, peering straight into my soul. "You managed to go to an entirely different country. I've only been able to move a few cities away."

"Why not go farther?" I'm hanging on to her every word, craving more of her intimate confessions.

"I can't afford it," she admits. Then she sighs. "But it's more than that. I don't think I'm capable of leaving. This is home," she repeats, but the declaration is soft with something like regret.

Does she feel trapped by her affinity for this place?

"That's why you favor the storms," I surmise.

Her paintings are beautiful, but her most powerful landscapes provide a glimpse into her tumultuous emotions when it comes to her home.

"Yes," she admits. "How did you manage it? Leaving home, I mean."

Something twists in my gut, a painful twinge. I breathe through the strange pain.

"Yorkshire is beautiful, but I'm not the sentimental type."

She's looking at me with that intent, open gaze. She's holding nothing back, and she expects the same of me.

"I didn't want my title," I confess. "The only way my father would accept that was to leave and not return."

"Why not?" She seems just as desperate to know me as I am to learn all of her secrets.

I find that I don't want to hide anything from her.

"My father is not a good person," I say, and it's almost as though the words are issuing from someone else's lips. "He uses his title and his wealth to cover his sins. He's a selfish, weak man. I refused to take up the same mantle. I want nothing to do with him."

For an awful moment, I see the blood, hear the incessant blaring of the car horn where my father's unconscious body is slumped over the steering wheel.

I shake off the childhood memory before it can fully form. I haven't thought about that night in years.

"And your mother?" Abigail asks softly, coaxing.

I sneer. "She just wants her comfortable lifestyle. She will accept anything my father does, as long as the family keeps up appearances."

As much as I loathe my father, I disdain my mother. He's a weak coward, but she's calculating. She's the one who ensures he goes unpunished and untarnished for his sins.

Abigail covers my hand with hers, calling me back to her. "I have a complicated relationship with my parents too."

Before I can press for more of her secrets, fat raindrops begin to fall. I realize that the other beachgoers have fled the storm, and we're alone. The waves creep closer, crashing in furious roars as the wind whips by us.

But the rain is warm. Cleansing.

Abigail closes her eyes and turns her face toward the sky, as though she's soaking in the storm. It suits her more than the sunshine.

Her hair is already drenched, the purple curl relaxing under the weight of the water. The rain runs down her cheeks like cathartic tears, and her expression is soft with something like rapture.

Hunger knifes through my gut, and I capture her nape to pull her to me for a vicious, covetous kiss. I want to consume her. I want to feel the depth of her emotions. If I kiss her deeply enough, maybe I can sink into them like she does. To lose myself in the terrible beauty of the storm and the calm that will come in its wake, when the wind and rain have swept the grime away from the world.

She opens for me, meeting me with equal fervor. Her lips are feverish on mine, wet with purifying rain. The storm has broken the midday heat, but fire courses through my veins. I'm burning for her, desperate for more of her sweetness, her purity, her darkness. She's the most delicious contradiction, the only puzzle I've never been able to solve.

Sheet lightning flashes behind my closed eyelids, and thunder cracks, far too close.

I want to linger in this moment, but her safety is more important.

I tear my lips from hers and gather her up in my arms, lifting her to her feet. We grab our soaked towels and start to run.

She tosses her wet hair back from her face and releases a joyous laugh as our feet pound the sand. It's the most beautiful sound I've ever heard, and it takes all of my considerable willpower to stop myself from pulling her into the dunes and fucking her while the storm rages around us.

Instead, I clasp her hand in mine, and my own laugh sounds a touch cruel as it wars with the thunder.

Mine. She's all mine.

23

ABIGAIL

The cool air conditioning in Dane's house is set to cut through the humid summer heat, but I'm soaked from the storm, so I shiver.

He wraps a protective arm around me and guides me up the stairs. "Let's get you warmed up, pet."

Another shiver races over me, but not from cold this time. Desire begins to pulse between my legs. We're walking into his bedroom.

Last night, I fell into a deep sleep after we had oral sex. My exhaustion from a week of sleepless nights had pulled me under, and I'd finally felt safe enough to sleep without nightmares haunting me.

But now, I'm acutely aware that Dane hasn't fully claimed me yet. The possessive flex of his hand on my waist lets me know that's about to change.

I soften and lean into him, silently communicating that I'm ready to have sex. After the way my body surrendered to him when he stretched me with his fingers, I'm confident that I'll be able to accommodate his huge cock.

He'll ensure that my body is ready to accept all of him.

I trust him completely.

My dark god.

My Master.

He's still shirtless from our beach date, and I marvel that this perfectly chiseled, gorgeous man wants me.

He guides me past the bed, and my heart sinks for a moment.

His low, arrogant laugh is the most addictive sound in the world. He told me he sees everything, and I'm starting to believe him. In my one moment of insecurity, he read my disappointment.

"I'll fuck you soon enough. I'm going to warm you up first."

We step into a massive ensuite bathroom, and he turns on the shower. Water sprays from three directions, and he tests the temperature with one hand.

When he's satisfied that I'll be comfortable, he leads me inside and closes the glass door behind me. We're still in our bathing suits, but they're already wet from the rain. The shower immediately chases away the chill that'd settled beneath the surface of my skin, and my muscles fully relax as my goosebumps subside.

His deft fingers find the ties at the back of my bikini, and within seconds, my sodden top falls to the tiles beneath us. My bottoms drop next to it, and I fist his swim trunks to tug them down his legs.

We're both naked, and for a few delicious seconds, we simply stare at each other, hungry eyes raking over what's ours.

Because even though I signed a contract giving myself to Dane, he's all mine too.

You make me feel things I didn't know I was capable of feeling. I recall his intense confession.

This connection between us is more potent than anything I've ever known, and I'm desperate to be impossibly closer to him. On the beach, he started to open up to me more about his fraught relationship with his family. One day, I might be ready to tell him about mine too.

But for now, I don't want that negativity to taint the sweetness of our new relationship.

He grasps my hand and directs my palm face-up so that he can fill it with sea salt-scented body wash. It's a masculine smell, but I don't mind the idea of imprinting some of his signature scent onto my flesh.

He puts more of the clear gel in his palms and rubs them together to create a lather. Then he starts skimming his soap-slicked hands over my body.

"Touch me," he rumbles.

I don't need further encouragement. I finally indulge myself, slowly exploring the swells of his corded muscles. They flex and bulge beneath my tender, reverent touch, as though he's under some unseen strain.

His hands massage my shoulders, and I tip my head back on a low moan of pure contentment.

His mouth crushes to mine, and he devours the sound of my raw pleasure. Our tongues tangle in a heated duel, each of us fighting to prove how much we want the other.

In the end, he fists my hair, and he wrenches my head back to expose my throat. His teeth graze the line of my vulnerable artery before sinking into the sensitive spot where my neck meets my shoulder.

Pain blooms beneath his possessive bite, but my core pulses with lust. I can't help pressing my hips to his thigh in a wanton attempt to stimulate myself.

I remember the way he commanded me to rub against his leg last night while he fucked my mouth. My cheeks heat with delicious shame and arousal. I marvel that this man can use me like his personal fucktoy but also make me feel utterly safe and cherished.

"Is my pet horny?" he murmurs against my throat, soothing away his bite with a flick of his tongue.

"Yes," I whine, griding myself against him. I'm his needy pet, his plaything. And I'm eager for more of his cruel passion.

He pinches my nipple in sharp reprimand, and I cry out.

"Is that how you address me when we're together like this?" he drawls.

"Master," I say quickly. "I'm sorry, Master."

"Better," he allows, brushing a doting kiss over my cheek. "I'll tame your mouth again if I have to, but I want your cunt today."

I swallow hard and tip my head back, meeting his sparking eyes. "I want that too. I want you, Dane. My Master."

My hand trails over his rippling abs, but before my fingers reach his hard cock, he grasps my wrist to stop me.

"I'm not nearly finished playing with you, pet. I won't be done with you for a long time. You'll be weeping for me by the time I finally fuck you."

My stomach flips—equal parts trepidation and lust.

He traces the shape of my parted lips before capturing me in a quick, fierce kiss. Then he pulls both of us under the cascade of water so that the last of the soap is washed from our bodies.

He turns off the shower and leads me onto the heated tiles. Even his towels are expensive, white and fluffy as clouds. He wraps me in one and insists on drying me off himself rather than allowing me to do it. He's almost fanatical about taking care of me, just as he vowed to do when he signed our contract.

The fact that we both agreed to this in writing allows me to give myself permission to just enjoy being with him. I don't have to stand on my own two feet. I don't have to insist that I can take care of myself. Dane knows I'm capable, but he wants it to be this way between us.

And leaning on him for support feels so good after years of bearing the burden of making my way alone through sheer stubbornness. I feel so free with Dane as my master that I don't stop to think about how I signed away my freedom when I gave myself to him.

When he's satisfied that I'm thoroughly dry except for my damp hair, he suddenly fists the wet locks. Little prickles of pain dance over my scalp as he pulls me down, forcing me into my knees.

"Crawl for me, pet."

Lust washes through me in a storm-tossed wave, a wild, undulating desire that makes my inner muscles clench and my clit pulse.

I release a soft moan at the intense hit of bliss and drop onto my elbows, eagerly complying with his degrading demand.

He keeps his grip on my hair as he takes a step forward, using the long strands as a leash to pull me alongside him.

The tiles are hard but warm beneath my knees, and they quickly give way to plush carpet.

My mind goes serenely blank as he leads me into the

bedroom, keeping my head high with his ruthless hold on my hair.

I'm panting by the time we reach the bed, even though it took less than a minute to cross the space. Being on my knees before my master feels right, and I revel in the release of surrendering control to him.

I've only ever known this wild, erotic abandon with Dane, and I never want it to end.

Suddenly, I'm in his arms. For a moment, I'm safely nestled against his hard chest. Then he drops me. My shriek of alarm almost immediately morphs into a giddy laugh when my back hits the soft mattress.

His massive body settles over mine, and his hand wraps around my throat.

"That's such a beautiful sound," he says, his voice taking on the soft, almost detached quality that makes my belly quiver. It's a bit unnerving, but I love the rush of fear that makes my fingers and toes tingle.

He's going to hurt me again, and I tremble in anticipation of the sweet pain.

"Your laugh is lovely," he says in that erotically disturbing tone. "But I think I'll like it better when you can't breathe unless I allow it."

His fingers tighten around my neck, pressing down on my arteries. Primal panic makes my hands fly to his wrist in a reflexive act of self-defense.

A cruelly beautiful grin stretches his lush lips, and he doesn't bother to restrain me. He lets me scrabble at his hand and squirm beneath him as he slowly increases the pressure.

"Dane..." His whispered name echoes in my ears alongside the desperate pounding of my own pulse.

"Yes, darling?" he drawls. "Do you want to say something?"

His palm presses down on my windpipe. Not hard enough to cause me pain, but just enough to restrict my airflow.

I'm writhing, but I'm rubbing myself on him. My nipples are hard peaks, and my arousal wets his thigh where I'm grinding my clit against his hard muscles.

My mind starts to float, and my fingers stop clawing at his wrist. He indulges himself in a long, tender kiss, exploring the shape of my parted lips as I struggle to draw in the small sips of oxygen he allows me.

"Are you going to come for me while I'm choking you, Abigail? Is your tight pussy aching?"

"Yes." My lips form the word, but no sound comes out.

My entire body is sparkling, and my mind is blissfully silent. There's only raw, animal need and his control over my body.

"Go on," he commands. "Make yourself feel good."

I rotate my hips, and pleasure bursts through me. I shudder beneath him as the orgasm wracks my body. Just as I reach the peak, he releases my throat. Blood rushes to my head, and blessed oxygen floods my lungs. I'm soaring, and the world goes white.

There's a scream tearing through the room. It echoes off the high ceiling like violent music, and I dimly realize I'm making the primal sound.

I'm shaking and utterly spent by the time the world comes back into focus. His green eyes are the first thing I see, staring into my soul with raw hunger. He's watched me come completely unraveled, and he's reveling in my total subjugation.

He finally breaks our intense connection when he focuses

on my wrists. I'm limp and trembling as he stretches my arms toward the bedposts and secures them there with waiting leather cuffs. They're attached to the sturdy mahogany frame with short chains, tucked neatly out of sight behind the mattress until he's ready to use them on me.

Once my wrists are bound, he makes quick work of shackling my ankles to the lower bedposts. Before I can fully catch my breath again, I'm spread out before him like an offering, completely helpless to resist anything he wants to do to me.

"You have such lovely breasts, pet," he says, his voice slow and deep, as though he's slightly intoxicated. "I want to know how sensitive those tight little nipples are. I'm going to learn every single one of your body's secrets. I own you."

I lick my lips, my own hunger for my dark god consuming me. "Yes, Master. I'm yours."

His nostrils flare like a predator catching his prey's scent, but he already has me snared. There's nowhere to run, no hope of evading him.

And I don't want to. Even though delicious fear is snaking down my spine, there's nowhere else I'd rather be.

I just orgasmed, but I'm already desperate for more. I want him to utterly devastate me.

He takes another deliciously tense moment to drink in the sight of my bound, helpless body before he goes to his nightstand. I crane my head to see what he's retrieving from the drawer, and something silvery glints in his hand. He mostly hides whatever it is in his fist and settles his body over mine again.

I sigh and relax under his weight, loving the feeling of being trapped by his strength.

His lips caress mine, a slow, indulgent kiss. I match his intensity, worshipping his perfect mouth. I trace the shape of his pillowy lips with my tongue, memorizing the feel of him. His scent enfolds me—slightly salt-kissed and uniquely *Dane* in the absence of his expensive cologne.

I tip my head back and invite him to kiss me more deeply, to consume me.

He palms my breast, and I gasp into his mouth as pleasure crackles in a sparkling line from my nipple directly to my clit. He hums his satisfaction at my response and tweaks the hard bud. A small flare of pain sharpens my pleasure, and my inner muscles clench.

He toys with me, pinching and tugging at my nipples until the pain and pleasure are inextricable. One can't exist without the other. I whimper and writhe, but I can't evade his onslaught.

I cry out at a particularly sharp pinch, but he doesn't release the tension. He keeps my sensitive nipples trapped in a cruel vise.

He pulls back slightly and cups my breasts, massaging gently. But the pressure on my tormented buds doesn't ease.

I glance down and find that small silver clamps are biting into my nipples while he tenderly strokes my breasts. The dichotomy of his gentle fingers with the cruel pinch fogs my brain. I can't process the dueling sensations; all I can do is endure his carnal game.

I release a shuddering sigh and fully submit, my attention harnessed by him. All thoughts float away, and there's only his control. I'll do anything to please him, suffer any erotic torment for him.

His triumphant grin is wickedly sharp, and I tremble in his shadow.

There's a slight tug, and the clamps tighten on my aching nipples. I gasp and arch my back to alleviate the pressure, but it's no use. The clamps are connected by a delicate silver chain, and he has it looped around his forefinger.

He's harnessed one of the most sensitive areas of my body with no more than a crook of his finger. His mocking smile tells me it's no effort at all to subdue me, to render me utterly helpless and desperate for him.

"What about your pretty little clit?" he taunts. I release a shocked cry when he taps the hard bundle of nerves. "Is it aching too?"

"Please..." I don't know if I'm begging for release or for more erotic torment.

But of course, there's more. This is Dane: my cruel master. My gorgeous, dark god.

A third clamp is attached to the chain.

"No!" I gasp, my eyes flying wide when I realize his intention. "I can't."

His emerald eyes blaze, burning into me. "You can, and you will. You'll take everything I give you, and you'll thank me for it."

"It's too much," I whimper. "Please."

"You seem to be harboring the mistaken notion that I'm a merciful master. Your pretty pleas won't move me, Abigail. I'm greedy for them, and I'm selfish enough to wring more desperate tears from your lovely eyes before I finally use your body for my pleasure. This is what it means to be mine: absolute submission. Now, take your pain like a good little pet, and scream my name when you come."

The clamp bites down on my clit, and stars burst across my vision. The pain is white-hot sheet lightning that flashes through my entire body, illuminating every inch of me with sizzling heat. Then he tugs the chain once, and ruthless pleasure wracks my tormented nipples at the same time.

My back bows in an effort to alleviate the pressure, but he's every bit as merciless as he promised. Two thick fingers slide through my wet folds, and he crooks them against that sensitive spot inside me.

"Dane!" His name is a rough, guttural cry that's barely human.

Ecstasy rips through my body with devastating force, and I'm flying. The world is bright white, and I'm purified by pain. Sparks dance over every inch of my sensitized skin as waves of pleasure roll through me.

Just as I'm starting to float in euphoria, he removes the clamps, and fresh pain assails me as blood rushes back to the abused buds. His thumb tenderly rubs my clit, and his tongue soothes the sting on my nipples. I melt away, until the only way I know I still exist is because he's touching me.

My entire body shudders as ruthless aftershocks ripple through me in cruel lightning strikes.

"Dane, Dane, Dane..." I'm murmuring his name over and over again, my own private litany.

He kisses my cheeks, and then I taste the salt of my tears when he claims my lips in a tender kiss.

"Good girl." His praise reaches deep inside my chest, wrapping my heart in gentle warmth. "Such a good pet."

Supple leather encircles my throat, and the soft *snick* of my collar locking in place calms me like nothing I've ever experienced.

I'm safe. Owned. Cherished.

I'm still floating in darkness, but I'm dimly aware of the sound of a condom wrapper ripping open. I force my eyes to open, blinking hard so that I can see my gorgeous master.

He looms over me, and he makes quick work of freeing my wrists and ankles.

"Hold on to me," he commands, and I cling to him.

I can't get close enough. I need him inside me, need our bodies entwined in the most intimate way possible.

He braces one arm beside me, and his free hand comes up between us so that he can loop his forefinger through the ring at the front of my collar. With no more than the slightest tug, he pulls me toward him for a deep, desperate kiss.

His hard cock presses into me, and my body yields to him as though I was made for him. My pussy stretches to accommodate his thick length, and he slowly fills me up until I'm hovering just on the edge of pain. It only sharpens my desire for him.

I boldly wrap my legs around his hips and press my heels into his sculpted ass, drawing him deeper. He enters me fully in one final, harsh thrust, and I cry out into his mouth.

His tongue strokes mine, encouraging me to relax and accept him. I marvel as my body softens further, and all pain dissipates. I'm almost unbearably full, but we fit perfectly.

"I knew you would be like this," he murmurs against my neck, dropping soft kisses on my sensitive skin. "So wet and tight. So perfect for me. My Abigail."

My inner muscles contract in a pulse of pure bliss, and he bites down on my shoulder with an animal growl. I tip my head to the side, welcoming him to ravage me, to mark me while he lays claim to everything that I am.

He starts to move inside me, careful, shallow thrusts at first. Then taking me with greater urgency as our mutual lust rises. My low moans seem to spur him on, and his teeth sink into my shoulder again as he thrusts harder, deeper. I lift my hips to meet him, urging him to take and take and take, until there's nothing left of me that doesn't belong to him.

"Yours," I pant. "I'm yours."

He tilts his hips, and his cockhead drags over the sensitive spot inside me. My fingernails score his back, and I release a sharp cry at the shock of pleasure.

"Mine," he snarls, slamming into me and stimulating the spot over and over again.

Pleasure builds like an unbearable pressure between my legs, and my inner muscles coil tighter and tighter with each ruthless thrust.

"Come for me, Abigail," he commands in a guttural growl. "Now."

My back arches on a scream, and I surrender to the tidal wave of ecstasy. My core contracts around him, and his roar mingles with my own blissful cry as we find our peak together. His cock pumps inside me, and a soul-deep satisfaction that I've never known before settles in my heart.

This strong, cruel, beautiful man has come undone for me. All for me.

"My Master," I sigh between languorous kisses. "Mine."

24

DANE

"It's time to wake up, my sleeping beauty." I brush a stray lock of dark, silken hair back from her cheek. "We need to get ready soon."

A soft smile curves her lips, and she snuggles into me. A warm glow suffuses my chest, and I pull her closer, wrapping my arms around her willowy frame in a possessive embrace.

Abigail has been my sweet pet for a week now, and she's only left my bed when we've both been forced to go to work. We stopped by her apartment once to pick up some clothes, but otherwise, she's stayed with me.

Today, she'll let me dress her up in an outfit of my choosing. I'm anticipating some resistance, but she will comply. It's past time that she accepts my money. I intend to spend it on her, and I won't tolerate further defiance.

She's accompanying me to my colleague's wedding this afternoon, and she will wear the designer dress I've chosen for her. She would be the most stunning guest in attendance even in one of her paint-splattered camisoles, but I'm proud to show her off in expensive clothing. I want everyone to see how I care for my woman.

"As much as I'd like to keep you in my bed all day, we have plans." I drop a doting kiss on her forehead, and she releases a happy sigh that I'm coming to find just as addictive as her laugh.

"Don't worry," she reassures me. "I'll be ready on time."

She stretches, and her delicious body arches against me.

I grip her hips and roll atop her with a soft growl. "Are you trying to tempt me, pet?"

She flushes the prettiest shade of pink and giggles. "Do you want me to?"

I brush my thumb over her smirking lips. "This mouth. How many times will I need to fuck you here to tame that sassy tongue?"

"At least once more," she says breathily, her pupils dilating with desire.

I groan and roll off of her. "What kind of master would I be if I give in to your tempting games?" I tap my forefinger to her nose in light reprimand. "Naughty little thing."

She snaps her teeth at me playfully, then laughs. The sound is pure delight, and it soars through me like the most exquisite song I've ever heard.

"Your pet bites," she warns, that little smirk still fixed in place.

Something dark stirs inside me. We've played twisted games all week, but this is the closest we've danced to the kind of dubious consent fantasies she used to exchange with GentAnon.

I climb out of bed and cock my head at her, considering her fate.

"I have a gag that would suit you nicely," I remark. "But I doubt you'd like to wear that to the wedding."

Her lips pop open in shock. "You wouldn't."

"Test me and find out." I don't bother to hide the dangerous threat from my cold tone.

In truth, I'd never allow anyone to see Abigail like that. Her subjugation is for my eyes only. But the little fearful tremor that races over her is absolutely delicious. I won't reassure her when she looks so beautifully frightened, those aqua eyes wide and glittering like gemstones.

"Go on," I prompt. "Take a shower. I'll make coffee."

She blushes and drops her gaze in submission. I'm almost disappointed when she obeys me, but I remind myself that we can't be late to Meadows' wedding. I might not feel friendship in the way most people do, but he's a good colleague, and the practice that we're building together here in Charleston is important to me.

Abigail sees this city as home, so it's time for me to put down roots here too.

I'm not going anywhere.

An hour and a half later, Abigail is wearing one of my oversized white bathrobes while she sips at the coffee that I made for her. She's just finished her makeup except for her lip gloss, which she said she doesn't want to smudge. Her hair is fully dry and naturally wavy, but she intends to perfect the loose curls before we leave at noon.

As promised, she's perfectly punctual—a quality I admire. She might be a bit haphazard when it comes to tidying her living space, but she's respectful enough of my time that she won't make us late.

"I'll need to stop by my place to pick up my dress," she says. "Just let me finish my hair, and we can go."

Her eyes rove over me, taking in my tuxedo. The wedding takes place later this afternoon, and the invitation said black tie attire. Meadows' family is old money, so I'm not surprised at the dress code.

"I bought a dress for you to wear," I say. "We don't need to stop by your place."

Her guard goes up immediately, her eyes shuttering and her mouth firming to a thin line.

"I have a nice dress," she replies defensively. "I won't embarrass you, Dane."

"You could never embarrass me," I assure her. "But I want to buy beautiful things for you. You are going to let me."

Her brows arch. "Am I? When did I agree to that?"

"When you signed the contract that says I'm responsible for your well-being." I let my tone drop lower in warning.

She straightens her shoulders. "There's a difference between my well-being and buying me expensive things that I don't need."

"This isn't about what you need," I counter. "It's about what I want. And I want to see you wearing the dress I bought for you."

Her posture goes rigid. "How can you make a gift sound so unbearably selfish? No, thank you."

"When did I ever give you the impression that I'm not selfish?" I drawl. "I've shown you exactly who I am. You chose me. You gave yourself to me. Would you prefer I pretended to be a soft, kind gentleman? No," I continue before she can open her mouth to respond. "You like me the way I am, and that means you'll do as I say."

Her eyes flash. "I don't think so."

Fuck.

I've let myself get too comfortable around her. My mask has been off for too long, and now, she's seeing a side of me that makes her angry when I'd intended to make her melt.

"Surrendering control when it comes to sex is one thing," she seethes. "I won't allow you to use your money to control me, Dane. Maybe you're the one who hasn't been paying attention to who *I* am."

My anger rises to match hers, but it's directed at her past abuser, not her. Whoever hurt her is responsible for this argument, not me.

I try for a placating tone that doesn't come naturally at all. Instead, my voice comes out gravelly. "Are you going to tell me who did this to you?" I challenge. "Why are you so scared of accepting my money?"

Her eyes cut away from mine, but her back remains ramrod straight. "Don't change the subject. You're being controlling, Dane. I don't like it."

I pause and consider my next words carefully. I am controlling, but I can't let the darkest parts of me scare her away. She's mine, but I want *her.* Not a mindless, spineless little plaything.

"I'm sorry." The words feel strange on my tongue, the shape unfamiliar. "I'm not explaining myself well because I'm angry at whoever hurt you." That much is true. "I don't want you to reject gifts from me because of some bastard's cruelty. I want to take care of you, and that includes providing for you. It's not about stripping you of your pride or forcing you to do something you don't want to do. Yes, I'm selfish, and I want you to wear the pretty things I buy for you. But never because you feel coerced or guilted into it."

I'm not above manipulation to get what I want, but I can hear the truth in my own words. I want Abigail to accept me and that includes accepting my gifts. I want her to trust that they won't come with strings attached. I want her to trust in me. In us.

Her eyes search mine, and after a terrible, tense moment, she relaxes on a sigh.

"It wasn't a man who hurt me," she admits. "It's my family. They wield money like a weapon. It took me years to understand it, and it's been incredibly hard to walk away from their financial control. When I dropped out of college, they threatened to cut me off if I didn't go back to my classes. So, I cut myself off before they could follow through. I got my barista job and started selling my paintings at the market. I've learned to survive on my own, and I've built a good life for myself. I'm not a famous artist with my own gallery, but I'm happy with my life the way it is."

I touch two fingers beneath her chin, and she doesn't flinch away. "Are you happy?" I challenge quietly. "Would it be so terrible to accept gifts from me? I will never ask for anything in return. I swear. Trust me."

Her teeth sink into her lower lip, and she hesitates.

"I left my family's wealth and expectations behind too," I remind her. "I've worked hard so that I can live comfortably without their support. Let me support you now. I can't think of a better way to spend what I've earned."

"I can't rely on you for everything," she counters, but I can sense that she's softening.

Our disdain for our families is a bond we share, and even

though I'm exposing my own vulnerability, I will leverage this to my advantage.

"I know you can take care of yourself," I say. "It's one of the reasons I admire you so much. You're tenacious and determined."

She offers me a shaky laugh. "That's a nice way of saying I'm stubborn."

My lips twist in a half-smile of my own. "I didn't say that."

She sighs again and shakes her head, capitulating. "Okay," she allows. "I'll wear the dress you bought for me." Her chin lifts. "I'm not going to let my past get in the way of our relationship. That's all behind me now, and I won't allow my family to control me anymore. I definitely won't let them be the cause of an argument between us."

I brush a kiss over her forehead. "That's my stubborn pet," I praise.

She laughs again, a sound of forgiveness. "It's only okay when I say it."

"It's a compliment," I assure her. "I meant it when I said I want all of you. Your sweetness and your stubbornness. I want everything."

She sways toward me. "You have me," she promises. "I want all of you too."

"Done." I seal my vow with a kiss, proving to her that I will honor the gift of her trust.

Our kiss deepens, and her breath quickens in between strokes of my tongue against hers. I tug the tie on her robe, and it falls open. She's only wearing a tiny scrap of white lace that barely covers her pussy.

My possessiveness surges, a carnal, primal hunger that overwhelms rational thought. I fist the delicate panties in both hands and tear them off her, revealing my pretty, pink cunt. This is all mine.

I grind my fingers against her clit, and I find that she's already wet for me. She cries out into my mouth, and I force a quick, brutal orgasm from her. Already, I know the exact way to touch her to make her come undone.

Her fingers bite into my upper arms, clinging to me as she greedily takes all of the pleasure I coax from her perfect body.

She whimpers, a pitiful plea for mercy that only enhances my cruel desire. Her clit is oversensitive from the ruthless treatment, but I'm not done with her yet.

I push two fingers into her tight sheath and stimulate her in the way she likes best. At the same time, I circle her clit with my thumb. My other hand tweaks her nipples, drawing out her pleasure with a fresh bite of pain.

My perverted pet moans and shakes, and she starts to grind herself against my palm.

As suddenly as I began, I withdraw, leaving her on the edge of release.

She lets out a delightful sound that's somewhere between an indignant shriek and a cry of loss.

I keep her locked in my cruel gaze as I lift her ruined panties to my face and inhale the scent of her arousal.

My cock is almost painfully hard, but we don't have time for me to use her to slake my lust. If I'm going to be denied, so will she. We'll both suffer through this wedding, but she'll be desperate for me by the end of the night. Her submission is so much sweeter when she's needy and begging for my merciful touch.

Her soft lips form a tempting *O* shape as she watches me shove the panties into my pocket. I'll keep my trophy close, and we'll both know what I'm thinking about every time I casually slip my hand into my pocket during the wedding.

I trace her lips with my tongue and claim one more kiss before I spin her around and deliver a sharp slap to her ass.

"Get ready, pet. You'll get your reward later."

Her indignant huff is entirely ruined by her flushed cheeks. My mocking laugh draws a light shiver from her, and I'm completely enamored with her responses to me.

We had our first disagreement, but I managed to soothe her without too much fuss. Abigail will wear the dress I bought for her, and we'll never have the same argument about money again. She'll let me take care of her, just as I've always wanted.

I'm a selfish bastard, and she still wants me.

I'm so savagely pleased at her submission to my will that I don't stop to think how much I've surrendered to her in return.

25

ABIGAIL

Dread is a lead weight in my stomach as we drive through the familiar gates of Montgrove Plantation.

Why didn't I think to ask Dane where the wedding would take place?

"What's wrong?" He touches my chilled cheek, attuned to my shifting moods as always.

I turn pleading eyes on him but keep my voice low. I don't want the driver to hear the tone of panic that I'm struggling to suppress.

"I didn't realize that your friend is Meadows Coatesworth."

I should've realized. It's not exactly a common first name, and Charleston is a small place when it comes to local families.

Dane's brows draw together. "Do you know him?"

Nausea tightens my gut, and I swallow hard against the burn at the back of my throat.

"Not well, but our families are in the same social circle. This isn't the first time I've visited their plantation."

My family's own planation, Elysium, is just another hour's drive down the coast. The beautiful, haunted, rotten place where I was raised is far too close for comfort. Years of distance have allowed me to see how fucked-up it is that my family lives in a place where so much evil took place, even if they hide it under the guise of a proud history.

"Meadows was six years ahead of me at school. I knew of him, but I rarely spoke to him," I continue. "But it's fine. I'll be fine."

I try to summon up my sunny smile, but my lips barely twitch.

"You're upset," he observes, eyes dark with concern. "Why?"

"My family will probably be here," I say, forcing the words through my constricted throat. "I haven't seen them in a long time."

The last time I spoke to my parents, it ended in a screaming match, and my father said he was cutting me out of his will. I told him that I didn't care, and I never wanted to see him again.

My mother called every day for a month after that, begging and then scolding and then threatening to get me to come back into the fold. To spare the family the embarrassment of an estranged daughter.

What am I supposed to tell the women at bridge club? she'd demanded. *What will I say when you don't show up at the next cotillion ball?*

I told her that was her problem, not mine.

Now, we haven't spoken in two years. We avoid one

another, and I've been careful not to do anything that might attract their unwanted attention.

It's why I didn't report the thief for stealing my purse.

And it's part of the reason why I didn't go to the cops after the masked man attacked me.

That, and my shameful physical response to being violated.

"Abigail." I flinch when Dane touches my hand. He frowns and folds his fingers firmly around mine. "You don't look well. I'll take you home."

"No!" I protest quickly. Dane can't miss his friend's wedding because of me. "I'll be fine. It'll be fine."

"Don't lie to me," he warns, but his voice is soothing rather than threatening. "If this is too much, we'll leave. I don't give a fuck about Meadows' wedding. I'm here because it's expected of me. I only care about you."

I draw in a shuddering breath, finding comfort in his fierce declaration. I squeeze his fingers in a pulse of reassurance.

"You saying that makes all the difference," I say. "But I can handle this. I won't run away from my family."

He captures my tilted chin between his fingers and gives me a proud smile. "That's my stubborn pet."

"Dane!" I scold under my breath and shoot a significant glance in the direction of our driver.

He chuckles and kisses me. "It's just a Yorkshire endearment, darling. No reason to get all hot and flustered."

I release an exasperated huff, and his grin widens.

Oh.

He's baiting me to distract me.

My heart gives an almost painful squeeze, and I crush my lips to his. He's still for a moment, surprised at my boldness.

Then his hand firms at my nape, and he deepens the kiss. For a blissful minute, I lose myself in him, and all of my anxiety melts away.

"Thank you," I whisper when we finally come up for air.

"I've got you," he promises. "Say the word, and we'll leave."

I straighten my shoulders. "I want to be here with you," I declare, finding strength in his staunch support. "I won't let them control me ever again. I'm not going to run away."

The car comes to a stop in front of the antebellum mansion. It's undeniably beautiful: a three-story manor with white columned porches and classic navy shutters. Live oaks surround the circular driveway, and Spanish moss drips from their elegant branches. The azaleas and hydrangeas are in full bloom, festooning the manicured gardens in shades of pink, purple, and blue.

It's a lovely day for a wedding, even if the setting disturbs me.

For a moment, I consider leaving on principle; plantation weddings shouldn't be a thing anymore, my own damage aside. It feels wrong to celebrate love here and pretend that nothing bad ever happened on this land.

"Are you sure you want to stay?" Dane asks, lingering with me in the stopped car. "We can go straight back home if you're uncomfortable."

I shake my head. "I am uncomfortable, but we're staying. I'm here with you. I can do this."

His eyes flash in response, and he lifts my hand to kiss my knuckles. I swoon for my dashing hero all over again. This gorgeous man has chosen to bring me to his colleague's wedding. I'll focus on that to get me through the event.

He gets out of the car first and then holds my door open

for me. I don't protest his gentlemanly treatment as he holds my hand to steady me.

I'm perfectly capable of getting out of the car on my own, but I'm starting to like leaning on Dane. He clearly derives pleasure from taking care of me, and I'm becoming addicted to his satisfied smile when I allow him to do so.

His hand spans my lower back as he guides me around the house and into the gardens. Hundreds of white chairs have been arranged in neat rows facing the back porch, where it seems the happy couple will say their vows. We're early enough that only about a third of the chairs are filled, and scores of other guests are milling around the green space.

A table is set up near the huge magnolia tree, and silver cups wait with mint juleps to keep us cool during the hot day.

"Do you want a drink?" Dane asks.

"No, thank you. I don't want any alcohol." If my family is here, I want my wits sharp.

He nods in easy agreement, and we find two seats on the final row. I know Dane should make a show of sitting closer to the front, given his close relationship with the groom, but he's making a silent gesture that I have an out if I need it. We can leave at any time, and it'll be easier to slip away unnoticed if we're behind the crowd.

The string quartet starts up, signaling that it's time for everyone to find their seats.

By the time the bride glides down the aisle, I finally start to relax. My family isn't here.

Dane's thumb brushes my palm in a pulse of comfort, and I lean into him. I know he must be hot in his tux, but he looks as cool and handsome as ever: an untouchable, perfect sculpture of male serenity.

I find that I'm grateful for the beautiful, lilac dress he

purchased for me. The sweetheart neckline is modest enough for a wedding while still giving my smaller breasts a feminine curve. The waist is fitted perfectly to my measurements, and the full skirt flows down to my ankles. Tiny, subtle purple flowers are embroidered into the lightweight fabric, spilling down the skirt like delicate wisteria.

In this stunning dress, I almost feel worthy of my dashing white knight.

And knowing that my ruined panties are in his pocket while I'm bare for him underneath the dress makes my pulse race. We're the picture of refinement, but we have a filthy, perverted secret that binds us together.

I touch my fingers to my throat, searching for the leather band of the collar that marks me as his. Of course, it's not there, so I drop my hand and place it back in his firm grip.

His keen eyes noted my gesture, and they glitter with desire. I wonder if he's thinking about my panties in his pocket too.

People are cheering. The ceremony is over.

I laugh, giddy at the intense connection I share with Dane and the fact that we made it through the ordeal without seeing my family.

He captures the sound of my joy on his lips, sweeping me up in a kiss that rivals the couple on the porch. But if anyone notices us, they don't comment. Everyone is too polite to stare. Besides, they're supposed to be focused on the bride and groom.

It's only when the guests are dispersing into the garden that I hear my mother's voice, and my stomach drops.

"Abby, honey! I didn't know you'd be here."

She sounds absolutely delighted to see me, but I know that falsely sweet tone.

I close my eyes and struggle to master the anxiety that rises up my throat like a choking vine. I should've known that she would be here; she was simply so late that she missed the ceremony.

She won't miss the opportunity to enjoy a night of gossip and an open bar.

I look into Dane's eyes and manage to arrange my features into my sunny smile before I turn to face her.

"Hi, Mama."

"Aw, sweetie," she practically coos, drawing me in for a hug. We barely make contact. Then she places her hands on my shoulders, and her pale blue eyes scour my face. "Your lipstick is smudged."

The criticism about my appearance comes under the guise of concern. It's all carefully calculated to set me off-balance at the outset so that she can politely eviscerate me.

"I think that's my fault," Dane says.

I blink up at him, surprised at his genial tone. He fixes my mother with a broad smile and reaches out to shake her hand.

"I'm Dane. Abigail is here with me."

Mama's eyes go wide. "Oh!" she exclaims. "I just love your accent. You must be Dr. Graham, Meadows' associate."

He nods, and it's almost a formal half-bow. I've noticed his imperious air many times, and the man standing beside me is every inch the perfect prince.

"I can see my reputation precedes me," he remarks.

She waves her hand, as though to dismiss any concern. "All good things, don't you worry, Dr. Dane."

"Just Dane is fine," he assures her.

I'm staring at them like they're both alien creatures. They're so natural together, their genteel exchange perfectly polite and impeccably charming.

"Abby." My father's voice is gruffer on my name than my mother's. "I didn't expect to see you here."

He steps up beside her, joining our nightmarish little circle.

And, oh god, my Uncle Jeffrey is here too.

"What a happy occasion to see your daughter," Dane says, all warmth despite the fact that it's almost a command. As though he can will my family to be happy to see me.

"Oh yeah, it's always a pleasure to see our little Abby." Uncle Jeffrey grins at me, and I suppress a cringe.

Dane angles his body slightly in front of mine. "I'm sorry, we haven't met." He extends his hand toward my uncle. "I'm Dane Graham."

"Jeffrey," he replies, squeezing Dane's hand in his usual macho style. "I'm Peggy's brother." He tips his head in my mom's direction. "But I'm more like a second father to little Abby, if you don't mind me saying." He glances at my dad, who nods absently. "We all spent a lot of time together when she was growing up. I live at Elysium with the family."

"Elysium?" Dane asks, managing to sound almost bored with a single, drawled word.

My mother's chest swells with pride. "Our plantation. It's just down the road, Dr. Dane. You'll have to come visit us sometime."

"I'll have to see what works for Abigail," he equivocates. "We're very busy in Charleston at the moment."

"Oh?" Mama's eyes fix on me, a shark sensing blood in the water. For two years, I've denied her any information about my life. Now, she's going to find some way to hurt me, a piece of information she can weaponize to punish me for my defiance. "What have you been so busy with, honey? Did you open that gallery yet?"

I try to ignore the stinging slash to my heart.

One of my final retorts to her was that I didn't need her money, and I'd find a way to open my own gallery one day.

Instead, I have a stall at the market and sell my paintings to tourists.

I lift my chin. "Not yet."

"Well," she says, all saccharine sweetness. "Let us know when you do. We'd love to attend the grand opening. You know how much your father loves your art."

I hate the tiny spark of hope that pings in my chest when I turn my gaze on my distant father.

Then I take in his slack, bored expression and the way his eyes are drifting toward the mint julep table.

My chest feels like it's caving in, but I keep my shoulders straight through sheer force of will.

He's never cared about my art. He only cares about how my success reflects on the family.

And now, he cares about getting a cocktail more than he wants to reconnect with me.

"Excuse me," he says. "I need a refreshment."

He doesn't wait for anyone to reply before he ambles off to get a mint julep.

"What have you been up to, Abby?" Uncle Jeffrey asks. "We sure have missed having you at the house."

"Abigail has been busy with her art," Dane says, sparing me the burden of a falsely cheery reply. "Her landscapes are stunning."

"Oh yes, our Abby is very talented," my mother says, and it almost sounds as though she means it.

Which makes it hurt so much more that I know she doesn't give a shit.

"But I'm sure you must be very busy too," she says to

Dane. "I hear your practice is doing very well. I might have to come in for a treatment." Her judgmental gaze rakes over my face again. "We could go in together, Abby. A mother/daughter day. I'm sure Dr. Dane could remove that freckle in no time."

"Abigail is perfect just as she is."

I stare at Dane. His voice has gone ice cold, and he's looking at my mother like she's a fruit fly he's found in his drink: insignificant but disgusting.

My mother takes a step back, and a beat of terrible silence passes before her high-pitched giggle grates down my spine.

"Aren't you the charmer?" she gushes. "Hold on to this one, Abby. You don't know when another man will come along who feels the same way."

"There won't be any other men in her life." Dane says it like a matter of cold, hard fact. "Excuse us."

His hand settles at the small of my back, and he steers me away from the awful scene. I lean into him, unashamed that I'm seeking his support in the wake of the painfully polite altercation.

Abigail is perfect just as she is.

The memory of his fervent declaration warms my heart, chasing away some of the chill that frosts my skin despite the warm day.

"I'm taking you home," he says, a decree rather than a question.

"I don't want to run away from them," I protest, even though I'm longing to do just that.

"You're not," he replies firmly. "I'm taking you away from them. Because if we have to breathe the same air as those people for another minute, I can't be held responsible for my actions. I'd rather not make a scene at my colleague's wedding."

"Oh," I breathe.

His fierce mood is shocking but deeply gratifying.

My steps quicken as we exit the garden. I'm eager to get away from this place. It's everything that I want to leave firmly in my past.

I'm ready for my future, and I want to share it with Dane.

26

ABIGAIL

We're safely back in Dane's bed when I start shaking. It's a small tremor in my hands at first, but then cold sweeps through my entire body. I wrap my arms tightly around my aching chest as a violent shiver wracks my frame.

"I'm sorry," I say through chattering teeth. "I don't know what's going on with me."

He tucks us both under the duvet and pulls me close. His square jaw is anvil-hard, but his hands are gentle as he rubs at my goosebumps.

"You're in shock," he says in his calm, bedside manner voice.

"What? No, I'm fine."

I shudder, and he cups my chilled cheek. His eyes search mine for the lie, but I'm being honest. I don't understand what's happening to my body.

He strokes his long fingers through my hair in a soothing

motion. "You clearly have trauma when it comes to your family. Seeing them put you in survival mode. But you're safe now, and your brain is struggling to process that."

"I didn't realize you're a psychologist." It's a weak attempt at a joke, and he doesn't laugh.

"What did they do to you, Abigail?"

I press my lips together, holding in the awful truths that want to spill out of me. My instinct is to bottle everything up, to force it down and ignore it until the ache in my chest subsides.

But I'm with Dane now. I can lean on him. He'll catch me if I fall.

"It's…a lot," I say softly. "I don't know if I'm ready to think about all of it."

"That's all right," he encourages. "Tell me what you can. I'm right here. You're safe."

Hope floods my chest in a forceful, hot wave that makes my heart strain against my ribs. I want to share this burden with him, and I know he's strong enough to help me bear it.

I take a deep breath and begin my confession. "I haven't spoken to my family since I dropped out of college two years ago."

He nods. "You said you didn't need a degree to prove you're an artist. But that's not the real reason you quit school."

"No," I admit on a tremulous whisper. "I failed out. I stopped going to class. My parents were furious. My dad was so disappointed in me."

Shame twists my gut on the admission. As much as I want to leave my toxic family in my past, some foolish, childish part of me still craves their approval and affection.

"Why did you stop going to class?" Dane presses gently. "I

know you're intelligent, so it has nothing to do with the difficulty of your course."

The compliment bolsters me. He wants all of me, and he deems me worthy of him.

"I was depressed," I say quietly.

He doesn't say anything. He simply holds me and waits until I'm ready to continue.

I sort through my muddled thoughts and decide to start at the beginning. For so long, I've been terrified that Dane will learn my shameful secrets, but we're beyond that now. I'm no longer afraid that he'll turn from me in disgust if he knows the truth.

"I was raped on the night of my debutante ball."

His body hardens to granite, and he's so still that I don't think he's even breathing. After a tense moment, he resumes stroking my hair, but his muscles ripple and flex around me with unspent aggression. I know it's on my behalf, and I don't feel so much as a flicker of fear.

I tuck my face into his chest and breathe in his spicy cedar scent, allowing it to ground me while I talk about what I endured.

"It was my date, Tom. He was two years above me at college, and I didn't know him well. My mom asked his mom if he would be my escort for the night, and he agreed. I thought he resented me. He seemed so angry all night."

I'm detached from reality, floating in a space that's neither past nor present. There's only Dane and my voice, recalling what happened to me in a flat, distant tone.

"Tom got drunk at the open bar, and towards the end of the night, he said I owed him. He was smoking in the garden behind the Azalea Club. The ball was still going on inside, so everyone was busy drinking and dancing."

The scent of cigarette smoke threads through Dane's comforting cedarwood smell, but I continue as though compelled. The truth is drawn from my soul like poison.

"He pushed me up against the bricks, and I didn't fight him. I just...let him do it. And I..." My throat closes, and nausea rolls through me. "I had my first orgasm."

Dane's hand stills in my hair again. He's rigid around me, his entire, powerful body coiled tight.

"Later that summer, I saw him at a house party." I'm no longer connected to my body. I'm just a voice, floating around us. "I knew he'd do it again. I *knew.* And I let it happen anyway. It felt good. So, it happened again a few weeks later." Another party, another shameful night of vicious pleasure. "And again."

"Where is he?"

It takes me a moment to work out that the inhuman snarl came from Dane.

"He's dead." My voice remains disturbingly flat. "He decided to drive drunk after the last party. He never made it home."

Dane's fingers bite into my skin for a bruising moment, and the small flare of pain calls me back to reality. I blink and focus on his face. It's carved in lines of rage, and his green eyes blaze with fury.

"So many times, I wished he was dead," I confess on a strained whisper. "That's why I became so depressed that I couldn't get out of bed. I knew that the only way it would stop was if he was gone for good. Because I kept letting it happen. I think part of me wanted it to happen. And then he was dead, and it was like it was my fault."

"Nothing he did was your fault," Dane growls.

I shake my head. "I liked it. You've seen how I am. You know now."

His eyes flash, and a shadow ticks at his jaw. "I am nothing like him. That's not how it is between us."

I shrink in his arms. "I'm sorry. That's not what I meant. I know you would never hurt me like that. Everything we do is consensual. I trust you. More than I've ever trusted anyone."

He captures my face in his hands, holding me like I'm his most precious treasure. "I will never betray you, Abigail. I will always protect you. Always."

"I know." I seal my promise with a kiss. "I'm safe with you."

I'm not shaking anymore. The cold that'd taken root in my bones has melted away, and I'm warm in Dane's embrace.

"That's why I don't talk to my family," I finish. "I've never told them what happened. But even if I did, they would still see me as a failure. I didn't live up to their expectations, so they threatened to cut me off. I cut them out of my life before they could follow through on their threats."

"You took back control," Dane says, his voice still rough with residual anger. "My brave, fierce pet." He caresses my face and stares into my soul. "You don't have to be alone anymore. I'm not going anywhere."

My eyes sting as relief floods me. I'd known that I could trust him with my darkest secrets, but his acceptance means everything to me.

I can tell him anything. One day, I might even tell him about the masked man.

But I'm too raw, too wrung-out. That's been enough emotional labor for an afternoon. For a lifetime.

I blow out a long sigh, releasing all of the remaining tension from the difficult day as I lean into him.

He cradles the back of my head, holding me firmly against his chest.

"I've got you," he promises.

I've never felt safer than I do in this moment. I'm protected in the cage of his strong arms, and there's nowhere else I'd rather be.

27

ABIGAIL

Dane holds me for hours, and I drift, simply indulging in his reassuring presence. I doze off for a while, and when I wake up, it's dark outside.

I blink, disoriented. "What time is it?"

He kisses my forehead. "Don't worry about it. Go back to sleep."

"You don't sound sleepy," I observe. "Have you been awake long?"

"I haven't been sleeping."

I sit upright and turn on the bedside lamp. "I'm sorry. You must've been bored. I didn't mean to drift off."

He strokes my hair back from my cheek. "You needed the rest. And I could never get bored when I'm holding you."

Pleasure flushes my cheeks. "That's very sweet."

Sometimes, I struggle to process his intense declarations and praise. No one has ever treated me like this, like I'm precious. Valued.

And after the awful altercation with my family, my old feelings of unworthiness are raw and exposed.

He hums, considering me as though he's trying to puzzle out my complex emotions.

"There's nothing sweet about me," he replies. "That's not a word I would use to characterize myself."

I giggle. "Are you offended? Should I say you're a very scary, very intimidating master?"

He grabs my hair, and suddenly, I'm trapped beneath him with his other hand around my throat. His wicked grin takes my breath away, even though he doesn't apply pressure with his fingers.

"Exactly," he drawls. "I'm very cruel and entirely selfish. And you love being afraid. You love when I make you tremble and whimper."

My heart flutters, and my blood heats, but I tip my chin back in an act of reckless defiance. In the wake of my difficult day, I want him to completely overwhelm me. I want to revel in the darkness we share, not hide from it.

I don't want to feel ashamed anymore.

"I'm not trembling," I challenge.

His eyes flash, and his grin sharpens. "Is that how you want to play tonight, my naughty pet? You've been so docile for me. Am I going to have to tame you?"

I suppress a shudder as desire courses through me, and I meet his glittering gaze without an ounce of fear. If he wants me to tremble for him, he'll have to make me.

I'm not truly afraid of him, and I'm ready to engage in a more twisted game. I'm completely safe with Dane, and I can push the boundaries of my darker fantasies without fear of judgment.

"Your pet has claws," I retort.

It's so similar to what I've said to GentAnon in the past.

But this is *Dane.*

This is real.

He quirks a taunting brow at me. "I don't feel you using them."

His fingers tighten around my throat. "You're so weak and fragile. What do you think you could possibly do to hurt me? To deny me?"

Blood begins to pound in my ears as he applies pressure to my arteries, but I can still breathe. I can still speak.

"I am not fragile."

I've never fought back in real life; the fantasies that blur the lines of consent have always been nothing more than words on a screen. But now, I'm safe enough to finally indulge in this game.

Summoning all of my strength, I bend my knees between us and try to leverage them against his abs to force him off me. At the same time, one hand shoves at his chest, and the other rakes red lines into his forearm with my nails.

He doesn't bother to restrain me further. He just laughs and presses me deeper into the mattress.

"Careful, pet," he coos. "I don't want to break you."

I'm starting to float, and black spots dance at the edge of my vision. My struggles grow more frantic as fear coils low in my belly. It snakes up my spine in a slow, slithering slide that makes me quake. My responses are becoming more primal, a true impulse to escape danger rather than a teasing game.

"You'll never break me," I manage to hiss through my constricted throat, and my fingernails dig into his wrist.

But his firm grip is unbreakable. The world is softening, sliding out of focus until the only thing I can see is his cruelly perfect face, split in an almost maniacal grin.

My fear morphs into a thrill that shivers through me. It undulates all the way to my fingers and toes, making them tingle as though my nerves are hypersensitive. My nipples rub against his chest as I writhe, and the forbidden stimulation is darkly erotic.

"No," he agrees softly. "I won't break you. I like you just as you are. But by the time I'm finished with you, you'll kneel at my feet and worship me."

It's a threat, but his intense declaration mirrors what he said in my defense at the wedding.

Abigail is perfect just as she is.

With that sweet reminder, he slips past my defenses, and I start to soften in his ruthless hold.

Or maybe that's the lack of oxygen flowing to my brain.

Darkness creeps in, gentle and alluring. I blink hard, desperate to keep his glittering eyes in focus. I don't want to lose sight of him. I need him more than I need the breath he denies me.

His grip loosens, and euphoria floods my system. My body is weightless, and my mind is floating. He presses a tender kiss to my throat, and the gentle flutter of his soft lips is an intoxicating contrast with the ruthless way he was handling my body only moments ago.

A low moan issues through my parted lips, and my core pulses in a heavy throb that matches my racing heartbeat.

He grabs my cunt in one hand, grinding his palm against my clit as his fingers easily slide inside me.

"So wet for me," he rumbles, dropping another featherlight kiss on my neck.

He strokes the sensitive spot inside me once, and my entire body convulses at the answering burst of ecstasy.

Then he withdraws entirely.

His weight no longer pins me to the mattress, but I'm limp, my mind still sapped by primal chemicals elicited by fear and lust. Adrenaline and oxytocin mingle in a potent cocktail, and I can't gather my wits.

I barely manage to stir by the time he retrieves the tools for my torment from beneath the bed.

My eyes widen when I see the gag in his hand. Earlier, I'd thought it was nothing more than a sexy threat.

"You wouldn't dare," I challenge, but it comes out as a breathy whisper.

I try to scramble away. I'm almost on my feet when he launches his bigger body across the bed. His arm loops around my waist, and he drags me back to him. I kick out at nothing and shriek my defiance. He pushes me onto my front, and his weight traps me again. His hand pins my nape, forcing my cheek into the pillow.

"I will do whatever I want," he says, a cool statement of fact. "And you'll take it for me like a good girl. I won't hear a word of complaint."

The gag appears in my line of sight, hovering near my face. I try to turn so that I can snap my teeth at his fingers, but his grip on my neck immobilizes me.

"No biting, pet."

The red ball presses against my lips. I grit my teeth together and growl in staunch refusal.

His hand leaves my nape, but before I can twist away, his fingers lock around my jaw, applying steady pressure.

My mouth opens despite my stubborn defiance, and I taste rubber on my tongue as it slides so deep that I almost gag.

He buckles the leather straps tightly at the back of my

head, and I struggle to draw in deep breaths through my nose to calm my mounting panic.

When I'm thoroughly silenced, his hand returns to my nape, gentler this time. He stares down at me with raw hunger tightening his square jaw. His other hand traces the shape of my lips where they're forced apart around the gag. My sensitive nerves tingle and dance beneath his reverent touch.

I still beneath him, and my eyes roll back as euphoria soars through me once again. The sense of complete helplessness is the greatest release I've ever known. I can't fight him. I don't have to pretend to be stubbornly independent.

I'm his, and there's nothing I can do but accept him as my master.

"Isn't that better?" he asks, as though his cruelty is a mercy. "My pet is so calm and sweet now."

I give a halfhearted jerk beneath him, and he shushes me gently.

"You don't need your pride." His low, accented voice is deeply alluring, drawing me into temptation. "You only need *me*. Submit."

A shuddering sigh convulses my chest, and he kisses the cathartic tear that rolls down my cheek.

His weight lifts off me, and I whine at the loss.

His arrogant chuckle rumbles over my skin like a caress, drawing a shiver from me. He grasps my shoulders and pulls me upright, so that I'm on my knees in the center of the bed.

I want to turn to face him, but I'm meekly compliant and don't try to defy him again. I'm bound by his will: his control chains my mind, and my body is now his to use however he wants.

Rope wraps around my wrists, and my elbows are forced to bend with my arms behind my back. I give the restraint a gentle tug, testing it. I relax further when it holds firm without biting into my skin.

My master might give me pain, but he will never cause me harm.

The rope winds around my chest, looping beneath my breasts. He weaves it around me in a complicated pattern that my mind is too hazy to follow. There's only the delicious tension of the hemp and his long fingers brushing over my sensitized skin as he slowly binds me. It's a sensual act, and my body flushes with carnal heat. Arousal drips down my thighs, and my swollen labia ache with every heavy beat of my heart.

He ties off his work at my back, and then he fists the complex web behind my shoulders. The rope draws tight around my chest, stimulating my trapped breasts until they throb in time with my core.

He reaches around me and tweaks my nipples, and my shocked cry of ecstatic pain is muffled by the gag. He toys with me, pinching and rolling the tight peaks between his deft fingers until I'm writhing in his ropes.

I try to plead for mercy, but I can only moan and whimper around the gag. His mocking laugh rumbles into me, stimulating my pussy like a vibrator pushed deep inside me.

"Are you going to come while I torture your pretty nipples?" he asks, giving them a particularly vicious twist.

Pain bursts through me, ravaging my psyche. My tormented mind interprets it as pleasure, and I scream out my orgasm. He rubs my abused nipples, and sparks dance directly to my clit. My release goes on and on, until I sob from overstimulation.

Finally, my master shows mercy and releases my breasts.

"I'm going to use you now, pet."

I close my eyes and float in a blissfully peaceful headspace, where nothing exists except for his will. More than anything, I want to please him. It's not even a coherent thought; it's a primal need.

He lowers me face-down against the mattress, but he grasps my hips so that I remain on my knees. My ass is lifted like an offering, my dripping pussy waiting for his cock.

I hear a condom wrapper tear, and then there's a quick spike of pain when he enters me in one deep, rough thrust. I release a raw, ragged cry, and he reaches around me to stimulate my clit.

I come again on a scream, my pleasure ripping through me in a tidal wave. My inner muscles contract around him. He growls, and his fingers bite into my hips, hard enough to leave a mark.

I want him to mark me. I love being owned by Dane, and I'll proudly wear his bruises.

As he fucks me hard and deep, I give myself over to him completely. I lose count of my orgasms. I'm not sure if they're even separate peaks. There's only relentless ecstasy, and every moment of him inside me feels like the most perfect peace.

My pussy flutters around him helplessly, and I sob into the gag as sensation and emotion overwhelm me.

He roars out his release, and he thrusts deep one last time. He keeps me pinned there for a long minute as his cock pulses inside me. We linger in our mutual pleasure, our bodies connected in the most intimate way possible.

This is exactly where I want to be.

I'm his, and he's mine.

Our souls are bound by darkness, and in this safe space, we can indulge in it together without shame.

28

ABIGAIL

I hum to myself as I fold my laundry, which is warm from the dryer. My headphones are on, and I do a little happy dance to the beat of my favorite alternative band.

I've never been so content in my life. Dane is perfect. He's my miracle, my gorgeous prince.

He likes me just as I am: a gift no one has ever given me. Not a romantic partner, and certainly not my judgmental, withholding family.

Anticipation buzzes through me, and I give an extra shake of my hips. I can hardly wait to see him again in a few hours. My short shift finished at noon, so I have to wait for him to get off work too. In the meantime, I decided to spend a little time at my place to catch up on laundry.

I might even paint if I have time.

It's been over a week since I last picked up my brushes, and even though I miss my art, I'm not desperate for the release of my inner darkness that I usually find at my canvas.

Instead of releasing it, I reveled in it last night.

My cheeks heat at the memory of the gag in my mouth and Dane's filthy threats. His condescending praise. The pleasure he wrung from my body.

I jolt when my headphones are tugged from my ears, and I whirl on a sharp yelp.

Ron, my creepy new neighbor, grins at me.

"No need to scream like that, Peaches." He lifts my headphones to his ears as though he has every right. "What are you listening to that has those hips swaying like that?"

I breathe through the burst of fear and lift my chin to stare him down. My shoulders straighten, and I hold out my hand.

"Give those back, please." My tone is cold, even if my words are polite.

I won't provoke him while we're alone in here, but I don't want him to think I'm remotely welcoming. His attention makes my skin crawl, and he's blocking my way to the door.

He gives me a rueful chuckle when he returns my headphones. I quickly toss them into my plastic hamper along with my laundry and hold it between us, forcing him back a step.

"Where's your fancy boyfriend?" he drawls, his eyes lingering on my breasts. My camisole has dipped lower than usual while I was bent over the dryer, and my cleavage is on display.

I can't tug my shirt up while I'm clutching the hamper, and I don't want him to know that he's getting to me. I sense that any sign of weakness will be interpreted as invitation.

"He'll be here any minute," I lie.

Dane won't arrive for a few more hours, but Ron doesn't need to know that. I'm hoping that the mere threat of my white knight's imminent arrival will make him back off.

Instead, he beams at me. "Oh good. We'll have a little time to get properly acquainted. I think we got off on the wrong foot before. We're neighbors. I want us to be friendly."

"I'd prefer if we were simply cordial," I reply coolly. "I'm sorry, but I'm really busy. I need to get this laundry put away before Dane gets here." I'm quick to remind him of my lie.

"Hey, I get it." Ron holds up his hands as though in defeat. "You're a classy lady, and he's a fancy man."

Then he takes a step toward me, and my stomach drops.

"But you have that sexy Carolina drawl, and you need a Southern man, not some foreigner."

"What I need is for you to leave me alone," I assert.

My butt bumps against the hot dryer. There's nowhere for me to go.

"Back off," I warn, and my voice doesn't waver.

I'm done being polite.

"There's no need to be rude, Peaches," he admonishes with a shake of his head.

"You're the one being inappropriate." I struggle to keep my tone calm and even when my heart leaps into my throat.

"Oh, come on." He's cajoling now, and he takes another step toward me. He's close enough that his weight presses my hamper into my belly, pinning me. "We could go up to my place. Have a drink. You'll see that I'm a nice guy."

My fingers are numb around the handles of the hamper.

"Let me out." The demand is a ragged whisper.

My twisted fear response is causing me to shut down. Forbidden lust doesn't stir this time, but I'm not running away from danger, either. As always, I freeze.

It's going to happen again, and I'm going to let him do it.

He shoves the hamper aside, and it clatters to the concrete

floor. My clean laundry spills everywhere, but my eyes are fixed on the threat.

"I knew you liked me," he says with smug satisfaction.

His breath smells like stale tobacco, and his lips taste bitter when they crush down on mine. The faint scent of cigarette smoke threads through my senses, and I'm not sure if it's coming from him, or if I'm getting dragged into the memory of Tom and my debutante ball.

I close my eyes, as though I can hide from what's happening to me.

Dane's fierce green eyes fill my mind. They glitter with possessive hunger.

I'm *his.*

Ron has no right to touch me.

For the first time in my life, I fight back.

My knee jerks up between us, slamming into his balls. He chokes against my mouth, then reels away. He doubles over and makes a pathetic retching sound.

"Fucking bitch," he wheezes, stumbling toward me.

I spin on my heel and run. I dart out of the laundry room and into the open breezeway on the ground floor. I'm at my front door in seconds, and I wrench it open. I slam it shut behind me and throw my weight against it, sliding the lock in place just as Ron's bulky body smacks into the wood.

"Come out here, you little cunt!" he roars. My entire door vibrates at my back. He's kicking it, punching it.

If he manages to get inside, he'll do the same to me.

The violence reminds me of a different night when I was pressed against my door, when the masked man pinned me here and violated me in the worst way.

My knees fold, and I sink to the floor as horrific memories threaten to pull me under.

I force my shaking hand to find my phone in my pocket. It takes a few trembling attempts to find Dane's contact information and connect the call.

He answers after three rings. "I'm at work. Can I call you back?"

I can't breathe. I try to speak, but all that issues from my throat is an awful choking sound. Ron pounds on my door, shouting curses at me.

"Abigail!" Dane's usually cultured voice is rough. "Where are you?"

"Home," I manage to wheeze.

I squeeze my eyes shut. My head is pounding in time with Ron's fists on my door.

"I'm on my way. Stay on the phone with me."

I can't do more than nod mutely.

"Tell me what's happening," he commands sharply.

"Ron..." His name is all I can force past the lump in my throat.

"I'll be there soon," he promises darkly. "Are you in your apartment? Is the door locked? Answer me, Abigail."

"Yes," I whisper, compelled to obey.

"Stay right where you are. Breathe. Just keep breathing. That's all you have to do until I get there, understand?"

I heave in a painful breath that's like a knife through my chest.

He must hear my attempt to comply because he praises, "Good girl. Another. Just focus on your breath."

His voice is my anchor to reality, preventing me from getting lost in awful memories. He continues to talk me through my terror, commanding each of my ragged breaths.

At some point, the hall outside goes quiet, and my door stops vibrating on its hinges. Ron has given up.

I'm not sure how much time passes before I hear Dane's voice at the door. It takes a second for me to realize that it's not coming through my phone.

"Let me in, Abigail."

I have to grab the doorknob to haul myself up onto my shaking legs, but I manage to unlock the door. It swings open to reveal my dark god, his heartbreaking face drawn in sharp, vicious lines of rage.

But his hands are gentle when he cups my cheeks, inspecting my face for signs of injury.

"He didn't hurt me," I say through numb lips. "I hurt him. That's why he was so angry."

Dane steps inside and scoops me up in his arms. He carries me into my bedroom in a few long, confident strides and lays me down on my bed. It's small, but he wraps his massive body around mine and pulls me close enough that we both fit.

I'm shaking, and he strokes my body in soothing caresses, imbuing me with his steady warmth.

After a while, my breaths come easier, and I melt into him, utterly wrung out and exhausted.

"Tell me what happened." It's a low order, and I'm compelled to reply.

"Ron cornered me in the laundry room again. I told him to leave me alone, but he wouldn't."

"Did he touch you?" The question rumbles like thunder.

"He...kissed me." I manage to speak through the nausea that surges at the visceral memory of his rank breath.

Dane's fingers flex into my arms, his entire body tensing with unspent violence.

"But I fought him off." Dimly, I marvel at the fact. I still can't believe I managed to kick him instead of freezing.

But I didn't freeze. I didn't let him take advantage of my body.

And it's all because of Dane. Because in my most panicked moment, I thought of him, and I knew he would never allow another man to touch me.

He wasn't there to save me, so I had to save myself.

I did it for him.

I did it for me.

"I'm yours," I promise, turning to face him so that he can read the depth of my devotion in my open gaze.

His eyes burn, and his hand curves around my nape. "I'll take care of this, Abigail. I'll take care of you."

"I know. I trust you. I..."

I trail off, holding back the words that tease at the tip of my tongue. It's too soon to say them, even if they run through my mind like a litany.

"I need you," I say instead.

His lips are hot on mine, and I open for him on a sigh. I welcome him into my mouth with a flick of my tongue, urging him to claim me more deeply. In the aftermath of the assault, I need to feel connected to my fierce protector. I need to bind him to me, to join our bodies as closely as our souls.

I tear at his clothes in a frenzy, and his hands fist in my camisole. After a few feverish minutes, we're both naked. He touches my pussy, and we both discover than I'm already wet for him. My body will always be ready for him, eager to join with him.

He reaches for his discarded pants and grabs a condom from his wallet. He sheaths his thick cock as he looms over me. I reach for him, tracing the harsh line of his cheekbone and the tight set of his jaw. His nostrils flare with desire, and he shudders at my tender touch.

I'm powerless to resist this man, my master, but I hold power over him too. It goes straight to my head, intoxicating. My fingers twine in his thick, black hair, and he allows me to tug him in for a fierce kiss.

His cock nudges my inner thigh, and I spread myself wide for him.

"Take me," I beg. "I need you inside me."

He eases into me in a deliciously slow slide, and my legs wrap around his hips. My fingernails bite into his shoulders, urging him closer, deeper, harder.

He groans into my neck and breathes me in, as though he can't get enough of my scent.

For the first time, there aren't any kinky games. There's no darkness between us. There's only carnal passion and fierce possessiveness as we lay claim to each other's bodies. I mark him with my nails, and he marks me with his teeth.

He pumps into me, his sculpted ass tight beneath my insistent heels as I drive him deeper.

Warmth floods my body, a painful heat. He's seared into my soul, my heart.

"I love you," I confess. "I love you, Dane."

His eyes flash, and his jaw goes slack with something like wonder.

Then he gnashes his teeth, and his handsome face contorts into something almost feral. He slams into me, lighting up my body with pleasure and sweet pain.

"Mine!" he snarls, his voice inhuman.

My heart swells. It's more than enough for me. He doesn't have to say the same words back to me. I can feel the depth of his affection for me in the rough thrusts of his cock and the bruising bite of his hands on my arms. He pins me beneath him and ravages me, fucking me in a frenzy.

I meet each of his harsh thrusts, showing him how much I want him, how I accept everything that he is. And how I willingly give all of myself in return.

We reach our peak together, our ecstatic shouts a violent crescendo to our vicious lovemaking.

He stays inside me even as he softens, and I keep him locked there with my legs around his waist.

Dane is mine, and I won't let him go.

29

DANE

Stalking my prey is almost too easy. Ron doesn't seem like a man with something to hide. He doesn't seem bothered at all by the fact that he tried to rape a woman just a few hours ago.

My blood simmers in my veins, already heating in anticipation of the violent retribution that's to come.

Abigail is safely in my home across town. I took her to our personal sanctuary after our intense sex at her place.

After she told me she loves me.

Something thuds at the center of my chest, an aching beat.

I choose to ignore the disconcerting sensation.

I'm not capable of love. She's introduced me to emotions I never thought I'd experience, but the depth of that feeling is impossible for someone like me.

Love is meant to be selfless, and that's something I will never be.

I'm a selfish bastard, and I'll covet Abigail's love for me, even if I can't return it in the same way. I'll cherish her and care for her. She will want for nothing.

That will have to be enough.

My job now is to ensure her safety. Ron will never touch her again.

I blink back the red haze that clouds the edges of my vision and find the cold, merciless truth at the core of who I am. Now isn't the time to indulge in rage. I need to be thoroughly in control.

The aged wood creaks beneath my boots as I stroll down the dock toward my prey. He turns at the sound, and his eyes narrow in a squint against the setting sun behind me.

As I draw closer, he blinks, and recognition dawns on his round face.

He drops his fishing rod and squares up to me in a pathetic attempt to make his weaker body seem intimidating.

I fix him with my most charming smile.

He draws back slightly, thrown off by my affable demeanor.

"What're you doing here?" he demands. "This is private property."

"Yes," I acknowledge. "I saw the signs. But it's not your property, is it?"

He scowls at me. "None of your business."

I shake my head at him, still smiling. "You snuck in. No one knows you're here."

The marsh is eerily silent around us, as though even the gulls have fled in the face of the threat I pose. I'm the most dangerous predator out here, and Ron finally seems to understand.

He swallows hard, but he manages a contemptuous sneer.

"What'd you do, follow me? If you're here because of your girlfriend, don't bother. I don't want that frigid bitch."

Fury swells my muscles, but I manage to maintain my composure.

"I warned you not to speak about her like that," I remind him coolly.

He rubs his jaw absently, as though it already aches from the impact of my fist.

"No," he retorts. "You told me not to say it around her." He spreads his arms wide, gesturing at the empty marsh. "She's not here."

"She's not," I agree. "There's no one here but you and me." I unbutton my shirt cuffs and casually roll up my sleeves. "She wouldn't like to see what I'm planning to do to you. But she'll never have to know. You'll never bother her again."

He takes a step back, then teeters at the edge of the dock. He throws himself forward to stop from crashing into the salt-water creek. He falls straight into my brutal punch.

His head snaps back, and he drops onto the aged wood. I pin him while he's stunned, pummeling his face until the lips that dared to kiss my Abigail are a bloody mess against his broken teeth. Warmth sprays my cheek, and my knuckles split at the force of my relentless blows.

I don't fight the red haze any longer. I sink into it, allowing it to suffuse my senses. I revel in the rush of vicious power that I've only known since meeting Abigail.

When he stops moving, I grab his curly hair and drag him down the dock. He releases a garbled shout through his broken jaw as thick splinters pierce his cheek.

Ron's boat shoes scrabble at the gravel as I pull him onto the rough driveway, as though he can run from the inevitable.

Then we're in the mud, my boots sinking into sludge as I pull him toward the dark water.

His hands scramble for purchase, and he screams when his palms are sliced open by the sharp oyster beds. He grabs at my arm, and his blood smears on my white shirt.

The water flows up to my knees, but he's trapped under my ruthless hands, his face shoved beneath the muddy surface. Out of the corner of my eye, I see a ripple moving toward us, and I recognize the ridged back of an alligator.

I won't even have to clean up my mess.

This fucker just needs to drown before the beast reaches us.

He thrashes in the water, the desperate sound calling to the gator like a school of jumping bait. Then his body convulses when he fills his lungs with saltwater. He jerks in my hold once. Twice.

He goes utterly still, and his bloody hands float at his sides. I shove his body in the direction of the alligator, and before I've managed to trudge out of the mud and onto the shore, Ron disappears into the murky creek.

He'll never touch my Abigail again.

30

ABIGAIL

"Are you okay?" Franklin's voice is rough with worry over the phone. "I just walked past your front door, and the paint is all fucked up like someone's been trying to kick it down. You didn't answer when I knocked."

"I'm fine," I promise, quick to allay my friend's concern. "I'm at Dane's place. There was an altercation with that new guy, Ron, earlier. But I'm fine now."

"What did that curly-haired creep do to you?" Franklin demands. "I swear to god, I will make his life hell until he moves out of this building."

My heart warms, and my lips curve in a small smile.

"Thank you. I'll take you up on that."

Franklin is a wonderful friend, but I know he's capable of chilling acts of passive aggression when someone crosses him. He can make Ron so uncomfortable that he'll move out sooner rather than later.

"But I'm safe with Dane. Plus, I kicked Ron in the balls. I don't think he'll try anything again."

"What? Who are you, and what have you done with sweet Abby? I mean, don't get me wrong. I'm glad you hurt the fucker if he was harassing you. But I didn't think you could hurt a fly."

"I didn't either," I admit. "But I'm glad I did it too."

"Good for you," Franklin approves. "So, you're across the street right now? Can I come see you, or are you busy with your gorgeous doctor? I haven't caught up with you in weeks."

"Across the street?" I'm not sure where he got that idea. "No, I'm at Dane's place."

"Right. The old powder blue house. I know the one."

"No," I correct him, confused. "Dane lives in Harleston Village."

There's a moment of silence. Then Franklin asserts, "I've seen him coming and going from the house across the street for months now. I noticed him when he moved in. He's too hot *not* to notice."

"You must be mistaken. I've never seen him in the neighborhood except when he's come to visit me."

"Okay, maybe he has an identical twin," my friend says slowly, but I can tell he's suspicious. "Because a man who looks exactly like him lives in the house across the street from our building. I thought you said you knew him because he comes into the café every morning."

"He does." My throat is getting tight, and my stomach churns.

I don't understand what's happening. Franklin has to be mistaken.

"The Sunny Side Café is three blocks away from where we live," Franklin reasons. "Nowhere near Harleston Village. I assumed Dane was a regular because he lives in the neighborhood."

"He just likes the café," I say.

"Is it near his workplace?"

"I...I don't know." I've never asked where Dane's practice is located.

A thought occurs to me. "Why don't you just ask him?" I suggest. "I'm sure there's a simple explanation. He should be at our building right now. He told me he was going to talk to Ron."

Another beat of silence. "Okay, let me check."

I hear Franklin's door open and close, and then he's knocking on Ron's door across the hall.

He knocks again.

And again.

My heart is in my throat.

"No one's here, Abby."

That can't be right. Dane's been gone for almost an hour now. It's less than a twenty-minute drive between our places, even with traffic. If he's not with Ron, he should be back with me already.

"Okay." My voice is a bit shrill. "Thanks for checking."

"Are you all right? Something weird is going on."

"Everything's fine," I assure him. "I'm fine. Listen, I'll have to call you back. I need to get in touch with Dane."

"Text me to let me know how it goes," my friend requests.

"I will."

I end the call, and my thumb hovers over Dane's contact. I'm about to message him, but I hesitate.

Something is wrong. I sense it in my gut, and I can't shake the slightly queasy feeling.

I take a breath and tell myself I'm being silly. Franklin is mistaken. There's no way Dane lives in the house across the street from our building.

An image flashes through my mind: Dane's living room the first time I ever came here. It was so clean. Sterile.

Like no one lived here.

It's different now. There are coasters on the coffee table downstairs, and a few crumbs litter the counter, despite Dane's fastidious nature.

Maybe I'm just messy, and I've made his house a little less tidy.

I'm being ridiculous. Dane will come back soon, and he'll explain everything.

I decide to text him.

ABIGAIL

When do you think you'll be back?
How's it going with Ron?

My phone pings seconds later with his reply.

DANE

Everything is fine. I'm sure Ron and I will come to an understanding. I'll be back as soon as I can. Don't worry, pet. I'll handle this.

My heart sinks.

But he's not with Ron. He's not at my building. Franklin just checked.

Dane is lying to me.

I shake my head. This is getting out of control, and I'm on the verge of spiraling.

I can clear this up easily enough. I'll just go to the powder blue house and find out who really lives there. Then, I'll come back here, and Dane will be waiting for me.

I look at his text again. He didn't say that he's with Ron right now. Just that they'll come to an understanding.

It's vague and a bit cryptic, now that I'm reading it with greater scrutiny.

Gathering my resolve, I open the app to call a car and head downstairs. Within minutes, I'm riding across town, back to my neighborhood.

I stare at Dane's text during the short drive:

I'll handle this.

I recall the way his eyes went ice cold when he threatened Ron in the laundry room.

Use that language with her again, and you'll end up with a broken jaw.

At the time, I'd swooned for his protectiveness. But now, I can't stop thinking about the dangerous glint in his eyes. How his face had gone blank and unnervingly devoid of emotion.

My stomach is churning by the time the car stops in front of the powder blue house. I straighten my shoulders and force myself to walk at a normal pace. I climb the three steps up to the wooden porch and ring the doorbell.

I note that the lights aren't on inside, but it's still bright enough out that the sunshine illuminates the space. There's a narrow, vertical window to the left of the front door. When no one answers the second ring of the bell, I press my face closer to the glass and peer inside.

I stop breathing. I recognize the painting that's hanging in the front hall. It's one of mine.

I swallow against the burn of bile at the back of my throat and reason that locals sometimes buy my art, not just tourists.

My footsteps are heavy with dread as I walk farther down the porch so that I can look into the larger window with a view into the living room.

My landscapes cover the walls. There must be a dozen of them crowding the small room.

Fear tingles down my spine.

This isn't right. I don't understand what's happening, what this means.

A wild, reckless impulse overtakes me, and suddenly, there's a rock in my hand. It smashes through the rectangular window beside the front door. I reach through the jagged hole I made and unlock the door from the inside. Broken glass scores my wrist, but I barely feel the sting of the cut.

I feel like I'm floating outside of my body, like this is happening to someone else.

The front door swings open, and I walk through the house in a daze, taking in my familiar style that's mounted on every single white wall. Otherwise, the space is unfurnished except for a small kitchen table.

And the bedroom.

The cramped space is dominated by a king-size bed, but I can't focus on that. More of my paintings hang on the walls. They're all images of storms.

That's why you favor the storms.

Dane knew so much about my work when we talked on the beach that day.

How did he know?

I sink down onto the mattress as my knees give out. My fists tangle in expensive sheets, as though I'm desperate to cling onto something solid, something real.

Because none of this seems real.

It can't be.

I suck in three deep breaths and force myself to think. There's nothing tying Dane to this place. Franklin thinks he's seen him in the neighborhood, but that's not proof that Dane lives here.

I grip the sheets more tightly, and my fingers clamp down on something soft and familiar.

A soft cry of pure horror bursts from my lips when I see my paint-splattered camisole in my fist. The one I thought I'd lost in the laundry.

Desperation claws at my insides, and I surge to my feet. A sort of fevered madness overtakes me, and I start tearing the room apart, as though I'll uncover some secret that will make sense of everything.

I wrench open the nightstand drawer, and my heart skips a beat. My fingers tremble as I reach out to touch the black wool. Part of me hopes it's a hallucination, but the material is all too real in my hands.

I stare down at the macabre skull that's painted onto the black ski mask.

My brain blanks. My body goes numb.

I can't process this. I can't accept it.

"You shouldn't be here, little dove."

I whirl, and Dane is standing behind me. He's covered in mud and something crimson that makes my stomach turn.

The man I love has blood on his face.

He's here. In this awful shrine to me.

Little dove.

He's never called me that before.

That's GentAnon's nickname for me.

"No." My tremulous whisper is barely audible.

It's *him.*

He's my dark god.
He's my online confidante.
He's the masked man who violated me.
They're all the same man. They're all *him.*

31

DANE

Something sharp pierces my chest, robbing my breath.

She's not supposed to be here.

She was never supposed to see this.

She was never supposed to know.

I came back here to get cleaned up, so that I wouldn't be covered in blood and grime when I returned home.

Now, she sees the ugly truth of what I am.

I'm her stalker.

Her attacker.

Her villain.

I was a fool to ever delude myself into thinking I could be something else to her, something more.

"Tell me it's not true." Her lovely eyes are shining, but her tears don't bring me a shred of pleasure this time.

"Abigail," I rasp.

My stomach knots, and I reach for her.

She cringes away.

"Tell me it's not true!" The words are a desperate shriek this time.

I grasp her shoulders, forcibly pulling her to me. Her fists beat at my chest like the frantic beats of a trapped bird's wings.

"Let me go!"

"No," I refuse. My fingers bite into her soft flesh, preventing her from putting an inch of space between us. "You love me."

If I say it, it might still be true.

Her cheeks are chalk white, and her jaw is slack with horror.

"You violated me."

The truth in her soft whisper hits me like a gut punch.

"It was you!" she rails.

The skull mask is still clenched in her fist, irrefutable evidence of my sin against her...

I wait in the midnight shadows of her apartment. Abigail will come home from the bar at some point, and I can be patient. Every moment that passes sharpens my senses, heightening my awareness of the world in a way I've never known before.

The thrill of hunting my pretty prey is the most addictive feeling I've ever experienced.

Abigail wants this. We've been exchanging dark fantasies for months.

Our desires are perfectly matched.

But I'm tired of keeping things virtual.

She'll find as much pleasure in this twisted encounter as I will. I'll make sure of it.

"You liked it," I say, even as my stomach lurches. "You came all over my hand."

She looks up at me like I've betrayed her on a level she never could've imagined.

The knife in my chest twists, an awful, shredding sensation.

"I knew we were meant to be together," I continue, as though I can salvage this. "That's why I came into the café and asked you out. You were meant to be mine."

"I'm not yours!" The words are wrenched from her chest on an anguished cry.

I wrap my arms around her, caging her in an unbreakable embrace. "You are. Nothing will change that. You love me."

She does love me.

She has to.

"I'm scared," she whispers. "You're scaring me. Let me go."

"I can't do that." It's a rough statement of fact.

I'm incapable of letting her go.

She writhes in my hold, and she opens her pretty mouth to scream.

I harden my resolve. If she sees me as her villain, then that's what I'll be.

I spin her around and clamp my hand over her mouth before she can cry out for help. My other arm captures her throat, applying pressure to her arteries.

We've played like this before, but this time, it's not a game.

Her fingernails rake red lines into my forearm, but I don't feel them any more deeply than a tiny kitten's claws. She's every bit as fragile as I've always said.

My breakable pet.

My little dove.

Her tears stream over my hand where it covers her mouth, and unlike her painless scratches, the tears scald me. I grit my teeth and force myself to maintain my ruthless hold on her delicate body.

She softens in my arms, and I catch her sagging, unconscious weight. I cradle her close to my chest and brush a kiss over her motionless lips.

"I'll keep you safe, Abigail," I swear. "I will do anything to protect you."

I will do anything to keep her for myself.

She said she loves me.

She'll say it again. She doesn't have a choice.

Abigail is mine: body, heart, and soul.

32

ABIGAIL

I wake up to a nightmare.

In the second between unconsciousness and waking, I believe that the awful scene with Dane was just that: a nightmare.

But then I realize that I can't move my limbs, and something soft is wedged between my teeth. The makeshift gag presses deep into my mouth, and part of my brain registers that it's one of Dane's neckties.

More silken material binds my wrists and ankles. They're drawn together at the small of my back, stretching my body in a hogtied position. I'm completely helpless to do anything but writhe on my side.

Fear crashes into me like the sharp slap of an icy ocean wave in January. Terror rips from my chest in a primal scream, but it's muffled by the knotted gag.

Dane shushes me gently, and I shudder in horror at the shadow of comfort that tempts me.

The man I love is the masked man who attacked me.

He's my online confidante, GentAnon.

He has scores of my paintings hanging in this house, the house across the street from my apartment building.

How long has he been watching me?

My mind races through all the times I felt shivery and trembled in his presence, even on our early dates. The images flicker in a nauseating film reel. Even then, my body recognized the predator. But I'm addicted to the fear, the threat.

He learned all of my darkest secrets, and he used them against me.

The mattress dips beside me, and my dark god appears in my line of vision, blocking out the view of my paintings.

We're still in the bedroom of the powder blue house, in the horrific shrine to me.

I can't have been out for very long. He caught me in a chokehold, but I don't feel bruises around my neck.

Dane wouldn't risk damaging his pet.

My stomach churns, and I taste acid on the back of my tongue.

Another scream tears from my soul—pure horror this time. Despair. Denial.

Dane's familiar, elegant hand is achingly gentle as he strokes my hair back from my cheek. His eyes are deep green pools, and fine lines sharpen his heartbreaking features.

"Hush now, pet. I'm not going to hurt you."

I shudder and cringe away, but I can't move more than an inch in my bound state. He has no trouble keeping me within his tender reach, and he caresses my cheek as though to prove my powerlessness.

"I didn't want it to be this way." His cultured voice is deep with something like regret.

The slightly rough tone threads confusion through my panicked, racing thoughts.

I don't know what's real anymore. Is he my protective, fierce lover? Or is he a heartless, calculating monster?

The memory of the woolen skull mask in my fingers is all too sharp.

I definitely didn't dream that.

"I can't let you go to the police," he reasons. He's unnervingly calm, and I recognize his bedside manner voice.

My vision blurs as tears surge. I desperately blink them away so that I can keep the threat in sight.

His thumb traces the line of my cheekbone as he wipes away the wetness on my cheeks.

My entire body goes cold, and a violent shiver makes my bound limbs quake.

"Don't be afraid," he soothes over the sound of my muffled pleas.

Let me go, I try to beg. *You don't have to do this.*

But the words are garbled behind the gag, and my assailant seems unfazed by my distress. He's still touching me as though he intends to comfort me, but he's coolly composed. I recognize the merciless, flat expression that sets his handsome face in stony planes. It used to make me tremble with desire. Now, I shudder in pure terror.

"Try not to struggle," he says, a gentle command. "You'll only strain your muscles. I have to go to my place to get a few things, but you'll be safe here."

He gestures in the direction of the nightstand. My phone is propped up against a lamp, the camera directed at me.

"I'll have you on video call the whole time." He says it like a reassurance. "I wouldn't leave you alone like this if I didn't absolutely have to. I'll watch over you, even when I'm not here."

Ice encases my bones. How long has he been doing just that: *watching over me?*

He twirls my purple curl around his finger before withdrawing regretfully. "I'll be back soon."

He stands and starts walking away.

Please! I scream into the gag. *Dane!*

He seems to recognize his name, because he flinches like I flung a knife that hit its mark deep in his chest. Then he shrugs and strides out of the bedroom, disappearing into the living room. I hear the front door open, then close. The lock engages.

I scream for help, for mercy, for salvation.

But no one hears my smothered pleas.

No one comes to save me.

I'M NOT sure how much time passes, but my muscles ache and my throat is sore by the time Dane returns.

He's holding a large, leather duffel bag in one hand. My passport is in the other.

My stomach drops, and I jerk against my restraints.

Why does he have my passport? How did he even get it?

I keep it in my nightstand drawer, and I locked my apartment door when...

My heart sinks as the awful reality of my situation weighs on my chest like a lead weight. Of course, Dane is able to easily access my apartment; he's the masked man. He's already been able to break in far too easily.

His sensual lips press together in a grim line as he sets the bag down and rummages in it for a few seconds.

My head starts swinging back and forth in horrified denial when I see the syringe he's holding.

"I had to get this from work," he explains, calm and cool. "It won't hurt."

He sits beside me and uncaps the needle. I writhe in a frenzy—prey caught in a trap.

One hand settles at my nape, pinning me with a firm but careful grip.

"Just a little pinch," he says, voice soft in that bedside manner.

I barely feel the needle slide into my neck, which only makes the horror of the drugs oozing into my system that much more potent. I shriek and jerk in his hold, but he might as well have a collar around my throat.

My limbs grow heavy, and darkness creeps in at the edges of my vision.

That featherlight touch on my hair again, petting me in a soothing rhythm.

"There's no point fighting it, Abigail," he admonishes. "The journey home will be much easier this way."

Easier for who? I want to rail, but my tongue is thick against the gag.

He's taking me somewhere, and I suspect that he doesn't mean my apartment when he says "home".

He has my passport.

We're going…

He's taking me…

I'm scared…

Even my disjointed thoughts float away, and his green eyes are the last thing I see before the darkness closes in.

33

ABIGAIL

I waver in and out of consciousness, completely disoriented. I'm only semi-lucid for a few minutes at a time before I feel the prick of the needle, and the world dissolves again.

DANE IS PLACING me in a plush seat and buckling me in. The floor tilts, and I dimly register the sound of a plane taking off. One big hand rests against the side of my head, gently urging me to lean on his shoulder. My eyelids droop, and I breathe in his spicy cedarwood scent as I float away.

DANE'S strong hands are on me, lifting me as though I'm a doll. Then I'm seated again, but the world is sliding past me.

Or I'm rolling forward. My head swims, so I close my eyes and drift.

"ABIGAIL IS MY PATIENT." I register Dane's accent, smooth and cultured as ever. "The flight was difficult for her after the procedure, so I gave her something to help manage the pain. I have her passport here."

My eyes flutter open, and I squint against harsh, sterile light. The uniformed officer looms over me, and I realize I'm still seated.

The man doubles in my blurred vision. He's looking down at the two passports on the desk between us.

Something heavy settles on my shoulder: Dane's hand. A reassurance? Or a warning?

Distant fear twists my belly, a fleeting twinge.

The officer glances up at Dane, then nods deferentially. "Welcome home, Lord Graham."

"My father is Lord Graham," Dane says smoothly, all charm and self-deprecating grace. "I'm just Dane."

The officer glances at me. "You're in good hands, miss. Get well soon."

A soft whimper catches in my throat. I don't understand what's happening or where I am, and my chest is getting too tight to draw in full breaths.

"It's all right," Dane soothes as the world starts to roll by me again. "We'll get you more meds as soon as we're out of the airport."

The rolling sensation makes my stomach turn. I close my eyes to hold back my rising nausea.

I barely feel the needle sliding into my neck, and then everything is warm and dark.

Dane's massive body cradles mine, and his unique, masculine scent enfolds me. I breathe him in, and calm settles over me. His deft fingers trail through my hair, skating over the silken strands in a soothing rhythm that lulls me into relaxation.

I'm somewhere between sleeping and waking. Being with him like this feels like the sweetest dream, and I distantly marvel that this is real: my dark god is holding me like I'm his precious possession.

You were meant to be mine. His fierce declaration rumbles through my thoughts, and my gut tightens.

You love me. His remembered words hold the ring of command.

As though I don't have a choice in loving him.

My stomach knots, and my muscles tense.

He shushes me gently and continues stroking my hair in that hypnotic rhythm. I squeeze my eyes shut, longing to stay in the peaceful space with the man I love.

I'll keep you safe, Abigail. I will do anything to protect you.

A sharp image coalesces in my mind: Dane, covered in mud and a crimson spray that I don't want to contemplate.

He'd promised to protect me while his heartbreaking face had been splattered with blood.

And then...

A strong hand clamps over my mouth, muffling my scream for help. Dane's arm catches my vulnerable throat with familiar pres-

sure, restricting my blood flow to my brain. I'm floating, but it's not a peaceful surrender. He's smothering me, subduing me.

The horrific memory layers over another dark night, the one that shattered my soul...

A gloved hand covers my nose and mouth, smothering my ability to draw breath. The shadows of my apartment close in, drawing me down into darkness. A low curse rumbles at my ear, and I'm suddenly released from the cruel grip. Oxygen floods my system, and my knees buckle. Strong arms catch me before I fall.

Dane's arms.

He's the masked man who violated me. He's GentAnon, my online confidante.

In all of those late-night correspondences with my anonymous, kinky kindred spirit, I revealed my most illicit, fucked-up fantasies.

And he made them come true.

You liked it. You came all over my hand.

The awful truth rakes at my heart with sharp black claws, and I choke on a painful gasp.

My first instinct is to jolt away from Dane, but I can already feel his bulky muscles coiling around me like a snake, ready to trap me in his perverse embrace.

I force myself to draw in a deep breath and keep my eyes closed. Disassociation comes easily. My mind goes mercifully blank, and my breaths come more naturally as I sink into nothingness. My body shuts down as though I was designed for this, and I'm too far gone to feel disgust over it. It's always been an act of self-preservation, a way to survive the horror of violation.

But I don't intend to surrender this time.

I allow the habitual disassociation to relax my body and

shield my mind from the terror that hovers just at the edges of my thoughts. In response, Dane's powerful body relaxes around mine. He's satisfied with my submission, and he doesn't expect me to try to evade him.

I have to figure out where I am. I have dim, disjointed memories of a flight and an airport. He was holding my passport, back in that awful shrine to me in the powder blue house.

I'm not in Charleston.

Before I blacked out, he mentioned a journey *home.*

My stomach churns at the suspicion that he's taken me out of the country, but I breathe through it and resolutely remain detached from my tumultuous emotions.

"Where are we?" My voice is soft and oddly flat.

Dane caresses my cheek, but I keep my eyes closed. I can't risk losing my tenuous, twisted form of serenity until I know more about my situation.

"We're in my family home in Yorkshire," he replies. "You'll be safe here."

Safe from who? The irate question flits at the periphery of my quiet bubble, and I choose to sink deeper into numbness.

"Don't worry, little dove. I'll take care of you."

Bile burns the back of my throat at the endearment; it's GentAnon's endearment for me.

The terrible reminder of what Dane really is shakes me to my core, and I suppress a shudder of pure revulsion.

"My friends will wonder where I am," I say, still soft and detached. "I can't be here."

He strokes my hair as though I'm an animal that could spook at the first sign of danger; as though I'm his pet, and he's keeping me calm.

"I used your phone to text Franklin. He knows you're on an extended vacation with me. And you don't need to worry about your barista job anymore. You can spend all of your time painting now."

My lungs seize for a moment, and I force in another breath.

"Stacy will expect me at the café," I try to reason.

"She's already accepted your notice." He says it like a reassurance, not a trap. "She's been worried about you, and she didn't even try to demand that you come in for your final two weeks. You're free, Abigail."

His declaration would be laughable if my situation weren't so horrific. I'm caged in Dane's corded arms, and he's whisked me off to another country. I'm an ocean away from my friends, and my family won't bother to ask after me. He's easily extricated me from my life in Charleston with a few messages from my phone.

Finally, I open my eyes to fully assess where he's trapped me. I know now that I'm isolated from anyone who might care to check on me.

He's behind me, one arm pillowing my head while the other is loosely draped over my waist. He could tighten those powerful arms in an instant, so it's imperative that I remain calm.

I blink and look at my surroundings. I'm in an opulent bedroom, and I instinctively know that this house is from another era. Everything is impeccably arranged. The furnishings are obviously antiques, and the cream wallpaper is decorated with vines and delicate birds—a style that's clearly not contemporary.

Dane said this is his family home, and I remember that he

told me he comes from nobility. This house is likely grand, which means I'll probably struggle to find my way out quickly.

But if I can make it far enough away from him to scream for help, surely someone will hear. Someone will find me and take me away from the monster who's holding me so tenderly.

I'm lying on a massive four-poster bed with intricate carvings on the dark mahogany. There's a matching nightstand just in my line of vision, and a heavy brass lamp with a stained-glass shade sits atop it.

The door to the room is farther away, at least ten long strides across the patterned blue and gold rug.

I have to get out. I don't know the layout of this house, and I don't know how far away I am from someone who might help me.

But I have to get away from Dane before he drugs me again. Or before he violates me like he did when he was the masked man.

For so many years, I've frozen when threatened.

Now, my freedom depends on fighting back.

I surface from my disassociated state like I've broken through a heavy wave, and the world comes into sharp focus. My hand shoots out, and my fingers close around the brass lamp. I twist in Dane's hold just as his arms begin to tense around me. I can't afford to hesitate, not even when his gorgeous eyes flare with something like betrayal.

The stained-glass lampshade smashes against the side of his head, and his grip around me loosens.

I scramble free and leap off the bed, racing for the door.

I'm in the hallway when he bellows my name like an enraged beast.

My stomach drops. I didn't hit him hard enough. He's coming after me.

His lumbering steps stomp behind me, uneven at first, then quickening to match mine.

"Abigail!"

Regal portraits flicker by me on either side like I'm running through an aged film reel. There's a grand staircase at the end of the hall, and the light is brighter there. I dash toward it, breath sawing in and out of my lungs as I push myself impossibly faster.

But his strides are so much longer than mine, and he's pounding closer with every agonizingly long second. The hallway seems to lengthen, the light growing more distant. A primal scream rips from my chest as I propel myself forward, desperation clawing at my insides.

Someone has to hear. Someone has to help me.

Because I'm out of time.

The first step of the staircase drops beneath me, but before my foot makes contact with the aged wood, the iron band of his arm loops around my waist. He drags me back into his hard chest, and I shriek in terror and defiance.

"Let me go!"

The world tilts, and my belly collides with his shoulder. He lifts me up as though I weigh nothing, and his arm clamps down on my thighs. My legs jerk uselessly in his cruel hold. I can't get the leverage I need to kick out at him.

I slam my fists into his back and scream out my impotent rage.

I hear the sharp crack of his hand before the answering pain flares on my bottom.

"Calm down," he growls.

He *spanked* me. As though I'm a child having a tantrum.

I fight harder, punching his lower back with all my strength. A feral, warning sound rumbles from his chest, but I can't stop trying to get free.

"There's no use screaming," he says, unnervingly matter of fact. "No one will hear you."

"Because you're going to drug me again?" I bite back, writhing in his grip.

"No. Because I sent the staff away, and my family summers in Spain. We're the only two people for miles. Now, calm down."

A shrill laugh fills the bedroom, and I barely realize I'm making the maddened sound. "*Calm down?* You kidnapped me, Dane. You drugged me and brought me to another country. Let me go!"

He obliges me, and my stomach dips as I drop.

The soft mattress cushions my fall, and I immediately try to scramble away from him.

The monster is on me before I move an inch. His long fingers encircle my wrists, shackling them above my head. His other hand curves around my neck, threatening to squeeze if I continue to defy him. The weight of his body pins mine, and I squirm uselessly in his restraining hold.

"I can't let you go, Abigail." It's a calm statement of fact.

His perfect features might as well be carved from ice: frigid and unfeeling. If it weren't for the way his emerald eyes blaze, I'd think he was completely devoid of human emotion.

Blood trickles down his cheek from a small cut at his brow. I managed to inflict some damage when I struck him with the lamp, but it wasn't enough to save me.

"I won't go to the cops," I promise desperately. "I won't tell anyone what you did to me. Just let me go home."

His jaw ticks, and his eyes flare with a dark possessiveness that I recognize all too well.

"I can't let you go," he repeats, and it holds the solemn ring of a life sentence.

He's insane. The man I thought I loved is absolutely insane.

"Get your hands off me, psycho!"

He flinches, but his fingers firm around my neck, choking off my ability to hurl insults at him.

"I never claimed to be sane. I've let you see exactly what I am, and you begged for more."

My lips part on shallow breaths that barely squeeze through my constricted windpipe.

"Please..." I barely manage to whisper the plea.

"You like this, Abigail." The words are a dagger to my thrumming heart. "You want me. The real me."

"I don't know the real you," I gasp.

I don't want this monster who's holding me captive. He's not the fiercely protective man I fell for.

"Liar," he accuses coolly.

He releases my throat, and oxygen floods my system.

Horror hollows out my chest when his touch trails lower. One strong hand keeps my wrists above my head, and the other deftly palms my breasts in the way I like best—just hard enough to threaten bruising pain.

My nipples peak against the inside of my bra, and a sickening pulse starts up between my legs.

"No," I moan in pure revulsion.

He knows my body. I told him my darkest secrets. He lured me into trusting him, and now he confidently manipulates pleasure from my deepest shame.

He's going to wield it against me like a weapon. It's far more devastating than the helplessness inflicted by the drugs.

"You do want me." It's a command, an edict. "You want it to be this way between us."

A drop of his blood drips from his tight jaw and sears my cheek. It mingles with my hot tears, and despair swallows me whole.

34

ABIGAIL

Dane frowns, and a furrow creases his brow.

I drag in a shuddering breath when he releases my breasts to brush away the wetness that sears my cheeks. He lifts his fingers to inspect them, and his frown deepens. His crimson blood is diluted by my tears, and the two mingle into a glistening red stream that rolls down his palm.

He looks...puzzled. Like he can't fathom why I'm so distressed.

Or maybe he can't believe that I actually fought back and made him bleed.

I lift my chin and glare up at him with open defiance.

"If you violate me, I will hate you," I hiss. "My body will respond, but I will hate you."

His eyes glitter when they fix on mine again. He's peering at me like I'm some alien creature he doesn't understand.

"But you like when I make you cry."

I gape at him even as my stomach turns at the truth in his words.

"Not like this." I force the denial through my constricted throat. "And never again. I trusted you. I thought I knew you."

His eyes flash. "You do know me. I've let you see me in a way I've never shown myself to anyone. You chose me. You love me."

"Stop saying that!" My words are roughened by desperation. I think I'll vomit if he says it again. "How can I love a stranger? How can I love the masked man who assaulted me?"

He shakes his head, as though my words irritate him like swarming gnats.

"You weren't supposed to find out about that."

"You think that's the problem here? That I found out, not that you attacked me in my home?" I glower at him, allowing him to see the depth of my disgust. "I know what you really are now. I could never love you after what you did to me."

He blinks, and his expression smooths to stony, unfeeling planes once again. "You're upset. I understand that you didn't agree to leave Charleston. But things will be better for you now. You don't have to scrape by with your barista job anymore. You don't have to live in that shitty old apartment. I'll provide a life for you that you deserve, Abigail."

My jaw goes slack for a moment. The depth of his delusion is truly unfathomable.

"I want the life I built for myself." I defy him. "I don't want anything from you. I want to go home and never see you again."

His eyes narrow. "That's not happening. You're mine. Nothing will change that."

"Saying I'm yours doesn't make it true," I shoot back. "I won't willingly give myself to you."

"You signed the contract," he reminds me.

"I signed a contract with the man I met at the café. I signed myself over to the Dane that I knew. The Dane who promised to protect me and honor my consent. You are not that man."

A shadow flutters at his jaw. "You didn't meet me at the café. You don't even remember the night we met because you drank too much and blacked it out. Do you know how maddening it was to see you all those mornings, and you looked at me like I was just another customer? Like we hadn't shared something unique?"

"What are you talking about?" I demand.

"We met at the bar a few nights after I moved to Charleston. You told me your dark desires, and I let you see a glimpse of the real me. You wanted me then, and I only let you go when I realized you were too drunk. I didn't want you to regret being with me.

"So, I found out where you worked. I approached you the next morning, and you had no idea who I was. What we had shared. What we could have been so much sooner if you hadn't been so stubbornly evasive."

My mouth opens and then closes. I'm not sure what to say in response to this new revelation. It's not completely unbelievable that I might've had too much to drink on a night out; I like a cocktail or three to ease my inhibitions when I go dancing.

I think back to that first morning I met him—the first time I remember meeting him.

He'd acted so strange at the café. Intense and familiar in a way that unnerved me.

But then, I convinced myself that I'd just been nervous because he's so gorgeous. I could barely look at him when he came in for his daily Americano because he's intimidatingly handsome.

Now I know that he made me nervous because deep down, part of me knew he was a predator. I have no idea what happened between us at the bar, but it must've been dark enough to set my senses on high alert in his presence. That giddy, fizzy hit of adrenaline had made me enamored with him on our first date.

I didn't recognize the thrill for what it was: a primal warning of danger.

My mind catches on something odd that he just said. "And how did you know where I worked?"

His gaze cuts away from mine for a heartbeat, and then his eyes narrow with something like defiance.

"I followed you home when you left the bar. You stumbled off before we could truly get to know each other. How else was I supposed to find you again?"

He makes stalking me sound so reasonable.

"You could have simply asked for my number, like a normal man."

His beautiful face hardens to a grim mask. "I am not a normal man. I thought you knew that. I thought you accepted me, just like I accept everything that you are. You're perfect for me, Abigail. Why are you denying us now?"

I shake my head. He's clearly insane, completely deluded. He seems incapable of understanding how stalking and assaulting me was a violation on the deepest level.

"There is no *us*." I try to speak as calmly as possible when my heart is hammering against my ribcage. "You're not the man I thought you were. Your belief that I love you won't change that."

He bares his teeth at me like a cornered predator, and for a moment, I think he's going to hurt me.

I cringe, and suddenly, his weight is gone.

He's standing three feet away from where I lie sprawled on the bed, completely disoriented by his abrupt decision to release me.

"You'll want to get freshened up before I show you around the estate," he says, the perfectly composed, genteel host. He tips his head in the direction of an ensuite bathroom. "Go on. I'll wait here for you."

Now that he's mentioned it, I become acutely aware of the fact that I've neglected my basic needs. How long was I unconscious?

My cheeks heat, and I duck past him into the bathroom.

Once I'm a bit more composed, I splash cold water onto my flushed face. The awful weight of my new reality presses down on my shoulders like a ton of lead, and it's all I can do to keep my shaking knees from buckling. I grip the sink for support. My knuckles are almost as white as the porcelain.

I'm alone with a madman on a remote estate. He's already proven that he's so much stronger than I am. Fighting him only gave him an excuse to pin me down and attempt to coax shameful pleasure from my unwilling body.

I won't make that mistake again.

Dane doesn't value my consent. That much has become painfully clear.

He thinks I love him. If I can convince him that I will never feel a shred of affection for him again, he might let me go. He seems obsessed with his misguided belief that I belong to him. Once he accepts that I will never surrender my heart, he'll grow tired of me. He'll release me, and I can return home to Charleston.

I straighten my spine and face myself in the mirror. I take several deep breaths and convince myself that my plan will work.

It has to work.

Because the ache in the center of my chest is from more than just the fearful pounding of my heart. I did love Dane, and the loss has shattered something inside me. Being near the monster who wears his face will be agonizing, but I'll have to bear it.

My freedom depends on it.

His soft knock on the door draws a shocked yelp from my tight chest.

"Let me in, Abigail."

"I'm coming out."

I don't want him to break down the door to get to me.

I slide the lock back, and he towers over me. I swallow hard and edge away from him. He follows my movement, staying resolutely in my personal space.

"What are you doing?" I demand breathlessly.

He gingerly touches two fingers to the bloody cut on his brow. "I need to get cleaned up. Stay."

He issues the command like I'm a wayward pet. I grit my teeth against the tirade that teases at the tip of my tongue.

I will remain compliant. I won't give him the excuse to manhandle me again.

My wits will get me out of this. I have to keep them sharp, and I know his unwelcome touch will devastate me.

He hisses softly when he cleans the cut I inflicted, but he doesn't rebuke me for attacking him. I'm relieved he doesn't lash out in reprisal for the pain I caused him.

My heart breaks all over again. The Dane I loved would've

done anything to protect me. He cherished me, and I trusted that he would never harm me.

This monster who kidnapped me is completely unpredictable. He was capable of holding a knife to my throat while he violated me. He could turn violent at any moment, so I have to remain calm and not give him any reason to harm me.

He doesn't look at me for the few minutes it takes him to find a pack of bandages in the medicine cabinet. It's almost as though he's ignoring me—if it weren't for the menace rolling off him in waves. His every movement is tense with barely leashed aggression, but, mercifully, he doesn't try to assault me again.

When he turns to face me, the blood has been washed from his face, and the only sign of the wound I gave him is a tiny bandage on his forehead. His midnight hair tumbles over his brow, almost concealing it entirely.

He sweeps the unruly locks back, smoothing them into his usual neat style. He's completely unruffled and utterly composed when he holds out his hand like a gentleman.

I stare at it, unwilling to place my hand within his grasp. My fists clench at my sides in silent defiance. His sharp gaze flicks over my rigid posture, and he shrugs.

He drops his hand to his side as though the tense exchange doesn't bother him in the slightest, but his jaw remains tight enough that a shadow flits at his cheek.

"I'll show you around the house," he says in a smooth cadence.

I get the bizarre sense that he thinks I'm his honored guest, not his captive.

The man truly is insane. How did I not see it before?

I recall the times his face went cold, and his eyes glinted with green fire. I'd trembled with fear-drenched desire, but that was when I trusted him implicitly. Before I found out that he's the masked man. Before I knew that he hid behind Gent-Anon's screenname to learn all of my most forbidden desires.

He claims that we met the night before he first came into the café. The fact that he stalked me on my way home and then followed me to work the next morning makes a chill pebble my skin.

All those months, he came into the café like clockwork every morning.

Until the day he finally asked me on a date.

The day after the masked man—*Dane,* I silently correct myself—attacked me.

"Why?" The single word is a razor blade in my throat, dragging its way out of me.

I don't think I want to know, but I can't help asking. I can still barely accept what's happening to me, and I'm desperate to understand.

"Why did you ask me out? Why do any of this?"

His green eyes blaze, burning into me. "Because you're perfect for me."

35

ABIGAIL

I press my lips together to hold back the defiant words that burn my tongue. Or maybe that's the bile that's creeping up my throat.

I swallow hard against my rising nausea and wrench my gaze from his burning green stare. The possessiveness in his eyes is terrifyingly potent, and I can't bear to maintain the intense connection for one second longer. He truly believes what he's saying. I'm not sure if it'll be possible to convince him that he's completely delusional.

He's decided that I belong to him.

When I look into his fiercely handsome face, I see the man I fell in love with. It's beyond horrific to know that man was never real. Everything moment we've shared has been a manipulation.

I hug my arms around my aching chest, as though I can hold the shattered pieces of my heart together.

"You must be hungry," he says, voice warm with concern.

I can't trust in that warmth. I've seen his cold, merciless

soul now. Any display of tenderness must be just another lie to lure me in.

I've always known that Dane is wickedly intelligent. I just didn't realize that he was using that razor sharp mind against me. He's a convincing enough actor that he tricked me into falling in love with him.

If I hadn't gone into the powder blue house and found out what he really is, I would still be in love with him. I'd be in his bed back in Charleston, calling him *Master* and giving my body to him eagerly.

I shudder at the thought. Because part of me wishes I could be that version of me—ignorant to Dane's true nature. His crimes against me.

"I don't feel like eating anything," I say truthfully.

I'm not sure if I can keep food down when my gut is churning so violently.

"You haven't eaten in nearly twenty-four hours." His voice is heavy with admonishment now. "Come with me."

He reaches for me, and I recoil. His hand clenches to a fist, then withdraws.

"You'll feel better once you've had food." He says it like I'm being unreasonable and providing me with sustenance will make me less cranky. "You will eat, Abigail."

I bristle at the command, and I keep my eyes trained on the black and white tiles beneath my feet. After a tense moment, I manage to force my head to dip in a jerky nod.

Remaining in this bathroom won't get me closer to freedom. If we truly are alone and isolated on his estate, I need to explore my cage. I won't try to run again unless I'm certain that I have a chance of evading him. For now, I'll remain complaint. He can compel my actions, but he can't rule my heart.

The sooner he accepts the fact that I will never love him—that I feel nothing but revulsion for him—the sooner he'll tire of me and release me.

He doesn't reach for me again, and I huff out a small, relieved breath. I keep my eyes averted from his powerful body as I follow him through the bedroom. My gaze catches on the shattered remnants of the colorful, stained-glass lampshade that litter the rug, and for an insane moment, I consider snatching up one of the jagged shards to wield it as a weapon.

I grit my teeth and force my reluctant feet to carry me away from temptation. I can't afford to attack him and lose.

We make our way down the long corridor, heading toward the staircase I never quite reached during my mad escape attempt. I focus on the layout of my surroundings, noting three closed doors that interrupt the lines of portraits on either side of me.

Dane notices my swinging gaze and explains, "There are four bedrooms in this wing. My brother, James, and I have rooms here. My parents occupy the east wing, although there are a further six guest rooms that remain empty. Not including the additional accommodations in the carriage house."

My heart sinks at the sprawling description of the manor. I'll have to rely on Dane to navigate the space.

We descend the wide staircase and cross a cavernous foyer. Natural light pours through large windows on either side of what I assume is the front door, making the wood paneled walls glow like they're burnished.

Dane leads me through a maze of rooms, and I commit the grand spaces to memory. There's a robin's egg blue sitting room with intricate crown molding. A dining room with a table long enough to host a feast like something out of a period drama. A library with thousands of books lining every wall on intricately carved shelves.

"I'll show you the billiards room and the indoor pool later," he says, making genial conversation. "There's a fully equipped gym, too, but we can exercise outdoors if you prefer. The Yorkshire Dales are too beautiful to waste time on a treadmill."

We enter a massive kitchen with modern appliances that have been tastefully chosen to complement the historic character of the space. Dark wood beams accent the cream ceiling overhead, and the massive stone fireplace beside a large, oval dining table is swept clean for summer. Across from the marble-topped island, the kitchen opens up into a glass-walled conservatory.

My breath catches when I get my first look at the countryside. Grassy hills roll to the horizon, and a narrow river is a shining blue ribbon that meanders between them. It spills into a huge lake that must be several miles away. I don't see any other houses—only dry-stone walls crisscrossing the hills, which are dotted with distant white sheep.

We truly are isolated in this gorgeous landscape.

My fingers itch for my paintbrush even as my stomach turns. The urge to capture the way the sunlight dapples the green hills is an ever-present, irrepressible artistic calling.

But the rural setting fills my heart with dread.

There's no one here to help me. No neighbors to hear me if I scream.

"I'll make us a proper fry-up," Dane says, calling my attention away from the terribly beautiful countryside. "It might take me a moment to get my bearings. Cooking in this kitchen is a novelty. All of my meals were prepared for me when I was a boy. In the years since I moved to America, I've learned to take care of myself."

His lopsided smile is so perfectly charming that I marvel at his ability to mask his monstrous nature.

"I can make a decent meal for you." He says it like a reassurance. "I doubt my brother could manage it. He's never worked at anything a day in his life."

"You brother still lives here? With your parents?" I try to keep my tone casual, politely interested.

He sees right through me. "Like I said, they're summering abroad. And no, my brother has his faults, but he has no desire to remain close to our parents. I believe he prefers to spend his time in the Wensleydale lodge. It's only about a half hour's drive from here, but it permits him some distance from our mother."

"You said you left your family behind when you moved to America for college," I say carefully. "Won't they want to see you now that you're back home?"

He scoffs. "If they knew I was here, they'd try to find a way to lock me down and prevent me from leaving. But don't worry. I paid the staff to keep quiet. They were happy to take an extended holiday."

"So, you're not planning to stay."

I have to get a sense of his plans for me. Does he intend to return to Charleston at some point? It certainly sounds as though he doesn't want to stay here for long.

He frowns and turns his attention to the fridge. He doesn't look at me when he replies, "You and I need to come to an understanding before we go back to the States. Meadows is pissed that I fucked off to England without notice, but he'll have to manage the practice without me for a while. I told him my grandmother had passed away. I just didn't specify when."

He keeps his focus on finding the pans he needs rather than looking at me.

"You think I'll turn you in for what you did to me," I surmise quietly.

In profile, I note the downward twist of his lips, as though he's bitten into something sour.

"I don't intend to go to prison." His voice is smooth and cultured as ever, entirely unruffled except for his frown. "You need some time to process what you saw. I understand that. It's regrettable that I had to bring you here, but it was the best option."

"You think kidnapping me was the best option." It's a dull, flat statement. I have to keep the shrill accusation from my tone if I'm going to reason with him. He has to hear how insane this is when I put it in clear, plain language.

He places several fat sausages and four rashers of thick bacon onto a hot pan, and the meat instantly begins to sizzle. He continues to focus on cooking, his movements smooth and utterly casual, as though this is a normal morning and nothing is troubling him.

"You don't have to continue with your menial job to make ends meet anymore," he reasons. "You can spend all your time focusing on your art. That's what you want, isn't it? I can give that to you, Abigail. I have given it to you. You're free to reach your full potential now."

"You stole my phone and quit my job for me." It takes all my willpower to remain calm and rational. "You made my friends believe that I'm on vacation with you. But you drugged me, and you're holding me against my will. That's not freedom, Dane. That's captivity."

He shrugs, a physical dismissal of my words. "You'll be

much happier now. You just need some time to adjust. I know what you saw upset you. I never intended to frighten you."

I can't hold back my bitter laugh. "Didn't you? You terrified me when you put on that skull mask and assaulted me in the dark. You threatened me with a knife."

"Just like you told me in your fantasies." He bites out the words, clearly agitated. "I acted out your deepest desires."

I breathe through my nose and suppress the urge to vomit.

He knows all of my secrets because he positioned himself as GentAnon.

"I confessed those fucked-up fantasies because I thought it was a safe space to express them. I thought I was talking to someone anonymous. Someone who understood me. I trusted you."

I told my illicit pen pal my most vulnerable secrets, and I'd felt secure in purging my inner darkness with him.

Instead, I made myself a target for a sadistic psychopath.

"How did you find my screenname?" I ask through numb lips.

My mind spins as I try to piece together what's happened to me. How long has Dane been watching me?

"You said we met at the bar before you came into the café for the first time. That was a few weeks before GentAnon messaged me. How did you find my erotica?"

He cracks an egg over the pan, a little too sharply. "You don't want to know that."

"Yes, I do," I insist, even though I really would prefer not to hear the sickening extent of his stalking.

But I have to understand him. I can't talk my way to freedom if I don't know everything about my situation.

"I've been watching over you ever since the night we met," he admits. "I think that much is obvious now."

"*Watching over me?*" I repeat, incredulous. "You mean *stalking me*."

His jaw tenses, but his movements are deft as he removes the cooked food from the pan. He places a full plate on the island in front of me, along with a glass of water.

Then he takes a knife and fork to cut my food into bite-sized pieces. He places the knife in the sink, well out of my reach.

Clearly, he's not going to tempt me with a potential weapon. Not after I attacked him with the heavy brass lamp almost as soon as I woke up from the drugs.

"Eat," he commands.

My stomach rumbles as the rich scent of bacon suffuses my senses. Even though I still feel queasy, I'm painfully aware of the fact that I haven't eaten in a full day. I have to keep my strength up and my wits sharp.

I take a bite of eggs. It tastes like ashes on my tongue, but I force myself to chew and swallow.

"Are you going to answer my question?" I press when half my plate is empty. "How did you know to position yourself as GentAnon?"

"No." He takes a bite of his own bacon, and I realize he's not planning to say more.

"No, what?"

"No, I'm not going to answer your question."

I gape at him. "You owe me the truth, Dane."

His brow furrows, as though he's struggling to process my declaration. It occurs to me that he probably doesn't think he owes me anything. Judging by his puzzled expression, in his mind, he's never owed anything to anyone.

"You're upset," he says after a long moment. "I don't want

to tell you when it will only make you more upset. I don't like how you're looking at me."

"And how am I looking at you? Like you're a monster who stalked and kidnapped me? Does that make you uncomfortable? Because I'm not remotely sorry."

I fix him with the full force of my defiant glower. I won't make this easy for him. If the way I look at him disturbs him, he'll be eager to let me go soon enough.

36

ABIGAIL

"Fine," Dane bites out, green eyes blazing. "You want to know how I became GentAnon? I borrowed your laptop and found your erotica."

I gape at him. "*Borrowed?* You mean you stole it. How? When?"

His gaze cuts away for an instant before snapping back to mine. "I went into your apartment and found your laptop two months ago. Is that what you want to hear?"

"You *went in?*" I press, forcing him to confront the softer language he's selecting over the harsh truth. "So, you broke into my home more than once."

"I told you that you don't want to hear this." He says it like I'm the unreasonable one.

I narrow my eyes at him. "Oh, I absolutely do. I want *you* to hear it. Listen to how crazy this is. How can you expect me to love you after everything you've done to me?"

He glares at me with open defiance. "Everything I've done has been for you. I had to make sure you truly wanted me.

The first night we met—the night you don't remember—you told me you wanted to be overpowered. Forced. I had to know that was real before I acted out the dark fantasy that we share. Both of us, Abigail. You wanted everything that I offered you. Or have you forgotten how many orgasms I gave you?"

My fingers shake with the rage that rushes through my system, so I curl them into fists. "You know I orgasm when a man forces himself on me. I told you what happened with Tom on the night of my debutante ball. How he did it again and again, and how ashamed I felt for letting it happen. You assaulted me, Dane."

His head jerks to the side in a staunch refusal of my accusation. "You're not thinking clearly," he says roughly. "I am nothing like him. I protect you from men like him. Just like I protected you from your neighbor, Ron."

The memory of Dane's blood-splattered face flashes across my mind. He'd said he was going to talk to Ron, and he returned covered in mud and blood.

"What did you do to him?" I ask, breathless with dawning horror.

Dark brows draw together in forbidding slashes. "I made sure he'll never touch you again."

"What does that mean?" I demand, voice going shrill despite my efforts to remain calm and rational.

"It means I'll do what's necessary to keep you safe," he snaps back, his composure slipping too. "This conversation is over."

"I don't think so," I hiss. "You don't get to tell me when to shut up. You don't control me. Not anymore."

He scowls. "I never tried to control you. How many times do I have to tell you that I want you just as you are? I expect obedience when we fuck because that's what we both like. We're perfectly compatible."

"You're delusional."

His face goes cold again, his eyes unnervingly calculating.

"I won't entertain this conversation further. Rail at me if you want. Get it out of your system. But I'm no longer participating."

I clench my jaw shut to hold in a scream of impotent rage. Shouting at him will get me nowhere. He seems convinced that I'm hysterical, irrational. After he stalked and kidnapped me.

Playing into his characterization of my behavior will only make him more convinced that he's right to hold me here against my will.

I watch in stony silence as he takes the plates to the sink. The dishes clatter a bit more loudly than necessary as he cleans up, tension clear in every taut line of his powerful body. And yet, he manages to carry out the chore with a completely blank expression.

He doesn't ask for my help as he dries the pans and puts everything neatly back in its place.

Something about the domesticity of the situation brings his psychopathy into sharp relief. He's holding me against my will, but instead of using violence to subdue me, he's cooking and cleaning for me. As though I'm a guest rather than his captive.

He truly thinks I'll just get over his heinous crimes against me. He's acting as though we can be together like a normal couple.

If anything, he's doting on me. In his twisted mind, he probably thinks that he's seeing to my every need.

He's incapable of understanding that what I need more than anything is to get away from him.

"Come with me," he commands when the kitchen is spotless. "I have something for you."

I cross my arms over my chest. "I don't want it."

His lips press to a grim line. "You'll accept it regardless. You don't seem ready to accept the fact that you don't have to work anymore to make ends meet. I'm going to show you how I will provide for you. You'll learn to embrace it, even if you have always been stubborn about accepting what my money can afford us. That ends now."

I never should've let him buy my drinks. I shouldn't have accepted the fancy dress for Meadows' wedding.

I'd been afraid that he'd wield his wealth as a weapon against me, just like my family.

I'd been right, but I hadn't listened to my gut instincts.

My back goes rigid.

"I told you that I won't be controlled financially ever again." It takes effort to maintain a calm, flat tone. "Whatever you have for me, I refuse to accept. You can't buy my affection, Dane."

He shakes his head sharply, the only sign that his irritation is breaking through his cold façade.

"This isn't about controlling you. It never has been. I want to take care of you. You're the one who's insisting on misunderstanding what I'm offering. I will never leverage my money against you. What I provide doesn't come with strings attached."

"No, you're misunderstanding." He truly seems to believe what he's saying. "You want to keep me captive. You think I'll soften toward you if you buy me things and ensure my comfort. That's controlling behavior, Dane. You have to see that."

"I will provide for you, Abigail. This isn't a negotiation. And it's not a manipulation. I told you from the beginning that I'm selfish. This is what I want: you, content and cared for in the way that you deserve. In time, I'll prove to you that I don't expect anything in return."

His eyes glitter with icy determination. "Now, are you going to come with me, or am I going to have to carry you?"

I fix him with an imperious stare that's icy enough to match his. "I don't intend to be spanked like an unruly child again. I'll walk."

He shrugs. "It's your choice."

I hold back the tirade that it's not a choice at all. He will take me wherever he wants to go, despite my protests. My only autonomy in this situation is whether or not I maintain some semblance of dignity.

He turns his back on me and strides out of the kitchen. It's a small mercy that he didn't reach for me, but I don't dare hesitate to follow him in case he changes his mind about touching me.

We go through the labyrinthine rooms again, making our way back to the cavernous, wood-paneled entry hall. He silently leads me up the grand staircase, and I realize we're heading toward his bedroom.

My steps falter. "I'm not going to have sex with you, if that's what you're thinking."

His shoulders stiffen, but he doesn't turn to face me when he replies, "I'm not taking you to my bedroom." He opens one of the doors we passed on our way down the long corridor with the portraits. "I converted this guest room into a studio for you while you were sleeping."

I hate the longing that tugs at my heart, even as my stomach churns. Dane knows my deepest dreams of being a successful artist, and he's using them against me.

"If you think I'll want you just because you've provided a space for me to paint, you're mistaken. This isn't a gift, Dane. It's a betrayal."

He finally turns to face me, pivoting in the center of the room, just beside the easel he's already set up alongside a table of paints.

"I'll tolerate your barbed comments because I appreciate the fact that the way I pursued you was unconventional. If you would take a moment to see things from my perspective, perhaps you wouldn't be so prickly."

I lift my brows, incredulous. "And what is your perspective? What mental gymnastics have you done to justify all of this?"

He lifts one finger. "You were so drunk that you forgot our initial meeting, so I couldn't ask you out." He lifts a second finger before I can respond. "You refused to make eye contact when I came into the café, but I knew you wanted me." A third finger goes up. "We both have dark, kinky fantasies that defy social norms. I had to be sure that you really wanted what I had to offer before I risked showing you my true self."

I cross my arms over my chest. "You're right. You are selfish. Everything you're describing is about what you want, about keeping you safe from judgment. You could've been vulnerable with me. You could have put yourself on the line and asked me out on a date. I should've had the chance to truly choose you, but you took that away from me. Everything we've shared has been a lie, a manipulation to get me into your bed."

He waves his arms at the room in a jerky gesture. "Getting

you into my bed would've been easy. Does this look like seduction to you? I'm offering you everything you could ever want. I'll offer you the world, Abigail. And I've offered you myself in return. My real, frightening, unmasked self. You saw what I am at my core, and you wept in ecstasy."

It finally registers that he must think he's made himself vulnerable. He keeps saying that he's revealed his true self to me in a way he's never shown anyone.

But that doesn't make him any less monstrous.

I just couldn't see him clearly before. I didn't have all the horrific facts to make a rational assessment of him.

"Just because it's not carnal doesn't mean it's not a form of seduction," I inform him. "You're trying to lure me in with every word, every tender action. Even offering me this studio is part of a twisted game to you. But you can't trick me into loving you again. I don't think I ever did love you, because I didn't know you at all. I loved an idea of you, but that man was never real."

His eyes turn stormy, and I know I've said the wrong thing.

"If you're feeling so emotional, I'm sure some time at your easel will help." He speaks in clipped tones, and his massive body seems even larger than usual as all of his powerful muscles flex with barely restrained aggression.

I take a wary step back, refusing to enter the studio with the beast. "Dane..."

"You will paint, Abigail."

"You can't compel my art." I swallow hard against my rising fear. "That's not how it works."

"I've seen your real masterpieces," he reveals coldly, no longer bothering to hide behind charm and beguilement. "The dark, erotic paintings that you keep hidden in your closet. But you don't have to hide your talent anymore."

The reminder that he's broken into my apartment multiple times makes bile burn at the back of my throat.

"Those are private," I choke out.

"Not from me. Any secrets you think you have, I know them. I know *you*. All of you. And I choose every part of you. I won't apologize for wanting you."

"That much has become clear," I reply bitterly. "I won't hold my breath for an apology."

He doesn't feel a shred of remorse for what he's done to me, for the countless violations that I can't even begin to fathom.

"Paint," he commands.

"No."

He can't make me. He could crush his fist around mine and force me to lift a brush to the waiting canvas, but he can't compel me to create art. My tumultuous emotions are my own to purge through my paintings. That part of me will never belong to anyone else. Certainly not the man who's betrayed me on a level I never thought possible.

"Abigail..." My name is a warning, but I refuse to heed it.

"I won't do it. I won't paint for you."

His brows draw together, forbidding. "You can come in willingly, or I can put you here." He points to the chair that's set up in front of the easel, presumably for my comfort. "If you won't do it for me, do it for yourself. You need this."

"You don't know what I need!" I fling the defiant words at him, losing my composure. "I need to get away from you. I need my freedom."

"I've set you free," he growls. "You just don't want to listen."

Rage curls my fists at my sides, and suddenly, I'm surging toward him.

"You want me to come to you like a trained pet?" I rail at him. "You think I'll roll over and do what you say?"

The canvas is in my hands, and I hurl it at his beautiful face.

"Fuck you!"

He bats the canvas away at the last second, and it clatters to the parquet floor. His lips peel back from his teeth in an animal snarl, and he lunges for me.

A defiant scream tears from my chest, and I grab the table where the paints have been neatly arranged for me. It's lightweight enough that I'm able to lift it, and I raise the delicate antique like an unwieldy bat. In a split second, I swing.

But he's too fast. Too strong.

He lifts one corded arm just in time to stop the impact to his head. He barks out a rough shout as the table splinters against his shoulder, and I'm not sure if it's a sound of pain or a predator's warning.

I lunge for the easel, desperate for another weapon.

Arguing was futile. My rationality is gone. His insane refusals to listen to reason have driven me to a purely primal, enraged state.

I'm not sure if I'm fighting to get away from him, or if some savage part of me just wants to inflict a fraction of the damage he's caused me. I want him to feel the pain that's shredding my heart. I know now that he's incapable of that kind of emotional agony, so I'll wound him physically.

His arm loops around my waist just as my fingers brush the easel, and he drags me back before I can fully grasp it. He tackles me with his full weight, and we're both falling.

At the last instant, he turns his body so that he catches the brunt of the impact with the hardwood floor.

I shriek and writhe in his arms, but he rolls on top of me,

quickly pinning me so that I'm face-down beneath him. My hands scramble for purchase, and my palms slip in something wet.

I've fallen on the canvas that I threw at him, and several paint tubes have been squashed under us. Blue splatter becomes a sapphire smear under my hands as I continue to struggle like a wild thing.

"That's it," he rumbles at my ear. "Fight me like you've always wanted to. Like you really mean it."

I scream again, a sound of pure fury. I've never meant anything more in my life than my desire to hurt him now.

His left hand is beside my scrabbling fingers, sliding in the paint so that his palm is coated in blue. His other fists in my hair, drawing my head back sharply to further restrict my struggles. Then he caresses my cheek, and the paint is warm on his broad palm. It slides over one side of my face, covering me from my brow to my jaw.

His grip on my hair shifts, forcibly tilting my head to the side and shoving me forward. My cheek presses against the canvas, marking it with my twisted expression of fear and impotent rage. I shriek and jerk in his cruel hold, but all I manage to do is spread more paint in manic swaths.

"I want an imprint of your pretty scream," he says, voice rough with desire. "I'll admire this masterpiece later. We both will."

I can't find the air to tell him that he's insane. My lungs seize, and my chest draws tight enough to crush my heart.

My fists pound the canvas, sending sprays of blue droplets flying.

"This is what you've always wanted." He says it like encouragement rather than a condemnation. "You want to know the difference between me and the men who violated you? Your body already knows. When they touched you, you shut down and surrendered. But with me, you fight back. You feel safe enough to challenge me because you know I won't truly hurt you."

"You are hurting me!" I wail, an agonized truth drawn deep from my soul.

No one has ever hurt me like this.

Because what he's saying makes some perverse sort of sense, and I can't accept it. If it's true, I'm just as crazy as he is. Just as fucked up.

He thinks I'm perfect for him, but that can't be real. I can't let it be real.

The prospect that I was destined to satisfy a heartless monster is too disgusting to process. I've always known that something is deeply wrong with me, but the Dane I loved made me feel like I could embrace every part of myself. Indulging in my dark desires had become empowering.

But I've never been more powerless than I am now.

"No, I'm not." He refuses to acknowledge that he's hurting me in the worst way. "I won't so much a leave a bruise on you to prove it."

Tears leak from my eyes, diluting the paint beneath my cheek.

"When you shared your fantasies with me online, you shared your true self," he reasons. "If I hadn't found your screen name, you never would've trusted me with your secrets in person. You want to know why I couldn't simply ask you out at the café? This was the best way. The only way. By the time you agreed to a date, I already knew exactly what you wanted. You wouldn't have opened up to me enough to sign our contract if I hadn't positioned myself as GentAnon. I have no regrets, Abigail. This is how it had to be between us. I will fulfill your every forbidden desire."

"I don't want you to," I counter in a ragged whisper. "Let me go."

"No. Not until you accept the truth of what we are, what we share. I'm not letting you leave this room until you scream my name while you orgasm."

"No," I moan in pure horror.

My revulsion is that much more acute because I'm starting to realize that the warmth flooding my veins isn't simply white-hot rage. Desire pulses between my legs, and my nipples are hard buds.

He keeps his firm grip on my hair with one hand while the other dips between my chest and the canvas.

"Hush now, pet," he soothes, dropping a tender kiss on my nape. "No more arguing. I don't want to hear another word unless it's my name on your pretty lips."

I want to defy him, to continue railing at him. But my screams stick in my constricted throat, and I can't manage more than a garbled groan.

It sounds unbearably erotic, and he drops another doting kiss on my exposed neck.

My cheeks flush with shame, and my clit pulses in response.

In this moment, I hate myself. I hate *him.*

His paint slicked hand wedges beneath me, sliding under the neckline of my dress to cup my breast. The pressure is uncomfortable, but the bite of pain makes my nipple throb where it's crushed against his palm. He squeezes gently, and I gasp into the canvas. I'm writhing, and I tell myself it's because I'm still trying to escape.

But my struggles only fuel my lust, just like in all of the terrible, forbidden fantasies I so foolishly shared with him.

"Dane…" His name is a whimper, a plea.

"Better," he praises. "But I want you to scream for me."

His other, unpainted hand finally releases my hair, but his bulky frame is heavy enough to keep me pinned. He traces the shape of my body with something like reverence, coveting every inch of me. When his fingertips skim my thigh, I tense.

"You're safe with me, little dove," he soothes. "Submit."

I choke on a sob, and pleasure sizzles through me when he pinches my nipple. He tugs and torments it in the exact way I like. He knows his clever ministrations will make me come undone.

My body uncoils for him even as my heart hammers against my ribcage.

His fingers skate up my thigh, easing my dress up to expose my ass. They dip between my legs, and he releases a low, satisfied hum at the slick arousal he finds there.

Mortification sears my cheeks when I realize that I've never been so wet.

He was right: he's unleashed something dark inside me that craves this cruelty, the struggle and forced submission.

"So soft and ready for me," he says with rough desire. "Is your sensitive little clit aching?"

"Don't…" I choke on the plea before I can fully verbalize it.

He shushes me again. "Only my name, remember?"

His fingers brush my clit, and I buck beneath him as stars burst across my vision at the punch of pleasure.

"Don't worry, pet. I'm not going to fuck you now. I won't break you."

The ragged sound that heaves from my chest is somewhere between a maddened laugh and a sob.

No, Dane doesn't want to risk breaking his precious pet. He said he wants all of me, and that seems to mean that he wants my mind intact.

How can he not see that he's destroying my soul with every tender touch and soft word of praise?

With every masterful brush of his hands over my most sensitive areas, I feel the caresses of the man I loved, the man I trusted with my whole heart. The fact that a monster is holding me instead is exquisite agony. My body welcomes the pain of his cruel fingers pinching my nipples, smearing paint over my breasts like I'm his most passionate work of art.

And my core is molten for him, my inner muscles contracting around nothing as he toys with my clit. I'm aching to be filled, but there's nothing I dread more than the prospect of his cock inside me.

He promised not to fuck me, but that doesn't mean this isn't a violation.

It's just like the night he attacked me as the masked man.

He hadn't taken his own pleasure in my body on that night, either. But I understand now that his carnal satisfaction was far more sadistic than simple physical release. Forcing orgasms from my reluctant body seems to please him on a primal, perverted level that only a complete psychopath could understand.

I can feel his thick erection pressing into my upper thigh. He's getting off on this: the control over me, my helplessness to stop my body from responding to him.

I'm on the cusp of the most powerful orgasm of my life. Pleasure coils low in my belly, and I thrash against the wet canvas. I fear that I'm no longer struggling to get away; I'm desperately seeking more stimulation. My clit is painfully hard as he teases around it in maddening circles. His low, arrogant laugh dances up my spine like a caress, and I shudder at the answering rush of pleasure that washes through me in a warm wave.

"Come for me, pet."

He slides two thick fingers inside me and crooks them against my most sensitive spot. At the same time, his thumb presses down on my clit.

My orgasm rips through me, and I scream in ecstasy and despair. I'm helpless to resist the bliss that shreds my psyche as it rakes through my body. My inner muscles contract around his fingers, clamping down hard to keep him inside me. The release goes on and on. Sheet lighting flashes over my vision, and I'm a whimpering mess, writhing on the horrific, perverted painting we're making together.

"That was very pretty, but you forgot something," he admonishes, continuing to wring ruthless pleasure from my core. "My name, Abigail. Say it."

"Please…" I can't. The surrender would be too shameful to bear. He has to allow me this last shred of my dignity, my autonomy.

"You'll get no mercy from me, pet."

His fingers finally withdraw from my pulsing pussy, but before I can heave in a gasp of relief, his touch trails upward.

I try to wriggle my way free, but his other hand releases my breasts to grip my ass cheek. His fingers dig into my flesh in a warning bite, spreading me wide open for him.

"You're mine," he declares. "Every part of you."

His desire-slicked finger presses against my asshole, and I try to buck away. He holds me steady, keeping me trapped for his amusement.

"You will submit, Abigail. Surrender."

"Dane. Please, Dane..." I'm babbling, repeating his name like that will earn his mercy.

But he has none.

"You'll have to come for me," he coaxes. "Come for me while I finger your tight little asshole, and I'll relent."

Something breaks inside me.

I don't have a choice. My mind accepts that my only way to escape this horrific ecstasy is to comply. And even if I didn't acknowledge that awful truth, my body would comply anyway.

Pleasure gathers low in my belly as his finger slips inside me. I clench around him, but my final efforts to resist him only awaken forbidden sensations I've never experienced before.

He bites out a curse and pushes deeper. "I'll stretch this virgin asshole with my cock soon enough. But I'll get you ready for me before I claim you. I'll never harm you, little dove."

I close my eyes and turn my face into the canvas, as though I can hide from what's happening to me. My body softens, and he begins to pump his finger into me in gentle thrusts.

"Good girl," he praises. "Such a sweet pet."

A strangled sound catches in my throat, a carnal groan. My core throbs with desire in response to his praise, and my clit pulses in time with my racing heartbeat.

He torments me with slow, terrible pleasure as he continues to toy with my ass, teasing me until I fully surrender. I'm not trying to squirm away from him anymore. Heat flushes my skin, and I practically pant with mounting lust.

"You're going to come for me just like this." His voice has

dropped to a deeper register, and he sounds almost drunk on his power over me. "I'm not going to touch your pretty cunt or your hard little clit. Only this."

His darkly perverse command shudders through me, and I weep into the messy painting we've made. The pleasure is so keen that it cuts my heart like a knife. My core is swollen and achy, as though his gentle fingers have marked me with bruises deep inside my pussy.

But, true to his word, he hasn't harmed me physically.

My soul is another matter entirely.

All of my muscles coil tight in anticipation of release. Sweat slicks my skin, and soft moans leave my chest with every heaving breath.

"Let go," he urges. "Give me everything."

I come apart on a scream, and his name echoes through the studio he's provided for me.

"Good girl." His warm praise layers over my sharp cry, and he pumps his fingers into me, drawing out my orgasm.

My scream melts into a sob, and I shake beneath him. I'm utterly spent and shattered beyond repair.

Dane commanded me to paint for him, and despite my refusal, he's compelled me to make a shameful, carnal work of art.

37

DANE

Over the last few weeks, it became clear to me that Abigail wasn't anywhere near ready to accept the fact that I'm the masked man who broke into her apartment. After she finally opened up to me about how she was raped by that fucker, Tom, I knew it was too soon to reveal the truth. Then Ron attacked her, and she was so distressed.

Even though she experienced intense pleasure when I forced her to orgasm under the threat of my knife, she hadn't fully embraced the darkest aspects of our connection. And when we fucked, she'd struggled in bed a few times, but she hadn't truly fought me.

Until she was ready to indulge in those darkest games, I knew it was too soon to tell her that I was the masked man.

But then she broke into my second home and found the skull mask in my nightstand, and the choice was no longer mine. She'd been horrified.

But after what we just shared, she'll understand.

In her new studio, we fully realized the powerful eroticism of dancing at the edge of consent. The sensual painting that we created is proof of that. Later, we'll both admire it.

But for now, she's shaking and spent. And she's covered in paint.

I gather her up in my arms and hug her to my chest. As I carry her out of the studio, I marvel at the stunning woman who belongs to me, irrevocably and completely. Her creamy skin is still flushed from her orgasms, a deeper shade of pink coloring her chest and cheeks. The lovely hue blends with the blue paint that I stroked onto her body like she's my own personal canvas. I'll never be an artist like Abigail, but she's my masterpiece.

I take my time carrying her to my bedroom, admiring my work. It'll be a shame to wash the paint away, so I etch the memory of her perfection into my mind.

She's *mine.*

I knew it was only a matter of time before she accepted our bond, my claim over her. She's been thorny since she woke up this morning, but now she looks serene. Subdued.

Her eyes are closed, and her breaths are deep and even. Her long, dark lashes fan her cheeks like a sleeping princess in one of her favorite animated musicals. That enchanting freckle on her cheekbone marks her as a unique, proud woman. I sensed it in her when I first laid eyes on her. Even then, my need to possess her completely had been inevitable.

My chest aches just looking at her. I want her so badly that my craving consumes me. My cock is still hard, but I have enough self-control to spare her from my selfish lust. There will be time for that later. She needed pleasure first.

I was right to seduce her in the studio. It served as a reminder of how good it can be between us.

Her accusations of stalking and kidnapping had stung a bit—as had the shocking blows with the lamp and the table—but I'm confident that I've done nothing wrong. She just didn't understand why I had to do everything that I've done to win her heart.

I meant what I said to her. It was the only way.

This is how it has to be between us: raw and dark and real.

Our connection is the only thing that matters to me now, the only real thing in my world.

She is my world.

My Abigail.

My sweet pet, my little dove.

All mine.

I step into my ensuite bathroom and carry her toward the bathtub. She's almost completely limp in my arms, so I carefully crouch down to turn on the water while I keep her in a firm hold. When I'm satisfied with the temperature, I ease off her dress and set her down so that she's reclining in the bath.

She's so still, and she allows me to position her like a doll.

My stomach knots.

What happened to my fierce pet who fought me with all her might? She should be looking at me with a lazy smile and utter devotion shining in her gemstone eyes.

"Abigail." Her name rasps from my tight throat.

She doesn't respond in any way. Her cheeks remain rosy from her orgasms and the heat of the rising water, but her expression is frozen.

I cup warm water in my hand and carefully wash the paint from her heartbreaking face.

It's not only her beauty that's making my chest ache now. There's a dull throb in my heart with each heavy beat.

"Abigail." Her name is almost a growl this time, a warning that demands her attention.

"What do you want, Dane?" The question is soft and flat.

She sounded like this when she first woke up in my arms this morning. I'd thought she was woozy from the lingering drugs. Now, I don't know what to think. I don't know how to interpret this strange mood.

"I want you to look at me."

Her eyes open, and they instantly shine with fresh tears. They mingle with the warm water as I wash the last of the paint from her cheek.

"You're okay," I soothe her. I suppose our scene in the studio was intense. Some residual emotion is understandable. "Stay here with me. You're safe."

She closes her eyes again and turns her face away from my tender touch.

She doesn't say anything in reply.

"Talk to me," I urge.

"What do you want me to say?" That flat tone sets me on edge. It's far more disturbing than when she was screaming at me.

"I want you to say that you're all right. You know I'll always take care of you. Tell me, Abigail. Tell me you're mine." The last is rough with something like desperation.

Her next breath shudders as she inhales, but that's the only sound she makes.

"Answer me," I command.

"I've never been less safe in my life."

Her whispered words are a dagger to my heart.

"No," I refute. "I will always protect you. Always."

I've killed for her. I would do anything to keep her happy and safe.

Her eyes remain closed, her expression completely blank. "There's no one here to protect me from you."

I reel back as though she's sucker punched me.

"You can't mean that." It's an order. I won't tolerate it.

I can't bear it.

"What do you want me to say, Dane? Just tell me what you want to hear, what you want me to do. You've made it crystal clear that my wishes don't matter. You won."

I bare my teeth like a cornered animal, but she doesn't open her eyes to see my anguished expression.

"This was never a battle of wills," I correct her. "I don't want to *win*. I just want you. All of you."

"And you have me right where you want me. You made sure of that."

She doesn't even sound spiteful. That detached tone makes my insides churn.

"Not like this," I insist.

She has to look at me. She has to come back to me. Because even though she's right beside me, we've never been farther apart.

"I'm sorry I'm a disappointment to you." Another tear rolls down her cheek.

"You could never disappoint me. You're everything to me. You're all that matters. Abigail!"

She flinches and hugs her arms over her bare chest, shivering despite the heat of the bath.

"Two days ago, that would've been everything I wanted to hear," she admits quietly. "You can't possibly understand how horrific those words are now. You are incapable of understanding."

"Then explain it to me," I insist.

Or am I begging?

"I've already explained it, and you didn't want to listen. Instead, you chose to violate me again. You forcibly subdued me to shut me up and make me a compliant, obedient little pet. That's what you wanted, isn't it?"

"No." The word is almost a groan. "That's not what I want."

"Well, that's what you got. That's all I have left. It's all I can offer you."

"Abigail..." I choke on her name.

I open my mouth to try again, but a sound deeper in the manor puts me on high alert. Someone is here.

Have the staff returned despite my bribes?

"Daniel! I know you're here. Come out and face me."

My chest tightens.

No.

My brother can't be here. He can't see her.

Especially not like this.

Not like I've...broken her.

The prospect makes me dizzy with nausea.

"Stay here, little dove. I'll handle this."

I don't want to leave her alone right now, but she can't be part of this confrontation. She's in a delicate enough state as it is. She doesn't need to witness a shouting match with my little brother. Or worse.

The last time I saw him, it came to blows.

He was just a kid, and still, he tried to take me on.

That was his mistake. I don't possess the capacity for mercy, not even when it comes to my own flesh and blood.

Especially not when it comes to them.

I straighten and force myself to walk away from her. She

doesn't protest or make a single sound of complaint when I leave.

She's probably glad to be rid of me.

Pain knifes through my chest, and for a moment, I think there might be something medically wrong with me. I've never felt this before. Surely, it's a sign of some terrible malady.

But I'm in excellent health.

A heart attack isn't at all likely.

I rub the center of my chest, straighten my shoulders, and stride out to face my brother.

He's standing in the corridor, waiting for me. I suppose it's a small mercy that he didn't barge into my bedroom. It's his house, after all. I surrendered my claim over it when I gave up my title and everything that went along with it.

"What do you want, James?" I demand, less coolly composed than usual.

The terrible confrontation with Abigail in the bath has shaken me to my core.

He eyes me up and down, then lets out a low whistle. "What the fuck happened to you? America not treating you well these days? Is that why you've come home? You look like shit."

"And you look like the same spoiled, arrogant little twat I left behind fifteen years ago."

He was only thirteen years old then, but he has the same dark auburn hair and eyes that match mine. A short beard covers his jaw now, but I still see a boy when I look at him.

His lips curl in a sneer. "Charming, as ever. Is this how you tempted your mystery woman to come to England with you? You must've truly swept her off her feet with your silver tongue. Or is it the family name you're trying to impress her with? You must've brought her to the estate for a reason. What's the problem? Is she not impressed with your massive...ego?"

The way he lingers over the insult makes it very clear that it's a slight against my manhood.

He knows about Abigail. That's far more worrying than his barbed comments.

"Who told you about Abigail?" I bark.

I don't want him to know anything about her, much less the fact that I brought her here against her will.

You kidnapped me, Dane. You drugged me and brought me to another country. Her accusation rakes through my thoughts, shredding me even as I attempt to gather my outward composure.

James' green eyes are wary on mine now. "You're different, big brother. I've never seen you worked up like this. America has changed you. Or is it her? Abigail, is it?"

"Keep her name out of your fucking mouth."

He takes a quick step back, then shrugs and returns to his nonchalant, spoiled prince posture. "Fine. Keep her secret. I really don't care. I only came to see if you were really here. I could hardly believe it when the groundskeeper told me this morning that you'd paid him to leave. Too bad you can't buy loyalty. You're not the heir anymore, Daniel."

"Yes, that's the whole point," I remind him coldly.

I didn't want to be the fucking heir. I refused to perform for them, to fit into the neat, small little box my parents designed for me. The cage they built with money and a "proud" lineage.

"But you're back," James counters. "Why?"

I hear Abigail moving around the bathroom: soft clatters of scented soap and the spray of warm water.

"Tea?" I ask blandly, gesturing in the direction of the grand staircase. "We can talk in the kitchen."

"I thought you'd never ask. I assumed you'd forgotten your manners."

Tea is always appropriate in England, even when verbally sparring with one of my oldest enemies. We can be civilized while utterly eviscerating one another.

38

ABIGAIL

I make quick work of washing the rest of the paint from my body, but by the time I'm clean and wearing a fresh dress, Dane is gone.

Someone else is in the manor. I heard them call out for Dane before he left me alone in the bathroom.

Or *Daniel,* as they had addressed him.

An old friend? Or a family member?

My first instinct is to scream for help, but no one is in sight.

Are they still here? Surely, they couldn't have left the estate already?

I recall the blood on Dane's face when he found me in the powder blue house, after he "talked to" Ron.

I will always protect you. Always.

If he thought that this unexpected intruder was a threat to me—or to his ownership of me—there's no telling what he might've done to them.

I force in a breath and try to get my brain back online in the wake of his devastating assault in the studio.

The assault that made me come harder than ever before.

Even when he was the masked man, my forbidden pleasure hadn't been so ruthless. Dane's sway over my body is like a hurricane: a destructive but awe-inspiring force of nature.

I shake my head to clear it.

I can't think about that right now. All I have room for in my brain is formulating an escape plan. This might be my only opportunity to get away from the monster who's holding me captive.

I tiptoe out into the portrait-lined corridor and find it empty.

I can't hear so much as murmuring voices in the distance.

Where is he?

If Dane catches me...

My heart hammers in my throat, and I swallow hard against rising panic. There's no time for terror to take hold.

I break into a light jog, making my way toward the grand staircase as quickly and as quietly as possible. When I reach the top of the stairs, I'm met with more silence.

Dane and the anonymous visitor could be anywhere on the estate now. This house is so sprawling that I haven't even begun to explore the extent of it. And there's no guarantee that he's inside.

If I venture into the open, he might see me.

My descent down the stairs is shaky. Somehow, I will my knees to support me, and I make it into the cavernous entry hall. Sunlight pours through the huge windows that frame the front door on either side. And through the windows, the countryside sprawls on for miles. And...

I clap my hand over my mouth to smother my gasp.

There's a Jeep parked in front of the manor. I don't see a silhouette through the passenger window; the vehicle seems empty.

Whoever came to see Dane drove here in this Jeep. And for now, they're both mercifully out of sight and earshot.

Keys. I need keys.

My frantic gaze rakes over my opulent surroundings, and I can scarcely believe my eyes when they catch on a shining silver car key. It's been tossed carelessly on a priceless antique table beside the front door.

For a terrified moment, I eye the key like it's a viper that might strike if I reach for it.

Is this some insane test? Another mindfuck from Dane?

I shake my head and lunge for the key.

It doesn't matter. I have to try, even if it is an awful ruse.

The metal bites into my palm as I clench my fist tightly. I won't let go of this key unless Dane pries it from my fingers.

I throw open the front door, choosing speed over silence. My bare feet crunch across jagged gravel, but I barely feel the pain. I'm at the Jeep in seconds, and I fling open the driver's side door. I climb into the seat and jam the key into the ignition. The engine roars to life.

I barely take the time to sling on my seatbelt before I throw the Jeep in gear and hit the gas. The tires spin in the gravel, and then the vehicle surges forward.

"Abigail!" I hear Dane's roar even over the revving engine, and I cast a fearful glance at the rearview mirror.

He's sprinting out of the house, chasing after me on foot.

As though he could possibly catch me now.

A giddy, mad laugh bubbles through the Jeep, and I increase my speed. Then I see the huge, iron gates ahead. They're closing. He's trying to lock me in.

He wants to keep me caged.

Not fucking happening.

The gates are only bracketed by a short brick wall that doesn't even extend fifty yards on one side. To the left is open countryside. This Jeep is more than capable of navigating the gently rolling hills.

I spin the wheel to the left, racing toward freedom.

My exhilarated laugh morphs into a sharp, short scream when the landscape drops out from under me. I'm airborne for a terrifying instant, and then the hood of the jeep tips downward. Bright green grass fills my view through the windscreen.

Metal crunches, the car horn blares, and pain explodes through my skull before everything goes black.

39

DANE

"Abigail!" I roar her name when the Jeep jerks sharply to the left, away from the closing gates. "NO!"

She doesn't know that the beautiful landscaping has been cut into a blind fence. The feature keeps troublesome sheep out of the estate while providing an uninterrupted view of the countryside. Instead of an unsightly fence, there's sharp a ten-foot drop that's unnoticeable if you don't know to look for it.

And she's racing right toward it.

My feet pound the curated lawn, but I'll never reach her in time. There's nothing I can do to stop her. My stubborn Abigail is about to crash the Jeep, and I can't prevent it from happening.

I can't save her. I can't protect her.

The disaster seems to happen in slow motion, each horrific moment imprinting on my brain to create nightmares that will last a lifetime. The Jeep is airborne for a split second.

Then comes the crash. The screeching metal. The blaring car horn.

I know what I'll find when I reach the wreck.

Blood. Death.

I'm as powerless as I was on that terrible night when I was five years old. Another crash, when I was a helpless child.

The sound that tears from my chest is something between a bellow of rage and a wail of anguish.

I can't lose Abigail.

I won't.

I refuse to live without her.

I swallow the copper tang of fear that coats my tongue and sprint toward the wreck. Whatever I find at the base of the blind fence, I'll have to face it head-on. If Abigail survived, she'll need medical care. She'll need *me.*

I can't allow old memories of long-buried trauma to rise up and consume me. I have to remain grounded in the present.

I have to save her.

She's alive. She's alive. She's alive.

I'm not sure if it's a prayer or an irrefutable truth that I'm willing into the world.

I finally reach the blind fence, and acid burns my throat at the sight of the wrecked Jeep. I curse my feckless brother for his carelessness in leaving his keys where she could easily find them. And for his foolish taste in vintage vehicles that lack modern safety features like airbags. A sensible car would've protected her from the worst of the damage, but this aged behemoth could've crushed her delicate body.

I leap off the blind fence and barely feel the pain that shudders up my left leg as my ankle twists. I manage to stumble toward her. I can see her lovely face in profile. It's covered in blood, and she's slumped over the steering wheel. Her eyes are closed. She's not moving.

Adrenaline increases my strength, lending me the leverage I need to wrench open the door. It screeches in protest, but I manage to get to her.

"Abigail. Abigail. Abigail..." I'm saying her name over and over, but she's not responding.

Her blood is hot and slick on my hand when I gingerly cup her cheek. My stomach turns in pure revulsion at the gory sight, but I force myself to study her wounds with clinical precision. She's bleeding heavily from a gash at her hairline. I can't tell how serious the damage is, but it's enough to have knocked her unconscious.

"Open your eyes, Abigail," I command. "Look at me."

But she doesn't obey.

The longer she remains unconscious, the higher the likelihood of brain damage. She could have a fractured skull. Internal bleeding.

All I can assess now is the fact that she fucking bleeding all over my hands, and she's as limp as a ragdoll.

I struggle to breathe through the fear that smothers my thoughts.

There's a pulse at her throat. She's breathing.

She's alive.

And she's going to be fine. I'll make sure of it.

"Daniel?" James calls down to me. "Oh, fuck."

As much as I loathe him in this moment, my voice is rough with desperation when I beg, "Help me."

~

With James' help, I'm able to get Abigail out of the wrecked Jeep and into another vehicle. I keep her gathered in my arms, murmuring reassurances to her as he drives the short distance from the base of the blind fence to the road.

We're in the back of one of my father's sleek black SUVs. If Abigail had chosen this for her insane escape attempt instead of the Jeep, she'd probably only have a few scratches.

Her escape attempt.

The thought makes my blood run cold. She was so desperate to get away from me that she risked her life. She'd begged me to let her go, but I'd selfishly refused because I didn't want to live without her.

Now that she might be bleeding out in my arms, I'm struck by the sudden, powerful realization that I *can't* live without her.

Abigail has given my life meaning. I won't tolerate a world without her in it.

I won't be able to endure it.

My vision blurs strangely, and I blink quickly to clear the burn from the corners of my eyes.

"Are you listening to me?" James demands. "The nearest hospital is almost twenty minutes away."

"She needs medical attention," I growl.

I'll do anything to save her, even if that means walking into a hospital and confessing my crimes against her.

"You're a fucking doctor," James shoots back. "We have first aid facilities at the house."

My mind races. The faster I get Abigail medical care, the better. I'm one of the best surgeons of my age. I'll care for her with far greater attention than she'll get at hospital.

Because our survival depends on her recovery.

Abigail has a deep cut on her forehead, but it won't scar, thanks to my neat stitches. The damage seems to be a flesh wound rather than a cranial fracture. Seeing her covered in blood had made me irrational, but now that she's stitched up and resting, I'm somewhat more composed.

She has bruised ribs and whiplash from the seatbelt cutting into her torso.

She'll be in pain for a while, but she'll live.

She will be okay.

And I will spend every day of the rest of my life making this up to her.

She stirs on my bed with a low groan, and I give her hand a gentle squeeze.

"You're safe, Abigail."

I'm right here, I want to add, but I swallow the reassurance.

When I'd washed the paint off her face, she'd said that she needed someone to protect her from me. My presence isn't a comfort to her.

But still, I can't let her go.

I know now that she's utterly essential to me; I can scarcely breathe at just the thought of losing her.

I rake my free hand through my hair. I've never felt so lost, so helpless. I don't know how to fix things between us. I can heal her body, but I fear I've done deeper, irreparable damage to her. To us.

"You're in love with her." James' quiet observation hits me like a blow to the gut.

I round on him with a glower. He doesn't understand the first thing about me. No one in my family has ever understood.

I'm not capable of love.

Obsession, yes. Possessiveness, definitely.

And above all, selfishness.

My absolute devotion to Abigail will have to be enough for her, because love is something I can never offer.

James holds up his hands in a show of surrender. "Fine. It's none of my business. I'll leave her in your capable hands now. And don't worry. I'm not going to run to Mum and Dad to tell them you're here. Let her recover fully before you go anywhere. I don't owe you anything, brother, but she doesn't deserve to be pulled into our family drama."

I narrow my eyes at him, usure if I should believe this show of goodwill. "And you're not curious about why she was driving away from me?"

He shrugs. "Like I said: none of my business. You're an arsehole. I'm not surprised you did something to make her pissed enough to leave you. But, Daniel." He pierces me with a dark green stare. "You can't keep her forever if she doesn't want to stay."

"You're absolutely right," I snarl. "My relationship with Abigail is none of your fucking business."

He sighs. "Arsehole."

I turn my attention back to my sleeping princess and barely register his retreating footsteps. For the foreseeable future, I'll have Abigail all to myself. I'll take care of her in her recovery. I'll prove to her that she can trust me.

She will love me again.

She has to.

40

ABIGAIL

The enormous weight of my failure makes my chest ache.

Or maybe that's the bruised ribs.

I barely managed to sleep through the night due to the fact that my entire body feels battered.

And the anxiety of sharing a bedroom with my assailant made me afraid to close my eyes. Even if Dane slept on a cramped, antique chaise that's far too small for him and doesn't look remotely comfortable.

When he stirred a few minutes ago, I closed my eyes and feigned sleep until he disappeared into the bathroom. I scarcely dared to breathe until I heard the shower running, and I knew that I was mercifully free of his presence for a short time.

I'm not ready for another confrontation. I'm not sure what he plans to do with me now that I tried to run away from him.

He'll probably find some other unfathomably sadistic way to make me suffer for daring to defy him.

I'm alone with him again on this vast estate. I have vague memories of another man hovering around my bedside yesterday. A man who closely resembled Dane, other than his auburn hair. They share the same striking, deep green eyes.

His brother was here.

And now, he's gone.

Did Dane hurt him? Did he make him disappear?

I shudder at the thought and suppress a wince at the answering flare of pain in my chest.

Surely, Dane's not capable of harming a member of his own family, even if they are estranged.

The latch on the bathroom door clicks, and I quickly close my eyes again.

"Abigail." He's using his disarming, bedside manner voice again. It's horrifically tempting to find comfort in it. "I need you to open your eyes. You hit your head hard enough to black out. I'll have to run some cognitive tests for a few days."

"I'm fine," I insist.

I don't want to interact with him at all if I can avoid it.

I hear him inhale deeply, as though he's struggling to maintain his calm demeanor.

"I need you to cooperate. Please." The last word is short and sharp, as though he's unfamiliar with the shape of it on his tongue.

I finally open my eyes and meet his gaze with defiance. "No commands this morning?" I ask bitterly. "What new mindfuck game do I have to endure now?"

His eyes flash with green fire, but his face remains impassive. "This isn't a game. You're injured. I'm going to take care of you."

"If I was hurt so badly, why am I not in a hospital?" I challenge.

He's too selfishly possessive even to take me for emergency medical care.

"It was too far away, and I ascertained that I'm capable of treating you here."

I glower at him. "At least be honest with me. You're too scared that if you take me to a hospital, I'll tell someone what you've done to me. You'll go to jail, and you don't want to risk that."

A shadow flickers at his jaw. "No one will care for you like I do."

I scoff. "Is that what you're telling yourself to justify this? I could've died, Dane. And you wouldn't have—"

"I know you could've died!" he thunders.

I cringe back into my pillows. I've never seen him so... feral. He's more unpredictable than ever, and fear prickles down my spine.

His entire body stiffens, as though he's willing himself not to move a muscle. I note that he hasn't approached the bed; he's maintaining several feet of distance between us.

Because he thinks he might hurt me? How tenuous is his control over his anger?

"Do you know how I..." He trails off and rakes a hand through his hair in a gesture of frustration I've rarely seen. "I can't lose you, Abigail."

"You mean you won't let me go," I counter acerbically.

He shakes his head, but it's not a denial. He looks almost weary. "I can't."

That's the only answer he offers me before he finally steps toward me. I flinch away. A scowl tugs at his handsome features, but he quickly smooths it away to a more clinical, calm expression.

"I'm going to do some tests now." It's a declaration, not a request.

So, we're back to subtle commands. He might try to pretend he's a good, compassionate man, but it's far too late for me to believe that carefully curated lie. He'll never ask me for anything; he'll simply tell me what to do. He expects mindless obedience, a pretty pet.

The pounding in my head is becoming too acute for me to argue further. Dane is a doctor, and there's no one else here to help me. After the crash, it would be stupid to deny medical treatment.

There will be time for defiance later. I won't try to physically attack him again, but I can go back to my original plan: make him grow bored of me.

I allow him to carry out the cognitive tests, and he seems satisfied with my responses.

"Where's your brother?" I dare to ask once he's finished.

His lips twist with distaste, but there's not so much as a flicker of guilt in his eyes. Either he's deeply psychopathic, or he didn't hurt his own kin.

With Dane, it's difficult to judge the situation. He's made it abundantly clear that he's a psychopath. What I'm unsure of is the depth of his condition. At times, he does seem to mean it when he's tender with me.

But that could be another part of his elaborate ruse, his sick mind games.

"James is back at his lodge in Wensleydale," Dane replies coolly. "He won't bother us again."

My brows lift. Maybe Dane isn't the only crazy one in the family.

"And he didn't care that you're holding me captive?"

The tiniest hint at a frown ghosts around his mouth, but he quickly catches it and returns to his calm demeanor.

"I didn't give him the details of our arrangement. He knows that you're mine, and he knows that you were badly hurt. We're safe to stay here until you fully recover."

"And then what?" I press. "What happens once I recover?"

He fixes me with a level stare. "That's up to you."

I press my lips together. I know he doesn't mean that I'll have the option to leave. He thinks he'll break me in the time it takes me to get better, and then I'll meekly follow wherever he leads.

"What do you plan to do to me in the meantime?" I challenge.

I won't give him a reason to assault me again, but that doesn't mean he won't expect sex.

"I plan to take care of you," he grits out. "You have nothing to fear from me. I'll prove it to you. Let me."

I huff out an incredulous breath. Is he really commanding me to trust him?

I don't bother to tell him that's not how trust works.

"I scared you yesterday," he says quietly. "I understand that now. You weren't ready, and I pushed you anyway. I didn't know how being together like that would upset you."

"You think I like it," I fling his sickening words back at him. "I don't."

His jaw tightens. "Now's not the time for this conversation. I don't want to argue. You need to rest and recover."

I bristle at the fact that he's essentially telling me to shut up again, but I swallow more defiant words.

He's right. I do need to recover. I can't get out of this nightmare if I'm injured.

"I'll get you something to eat," he says. "Food, then painkillers. I don't want to see you suffering."

Again, it's all about what he wants. Not the fact that I'm in pain. He's incapable of true empathy.

I close my eyes again, shutting him out in the only way that I can. He doesn't make a sound for several long seconds, but finally, I hear him stomp out of the bedroom.

I know my reprieve will be short; he'll come back with breakfast in a few minutes. Without his infuriating presence to draw my ire, pain consumes me.

AFTER BREAKFAST, the painkillers finally start to take effect. I ease back into the pillows, cushioned in fluffy clouds. The absence of pain is almost euphoric, and some part of me registers that I'm probably a little high from the strength of the drugs he gave me.

But I'll take the dulled awareness over the pounding in my head and sharp stabs at my ribs with every shallow breath.

"Screen time is inadvisable," Dane says. "I'll read to you so you don't get bored."

I blink and manage to focus on him. He's sitting on the too-small, pale blue chaise, his massive body almost comically oversized for the delicate antique.

I instantly recognize the book he's holding, even though his hand conceals most of the title.

The Invisible Life of Addie LaRue.

"Why do you have my favorite book?"

He cuts his eyes away. "I think you know."

Yes, some part of me did already know. He's broken into

my apartment. He must've seen the book at the top of my stack.

Uncomfortable silence stretches between us. I don't have to reply or ask more questions.

He's my stalker, my attacker.

And yet, when he starts reading aloud in that deep, rumbling voice, I sink into the familiar story.

It's so much easier than facing the horrors of my reality.

"You'll want a bath. You'll have to be careful with your stitches, but you can get properly cleaned up."

My stomach turns. "I have no interest in getting naked with you."

His nostrils flare with irritation. "I didn't ask you to get naked with me."

"No, you didn't ask at all. Do you even know how to make a request? How to ask for my consent?"

He sighs. "I'm tired of arguing. It doesn't have to be so contentious between us."

I lift my brows at him but don't say anything in response. I will not make life easy for him.

"I don't intend to bathe you, as much as I would like to." At least he's honest enough to make the admission, even if he is making a concession for once. "You need to rest and recover. I'm not going to cause you distress."

"Of course," I say dully. "This is about making sure your pet recovers."

He sighs again, a more exasperated exhalation. "I do want you to recover, Abigail. Is that so terrible?"

"Depending on your reasoning, yes. It can be."

"My only desire is to see you healthy and whole. Your pain is unbearable to me."

I eye him with suspicion. It almost sounds as though he truly cares.

But I can't trust a word that leaves his lips.

I am in pain, and I do want a bath. After the crash yesterday, I was too woozy take care of myself, and Dane was merciful enough not to bathe me.

"It's been over twenty-four hours since you hit your head," he says, the reasonable doctor. "I'll need to monitor you closely for the next few days, but you're well enough to see to your own essential needs. However." That one word fills me with dread. "I don't intend to leave you completely on your own. You're still a fall risk."

I eye him warily. "What are you planning to do to me?"

Something like pain tightens his features. Have I managed to wound him?

"I'm going to help you walk to the bathroom," he explains, soft and placating. "Nothing more."

I grit my teeth and accept his help getting to my feet. After a brief dizzy spell, I'm able to walk the few steps to the ensuite. He hovers at my side, allowing me a modicum of personal space while remaining close enough to catch me if I stumble.

It's almost as though he's keeping a respectful distance.

I don't know how to process that, and my head hurts too much to puzzle it out.

When I enter the bathroom, he doesn't leave, but he does turn his back.

"I'll be right here if you need me." He says it like a reassurance.

And maybe it is. I don't want to be with him, but he's not

forcing himself on me. He's remaining nearby in case I get dizzy again.

I can't succumb to his tender care. It's rooted in selfishness, not true concern for me. If he really cared, he would take me to a hospital. He would walk away and never show his face again.

But I know that won't happen.

So, I strip and carefully step into the bathtub, which is already filled with warm water. Dane set it up for me.

He doesn't care, I remind myself.

I can't forget his true nature for one second.

Even when he retrieves the worn copy of *Addie LaRue* where it was waiting on the sink and begins to read to me.

It's not my own copy—I've memorized every crack in the spine of my beloved book.

That means Dane's the one who's worn down the book in his hands. How many times has he read it?

It's another puzzle that I can't bear to contemplate for long.

He's not the only one who's tired of arguing.

I relax into the warm water and allow my mind to drift as his voice fills the room in a cultured, soothing cadence.

41

ABIGAIL

The studio is the only place in the manor where Dane leaves me alone. Over the last three weeks, it's become my personal haven.

Otherwise, he's a constant presence—he cooks every meal for me, cleans up after us, and reads to me for hours. We've moved on from *Addie LaRue* to one of my favorite fantasy romance trilogies. He doesn't seem to mind the romantic content, and the steamy scenes read aloud in his deep voice makes something flutter between my legs despite my best efforts.

He hasn't tried to touch me more than absolutely necessary in that time, and he's slept on the tiny chaise every night. He says he doesn't want to disturb my sleep, but sometimes I wonder if he has other reasons for giving me space.

My plan from the very beginning was to make him understand that I will never love him again. Perhaps my escape attempt—and the desperate risk I took—has given him some perspective. It might actually be sinking in that I don't feel anything for him but loathing and resentment.

I can see that it bothers him.

Good.

He deserves to feel disturbed for what he's done to me.

I'm not delusional enough to think he experiences guilt, but he does seem uncomfortable and off-balance around me in a way I never would've expected.

I've spent long days in the studio working through my physical pain so that I can spend time at my easel.

Dr. Graham approves of my efforts to return to gentle daily activities as part of my recovery, even if he does appear genuinely bothered by my winces at sudden movements. A few times, he's reached for me during particularly intense spikes of pain, but he always withdraws when I flinch.

Today, I'm putting the finishing touches on the painting I've struggled to express on my canvas. The agony of it was far deeper than the ache in my ribs when I lifted my arm or shifted my weight too quickly.

I set my brush down and sit back, taking in my work. It hasn't been a cathartic project; it's been an act of anguish.

But it's finished. I can show it to Dane now.

I cross the parquet floor and open the door to the portrait-lined corridor.

"Dane?" I call out.

Heavy footfalls immediately rush toward me. He appears out of his bedroom and storms down the corridor. His dark brows are drawn together, and his eyes are almost feverish with worry.

"What's wrong?"

I take a step back from his potent aura. I don't understand him when he's like this, and it scares me. I can't predict his actions when he shows a semblance of human emotion. Will he tackle me to the floor again and force himself on me in a moment of twisted passion? Or will he snap back to his cold, clinical default state? Both are equally terrifying.

I swallow hard, and he halts as though he's hit a brick wall, stopping several feet away from me. His beautiful eyes rake over my body, assessing me for signs of injury. Then his shoulders slump slightly.

"You're all right."

"I have something to show you," I say instead of responding.

I'm not all right. My heart throbs as though it's as battered and bruised as my body after the crash. The painstaking work of finishing my painting has left me wrung out and emotionally exhausted, but I have to see this through.

I take another step back, but this time, I'm welcoming him to enter the studio. The moment he sets eyes on my art, he freezes again.

"Abigail..." He breathes my name. "What is this?"

"It's me," I answer quietly.

On the canvas, I've captured all of my pain and impotent rage, my fear and desperation. My face is contorted in an anguished scream, and blood drips from my split lips. My face is bruised almost beyond recognition, and my fingers are knotted in my hair, tearing at the delicate strands. More bruises encircle my throat—the violent marks from Dane's fingers imprinted on my pale skin.

"Why?" he asks, his gaze transfixed on the disturbing image like it's a car crash he can't look away from.

"This is what you did to me." It's meant to be a flat statement of fact, but the lump in my throat makes the words strained.

"No," he refuses. "You're getting better. You're healing. This didn't happen in the wreck."

"It's how I feel inside." Tears burn my cheeks. I blink rapidly, but I can't stop the steady stream as my tumultuous emotions leak out of me.

He shakes his head sharply, a willful rejection of the truth. "I know men have hurt you," he growls. "I know you've felt shame and self-loathing. I never want you to think of yourself this way."

"No, Dane. This is what *you* did to me."

He rounds on me, and I can't help cringing away. His entire body coils tight, and I'm not sure if he's preparing to launch himself at me or if he's wrestling with his own shadows of emotion. The only ones he's capable of experiencing.

"I would never hurt you," he vows. "Never."

"You have hurt me more deeply than anyone in my life. Worse than Tom when he raped me. Worse than my family with their years of psychological and emotional abuse. You made me believe I loved you, but it was all a manipulation to get me into your bed. It was all a sick game to you." I dash the tears from my cheeks so I can look him squarely in the eye. "You broke my heart, Dane. You broke *me.*"

His skin is unusually pale, and he looks like he might vomit. "I wouldn't. I haven't."

"Look at me." I gesture at the painting. "Look at what you've done to me, and tell me you would never hurt me. Tell me you truly believe that you haven't shattered me. Lie to us both if you want, but I'm done being gaslighted by you."

He stares at the painting again and shakes his head. Then he stares some more. The silence is thick between us, and I let him stew in it.

I'd expected to feel vindication in this moment, but all I feel is soul-deep grief.

Grief for what I thought we could be together, and for the devastating loss of love when I learned the truth about Dane.

"I wanted to die," he rasps.

"What?" I ask faintly.

He finally turns to face me, and his eyes are dark with agony. "When you crashed the Jeep, I thought..." He swallows hard. "All that blood. You weren't moving. You didn't answer me when I said your name."

His jaw firms, and he fixes me with a fiery stare that's so intense I can hardly bear to maintain eye contact.

"If you had died, I would've opened my veins and laid down right next to you. I realized that truth in the moment I thought I'd lost you."

Shock punches me when he drops to his knees and takes my chilled hands in both of his. My fingers are trembling, but not from fear.

"I told you I can't live without you. I mean it in the truest sense of the words. You've made me *feel* for the first time in my life. I wasn't living before I met you. My life has no meaning without you in it."

My lips are parted on panting breaths, as though I've been sprinting for miles rather than standing frozen in the beautiful studio that he made for me.

"I know I've hurt you. I can see that now. I will spend every day of the rest of my life making it up to you. Name anything you want, and I'll give it to you. I'll give you the world, Abigail. I would give you the blood from my veins. I would give you my heart, but I can't promise you something I don't have. You want the organ that keeps me alive? I'll cut it out of my chest for you. Because without you, I don't need it."

He rubs his thumbs over my chilled knuckles. "I'm scaring you. I don't want to, but I won't lie to you. I'm obsessive and cruel and every bit as selfish as I've ever said. I won't ask you to forgive me. I can at least spare you that selfish request." He lifts my hands and kisses my palms with reverence. "I'll be better for you, Abigail. I will never be worthy of you, but I'll be better. I swear."

His pain pierces my heart like a knife, twisting and shredding. Even after everything he's done to me, bearing witness to his anguish is my own form of agony.

I want him to be the man I fell in love with so badly.

And this version of Dane who's on his knees before me looks so much like him.

I know deep in my bones that this isn't a trick. It's not another manipulation.

He said he would die without me, and I believe him.

I don't know how to process it.

I hate him for what he's done to me, but how can I still feel yearning for the man who assaulted me?

The depth of his obsession is terrifying. His confession should only make me more wary of him, but my tattered heart tugs toward his in an echo of the love I used to feel.

"I don't know what to say," I finally admit on a shaky whisper.

He grasps my hands closer to his chest. "You don't have to say anything. You don't owe me anything. I'm the one who should speak now. And I want to say I'm sorry. I'm so fucking sorry I hurt you like this. Never again. I swear."

I'm stunned at his apology. It seems impossible, surreal, that Dane is on his knees telling me he's sorry. I didn't think he was capable of remorse.

But he's still not promising to let me go if that's what I ask of him. He said he won't live without me. That means I have no hope of escape.

My heart breaks all over again.

I'm still trapped with the madman who wears my love's face. And his devotion to me is more fanatical than I ever could've imagined.

He'll keep me in this gilded cage forever, and I fear that one day, I may no longer want to fly away.

He reaches up and brushes the tears from my cheeks with his thumbs.

"I don't want to make you cry."

Now I'm the one sinking to my knees. They're too shaky to support me. My chest convulses on a harsh sob.

I want him, and I hate myself for it. No one has ever cared about me the way Dane does. It's tempting and terrifying in equal measure.

His arms close around me, strong enough to support me but gentle with my healing body. True to his word, he's not causing me an ounce of physical pain.

My tormented soul is another matter entirely.

"I've got you," he promises.

"I know." I choke on another sob. "I know."

42

DANE

Blood. So much blood. It's splattered across my face in droplets that are beginning to cool. It's wet and sticky on my hands where I'm grasping my sister's dress. I'm shaking her, screaming at her.

Katie isn't breathing. She doesn't answer when I say her name over and over again.

How can she answer when half her face is missing?

A car horn blares incessantly, deafening me. I shake my head sharply, as though I can toss the maddening sound from my ears.

I can't escape from it. My seatbelt is stuck.

If it weren't, I would've tumbled into my sister.

The Jeep is on its side. We rolled off the country lane and down a steep hill when my father took a particularly fast corner.

I don't know how long we've been here, but it's dark outside, and my voice is raw from screaming.

No one has come to save us.

No one has come to save Katie.

My father is slumped over the steering wheel. It's not an unfa-

miliar sight to see him passed out after a night of drinking, but this time, there's a thick crimson stream that flows down his slack face.

The car horn rings in my ears. I'm clawing at them, raking my hands through my hair as though I can pull the sound from my mind.

Katie is looking at me with one eye, but she doesn't see me. She doesn't see anything.

I cry out for help, for salvation, for mercy.

Anything to escape this nightmare.

After a while, I go quiet. I accept that no one will come for me.

No one will bring my twin sister back to me.

I don't yet know a word for what's happened to her, but I know she's gone forever.

The doctor won't be able to fix her.

There's nothing I can do. I'm powerless. Helpless.

Alone.

"Dane." A soft hand shakes my shoulder.

I grab the delicate wrist and force the tender touch away.

Abigail reels back into the shadows of my bedroom. I shove upright off the cramped chaise and blink hard to focus on the present.

I run a hand over my face and find that my brow is slick with sweat.

"I'm sorry," I murmur into my palm. "I didn't mean to lash out at you."

I'm not ready to face Abigail. Not when she'll look at me with fear in her eyes.

"You were having a nightmare," she says gently.

The bedside lamp turns on, chasing the shadows away. I keep my face in my hand and apply pressure to my closed eyes, as though I can wipe the macabre images from my mind.

"You're shaking," she observes, voice soft.

I rub my temples and keep my eyes closed. "I'm fine. Like you said. It was just a bad dream. Go back to sleep. I'm sorry I woke you."

"Who's Katie?"

I freeze. No one has said my sister's name aloud since her funeral. Certainly not in this house.

She deserves better than that. She deserves to be remembered.

And I've spent years trying to forget.

I haven't thought about that crash in a long time, and nightmares about it haven't troubled me since I was a child. I never needed to be coddled or comforted when I was distressed in the middle of the night; I learned to overcome the fear on my own.

Comfort wouldn't have been forthcoming, anyway.

"My sister," I admit. "My twin."

"I didn't know you have a sister. You've never mentioned her."

"That's because she's dead." The words are flat and utterly devoid of emotion. "She died when she was five years old."

Her small gasp makes something twist in the center of my chest.

"I'm so sorry." She sounds like she really means it. My sweet, compassionate Abigail. "You were having a nightmare about her? You said her name in your sleep."

I press my lips together for a moment, reticent to reveal the terrible extent of it. My father's carelessness. My mother's coldness. The fact that they replaced my dead sister with James and acted as though she never existed.

But Abigail doesn't have an ounce of cruelty in her. She won't dismiss Katie's memory as an inconvenience.

I can trust my little dove.

"I was dreaming about the night she died," I say after a long, heavy pause.

"You were there?" Abigail's voice is soft with horror. "When you were only five?"

I nod absently, detaching myself from the volatility of that night and looking at the memory with cool, clinical eyes.

It can't hurt me if I don't relive it.

"My father was driving drunk. A bad habit of his. He thinks he doesn't have to follow the law when it's inconvenient to him. He was driving us through the Dales when he took a corner too sharply. The Jeep rolled a few times. My father was unconscious for several hours. Katie didn't make it."

"Dane..."

My name wavers, and I finally look up at Abigail to find that her eyes are shining with tears.

Tears for my sister.

For my loss.

My chest aches, and it's all I can do not to reach for her when I know she'll recoil again.

"Is that why you..." She trails off and then tries again. "When I crashed the Jeep. I understand why that must've been so upsetting for you. I didn't know."

I try to shrug, but it's a sharp movement to throw off her empathy. I can't allow her emotions to bring out the new feelings she evokes in me.

Not when it comes to this.

Because if I feel what I felt that night, it'll destroy me.

Maybe it already has.

Then, by some miracle, she's closing the distance between

us. She sinks down onto the chaise beside me and places a tentative hand on my knee.

I can't help grasping it and pressing her palm directly over my aching heart. She doesn't pull away.

"When I saw you covered in blood..." My breath shudders. "I wasn't rational. I was consumed by the fear of losing you. If James hadn't snapped me the fuck out of it, I wouldn't have been able to help you. I'm sorry."

"You did help me," she says with the weight of a promise. "You healed me and took care of me. You are taking care of me. I'm right here, Dane."

She places her other hand on my cheek, and I forget how to breathe.

"What you went through is terrible. No one should endure that."

"I couldn't save her," I confess. "I didn't know how to fix her."

"You were a child." Her thumb caresses my cheekbone, keeping me grounded to her. "Is that why you became a doctor? So you can fix people?"

I try to scoff. "I've told you before that there's nothing altruistic about my career."

"But you could, if you wanted to," she counters quietly. "You have the knowledge to save someone if they're seriously injured. You saved me."

I wish that were true. I want to be the man she's describing, but it's just not who I am.

"You were never in danger of dying. I just patched you up."

"But you didn't know that when you first found me in the Jeep. You said there was a lot of blood. I was unconscious. I know that must've been traumatic for you." She increases the pressure of her hand over my heart. "I'm safe now, Dane. You can breathe."

Bright, hot hope sparks in my chest.

She said she's safe with me.

Before, she'd said that she needed protecting from me.

Has something changed her mind?

I scour my recent memories to understand this change in her. Maybe my unnervingly intense apology hadn't frightened her like I thought. Yesterday afternoon—after she showed me her nightmarish self-portrait—I'd thought she'd been distressed. I overwhelmed her and made her break down sobbing.

No. That can't be what's changed her mind, no matter how sincere my apology was.

It must be this: the fact that I've told her my worst trauma.

I've made myself vulnerable with her.

The power she holds over me should be terrifying, but I want her too badly to care. She's looking at me with that clear, open gaze for the first time since I brought her to England. She *sees* me in a way no one else ever has. No one has ever bothered to try.

I obey her gentle urging and draw in a deep breath. Calm settles over me, and my eyes droop closed with a sudden wash of exhaustion.

Her hand turns in mine, pulling away from my chest. My fingers tighten around hers, but she's not trying to escape me; she's urging me to follow.

"You should sleep in the bed," she says. "That chaise can't be comfortable."

I look at her with wonder. Is she offering me absolution? Or at least acceptance?

I scarcely dare to hope.

"I don't want you to pity me."

"This isn't pity," she assures me and climbs into bed, making room for me beside her.

I join her before she can change her mind. She scoots back slightly, and I get the message: I can sleep beside her, but she still wants space.

I can give her that.

For now.

I'll win her back, no matter how vulnerable I have to make myself. Nothing matters but having her.

"My father likes to drink too," she says after we settle down, inches apart. "And he doesn't care who he hurts when he's drunk. Usually, it's verbal cruelty. But it still hurts." She places her delicate hand over mine again, the lightest contact. "I'm sorry for your loss. I'm sorry about Katie."

Just the sound of someone else saying her name in this house, acknowledging her existence, is enough to make my eyes burn strangely.

"Thank you. I am too."

Another beat of silence passes before I growl, "You said *usually*. Has your father ever laid a hand on you?"

"I don't think we should talk about this."

"Why not?"

She's looking at me with that clear-eyed gaze again, and it takes everything in me not to glance away from the power of her guileless stare.

"Because I don't know what you might do to him if I tell you."

That answer is enough to seal his fate, but she won't want to hear that.

"I'm serious, Dane." She reads me so easily. "You can't hurt my father."

I decide to bargain with her. "I won't, if you tell me what he did."

She considers me for a long moment, assessing my honesty. Whatever she sees in my expression, she must decide that she believes me.

"It hasn't happened since I was about ten," she begins. "But he used to belt me if I disappointed him. Or angered him. He got angry a lot when he was drinking. At some point, I guess he decided I was too old to discipline me like that anymore. The cruelty was verbal after that. He would yell, and then my mother would dictate the terms of my punishments."

"And what did she do to *punish* you?" I can't quite keep the dangerous edge from the question.

"You can't hurt my mother either."

I growl, then catch myself. "Fine. I won't hurt anyone in your family. No matter how much they deserve to suffer."

"Swear it."

I narrow my eyes at her. I don't want to agree to this blanket pardon of her loathsome relatives.

But she would be troubled by their suffering. She's so soft-hearted and good to her core. She would shed tears even for her abusers, just like she said she cried over her rapist's death.

I won't allow the monsters who raised her to cause her one more shred of grief. And she would grieve them if I killed them for her. She would probably feel responsible.

I won't do that to her.

"I swear I won't hurt anyone in your family."

She nods, accepting my promise.

"My mother's punishments were erratic," she admits. "Sometimes, I wouldn't be allowed to leave the house for a week. Other times, a simple slap to the face was enough to satisfy her. There was no rational pattern to the severity of the consequences."

"The chaos was designed to keep you on edge." Her mother is a narcissistic piece of shit. I'd known as much after spending five minutes in her presence at Meadows' wedding.

But learning the extent of her cruelty to my Abigail is enough to make me see red.

"Dane." My name is laced with warning, and I realize my hand has fisted beneath hers.

I force my muscles to relax.

"I'm not in that house anymore," she reminds me. "She can't hurt me."

"And you'll never step foot inside it again." I try to keep the ring of command from my tone, but I don't quite succeed.

"I don't intend to."

"I'll protect you from them," I vow. "I'll make sure they never bother you again."

"You can't guarantee that," she counters, but she doesn't seem troubled by my fierce countenance. "I can handle them."

I remember the way she wilted like a cut flower in her mother's presence at the wedding.

"You don't have to handle them alone. Not anymore."

She stares at me for a while, and I realize she's not going to respond to my intense declaration.

"We should get some sleep," she says instead. "I'll be here if you have another nightmare and want to talk."

I marvel at how she's softened toward me.

Maybe she won't hate me forever.

Maybe she'll love me again one day.

43

ABIGAIL

I*'m safe now, Dane.*

I can hardly believe I said those words to him last night. They'd been automatic, an irrepressible urge to comfort him in the wake of his nightmare about losing his sister.

But had I meant it?

Yesterday, he confessed that he would die without me. The man who fell to his knees and literally offered me his heart wouldn't hurt me. He wouldn't be capable of it.

Nothing will erase the pain he's caused me. Nothing can undo the stalking and kidnapping. The lies and the heartbreak.

But I don't think he'll hurt me again.

When he first brought me to England, I railed at him that he was tormenting me, that he was my own personal monster. He hadn't listened. Convincing him that he'd wronged me seemed impossible.

Now, he's apologized. He acknowledged that he caused

me immense pain. And it was so much more than a simple *I'm sorry*.

I'll be better for you, Abigail. I will never be worthy of you, but I'll be better. I swear.

And last night, he was so raw. He told me how he watched his twin sister die because of his father's carelessness. He welcomed my comforting touch, as though he needed to feel me.

I thought he was a complete psychopath. But he does seem to feel something for me. Maybe it's every bit as cruelly possessive and obsessive as he claimed. That doesn't change the fact that my ravaged heart feels tethered to his by a gossamer thread.

We both have emotional wounds inflicted by our families. It was one of the first things that bonded me to him.

That had nothing to do with his stalking, nothing to do with the thrilling fear I experienced around him—the fizzy sensation I'd mistaken for lust.

This part of our connection has always been real: we've both been subject to abuse.

It made me kind, but it made him cold.

I never want to hurt anyone the way my parents hurt me. But Dane seems to have shut off his feelings entirely to avoid the pain.

He was only five years old when he watched his sister die. I can't imagine the psychological damage that inflicts on a child.

"What are you thinking about?" Dane's eyeing me almost warily.

I realize I've fallen a few steps behind him, and I've been staring at him like I can peer into his mind if I just look hard enough.

I cut my gaze away and study the stunning landscape. We're walking along a vaguely marked footpath through an idyllic field dotted with sheep.

Dr. Graham has deemed that I'm well enough for light exercise, and I jumped at the chance to explore the countryside. For weeks, the views from the manor's windows have been tempting me to paint the rolling hills, but I was too focused on my anguished self-portrait.

"Can we talk more about last night?" I ask after a moment.

He pauses, then leans back against a dry-stone wall. His posture is casual, but there's a defensiveness in his crossed arms.

"What do you want to know?"

I know this topic will be painful for him, but I have to understand him better. And not just so that I can formulate an escape plan. I'm starting to accept that I simply long to know everything about him.

Some secret part of me wants to justify opening my heart to him.

I'm nowhere near loving him again, but I do feel compassion for him.

And yearning for the man who knelt before me and promised to give me the world. All he wants is me. The knowledge is heady and terribly tempting. I've been alone for so long, and Dane promises complete and utter devotion.

I consider my next question carefully. I could ask why he decided to assault me as the masked man again, but I fear that his answers will be the same as before. He thinks it was the best way to win my heart.

That subject is too painful to contemplate, so instead, I ask, "What were your parents like with you? After Katie died?"

His brow furrows. "Why would you ask me that?"

"I told you how my family treated me when I was a child. Is it too much to ask for the same in return?"

He manages a halfhearted smile. "Do you promise not to kill them if I tell you?"

It's not funny, but I return his smile, my lips twisting with sorrow for the abused child he used to be.

"I promise," I vow needlessly. His family is in no danger from me, no matter how awful they are. I hope to never meet them.

"They didn't beat me, if that's what you're asking," he says, tone light.

"That is what I'm asking," I confirm. "So, what did they do to you, Dane?"

His eyes focus on something beyond me. "It was the opposite of what you experienced. Your father belted you, and your mother punished you. They controlled you with physical and verbal violence."

"What's the opposite of that?" I press.

"Complete indifference. Duty and expectation. Raising me like I was nothing more than an extension of their own vanity. Everything for appearances, nothing real. Nothing raw."

"No emotions," I surmise.

He sneers. "What good are emotions if there's no one there to bear witness to them? Why bother with the theatrics when you're alone? Why suffer through them when they're of no consequence?"

My heart bleeds for him. For years, I've felt so alone.

His damage matches mine, even if it shaped him differently.

Suddenly, he pushes away from the wall and closes the

distance between us. He takes my hands in his, but he doesn't force me closer.

"You *see* me, Abigail. Ever since the night we first met. You make me feel things I never thought possible. No one has ever given me that gift. I don't think anyone else can. There's only you. You're all that matters to me."

Longing floods my chest in a surging wave that's strong enough to make my healed ribs ache. My head tips back, and for the first time in weeks, I allow myself to truly breathe in his salt-kissed cedarwood scent. Comfort blankets me, even as my body heats in response to the scent memory.

Before the terrible night I stepped into the powder blue house, this was all I wanted: Dane's arms enfolding me, keeping me safe and giving me more pleasure than I imagined possible.

I still want that. I still want him.

Not the monster who kidnapped me.

Not even the man I thought I loved back in Charleston.

But *this* man: the real Dane.

Nothing about him is a lie. He's raw and vulnerable. He can't live without me.

"What are you thinking?" he asks me again. He's staring at me so intently that I shiver like his gaze is a palpable caress on my soul.

"I don't want to think anymore."

It's foolish, reckless. But I cup his beautiful face in both hands and draw him toward me for a fierce kiss. I don't stop to consider what this means. What the consequences may be.

I melt into him, wrapping my arms around his shoulders to pull him even closer.

He meets me with the hungry growl that makes my insides quiver with fear-edged delight. His lips are so decadently soft on mine, worshipping the shape of my mouth. Tasting me with teasing flicks of his tongue, testing my welcome.

I open for him on a sigh, completely surrendering to my desire for him.

His tongue surges into my mouth, claiming me in deep, domineering strokes. I'm dizzy from his kiss, the passion we share.

How could any woman give this up? How can I walk away from such perfect chemistry?

He no longer allows me room to resist, and I don't want to. His arms are iron around me, immovable but cradling my body with care. One hand grasps my nape in a firm grip, holding me in place so he can ravage my mouth.

My fingers spear into his thick, midnight hair, and I drag him to me, urging him to take me more deeply. I share every breath with him, and my heart races for him.

Rain begins to fall, and I welcome the cooling mist on our heated skin. It dampens his hair, and the thick, short waves tighten into loose curls. I twine them around my fingers, reveling in the feel of him against me.

It feels like a cruel eternity has passed since our last kiss. I'm a different woman than I was then. This is a different life.

One that I'm sharing with him, whether it's by my own choice or by his will.

In this moment, I choose to be with him. To stop twisting myself in knots and just let go.

And it feels so blissful that my eyes sting with the force of my emotional release. I close them and kiss him like I need him more than oxygen.

The rain is falling in fat, cool drops, and I shiver despite the heat between us.

Dane breaks the kiss, fixing me with a cocky smirk at the sound of my small whimper of protest.

"Let's get out of the rain. Come on."

"I don't mind," I insist, wanting to stay in this surreal, peaceful bubble with him for a while longer. "It's at least half an hour to walk back to the house. We're wet anyway."

"There's shelter nearby. The rain will pass soon, and then we can walk back." He grasps my hand and starts walking. "No more arguing, Abigail."

I huff out a breath, but I don't really feel annoyed. I'm still burning for him, and I remember the pleasure I used to experience when I obeyed his every wicked command.

"I don't like it when you tell me to shut up," I inform him.

He quickens our pace as the rain falls faster. "I would never tell you to shut up. I love the sound of your voice too much. I simply don't want to argue."

I love the sound of his voice too. That gorgeous, lilting accent when he caresses my name with his tongue. The way his tone deepens when we're intimate. The way he rumbles when he reads my favorite books to me, like rolling thunder during a warm summer storm.

We arrive at a tumbledown stone building that used to be some sort of barn or small enclosure for sheep. Now, half of the roof has fallen in, and it obviously hasn't been functional in many years.

"It's safe," Dane reassures me as we duck under the remaining shelter. "I've been coming here since I was a boy, and it hasn't changed one bit."

"Your home is so beautiful," I say with fervent sincerity. This estate has some of the most striking landscapes I've ever seen. I can hardly wait to paint them.

He chuckles. "We're standing in a ruin during a downpour. It's soggy and gloomy. I'd hardly consider that beautiful."

"You're just not looking properly," I tease. "Don't you see the way the sunlight plays over the hills?"

He steps toward me, and for a moment, I think he's going to kiss me again. His face is sharp with hunger, and I tip my head back to welcome his claim.

Instead, his hands bracket my waist, and he spins me so that I'm facing away from him, looking out at the landscape. He pins me to his front with his firm grip on my hips.

His breath warms my rain-chilled neck as he murmurs in my ear, "Tell me more. Describe it to me."

I'm compelled to respond. Not by his commands, but because I hear the yearning that roughens his voice. He wants to see what I see.

I lean back into his strong body, and just like on our first dates, the world comes into sharper focus. The rich green color palette turns almost surreal.

I point down the length of the valley. "The river looks so blue at this distance, like a shiny, navy satin ribbon that some careless goddess has dropped between the hills. And the way the afternoon light hits the lake makes it glitter with gold sparks." My gesture shifts to the rolling hills. "It's gloomy here, but farther away, you can see the shadows of the incoming rainclouds dappling the grass. How many shades of green do you think I would need to paint to capture it? I'm not even sure if I can."

"You can," he says fervently. "You are remarkable, Abigail." He nuzzles my hair and twines my purple curl around one elegant finger. "I've never seen the world the way you do. You make it brighter and more beautiful than I ever thought possible."

"Dane..."

The way he talks about me is overwhelming, like I'm his own personal miracle. He believes in my art. He understands me like no one else.

He applies steady pressure to my curl, tugging gently until I turn my face to his. He captures my lips again, and I don't hold anything back. I pour all of my tumultuous emotions into the kiss: my longing, my pain, my turmoil. And above all, desire. It's carnal and desperate, hot enough to sear away reason and self-doubt.

I don't break the kiss as I turn into him, pressing my chest to his. My nipples are hard, aching peaks against the inside of my bra, and I wantonly arch into him to seek stimulation. His hand snakes under my cotton shirt, and he palms my breasts with a squeeze that takes me to the edge of pain.

His cock presses into my thigh, hard and insistent.

But he doesn't try to force himself on me. He doesn't take anything more than what I'm offering.

He seems to read my moment of worry, because he breaks the kiss to promise, "Tell me to stop, and I'll stop. No need for a safe word. This isn't a game. I need your consent. I can't hurt you again."

He says it roughly, like the thought alone threatens to break something in him.

The belief that he won't hurt me settles in my heart and takes root. He truly means it.

And my body is still thrumming for him.

"Yes," I pant against his lush mouth. "Yes, I want this. I want you, Dane."

His low groan rumbles into my chest when he captures me in another fierce kiss. My fingers fumble at his belt, and his free hand shoves at my jeans. He finds my hard clit and rubs in a firm rhythm that I like best. At the same time, he tweaks my nipple in a cruel pinch.

A sizzling line of fire races straight from the abused bud to my stimulated clit, and I hit my peak with shocking speed. The orgasm crashes through me, and I claw at his jeans as my fingers curl with the force of my pleasure.

I start to come down from my quick high, but we're not nearly finished. He tears at my clothes, stripping off the sodden garments until I'm naked for him. My flesh pebbles in the slight chill, but I grab his hand and drag him out from under the sheltered part of the barn. We're still in the stone walled enclosure, but the rain falls down on us in fat, heavy drops. The cool contrast with my desire-heated skin makes every inch of my body hypersensitive.

He barks out a delighted laugh and joins me in the deluge, stripping off his shirt and baring his chiseled chest. Rain runs down his rippling muscles in enticing rivulets, and I grab him closer so I can trace one with my tongue.

He bites out a curse, and I smile against his hard chest.

I can make this fierce man come undone. I make can make him laugh. I can make him *feel.*

I'm giddy with the knowledge, the power I hold over him. He could subdue me in a moment, but he won't. Not without my consent.

I'm safe here, in this wild, gorgeous landscape with the most beautiful man I've ever known.

He frees his cock from his jeans and grabs my waist, yanking me into him. Then he lifts me up, and I wrap my legs around him for support, clinging on tightly. My shocked laugh mirrors his, a sound of release and merciful joy after long weeks of pain and anguish.

He backs me up against the aged wall. The stones are slick

and rough against my back, but his big hands cushion my ass and shoulders. He won't let me get so much as a scrape while we're together.

His cock presses at my entrance. I'm wet and ready for him after the ruthless orgasm he wrung from my body.

He pauses, brow furrowing. "I don't have a condom."

"I trust you," I promise.

That's a worry for later. Right now, I need him inside me more than I need my next breath.

With my vow of trust, he enters me in one swift thrust. I cry out at the shocking penetration, and he stills, fingers flexing into my skin.

"I'm okay," I assure him. "It's good. So good. Don't stop."

We're a perfect fit, his huge cock stretching me just to the edge of pain with his deepest thrusts. I remember the first time we had sex, when he'd made sure I was relaxed and ready to accommodate him. He'd been ruthless with my body back then, too, but he'd ensured my pleasure. So much pleasure that I'd wept for mercy.

I shudder at the bittersweet memories. The man fucking me with such passion now is the same person. The way he's holding me, sheltering me, is the same. I didn't fully know Dane back then, but this hasn't changed.

Our chemistry is as potent as ever.

With each harsh thrust, pleasure builds at my core. My fingernails dig into his shoulders, and he releases a primal snarl. His teeth nip my lower lip in punishment, but I claw him harder.

"Abigail!" I think it's meant to be a warning, but it comes out as a feral roar.

The sound of Dane coming undone for me pushes me to the peak. Rain splatters my upturned face as I scream out my release. He fucks me harder, his lips pulling back from his teeth like a beast as he resists his own orgasm so that I can reach completion.

When he can't take it anymore, he pulls out, and hot cum lashes my belly and thighs. The rain immediately begins to sluice it away, erasing his mark. The loss draws a soft cry from my chest.

He cups my cheek and studies my face like I'm his greatest treasure. "Are you all right?"

"Yes," I promise, placing my hand atop his to anchor him to me. "You didn't hurt me."

And now, I'm sure that he never will.

44

DANE

Two Weeks Later

I can hardly believe that Abigail willingly sleeps in my bed and welcomes me into her body every night. Only a few weeks ago, that seemed like an impossibility. After the crash—when she'd tried so desperately to get away from me—I'd been determined to keep her. But I hadn't been sure if she would give herself to me ever again.

My sweet, compassionate Abigail still wants me. It wasn't my mastery of her body that made her surrender; it was my vulnerability. Raw honesty.

I'll answer any question she asks of me if it means more intimacy with the woman who is my everything.

Her birth control shot should be effective by now, so I won't have to use the precaution of condoms anymore. The feeling of her wet cunt gripping my cock when I claimed her in the rain was the most exquisite ecstasy of my life.

She didn't ask where I obtained the shot, and I chose not to tell her about the delivery. I think we're both avoiding difficult topics.

Like the fact that I won't allow her to leave me. I won't risk her running to a driver to ask them for rescue.

She seems completely absorbed in her work, shutting herself away in her studio for hours every day. It wasn't difficult to get the shot delivered while she was painting. I have the necessary professional documentation to obtain what I wanted. The arrangement was easy enough.

And it'll be well worth it when I get to fuck her without the barrier of a condom separating us.

We haven't engaged in anything more than slightly rough sex since that day in the rain, but I know she needs more. I worry that she's not ready to accept the darker things we both enjoy, but I can tell she's not fully satisfied. I've seen Abigail when she's utterly spent and sated, and I'm determined to make her that blissful again.

I have a plan in place to coax her darkness back to the surface, but that will have to wait for tomorrow.

No matter what happens, I will not force her again. She'll get her safe word back, and I will honor it.

I'll do anything to keep her trust.

"Dane?"

I'm rushing toward her studio without hesitation. She doesn't sound distressed, but I can't help feeling on edge whenever she's out of my sight. After the crash...

I shake off the bloody memories and focus on her smile.

"I'm fine," she promises, reading the worry that lingers around my brow. "I want to show you something."

She steps back, inviting me into her private haven.

For a moment, I falter. The last time she showed me something in her studio, it was her horrific self-portrait. That confrontation had shredded me. These last two weeks together have been so wonderfully easy. I don't want to go through another difficult conversation like that.

"Don't worry," she soothes. "It's nothing bad. Well, I hope you think they're good. I've been working really hard, and I'm feeling so inspired. But they're nothing special. I like them, though. What do you think?"

She steps back, revealing three small impressionist paintings. One is still on the easel, and the other two are propped against the wall on either side of it.

"Abigail," I breathe.

"I know they're not masterpieces or anything," she rushes to downplay her art. "But it's just so beautiful here, and I wanted to try to capture it. They're silly. I don't plan to frame them or anything like that. They're just for me. But I wanted to show you."

"Abigail." Her name is a quiet interruption this time. She's babbling because she's anxious about my reaction, but I'm speechless.

I stare at the paintings, and something tugs at the center of my chest.

The one against the wall to the left of the easel is the view through our conservatory—probably her first glimpse at the Yorkshire Dales from the kitchen.

The painting to the right is a close-up of a grey stone wall. She's captured the dull sheen from the rain, and a broad, masculine hand is splayed against the wall. Thick veins stand out on the back of the hand, and the fingertips curve as though clawing at the stone for purchase.

It's my hand. When I braced myself after fucking her against the wall in the ruined barn.

The third painting holds my attention the longest. It's the scene from the barn, the one she so eloquently described with her artist's eye. But the perspective is slightly different. The rolling, sun-dappled hills are the same, as is the blue river and the glittering lake.

It's the two figures in the foreground that fascinate me. Their backs are to the viewer, but a tall man with dark hair is embracing a smaller woman. She's barely visible—the only hint that she's there is the perfect purple curl that's twined around his finger.

They look like they belong there.

Like it's home.

"What's wrong?" she asks. "Did I not get it right?"

I shake my head, struggling for words.

"That's not me," I finally manage, pointing at the man in the central painting.

"What?" She peers at her work with a critical eye. "There's something off about your hand. I know. I worked at it for days, but it's just not—"

"Your art is perfect," I assure her. "But I'm not... This isn't my home. I don't want it to be."

Her lips part, and her eyes shine for a moment before she blinks quickly. "I didn't mean to upset you. I'll put these away."

Fuck. I'm saying all the wrong things when she was making herself vulnerable by sharing her work with me.

"Your paintings are masterpieces, and I intend to frame each of them," I say sternly.

If I have my way, she'll be featured in a gallery soon. But she's not ready to accept that yet.

"This place is messing with my head," I admit. "I chose to walk away from my title and everything that comes with it, including the estate. I hated this place when I was growing up. But you see it so differently than I do." I gesture at the painting again. "I don't belong here."

Her features are pinched with concern. "It doesn't have to be your home if you don't want it to be. You can choose your home. I chose mine. Back in Charleston."

She cuts her gaze away, and for a moment, I think we're going to return to the thorny issue of her leaving Yorkshire. Without me.

"This place holds nothing for me but memories of cruelty and blood," I say before she can go down that road.

Her eyes snap back to mine, bright and incisive. "You're talking about your sister's death? The car crash?"

I run a hand through my hair, and now I'm the one to look away. "Yes."

"But it's more than that." She sees right through me. "You can talk to me, Dane."

I don't want to tell her some of my darkest truths, but I have to prevent her from thinking about Charleston.

"I was a violent child," I admit. "I was the cruel one. Well, we all were, I suppose. Except maybe James. He's just a spoiled little prince." I force myself to meet her eyes. "My parents are cold and narcissistic, but they never beat me. My mother always said she didn't know where I got it from, and I guess that doesn't really matter. The fact is that I was dangerous. It wasn't until I was eleven that I realized I had to hide that part of myself."

"Dangerous, how?" she asks carefully.

"I lashed out at other children. I hurt them."

All those times I came back with little spots of their blood dotting my shirts, and my mother would berate me for ruining my pristine clothes. Not because we couldn't afford more, and not because she cared about the other children. She only cared about what other people would think if they found out.

At least, the people who *matter.*

If the children of staff members had "accidents" around the estate, my parents didn't give a fuck. And if their parents put up a fuss, hefty bonuses made the problem go away. Or outright dismissal if my mother was irked enough.

"What changed when you were eleven?" Abigail presses gently. "Why did you stop being violent?"

"I almost killed another child. A child who *mattered*, according to my mother."

I force myself to continue over her horrified gasp. I'm staring at the painting of us together, the one that looks so right but all wrong at the same time.

"Peter was a bully," I explain. "He often picked on me for being a freak. The other children were right to sense something off in me. I wasn't good at concealing it back then. I didn't even try.

"I never retaliated at school because I knew better than to get caught. But then one day, Peter was tired of never getting a reaction from me. So, he ran his mouth about Katie. He said I'd probably killed my sister. He said it was my fault she was dead." I glare at the painting. "I shoved him out of the window. He spent two weeks in hospital."

Abigail doesn't seem to have the words to respond to that cold declaration, so I carry on.

"The police were called. I was questioned. Mum made it very clear that I would be locked up if I didn't figure out how to mask my true nature. She said I was lucky that Peter's family accepted a payoff and a few threats with the weight of the family name behind them." I sneer around the last. "She thinks she can buy anything she wants. People. Freedom. Forgiveness."

I stop talking. I've said too much.

Abigail is far too quiet, and I don't dare to look at her and see her expression of revulsion.

"You were a traumatized child." Her softly spoken words hit me like a blow to the chest. "It sounds like you didn't have any support after you saw your sister die. Your father was responsible for her death, and he didn't suffer any consequences, did he? That's what you mean when you say your mother thinks she can buy anything. Isn't it?"

I stare at her with open awe. "You're not... You don't think I'm a monster for what I did to that boy? I hurt people, Abigail. Children."

"You were a child yourself. You had witnessed something horrible, and you were living in an emotionally abusive home. It doesn't sound like anyone showed you another way to behave, and you lashed out."

"That doesn't scare you?" I challenge, hardly able to believe she's not cringing away from me.

"There have been plenty of times when you've scared me, Dane. Now isn't one of them. I'm not afraid of the boy who suffered so much pain. I'm sorry you went through that."

I just told her I almost killed a child, and she's apologizing to me.

She truly is my miracle.

I decide not to say anything else that might change the way she's looking at me right now: like I'm worthy of compassion. Empathy. Affection.

"I didn't know you felt that way about the estate," she says.

"I can change the painting. I can destroy it if you want me to. We can burn it together."

I grasp her hands in mine, pulling her close. "No. Never destroy anything you create. Especially not on my account. The world needs your art."

Her cheeks color my favorite shade of pink. "I'm really not that talented."

"Yes, you are." I look at the central painting again, the one of us standing together, looking out at the countryside. "You made a place I loathe look like home. That's a gift, Abigail. Don't you dare hide it or destroy it."

The longer I look at the painting, the more it feels right. And I start to realize that maybe it's not the setting that makes it feel like home. Maybe it's that perfect purple curl curved around my finger.

45

ABIGAIL

"Where are we going?" I ask warily.

Dane has been enigmatic about our destination, and his teasing non-answers are starting to grate on me.

"Back to Charleston?" I ask, but I don't sound as hopeful as I should.

I tell myself that's because it's highly unlikely, not because some part of me doesn't want to leave this peaceful space I've found with him. As long as I don't think too hard about going home, I'm able to indulge my growing, irrational desire to stay with him, despite everything he's done.

"Do we look like we're dressed for travel?" he drawls, shooting me an unbearably sexy smirk from the driver's seat of the sleek black Porsche.

I huff an exasperated breath, and he chuckles.

He's wearing a sharply tailored tux, and he's dressed me in a daring silk gown. The neckline drops down almost to my navel in a deep V, and he's chosen a gorgeous purple tone that's so dark it's almost black. I didn't argue when he gave me the obviously expensive garment. We're past that now.

I'm so tired of arguing with him, and I believe him when he says that his gifts don't come with strings attached. After his intense revelations about his abusive family and his choice to walk away from them, I know he would never try to control me like that.

And he'd wanted to hurt my parents for their controlling behavior. I'd had to make him promise not to go after them if I revealed the depth of their cruelty.

This isn't about controlling you. It never has been. I want to take care of you.

I didn't understand him when he made that fierce declaration, but I know him better now. I *see* him: the devoted lover and the fierce protector. And I see the pain that shaped him into a selfish psychopath who learned to turn off his emotions entirely in order to protect himself.

That side of him doesn't scare me anymore.

"We're almost there," he promises.

"Almost where?" I demand, irritated and more than a little nervous. Anxiety tightens my stomach, and a familiar, giddy thrill races through me at the hint of fear.

"You'll see."

"Dane."

"Abigail."

I throw up my hands and ignore the way that stern, deep tone makes my core heat.

We've been driving through the countryside on a narrow, winding road for nearly an hour, and the sun is setting.

The headlights turn on, illuminating a twilight-dim turn onto an even narrower driveway. We pass through open iron gates.

Is this another family estate?

After a further five-minute drive, we slow behind a line of other cars. Ahead, the vehicles curve around a circular driveway in front of a grand, sprawling house that almost rivals the Graham family manor.

My jaw drops.

He's going to take me somewhere public? Where I can ask someone for help?

I narrow my eyes at him. The arrogant bastard must think I'm beyond that now. He must've decided that I don't want to escape from him.

I cross my arms over my chest.

Don't I?

I'm no longer sure if I do, but my heart longs to return home to Charleston. I can't stay in this surreal state with Dane forever. No matter how much I'm coming to care for him, I can't just abandon my life. I won't live to suit his every whim. If I choose to stay with him, that's not how it will be between us.

He's insisted that he wants *me* so many times. Not a mindless, obedient pet.

He hasn't even called me *pet* in weeks, not since I crashed the Jeep during my escape attempt.

I almost miss the kinky endearment.

I press my lips together to hold in further questions. I'm not sure what I want to say.

And I'm not sure what I'll do once I'm surrounded by people who can possibly help me get back home to Charleston.

Without Dane.

We come to a brief stop behind a yellow Lamborghini.

He takes the opportunity to turn toward me and grasps

my hand. He lifts it to his lips and brushes a gentlemanly kiss over my knuckles. For a moment, he's my dashing, perfect prince again: the man I fell for all those weeks ago.

Then his wicked grin reminds me that he's a rakish villain too.

They're both the same man. Exactly how I used to fantasize about him when he was just a customer, an untouchable, beautiful god.

His thumb brushes my palm. "I trust you, Abigail. I trust in *us.*"

My heart skips a beat.

If I betray him now, he'll end up in prison. I'll never see him again.

The thought makes my stomach knot.

"You'll need this," he says, releasing my hand.

I instantly miss the reassuring warmth of his tender touch. My fingers furl and unfurl, as though grasping for him.

His attention is on something in the glove box, so he doesn't see my involuntary, embarrassing display of desperation.

Something glints in his hand: a golden masquerade mask.

His soft fingers brush my cheeks as he lifts it to my face, and his touch is so alluring that I don't try to pull away when he fixes my mask in place. It covers my features from my cheekbones to my brows. Someone who knows me well could probably recognize me, but a stranger won't be able to make out all of my features.

Dane puts on his own mask. Unlike mine, it's black, but it glints dully like carbonite. It only covers the upper half of his face as well, but it's been molded to subtly mirror the shape of a skull.

He looks like a beautiful demon, some sort of terrifying incubus that's designed to lure me in and ravage me.

My mind flashes back to a different night when he donned a skull mask. It'd been stark white, and it'd completely concealed his face.

I shiver, but I can't stop staring at him: my dark god.

"Are you frightened?" he asks, voice low and intimate.

"Yes." The affirmation shudders from my chest.

"Are you turned on?"

My cheeks heat, and I glance away, hiding from him. Hiding from the truth.

Two fingers curl beneath my chin, and he redirects my gaze to his. In the dim lighting, his eyes are almost black, enhancing his aura of otherworldly danger.

My heartbeat ticks up a notch, and I feel an answering pulse between my legs.

"What are we doing here?" I ask instead of answering his lewd question.

He traces the shape of my mouth with his thumb, and my lips tingle with sensual awareness.

"I'm going to remind you of how it should be between us. I'm going to give you what you really want."

"Dane..." His name is a protest. I can't bear it if he forces himself on me again.

"You have your safe word," he promises. "Use it, and everything will stop."

I shake my head, so he cups my cheeks to still the sign of my fearful denial.

"Tell me that what we've shared over the last two weeks has been enough for you," he challenges gently. "Tell me you don't want me to take control. You don't want me to ravage you."

My chest tightens. It's been blissful to be back in his arms, to have him inside me. But I haven't experienced the transcendent ecstasy that once consumed me.

But that was before I knew what he did to me. Before I knew how dangerous he truly is.

"I will never hurt you," he reminds me. "Trust me."

"Dane, I..." I can't find the right words. My mind sticks on the decision.

It's foolish to give in to this, to give in to *him*. He's my stalker. My kidnapper.

And yet, I know deep in my bones that he'll do anything to keep me safe. Even from himself.

He brushes another kiss over my knuckles. "It's your choice."

We've reached the front of the line of cars. He gets out, circles the Porsche, and opens my door for me. A valet takes his keys, and Dane places his hand at the small of my back.

Butterflies beat their delicate wings in my stomach, a slightly desperate, fearful thrill.

He pauses and snaps his fingers. "How could I forget?"

The slightly cruel tilt to his smile tells me that he didn't forget at all; this moment is designed to keep me on edge.

He reaches into his pocket and pulls out my black leather collar with rose gold accents. The one that used to mark me as his submissive. And he was my master.

I try to take a step back, but his strong arm snakes around my lower back, trapping me. He pulls me in close, and his murmured words are hot on my neck.

"Are you going to be a good girl and lift your hair for me? Or am I going to have to pin you down to lock your collar around your pretty throat? One way or another, you'll accept it. You'll accept *me*."

My lips part in shock, and I stare up into his glittering green eyes that peer through the black skull mask.

"It's your choice," he says again, but there's a mocking lilt to his tone this time.

I can't allow him to physically subdue me like that. I can't bear it. Especially not when there are other people around to witness my degradation.

My hands shake as I lift my hair, but I glare at him with open defiance.

He grins. "There's my fierce pet. You're being such a good girl for me now. When will you show your claws?"

"I'm not playing this game with you," I hiss.

I can't.

Not after what he's done to me. Not after that awful scene in my studio, when he forced orgasms from my unwilling body.

He drops a kiss on my chilled lips, and the ice that was beginning to frost my skin melts away.

His hands encircle my throat, and smooth leather touches my neck. The familiar feel of it buckling into place is bittersweet, and tumultuous emotions surge.

I can't do this. I can't want this.

But I don't fight when he slips the delicate padlock through the metal loop at the back of the buckle. It clicks closed, and the collar seems to meld into my skin, becoming part of me. As though it belongs there.

As though I belong to him.

I'm so absorbed by my internal conflict that I barely register the glint of silver before the cuff closes around my right wrist.

"What are you—"

The question dies in my throat when I see him lock the

matching cuff around his left wrist. We're tethered together by a short chain.

"You're not going anywhere, pet."

I straighten my shoulders. "You can't do this to me. I won't walk into a room full of strangers wearing a collar and handcuffs."

"I absolutely can." He chuckles, a sound of arrogant amusement. "Try to stop me. Give me the satisfaction of clipping on your leash and making you crawl."

I narrow my eyes at him. "You can't make me do anything."

"Oh, little dove," he croons. "I definitely can. But for now, I'm giving you a choice."

"These aren't choices," I shoot back. "It's coercion."

With every "choice" I make, I'm making myself more vulnerable. I'm surrendering to him just a little bit more.

He traces the curve of my purple curl. "And you love being coerced."

You liked it. I remember how he justified his actions as the masked man. How he justified what he did to me in the studio.

The chill is closing in on me again, and my throat tightens to restrict my breathing, as though his long fingers are squeezing my neck.

He kisses me again, taking his time to caress my lips with his, imbuing me with warmth.

"Time to join the other guests, pet."

I try to stall, but he strides forward. The metal cuff tugs at my wrist, dragging me in his wake.

"This is crazy," I insist.

I'm wearing a collar and handcuffs. I can't be seen publicly like this.

He laughs again and doesn't slow his confident pace through the massive, open front doors. "Don't worry. You'll fit right in."

Dozens of people wearing fine clothes and elaborate masks fill the foyer. Several curious glances rake over us, witnessing the embarrassing spectacle we're making.

To my horror, I feel something slick between my thighs with every shaky step. I'm getting turned on by this humiliating scene.

I lift my chin and school my features to an impassive expression that's far better at concealing my emotions than the gold mask.

"My proud, brave little pet." Dane says it like praise, not mockery. "You'll enjoy yourself tonight. I guarantee it."

As we near the other guests, shock makes my feet stick to the marble floor.

Their outfits are obviously expensive, but several of them are dressed in leather and latex rather than fine silk. A statuesque blonde wears a corset over her voluminous taffeta skirt. Her breasts are almost spilling out, and the skirt is open at the front to reveal sheer white tights. She's not wearing underwear.

I gasp and tear my gaze away. It falls on the man to her left. What I originally thought was a formal kilt is actually crafted in leather, and his loose-fitting white shirt is unbuttoned to reveal masculine chest hair. He's holding a leash causally in one hand. The other end is clipped to a collar on the corseted woman's neck.

"What is this, Dane?" I ask breathlessly.

He fixes me with a wicked smirk. "It's a party, darling. Haven't you always wanted to go to a ball like one of your fantasy princesses?"

I gape at him. There's nothing romantic about this. It's deviant. Carnal.

Perverse.

And my blood is humming through my veins.

"That's one of my favorite colors," Dane rumbles, caressing my heated cheek. "Almost as pink as your pretty cunt."

"Dane!"

Judging by the kilted man's smirk, he heard that scandalous remark.

A server carrying a silver tray with champagne flutes pauses to offer us a drink. Dane assesses me, reading every nuance of my jittery, indignant mood.

He selects a glass for himself but doesn't offer me one.

"I'd rather not end up with champagne in my eyes," he teases. "I have a feeling you'd toss the drink in my face as soon as it was in your hand."

"Good idea," I mutter.

"Sorry to disappoint you. Now, do you want a drink?"

I blink at him. He just said I couldn't have one.

"Yes," I reply before he can change his mind. Now that he's mentioned it, I would very much like to throw champagne into his smug face.

One of his big hands slides into my hair at my nape, anchoring me in a firm grip. He applies steady pressure and tugs my head back slightly. He lifts the glass to my lips.

"You wouldn't," I insist.

He won't actually give me a drink from his hand like I truly am his helpless pet.

"Your choice," he says again, but he doesn't lower the glass.

I press my lips together in denial, but I can't shift my head.

The glass tilts despite my glower, and champagne spills down my chin, dripping onto my chest.

I open my mouth, cheeks flaming. Having him pour the drink down my chest feels more embarrassing than accepting the drink. The fizzy liquid bubbles over my tongue, reminding me of the drink he bought for me on our first date.

That memory is so terribly tempting, and for a moment, I want to give in.

I want to belong to Dane again. In every way.

But the champagne is still spilling from the corners of my lips, and I realize he's doing it intentionally.

"Not too much," he chides, as though I have a choice in how much I'm drinking. "I don't want your senses impaired."

I consider spitting the champagne in his face, but it's too late for that. He pulls the glass away, and I'm left panting for breath and covered in expensive wine.

His eyes darken when they fix on my chest, and I realize my nipples have pebbled to hard, aching buds. They're clearly visible against the dark purple silk. It clings to my breasts now that the material is wet.

"I want a taste," Dane rumbles, but he sets the half-empty glass on to a passing server's tray.

I try to ease away from his predatory energy, but the handcuff keeps me closely bound to him. And he still hasn't released my hair.

He tugs sharply, forcing me to expose my throat. His lips are unbearably soft against my sensitive skin, and his tongue brands me when he licks the line of my vulnerable artery. He takes his time sampling the champagne on my skin, making his way lower down my chest with a trail of hot, hungry kisses.

"No." My protest is so breathy that it might as well be a welcoming purr.

His lips close over my nipple, his teeth grazing it through the thin barrier of my wet dress. Pleasure floods my body in a strong wave that crashes from my breasts all the way to my fingers and toes. It goes straight to my head, and for a moment, I'm euphoric. Desire layers over my embarrassment, and sparks dance down my spine to heat my core.

"Lovely." The woman's voice is far too close.

Oh, god. I remember all of the people that surround us. They're all bearing witness to my shameful, wanton responses to Dane's cruel game.

I lift my free hand and try to shove his head away from my chest. He bites my nipple in sharp reprimand.

I yelp, and the woman giggles.

I turn desperate eyes on her and suppress a whimper as Dane returns to teasing my tight, sensitive bud with his tongue.

"Help me," I beg. I can't bear further humiliation, no matter how my body is humming for him. "I don't want this."

Dane nips at me again, and my knees almost buckle. He steadies me with an arm around my waist and continues to torment my breasts as though this is completely normal and natural.

The blonde fixes me with an indulgent smile, and one blue eye winks through her silver mask. "Of course you don't."

"You don't understand," I insist, and the words are almost a desperate groan. "I don't want to be here."

The woman's smile tilts. She thinks this is a game.

And Dane is still tormenting my nipples in the way that makes me come undone for him.

"No," I moan, equal parts horror and lust. I try to keep the woman in focus when my eyes are threatening to roll back in my head. "I'm here against my will."

She giggles again and sips her champagne, indulging in the carnal scene like a spectator at a particularly sensual play.

"He kidnapped me!" I burst out.

Someone has to help me. This has to stop.

But Dane doesn't stop. He drags his tongue up my sternum before his teeth graze my throat in warning.

"Please," I beg the woman. "This is real."

She just continues to smile at me. "I'll leave you two to enjoy yourselves."

"No! Wait!"

But she doesn't listen.

No one listens to me. No one will help me.

The cruelty of Dane's dark game crashes down on me, and I shriek out my frustration. Several people look at us, but they don't seem alarmed in the slightest. Instead, they're merely curious. Interested to see what Dane's *pet* will do next.

My right hand is cuffed to his left, and his free hand is still in my hair.

My left hand slaps his stunning face with a shocking *crack*.

I immediately regret it.

His wicked grin is far more terrifying than a thunderous scowl.

"Are you ready to struggle, little dove?"

"I want to leave," I insist, my chest rising and falling on rapid, heaving breaths.

"It's too late for that," he admonishes. "Do you really think I'll let you go unpunished?"

"Don't do this," I beg. "Not in front of all of these people."

His fingers soften in my hair, and he massages my scalp in

soothing circles. "Is it the audience that bothers you so much?" he croons. "Beg, and I might show mercy."

I lick my lips, shame searing my cheeks. I don't want to beg him for anything, but I can't endure more of this erotic torment.

My pride makes my spine stiffen, but I force out through gritted teeth, "Please. I want to leave."

"You didn't ask very nicely, but you'll do better by the end of the night."

For a moment, I think he'll refuse. I think he's going to force me to remain here where everyone can witness my degradation.

Then he lifts me over his shoulder and strides out into the night.

I huff out a relieved breath, but I don't yet realize that this isn't over. It's barely even begun.

46

ABIGAIL

"Where are you taking me?" I demand.

"You asked to leave the party," he reminds me, like he's being completely reasonable.

"Take me back to the car."

"I never agreed to that." His low laugh is infuriating, and my inner muscles clench.

I cover my face with my free hand, relieved that he can't see my chagrin when I'm slung over his shoulder.

He's taking me somewhere deeper in the shadowy grounds of the grand estate. Night has fallen, but Yorkshire is far enough north that the sky is still dusky despite the late hour. I've seen enough to know that we're in a curated garden; I noted perfectly pruned rose bushes and a neat hedge in my peripheral vision. Otherwise, I'm looking down at the dirt path beneath Dane's designer shoes.

Too late, I realize that the hedge has risen up on either side of me. I've been so absorbed in my inner turmoil that I didn't pay enough attention to my surroundings.

We're in a hedge maze, and I'm already hopelessly lost.

Dane seems to know exactly where he's going.

"Put me down. I don't like this," I say shakily.

"Liar," he drawls.

His restraining hand eases up my thigh to caress my swollen pussy through my thin dress. I gasp at the answering burst of pleasure and buck over his shoulder. His only reply is another arrogant chuckle.

"Bastard," I hiss.

"I'll enjoy taming that pretty mouth later. I have other plans for you now."

He finally sets me down, and I'm disoriented for a moment at the shift in perspective. I blink and realize we're in the center of the maze. A bubbling fountain featuring giggling cherubs is illuminated to our right. The small statues seem to mock me with their sly smiles.

Dane bends down and rummages in a waiting black duffel bag.

"What's in there?" My voice is a touch higher than usual.

"You'll find out soon enough."

"You planned this," I accuse. "You've arranged all of this in advance."

He quirks a single dark brow at me. "Of course."

"You knew no one would help me."

His sensual smirk is pure, masculine satisfaction. "I have you right where I want you."

I lift my chin and glare at him. "You wouldn't put me in a scenario where you could get caught. I thought we were building trust, Dane."

"That's exactly why we're here," he explains calmly.

He's holding a short coil of rope in one hand. My stomach flips, and I try to edge away from him.

What else is he hiding in that bag?

"If you think I'm just going to stand here compliantly while you tie me up, you're mistaken," I defy him. "I won't let you."

He pins me with that wickedly sharp smile. "I'm counting on it."

His hand jerks to his side, and my cuffed wrist forces me close to him. Before I can reason through how I can deny his twisted game, he twists my arm behind my back and grabs the other. Rope loops around my wrists, binding them together at the small of my back.

"No!" I try to twist away.

Which is exactly what he wants. He wants me to struggle, to indulge in his dark mindfuck.

I know this, but I don't soften and submit.

I can't. My pride won't allow me to surrender so easily.

And some secret, perverted part of me doesn't want to remain meekly compliant.

The metal cuff unlocks, dropping to the dirt path. But my wrists are even more securely trapped than they were before.

I lunge forward, propelling myself away from him. He hooks an arm around my waist and drags me back.

"No running yet. We're not finished here."

My heart hammers against my ribcage.

Yet.

He's going to chase me through this maze, and I have no idea how to get out.

I harden my resolve and try to elbow him in the ribs. His sharp exhale is my only reward before I'm shoved to my knees. He grabs my shoulders and forces me down onto my back, trapping my hands under me. His weight settles over my hips, just heavy enough to pin me without causing me pain.

I writhe in the dirt, but when he fists my dress in both hands, I arch toward him. With one jerk of his powerful arms, the delicate material tears, baring my breasts to him. He cups them with reverence, teasing my nipples with his thumbs.

Pleasure sparks beneath his tender touch, and I swallow a whimper.

"No one else will ever see you like this. You're all mine, Abigail."

We're alone out here, completely isolated from the rest of the party. I don't have to worry about anyone witnessing my humiliation anymore.

"No one will save you from me," he warns, and I shudder.

He keeps me pinned and reaches into that damn bag again. Something jingles softly when he pulls it out. I instantly recognize the silvery glint of nipple clamps.

This isn't the first time I've seen them, but they're different from the ones he's used on me before. These are connected by a black leather cord, and three delicate silver bells hang from it.

"Don't you dare."

"How else am I supposed to keep track of my pet when she runs away?" he taunts.

"I'm not your pet," I seethe, wriggling beneath him.

All I manage to do is stimulate my clit against his growing erection.

He hisses in a sharp breath as his own lust torments him, but he doesn't have an ounce of mercy in his hungry gaze. The light from the fountain catches in his eyes, illuminating the dark green pools so that they practically glow.

He hums in false consideration. "Aren't you? Pets wear

pretty collars, just like yours." He leans in close, his lips teasing mine as he says, "Pets obey their master."

I snap my teeth at him, and his eyes flash with delight.

He grips my jaw, holding my head still so that I can't sink my teeth into his perfect mouth.

"No biting," he admonishes sternly. "I'll tame you again, Abigail. It will be my pleasure."

Wanton arousal wets my thighs, and my clit pulses madly against his erection. I barely prevent myself from rubbing against him like a needy kitten.

He plucks at my nipples, drawing a reluctant moan from my chest. His deft fingers feel so decadent, tormenting me with pain that blossoms into forbidden pleasure.

I throw my head back on a sharp cry when he captures them in the clamps. They bite down on my sensitive nipples, and I squirm in the dirt. I must be getting filthy, but he wants me this way: dirty and degraded. I never knew how the humiliation could make me burn for him.

He stares down into my eyes and twists the screws on the clamps, adjusting them until they're tiny vises on my throbbing nipples.

When he's satisfied with my squeak of discomfort, he relents and flicks the bells that are draped between my breasts on the leather cord. The melodic jingle mingles with his cruel laugh.

His hands close around my shoulders, and he drags me upright. With my hands bound behind me, I have to rely on his support to get to my feet. My torn dress slides down my body, pooling on the ground and leaving me bare before him. A scrap of black lace is my only bit of modesty, and judging by his possessive gaze, the lingerie only entices him more.

I glower at him, allowing the full force of my defiance to pierce him like a knife.

He simply smiles and caresses my cheek. "So beautiful. My pretty pet."

"Stop calling me that," I seethe.

He cocks his head at me, and midnight hair tumbles over the black skull mask. "Say the word, and this will end. You do have a choice, Abigail. Always. I'll never take that from you again."

My ire melts away. He's asking for my trust.

He said that he brought me here for a reason. He wants me to remember how good it can be between us when we both indulge in our mutual darkness. My soul matches his in so many ways.

My heart tugs toward his, stronger this time. I yearn for him, for us. I want to engage in this twisted game, but I'm frightened.

"I'm scared," I admit, my voice small.

His jaw firms, but his hand on my cheek remains achingly gentle. "I never want you to be scared of me."

"I'm scared of *me*. I shouldn't want this. It's sick and wrong."

"Nothing about you could ever be wrong. You're perfect, Abigail."

He tips my chin back so that he can stare down into my soul. "Do you want to stop?"

That question makes all the difference. I settle into my decision, accepting everything that we are. Accepting *him*.

And myself.

"No," I breathe. "I don't want to stop."

He leans in close, and his lips brush the shell of my ear when he commands, "Then run, little dove."

He steps back, watching me with open curiosity for my next move.

I straighten my shoulders and kick off my high heels. The dirt path is cool beneath my feet. The earth is hardpacked; it won't hurt my bare soles.

His tilted grin is pure, maniacal pleasure. "You have thirty seconds, and then I come after you."

"Aren't you going to untie my hands?"

"And let you pluck off those lovely bells? I don't think so."

I hesitate, torn between denying him his fun and wanting to unleash my most primal urges. This is a battle of wills, and even though there's no way I will win, I'm determined to engage in the fight. The struggle. The inevitable, ecstatic defeat.

"Twenty seconds now," he warns.

I start running. I have to get as far away as possible before slowing down; the damn bells will give me away if I continue sprinting, and I already know he's faster than I am.

I hurtle down the path, willing my eyes to adjust to the darkness as I run farther away from the light of the fountain. The maze opens up to my left, and I choose to take the turn rather than going straight. There's no way to know how to get to the exit, and Dane is well aware of that fact.

My fate is already sealed, but I grit my teeth and increase my speed.

He wants a hunt? I'll give him a hunt. He'll have to work for it if he wants to capture me.

With every pounding step, the bells sway on the cord between the silver clamps. The weight of them tugs at my trapped nipples as my breasts bounce. My blood runs hotter in my veins, and it's not just from the exertion of evading him. The torment to my nipples is unbearably erotic, and my inner thighs are wet with my arousal. My swollen labia throb with every stride, and I'm achingly aware of how empty I am without his cock filling me up.

"Abigail!" He roars my name from the center of the maze, and I know I'm out of time.

I duck down an opening to my right, winding my way deeper into the maze. I take turn after sharp turn, until I'm dizzy and my breath burns my lungs. He can clearly hear the jingling of the traitorous bells, but I think my path has been erratic enough to confuse him.

For a while, at least.

I slow down and struggle to breathe as shallowly as possible so that the bells won't jangle. My steps are light and careful, and I manage to take another turn without making a sound.

I'm not sure how long I manage to keep quiet before he calls out for me again.

"I know you're nearby, Abigail. Such a clever little pet. You're lost, but I'll find you."

He says the last like a mercy.

His voice is far too close. I have no choice: I have to start running again.

He barks a laugh when the bells chime, and a mix of defiant rage and desire heats my flushed cheeks.

His arrogance is galling, but my body craves him.

I deny my base, carnal needs and increase my speed, rounding another corner. Seconds later, I cry out before I can stop myself.

I've hit a dead end. And I can hear his heavy footfalls pounding closer.

I whirl, and his massive, shadowy form is barreling toward me, cutting off my exit. I scramble back, but I collide with the hedge. Branches prickle my bare skin, scratching my sensitized flesh like a sharp caress.

He slows as he closes in, and his white teeth flash in a feral smile through the darkness.

"Little dove," he coos. "Are you trapped?"

"Don't touch me," I snap, pressing myself deeper into the hedge.

"Poor little pet. All alone out here. So lost and afraid."

"I'm not afraid," I lie. Fear thrills through me in a tingling wave, setting all of my senses on high alert.

"You don't have to pretend with me." He says it like a reassurance that's belied by his mocking tone.

He's right in front of me, his massive body blocking any hope of escape.

"You seem to be caught in a snare. Let me help you."

He moves lighting fast, grasping my shoulders and tearing me away from the hedge. He tackles me to the ground, angling us so that his body takes the impact.

Then he rolls atop me, forcing me onto my front. The clamps bite into my nipples. With my hands bound behind me, there's nothing I can do but kick and scream.

My defiant shriek dies in my throat when I catch the glint of the blade out of the corner of my eye.

"Dane!" True, potent terror claws at my insides.

I crane my neck back so that I can keep the wickedly sharp hunting knife in my line of sight.

The last time he held a blade to my throat, he was the masked man. He terrorized me and violated me.

He's wearing a different skull mask now. The image of my alluring demon morphs into a horrific, macabre memory.

He strokes the length of my spine with his free hand and shushes me gently. The knife is nowhere near my skin; he's holding it at least two feet away from me, and it's pointed outward, not toward me.

"I took this fantasy from you," he rumbles. "I want to give it back."

My chest convulses on a shuddering breath. Terror still rides me hard, but his words touch something deep inside me.

He wants my consent. I could stop him right now if I wanted to.

But I don't speak. I don't use my safe word.

I want to take ownership of this fantasy too.

I close my eyes briefly and breathe through the worst of the clawing horror, until it subsides into fizzy, thrilling fear once again. I allow myself to sink into the giddy sensation, like I'm riding a rollercoaster.

I'm safe with Dane.

"Good girl," he praises. "So brave for me."

My eyes flutter open, and the blade glints in the moonlight as he slowly moves it closer to my body. When I don't scream or cringe away, he grasps my wrists with his other hand. The rope tugs slightly as he slips the knife through the knot.

I go utterly still.

"Be careful, little dove," he warns gently. "I don't want to accidentally clip your wings."

The blade slices upward, away from my body. The rope falls from my wrists, but I don't dare to move. I'm hardly breathing, and I'm becoming lightheaded from lack of oxygen.

He shifts behind me, and I'm on my back.

The knife is still in his hand, and this time, the tip is pointed at my chest.

"Dane..." His name is little more than a pleading whisper.

"*Master*," he corrects me. "You're mine, Abigail. It's time you remembered what that means."

The knife flicks beneath the leather cord that connects the nipple clamps. The bells jingle softly as he slowly draws it upward on the flat of the blade.

"I wonder what will happen first," he muses, eyes glittering with cruel fascination. "Will the cord be severed, or will those tight little clamps be tugged off of your nipples?"

"Don't." I dread the pain of the latter threat.

"You do beg so sweetly, but that won't spare you. You're my helpless little plaything now. Mine to toy with however I want."

He slowly raises the knife, increasing the pressure on the cord. It begins to tug at the clamps, pulling on my abused nipples. Pain spears through me in sharp spikes that somehow turn to pure pleasure when they reach my core. I cry out and arch my back, desperate to alleviate the strain.

"Would you like that?" he taunts. "You could be my obedient little fucktoy. Or you can continue to suffer for me."

I growl through gritted teeth, the only sound I'm able to make when pain rakes at me, commanding most of my attention.

"You brought this on yourself,"

That's my only warning before he jerks the knife away from me. He doesn't turn it to sever the cord with the sharp edge. My scream fills the maze when the nipple clamps are yanked free. The searing shock of pain makes my vision flash white for an instant.

I blink rapidly, and tears stream down my temples to wet my hair. The world comes back into sharp focus when I see the knife hovering just above my stinging nipple.

Fear shudders through me, a primal response to danger. "Please..."

"I would never damage your beautiful body," he reassures me. "But you're going to have to remain very still for me. I'll make the ache go away. I know you're hurting."

My nipples throb as though I've been stung by bees, but that doesn't ease my spike of terror when the cold flat of the blade touches one tight peak with the lightest pressure.

All of my muscles lock up tight. A small, pitiful whimper eases up my throat, but the tiny exhalation is the only move I dare to make.

He stares down at me, eyes dark pools in the shadows of his mask. His beautiful face is drawn into stony, merciless planes, and his cock is hard against my thigh.

He's getting off on this, reveling in his sadistic power over me.

And I'm molten for him.

My body relaxes, all of the fight going out of me as I submit. The blessed release of surrender is pure bliss, and it pulses through my body like a drug.

"So perfect," he breathes. "My Abigail."

"Yours." My lips shape the word, but I don't have enough air to speak. Not with the knife so perilously close to my vulnerable nipple.

He shifts the blade to my other breast, further soothing the sting from the clamps with cold steel. He keeps it there while he reaches between us, his free hand dipping under my soaked thong. He groans when he finds the wetness that coats my inner thighs.

"Stay just like that," he orders, and he sounds like he might be drugged too. "Don't move."

The knife is at my throat, sending a fresh burst of fear fluttering through my system. I float in it, riding the thrilling high.

I draw in shallow, careful breaths as he teases my swollen pussy with a featherlight touch.

"Please." I mouth the plea, but I'm no longer begging for reprieve. I crave more: more fear, more pain, more pleasure.

I'll take everything he wants to do to me. I'll offer him anything he desires.

He's my dark god, my master.

My everything.

And he's looking at me like I'm the only person in his world. The only thing tethering him to sanity. He needs me so deeply that it transcends the bounds of physical lust. He yearns for me, just as I long for him, for this connection that we share.

Two thick fingers ease into my tight sheath, and he applies firm pressure to the sensitive spot inside me. The stimulation is slow, tender. So at odds with the violence of the knife at my throat.

My lashes flutter as primal chemicals mingle in my system. I'm no longer sure of the difference between fear and desire. There's only the burning need for him and the euphoric release of submission.

"Stay with me," he murmurs. "Keep breathing."

I realize I'm dizzy from lack of oxygen, so I draw in a careful breath. His will compels me, and I'm his to command. I'll do anything for him, suffer any torment. Because I know he'll give me exquisite ecstasy in return.

"Now, come for me."

He presses down on my clit and rubs my g-spot.

I don't have enough air to scream, and I don't dare to so much as writhe as cruelly potent pleasure rips through me.

He watches me come in tormented silence, as though I'm the most fascinating, breathtaking thing he's ever seen.

The cold kiss of the blade is gone, and he tosses the knife far away from us. I immediately start shaking, my entire body trembling with the force of my residual fear.

He strokes my hair back from my sweat-slicked brow and crushes his lips to mine, devouring me. I groan into his mouth, a purely wanton sound.

I came only seconds ago, but I'm still throbbing for him. I crave him inside me, joining us in the most intimate way.

He can't seem to wait another moment, either. He unbuckles his belt and frees his cock. It presses at my slick opening, and I shift my hips up to welcome him. He slides in to the hilt, stretching me in one smooth thrust.

He breaks our kiss so that he can grasp my thighs. He directs me to lift my legs between us until my calves rest on his shoulders. He leans into me, and his cock sinks impossibly deeper, hitting a spot inside me that's almost painful. It adds the sweetest edge to our connection, and I tip my head back on a guttural moan.

I'm trapped beneath him, pinned by his strength. He grasps my wrists and holds them above my head. His other hand closes around my throat, squeezing gently.

He begins to claim me in long, hard thrusts that jar my entire body when he drives deep into me. My muscles coil tighter as my pleasure crests once again, and my inner walls clamp down on his cock. He snarls and increases his pace. With each possessive thrust, his fingers tighten around my throat incrementally.

Blood pounds in my ears, and the shadows of the maze draw closer. I can still breathe, but the pressure on my arteries restricts the blood flow to my brain.

"Scream for me," he growls. "Give me everything."

"Master!" I cry out, acknowledging his claim over me.

His title is a trigger, and my orgasm hits me with brutal force. Fireworks burst over my darkening world, and my scream fills the maze.

"Abigail!"

His cock pulses inside me, and for the first time, his hot cum lashes into me, marking me as his.

"I'm yours," I sob as bliss consumes me and the shadows lengthen.

Just before I float away entirely, he releases my throat. Oxygenated blood surges back to my brain, and the world turns surreal. The only thing tethering me to reality is Dane's soul-searing green gaze.

"Mine." He seals the promise with a fierce kiss.

47

DANE

It's past noon when Abigail finally stirs in my arms. She turns toward me, and her stunning, aquamarine eyes open. She offers me a lazy smile and stretches like a contented cat.

I marvel at her. I can hardly believe she's given herself to me after all of my crimes against her.

I was incapable of understanding how I'd wronged her until she showed me her powerful, disturbing self-portrait. She makes me see the world in ways I never thought possible. She is my world now. I'm no longer limited to my mundane, tedious existence when I experienced nothing but idle amusement in manipulating others. For the first time in my adult life, I care about someone other than myself.

Abigail is mine to covet, mine to shelter and protect. I'll do anything to keep her happy in my arms like she is right now.

Last night, she placed her full trust in me. I'll never betray that trust.

I press a kiss to her forehead. She hums happily and wraps her arms around me.

This might be the most perfect moment of my life.

"You need to eat," I murmur into her hair.

She cuddles closer. "Let's stay in bed for a while longer."

I can't deny her anything.

I'm not sure how long we hold each other in contented, companionable silence. This is how it's meant to be between us. This is how it will be. Every day for the rest of our lives.

"Daniel!"

Panic spikes through me, and I jolt upright.

That's my mother's shrill voice, echoing down the corridor.

No. She can't be here. James said he wouldn't tell our parents that I'm home.

But there are several sets of footsteps approaching my bedroom. Mum isn't alone.

I surge out of bed and quickly find my sweatpants, tugging them on to cover my nakedness.

"Who is that?" Abigail asks, her voice touched with alarm.

"Stay in here," I command.

I don't have time to explain.

I dart out of the bedroom and shut the door behind me, shielding Abigail from my family.

Dread is a lead weight in my stomach when I see both of my parents, flanked by my traitorous brother. I glower at him, and my fists clench at my sides.

"What the fuck, James? You said you wouldn't tell them I'm here."

His mouth is set in a grim line when he comes to a stop a few feet away from me. Just out of punching distance.

"That was before I knew you'd kidnapped Abigail."

"What?" The question is a touch breathless.

How can he know?

He sneers at me. "Do you think you have the monopoly on depravity in this family? And did you really think that mask was enough to conceal your identity last night?"

I rake a hand through my hair. This can't be happening.

"I heard her say that you kidnapped her. I heard her scream."

"Everyone else there knew it was just a game," I growl.

"They didn't see her after she wrecked my Jeep," he informs me coldly. "She was clearly desperate to get away from you that day. I thought you must've had a bad argument, but when I saw her last night, I finally got the full picture."

I fix him with the full force of my loathing. "Why couldn't you just ask us about this last night? Why didn't you talk to me about it like a man instead of tattling on me to our parents?"

James scoffs. "You had clearly coerced her into being at that party. I couldn't trust a word you said. And you carried her off somewhere before I could approach you. You left me with no choice."

I bare my teeth at him. "You didn't have to call *them.* You still could've come here on your own to ask me about it."

He shakes his head. "I am not Lord of this house yet. Dad is the one with the power to kick you out."

"What have you done this time, Daniel?" my mother demands shrilly. "And what on earth was that party you went to?" She rounds on James, including him in her censure. "Am I right in understanding that both of my sons attended some sort of sordid function last night? That you put the family name at risk of public scandal?"

James waves in dismissal, even though his cheeks flush.

"Everyone was wearing masks," he says quickly. "We don't need to go into the details."

She narrows her beady green eyes at him. "We will return to this conversation later." Her sharp gaze pins me again. "Explain yourself. Where is the woman you've supposedly kidnapped? Will she go quietly if we pay her? How much will your latest sin cost this family?"

"I don't want your money," I bark. "I never have."

My father speaks up for the first time, his words slurring slightly from his chronic alcoholism. "We'll bail you out if we must," he asserts. "Just like all the other times. This will not get into the news cycle. You're still a Graham."

The prospect of accepting anything from them raises my ire. Especially when my father is the one talking about bailing me out. Just like all the times he's been bailed out of sticky situations to escape punishment for his crimes.

"I am not part of this family," I seethe. "I gave up the title."

"And yet, here you are," Mum accuses. "Making yourself at home like the manor belongs to you. You're either in or you're out, Daniel. You've chosen to come back in. That means your actions reflect badly on the family. You will accept our money to pay off this woman. Make her go away."

"Abigail isn't going anywhere!" I thunder.

James is the only one with the good sense to take a step back from my volatility.

My mother and father remain coolly composed, completely unruffled by my uncharacteristic outburst. As though I'm still a child, and I'm incapable of controlling myself.

The awful memories that unlocked when I found Abigail bleeding in the wrecked Jeep rise up to take hold of my mind, my tongue.

"You think you can buy your way out of everything," I hiss at my father. "Just like you bribed the police not to arrest you for killing Katie. You murdered my sister, and you never paid for it."

"Daniel!" Mum's tone is a sharp rebuke. "You know we don't say that name in this house. It upsets your father."

"And you." I narrow my eyes at her. "You thought you could just replace my twin with another spare? With *him*?" I gesture sharply at James, and he pales.

"Let's just take a moment," he cajoles. "We can all have a cup of tea and talk about this rationally."

I bark a bitter laugh. "You think tea is going to help fix this? My sister is dead because of them. I watched her die. I was trapped with her dead body for hours, and none of you ever gave a shit."

"Really, Daniel." My mother sounds scandalized. "There's no need to make a scene. That was years ago. You're not a child anymore."

"I hate you." My tone goes cold and flat. "I thought I felt nothing for you at all, but I truly hate you. Stay the fuck away from me."

"You're the one who came back," my father reminds me with a scowl. "We didn't invite you here."

"I'm leaving," I snap. "I never want to see any of you ever again."

"I don't think so," Mum refuses. "You brought this mess to our doorstep. We're going to clean it up before anyone finds out what you've done. Now, where is this woman you've kidnapped?"

She says it with irritation, not horror. She's not remotely surprised or bothered by the fact that I could commit such a crime. It's simply the optics she's worried about.

Everything for appearances.

"I'm right here."

I whirl and find Abigail standing in the open doorway to my bedroom.

"You can't be out here," I say, gentling my tone when I address her. "Go back inside. I'll handle this."

The last thing I want is to subject her to the cruelty of my relatives. She's already suffered so much at the hands of her own parents. I'll shield her from mine.

My brave, stubborn Abigail lifts her chin and steps up beside me. She fixes my family with an imperious stare and takes my hand in hers.

"I'm with Dane willingly," she asserts.

My heart skips a beat.

Last night, she gave herself to me willingly, but until this moment, I wasn't sure of her loyalty. I wasn't certain that she wouldn't try to leave me again if she had the opportunity to be free of me.

I never intended to give her that choice, but I still didn't know if she would challenge me over it.

"I'm sorry we came here unannounced." Her voice is frosty as she continues to address my parents. She's perfectly poised and icily polite. "We'll leave now."

"Wait just a minute!" Mum insists, bristling at the challenge. "My son isn't going anywhere." She looks at me again, eyes glittering with accusation. "Do you know how difficult it's been to excuse your absence for all these years? To conceal our estrangement? You've come home, and now you're staying."

"You're distressed," Abigail remarks coolly. "I understand. It must be very difficult to have a son who hates you. Maybe you should go have that cup of tea while we pack. I've heard it's good for the nerves."

My mother's face has gone beet red, and she splutters, "You... How dare... In my own home?"

"Americans." My father spits out the word like a curse, a condemnation. "Bloody upstarts."

"Yes, I'm sure we'll all be happy to part ways," Abigail continues smoothly. "Dane and I just need a few minutes to collect our things. Then we'll be out of your hair." She pointedly glances at my father's balding head.

I grin. She's good at this.

I lost my composure, and my fierce Abigail has come to my defense.

How could I ever deserve this woman?

"Come on." James finally speaks up again. "Let's have that cuppa. Now, Mum."

He gently grasps our mother's shoulder and turns her away from me.

"Dad," he calls back over his shoulder as they head for the stairs. "I'm sure there's a bottle of whisky somewhere in the kitchen."

The promise of alcohol moves him like nothing else. My father gives me one final contemptuous sneer. Then he turns and walks away too.

I turn to my woman, my miracle, and trace the curve of her amethyst curl that fascinates me endlessly.

"Thank you," I say. I don't have the words to express the depth of my gratitude, my admiration.

She waves off my thanks. "You're welcome. They deserved it. Now, we need to get the hell out of here. Do you have your own car?"

I nod and trail her into the bedroom to pack. Wherever Abigail goes, I'll follow.

48

ABIGAIL

"It's so beautiful," I gush, spinning in a circle to take in the stunning, historic city of York. "I can't believe you grew up here. It's magical."

Dane is staring at me, not the imposing, centuries-old Minster. I've been studying the intricately carved masonry, and my fingers itch for my paintbrush. I'm not sure when I'll have the opportunity to express this scene on my canvas, so I'm doing my best to commit it to memory.

"Yes," he says softly. "I suppose it is a bit magical."

"A bit?" I tease. "There are medieval buildings lining every cobbled street. It doesn't seem real. It's like we've stepped back into another time."

His mouth tips in a lopsided smile that makes my heart flutter. "Is it?"

He gestures at the man who's painted in purple from head-to-toe, trying his best to remain stationary on a bike.

I've seen better human statues, and I can't suppress a giggle. Dane isn't remotely impressed by the man.

I decide to include the street performer in my painting. The juxtaposition with the historic Minster is whimsical, charming. I'll try to capture Dane's expression of pure bafflement too.

I loop my arm through his, steering us away from the spectacle. "You just don't understand art."

"That's not art."

"You have to open your mind," I urge, but I'm only half-serious. Bantering with him is fun. "Anything can be art."

He scoffs. "Now you're just making up meaningless platitudes. There is no comparison between your work that that purple man."

"Beauty is in the eye of the beholder." I shrug.

He pauses and urges me to face him. One dexterous hand brushes my hair back from my cheek. "There's only one beautiful thing I see here."

I flush with pleasure and cut my gaze away, flustered.

He cups my jaw, urging me to tip my head back so that I have no choice but to look up at him.

"You are the most stunning, remarkable woman I've ever met," he says solemnly. "The way you defended me in front of my parents…" He trails off for a moment and traces the shape of my lips with his thumb. "I can never express what that means to me. How proud I am to call you *mine*."

"They were being cruel to you," I say quietly. "I would do it again a hundred times over. I won't let them hurt you anymore."

His eyes flash. "And I won't let your parents hurt you," he vows in return. "When we get back to Charleston, I'll make sure they won't bother you."

My heart lifts. "We're going back to Charleston?"

He nods. "I booked our tickets from London. We fly out in

a week. I know you want to go home, but there's something I want to show you in York first."

"What is it?" I ask.

I don't mind the short delay. The promise that we're going home is enough for me. I trust Dane to keep his word.

I'm not sure what my life will look like when I return to Charleston—the small, quiet little life I built for myself after college is over now. Dane forcibly removed me from it, but I no longer feel resentment over his decision to take me away. I understand him now. Despite everything, I've chosen him.

He respects me and treats me as his equal. If anything, he reveres me and places my needs above his own.

"It's just there," Dane answers me, pointing at a large red building with white accents.

It looks Victorian, and it probably is. Dane said the Romans were the first to build York's city walls. The Victorian period came nearly two millennia after, even if that era seems like a long time ago to my American sensibilities. Everything in York is frozen in its own time period.

I sigh and lean into Dane, admiring the beauty of our surroundings all over again as we walk the short distance to the red building.

When we approach the front door, I notice the sign in large gold lettering: The Howard Gallery. Dane is indulging my love of art, even though I know he doesn't connect with it the way I do.

"Thank you." I squeeze his hand in a pulse of gratitude as we enter the building.

"Don't thank me yet."

I shoot him a puzzled look, but before I can ask what he means, a tall, slender man in a waistcoat steps into our path.

He's probably in his late twenties, with sandy blond hair

and understated, round glasses with a thin wire rim. He offers me a warm smile.

"You're Abigail Foster?" He extends a hand. "I'm Stephen Lansing."

"It's nice to meet you," I reply automatically, even though I'm somewhat taken aback by his familiarity.

"Dane Graham." Dane's voice is a touch cool when he introduces himself, and he's eyeing Stephen's hand grasping mine.

The younger man quickly releases me to shake Dane's hand instead. "Yes, we spoke on the phone. It's good to meet you in person. I'll be your point of contact at the gallery."

Dane doesn't look impressed. "Shouldn't Abigail be speaking to the owner?"

Stephen lifts his chin. "My father is very busy. He trusts me to manage the collection. I just finished my PhD at the University of York. I'm more than qualified."

"I'm sure you are," I say politely. "Would you mind explaining how you know who I am? I'm a little lost here."

Stephen glances from me to Dane and back again.

"This is a surprise," Dane explains. Then he turns to me. "Your work will be on display here starting this week. It will remain in the gallery for the summer."

I gape at him, then manage to ask, "What work? All of my paintings are back in Charleston."

Stephen looks confused. "You sent pictures," he says to Dane. "The three paintings of the Yorkshire Dales and the self-portrait."

I blink at Dane. "You didn't."

He grins at me. "I did."

My heart lifts. I've never been featured in a gallery before. And I never would've submitted those pieces for consideration myself. I felt they were imperfect, nothing special.

A troubling thought occurs to me.

Dane arranged this. Not me.

I didn't get here on merit.

"How much does it cost?" I ask Stephen, and Dane's hand tightens in a vise around mine.

"Cost?" Stephen is completely befuddled by this entire interaction. "If you choose to sell the paintings to interested buyers, you can name your price. We take a ten percent commission."

"No," I correct him. "I mean, how much did it cost for you to agree to feature my work?"

"I didn't pay him, Abigail," Dane says, voice rough with frustration.

And maybe a touch of hurt.

Oh.

"I'm sorry." I look at Dane when I apologize and brush my thumb over his palm. "I didn't understand the arrangement. Thank you for submitting my work." I turn a friendly smile on Stephen. "I'm thrilled to have my work in your gallery. What do you need from me?"

He returns my smile easily. "Come by sometime tomorrow after close, and we can discuss how you would like your paintings displayed. Is eight o'clock too late for you?"

"Not at all," I confirm. "Eight sounds perfect."

I truly am thrilled to have my work in a real art gallery for the first time in my life, but I'm mostly preoccupied with worry that I've upset Dane.

"I'll see you then," I promise, ending the meeting so that I can be alone with him.

I'll prove to him just how much this means to me.

~

"I'M SORRY." I apologize as soon as we're in the privacy of our rented penthouse.

The view through the floor-to-ceiling windows is surreal. The city of York with its historic architecture is defined by the Minster and Clifford's Tower, the remnants of a Norman castle. We can see for miles beyond the city walls, all the way out to the rolling green hills of the Yorkshire countryside.

But for now, the scene doesn't hold my attention like it did when we checked in several hours ago. I'm too concerned that I've hurt Dane.

"There's no need to apologize," he reassures me, but tension lingers around his jaw.

"I shouldn't have assumed that you paid for me to be featured in the gallery. I know that bothered you."

He caresses my cheek, and I'm easily forgiven.

"Your work speaks for itself," he assures me. "They were all too eager to feature you. If you do choose to sell, I'm sure they'll earn a hefty commission. Although, I would like to request that we keep the self-portrait."

My brow furrows. "Why? Doesn't it disturb you?"

I place my hand over his heart, securing our connection as we both think back to the painful day when I showed him the painting of my anguish.

"No," he replies firmly. "It's the most powerful piece of art I've ever seen. You deserve to share your talent with the world. You deserve to be seen. Celebrated. Your paintings will be in galleries in London and New York. We can travel anywhere you need to go to establish your career. I know you have difficulty accepting my money, but let me do this for you, at least. I'm sure you'll have plenty of your own funds soon enough."

My heart soars, and my eyes sting with a swell of emotion that I fear I recognize.

It's too soon to say it, but I've felt it growing in me every day since he dropped to his knees and said he can't live without me.

It would be so easy to love Dane again.

I think I already do.

But I need to assert my independence first. I need to go back home and build a new life for myself, one that I share with him.

"All I want is to start my own gallery in Charleston," I say instead. "I don't need London or New York. I just want to be home."

I want to put down roots, to feel the security of a home that I never experienced in the house where I was raised.

I think I can have that with Dane. We can share a home together. The first one either of us has ever truly known.

He curves my purple curl around his finger. "Home," he agrees. "We're going home. You'll have your gallery, Abigail."

"It's just a loan," I say firmly. "I'll pay you back."

He shakes his head. "What's mine is yours."

I lift my chin. "I don't have any money to offer now, but the same goes for you. Anything I earn, I'll share with you. We're equals, Dane."

He cups my nape, drawing me closer. "No, we're not. You are so much more than I could ever be."

He crushes his lips to mine, consuming my soft gasp. He worships me with his mouth, his tongue, his teeth. I belong to him, but I've never felt freer than I do in this moment. Empowered. Cherished.

I kiss him back, matching his intensity as I silently pledge my love to him in return.

We move into the bedroom in a frenzy, tearing at each other's clothes. By the time he tosses me onto the bed, I'm naked. He fixes me with a wolfish grin and steps out of his jeans.

He towers over me, completely bare and glorious as a god. His powerful body is so much stronger than mine will ever be.

But I hold my own, softer power over him.

I extend my hand, beckoning him to join me on the bed. He grasps it and kisses my palm.

"One moment, pet."

He steps away, and I whine, "I need you, Dane."

He smirks at me as he rummages in his duffel bag. "So impatient. You'll get my cock in your tight cunt soon enough. I want to play with you first."

When he returns to the bed, he's holding a long coil of rope. Anticipatory pleasure races over me in a light shiver.

I love when he ties me up so that I'm helpless to resist him.

But I'm craving something sweeter today, something more sensual.

"I don't want to fight you," I admit. "I just want us to be together."

He drops a kiss on my forehead. "I'm feeling the same way, little dove."

"Then why do you need the rope?"

"Because even though you're not going to struggle, I'm still in control. And I want to bind you."

I huff out a breath, but I'm not really exasperated. "So selfish," I tease.

"Don't worry. I'll still make you come so hard that you'll weep in gratitude. I'll always take care of you."

I release a contented hum. "I know. I trust you."

He climbs onto the king-size bed with me and grasps my waist, dragging me to the center of the mattress.

"Kneel," he commands.

I obey easily. I have no desire to challenge him today. I simply want to please him. And to be worshipped in return.

"Put your hands behind your head, and keep them there."

When I'm in the position he desires, he settles behind me. His thighs are on either side of my own, and his broad chest cradles my back. He presses one big hand to my sternum, urging me to lean into his strength.

I melt against him with a sigh.

"Breathe with me," he murmurs, nuzzling my hair and inhaling my scent.

Salt-kissed cedarwood enfolds me, and I relax deeper into his embrace.

Our chests rise and fall as one as we take deep, even breaths together.

My heartbeat is slow and steady beneath his hand. I wonder if his matches mine.

A sense of intimacy blossoms between us. I've experienced carnal bliss with him many times, but this bond is so intense that it's almost painful. My body hums for him, but I'm not throbbing with desperate lust. I could simply stay in this peaceful space with him for an eternity.

We drift for a while, and my eyes slide closed as my head drops back against his shoulder. He presses tender kisses along the column of my throat, warming my body with simmering desire.

His broad palm remains pressed over my heart. His other hand is wrapped in rope, and when he drags his knuckles beneath my breasts, the slightly rough hemp stimulates my sensitized skin. I'm hyperaware of him, and my nerves sparkle and dance everywhere the rope grazes me.

I release all of the lingering tension in my body on a low moan and surrender to him completely.

"Good girl," he praises. "Such a sweet pet."

The rope wraps around my chest in a slow, sensual embrace. His hands never break contact with my skin while he binds me. We're constantly connected, melting into one another.

My heart beats for his.

The rope winds around my chest, knotting in an intricate pattern that I can't quite follow. Dane handles me with quiet confidence, and I simply allow myself to be with him.

I don't have to fight. I don't have to say anything.

All I have to do is remain where he's positioned me and breathe with him, just as he's commanded.

But as the rope coils tighter, my chest is constricted incrementally. I try to match his breaths, but my lungs can't fully expand beneath the steady pressure of the rope cage he's weaving around me.

"Dane." I pant his name and draw in a sip of oxygen.

"Your body is mine," he intones, tugging the rope a fraction tighter. "Your breath is mine." Another tug, another shallow breath. "Your pleasure is mine."

"Yes," I whisper.

I've entered an almost meditative state. All that exists is my breath and his hands on the ever-tightening rope.

My lashes flutter, and my mind floats.

The pressure stops increasing, but the tension doesn't ease. He ties off his work, leaving me in the restrictive embrace of his cruelly sensual rope.

He hasn't bound my limbs at all. I could try to run away if I wanted to. I could try to free myself from his knots.

But I'm thoroughly subdued by his will. I submitted as soon as his hand settled over my heart.

He gently grasps my wrists and directs my arms to drop. "On your hands and knees."

The murmured order sinks into me, and I float into position. As I move my body, the rope shifts around me in a tight caress. His hand settles on my back, stroking the length of my spine, and I arch into his touch.

My pleasure is warm and pleasant, like a perfect summer morning on a pristine beach. I bask in it, reveling in the beauty of this moment with him.

His touch trails lower, tracing my swollen, aching folds. I'm wet and ready for him, and he growls his satisfaction when he tests the slickness between my legs.

He takes his time toying with me, playing with me like he has all the time in the world to explore my pussy. He seems intent on memorizing each of my shallow sighs and quiet whimpers in response to his teasing touch.

My body hums for him, bliss illuminating every inch of my flesh until I'm incandescent with pleasure.

"Master." My lips form his title, but barely any sound escapes from my restricted chest. "Master, Master, Master..."

It's beyond an orgasm. There is no building tension, no vicious, cresting wave of ecstasy. I am a being of pure pleasure, endless and complete.

He plays with all of me, exploring my ass as well as my pussy. He tests me, entering me in teasing strokes before pushing deeper. Stretching wider.

Something cool and wet drops onto my asshole, and I

shudder at the intensity of carnal sensation when my body is alight with sensual awareness.

A larger intrusion presses against my tight hole, and I know it's not his finger this time.

"Relax," he coaxes. "You can take the plug. I want to fill you up while I fuck your cunt."

I've never experienced anything like this, but I trust him implicitly. My body softens to accommodate the intrusion. He pumps it into me in slow, short strokes, stretching me wider with each gentle thrust. Pain edges my pleasure, and my fingers curl into the sheets.

"Almost there," he urges. "Good girl. Take it for me."

He tweaks my clit with his other hand, and my inner muscles contract. The plug slips into me fully, and the pain abates as it settles deep inside me.

The penetration is strange, but not entirely uncomfortable. And as he continues to stroke my clit, the pleasure that fills my entire being begins to concentrate at my core.

"Are you ready for me?"

"Always," I whisper.

He kneels behind me and lines his hard cock up with my wet pussy. Now that he's almost inside me, I'm desperate for him to fill me. He enters me in one long, slow slide, then stills. I lift my hips in wanton invitation for more, and his fingers dig into my butt, holding me still with a bite of bruising pain.

He stretches me wide open and simply stares down at me, indulging in the lewd sight of the toy filling my ass while his cock is buried deep inside me.

I begin to quiver. I've never felt so unbearably full, and the erotic stimulation is becoming too intense to bear.

He taps on the base of the plug, and I cry out as forbidden

pleasure shudders through me. It undulates through my core, and my inner walls contract around him.

He hisses out a sharp curse, and his fingers flex into my tender flesh.

Finally, mercifully, he starts to move inside me. His cockhead drags across my g-spot, and I shake with the force of the ecstasy that rolls through me in relentless waves. Each time he thrusts deep, he pushes on the base of the plug. He lays claim to my body, just as he promised from the very beginning.

Tears gather at the corners of my eyes; the strength of my emotions is too intense for me to contain them within myself.

He takes me in a merciless rhythm, using my body for his own pleasure. I'm lost in a flood of euphoria, and I fall out of time and place. All that exists is Dane.

He comes undone on a roar, and his hot seed lashes into me, branding me. His name shudders from my constricted chest on a choked cry.

He catches me as my muscles give out, holding me beneath him to keep us joined for a few moments longer.

"No," I whimper when he finally pulls out.

He shushes me gently. "I promised to take care of you," he reminds me. "You need to breathe properly."

His hands are on me again, tugging at the rope.

"I've got you," he promises, slowly uncoiling the length from around my body.

As it loosens, my breaths come deeper, slower. I remain cocooned in my transcendent state, on my own personal plane of being where only Dane and I exist.

He holds me, his massive body enfolding mine from behind. The rope has fallen away entirely, and his hand has returned to my heart.

We breathe together in perfect time, our souls a perfect match.

49

ABIGAIL

"That's brilliant." Stephen grins at me and scrawls a final note on his tablet. "I think the lighting here will really make your landscapes pop."

We've spent the last two hours walking through the gallery and reviewing the best placements for my paintings. I'm deeply gratified at the time he's putting into making the arrangements. It's nearly ten PM.

"I've kept you too long," I say. "If that's everything, I'll get out of here so you can lock up."

"It's been a pleasure getting to know you better," he replies, dismissing my assertion that I've taken up too much of his evening. "And it's always exciting to meet an emerging talent. We're lucky to be the first gallery to feature your work."

I duck my head. "That's very kind of you to say."

"I mean it." He sounds sincere. "Come to the office with me for a minute. We'll have a drink to celebrate. I have a beautiful fifteen-year-old whisky. Do you like whisky?"

"Not really," I equivocate. I don't know if it feels entirely appropriate to have a drink at the gallery. "I like sweeter drinks."

His broad smile doesn't waver, and he gives me a conspiratorial wink. "Don't tell anyone, but I do too. I have plenty of soft drinks we can use as mixers."

"With your nice whisky?" I attempt a polite way to decline his invitation. "Isn't that basically a crime in the U.K.?"

He laughs. "I think it's considered a crime anywhere in the world, but I can keep a secret."

"All right," I capitulate. "Just a little splash for me, please. I really don't like the taste of alcohol."

This is my first big break, and I don't want to offend the young man who's taking a chance on me. His father owns this gallery. It reeks of nepotism, but I've been genuinely impressed by Stephen's knowledge and eye for detail. I'm confident leaving my work in his capable hands for the summer.

I follow him back to his office, and I wish I had my phone to text Dane that I'll be late. He's expecting me back at the penthouse around this time, and I don't want him to worry.

But my phone battery died weeks ago. Dane didn't bother to bring the correct charger from America once he messaged my friends to allay their concerns.

He's assured me that I'll have my phone back as soon as we return to Charleston, so I haven't been too concerned about it.

But it would be good to text him now. I'd rather not have him break into the gallery to get to me if he thinks I've stayed too late.

Even as I think it, a small smile plays around my lips. He might be overbearing at times, but my fiercely possessive lover would do anything to protect me.

Still, it's best to make this a very quick celebratory drink.

I don't actually want Dane to kick down the door.

"Please, sit." Stephen gestures at the small couch in the cramped but tastefully furnished office.

I oblige him, sitting down while he goes behind the desk to retrieve his stashed whiskey.

"Just a tiny splash," I reiterate when he pulls out a half-empty bottle.

His brow furrows, and he looks confused for a moment. Then he smacks his hand to his forehead.

"Idiot," he mumbles. He offers me a rueful smile. "The cups are in the kitchen with the soft drinks. I hope you don't mind a mug."

"You really don't have to go to all this trouble," I say, giving him an out. "I'm fine without a drink."

"We have to toast to your success," he insists. "I'll be right back."

True to his word, he's gone for less than two minutes before he returns with two mugs filled with soda. One has a pug dog with a monocle, and the other features kittens dancing on a rainbow.

He tips the tiniest splash of whiskey into the kitten mug for me. That amount of alcohol should be easily manageable. The ride back to the penthouse will take less than ten minutes, and there's a taxi rank right outside the gallery. I can get back to Dane quickly once I down this drink.

"We used to have a mug that said, 'Gough hard or Gough home,' but I smashed it last week," Stephen says as he presses the kitten mug into my hand.

Our fingers brush accidentally, and I almost spill my drink in my haste to withdraw from the awkward moment.

"Sorry," he says with a shaky laugh. "I always get nervous around beautiful women. I'm talking bollocks."

That comment makes me more uncomfortable, so I edge away from Stephen and take a gulp of whisky-tinged soda. It's sweet and goes down easily.

"Ah, shit," he continues. "I'm being awkward as fuck. I'm sorry. I spend so much time working at the gallery that I think I'm forgetting how to socialize like a normal person."

I offer him a polite smile. There's no need to antagonize him after all the work he's putting in for my art, but I won't encourage him, either.

"Have you worked here long?" I make small talk instead of reassuring him that his comment was acceptable. "You said you recently finished your PhD, right?"

I take another big sip of my drink. I don't want to appear like I'm rushing to get away from him, but Dane really will start to get worried soon.

And I'm liking Stephen less and less with every passing minute.

His eyes flick to my lips and then back to my eyes. I pretend I didn't notice, but I let my smile drop.

"Yeah," he replies, chest puffing with pride. "I'm Dr. Lansing now. You know, I have a lot of connections in London. Some of my uni mates live there now. I could make some calls if you want."

I take another sip of my sweet drink. I wish Stephen had put some ice in the mugs. It's too warm in this cramped office, even though the temperature must be dropping outside.

"That's okay, but thank you." I refuse his offer. "I have plans to open my own gallery in Charleston. I won't have time to travel to London."

"There's no need to be coy." His voice drops deeper, and I

don't trust the slightly husky edge to his words. "I'm happy to help you out."

My mug is over half-empty now, thank goodness. I'm ready to leave. I don't like how pushy he's being, even if he has helped me a lot today.

"Like I said, I don't have the time. But I appreciate the offer."

My skin is getting sticky with perspiration. I really should step outside sooner rather than later.

"Are you okay?" Stephen asks, brow furrowed with concern.

Heat rolls beneath the surface of my skin in a nauseating wave.

"Actually, I'm feeling a little lightheaded," I admit. "I need some fresh air."

"Drink some more. It'll cool you down. And it's mostly soda. The sugar should help."

I suppose I haven't eaten enough tonight, since this meeting is running far later than planned. Sugary soda isn't going to help all that much, but I drain the last of my drink anyway. I'm so hot, and I need to get outside into the cooler night air.

"Stay for a little while longer," he cajoles. "We should talk more about your career."

He slides out of focus for a second.

I'm more than just lightheaded. I'm getting dizzy.

I wish I could call Dane to come pick me up.

I close my eyes and draw in a deep breath, willing the room to stop spinning.

"You should let me make those London calls." Stephen is still talking to me, but his voice sounds oddly far away. "I really can help you out."

His hand is on my knee.

What the hell?

My eyes snap open, and I surge to my feet.

The world tilts, and Stephen catches my elbow to steady me.

"Whoa." He laughs. "Steady on. How much of a lightweight are you? I knew you Americans can't hold your drink, but this is ridiculous."

I shake my head. "You said it was just a splash. I saw you..." My tongue is thick in my mouth. "I saw you pour it."

I'm on the couch again. Stephen's leg is pressed against mine. He brushes his hand over my hot cheek and tucks my hair behind my ear.

"You really are beautiful," he says. "And so talented. Any man would be lucky to have you."

"I'm with Dane." My fierce declaration comes out soft and slurred. "Get away from me."

His hand is on my thigh. "Your boyfriend doesn't have to know. This is our secret, right? You agreed."

I shake my head again, and the room spins. "I didn't. Just a drink."

"You're talented, but you won't get ahead in your career without the right connections. I'm a useful person to know. We should have a good relationship."

"No." It's all I can manage when everything is swirling around me.

Cool air hits my chest.

"You're so flushed," Stephen says as he parts another button on my blouse.

I try to bat his hands away, but he easily brushes me off.

"Stop." It's little more than a slurred whisper.

My stomach churns, heightening my nausea.

The cool air caressing my bare stomach is a blissful relief from the heat that's surging beneath my skin. I groan at the sweet reprieve, and my muscles relax.

"That's better," Stephen praises. "I knew you could be friendly. There's no need to be so uptight."

Tears wet my lashes, blurring the spinning world.

Dane. I want Dane.

The hands that are touching me are all wrong. The fingers are slenderer, the palms slick and clammy. He gropes at me without finesse, exploring my body for his own pleasure rather than mine.

My eyes slide closed, and my low moan of despair fills the cramped office.

50

DANE

The sign on the gallery door is flipped to *closed*, but the door is unlocked. Abigail must still be here with Stephen.

Irritation tightens my jaw. She was supposed to return to the penthouse nearly twenty minutes ago. I've tried to give her space to work—I have to respect her independence—but I can't wait any longer.

I should've given her a damn phone so I can reach her whenever I want.

Or I should've just accompanied her to her meeting at the gallery. I should've stayed by her side, where I can watch over her. I should keep her on a leash so that she's never out of my sight.

I shake my head sharply and push open the door. She won't thank me if I burst into her meeting like an enraged, possessive brute.

But I can't bring myself to put on my civilized mask, either.

Stephen will have to deal with the cold, clinical monster at my core. It's the best I can do at the moment when all I want is to punish him for keeping Abigail from me.

I walk through the gallery, searching for them. The lights are still on, but I don't hear their voices echoing from any of the spacious rooms.

I scowl and find a narrow corridor on the ground floor that's marked *staff only*. They must be somewhere in the back offices.

Just the thought of that little fucker being alone with Abigail in private makes white-hot rage pulse through my veins.

I remind myself that she won't like it if I punch the gallery owner's son in his entitled rich kid face. No matter how much I would enjoy smashing those pretentious glasses with my fists.

A low moan rolls from the back office, and I immediately know it's hers. I live for that sound.

And she's making it for another man.

My chest hollows out, and the ground shifts beneath my feet.

This can't be real. She wouldn't.

She gave herself to me.

The corridor blurs around me as I surge toward them. All of my muscles coil tight, ready to unleash my fury in a burst of violence.

I storm into the office, and my stomach drops at the sight of them together on the small couch.

She's beneath him, her blouse unbuttoned. His hands are on her breasts, and his lips taste hers.

He'll die for this. And Abigail...

I'll think about her punishment later.

Because I can never hurt her. Never.

Back in her studio, I offered her the heart from my chest. She might as well have ripped it out with her bare hands.

I bellow at the agony of her betrayal.

Him. I focus on *him.* He'll suffer and scream before I end his miserable life.

He tears his lips from hers, and his brown eyes are wide behind his large glasses when he sees me surging toward him.

"Wait!" he gasps, but he'll get no mercy from me.

I grab him by his shirt and yank him off of her before tossing him across the room like garbage. His filthy hands touched her. His taint mars her perfect skin.

He scrambles away from me, but there's nowhere for him to go. I lash out, my boot connecting with his jaw. It shatters at the impact, and he screams. I stomp my heel down on the back of the hand that touched what's mine. The fine bones crunch beneath my heel.

Before I can destroy his other hand, Abigail moans again.

In horror at my violence?

I stiffen. I shouldn't be affected by her fear. She should be afraid of me.

I'm the monster out of her worst nightmares. I always have been.

"Dane..." My name is slow and oddly slurred.

I whirl to face her, panic spiking through my system. Did I injure her somehow when I tore that bastard off of her? Even in my rage, the thought makes my stomach lurch with a surge of nausea.

Her lovely eyes are unfocused and strangely dull. It's inherently *wrong.* She's peering at me like she can't quite see me.

She's sprawled out on the couch exactly as she was when I

stormed in. She hasn't tried to cover herself. She hasn't moved at all.

Her hand twitches toward me, and her soft whimper of distress shreds me.

A red haze descends over my vision.

He drugged my Abigail. He touched her. He violated her.

And I failed to protect her.

So many men have wanted my beautiful pet. Sick bastards who would do anything just to touch her. Taste her. Fuck her.

Whether she wants them or not.

I may be a monster, but I'm *her* monster.

I grasp her chilled hand and brush my lips over her knuckles.

"I've got you," I promise. "You're safe."

Behind me, Stephen groans through his broken jaw.

I carefully button her blouse so that she's covered, hiding her from his covetous eyes.

The eyes that I'm about to pluck out.

"Don't watch, Abigail," I command softly, stroking her hair back from her cheek. Her lashes flutter. "That's it. Close your eyes for me. I'll take care of this. I'll take care of you."

I drop a kiss on her lips, and they're far too still beneath mine.

Rage surges back to the fore, and I round on my enemy.

He's crawling away from me, dragging himself along the aged cream carpet with his unbroken hand.

I smash his delicate bones with my heel, ensuring he'll never hold a pen again.

Not that he'll need to.

He'll be dead within minutes.

A savage rush soars through my system, and if it weren't for Abigail's distress, I would bark a cruel laugh at the incredible high. As it is, I focus my righteous fury on the only thing that matters now: making him suffer in the short time he has left.

I surrender to the red haze, and I take out my retribution in blood.

When I return to Abigail, my hands are coated in gore. I frown down at them. I can't let his filthy blood mar her body.

Now that I'm coming down from my vicious high, some of my rationality is returning.

There's a dead body to deal with.

Ron was so easy to dispose of. Back in Charleston, the natural predator had done all the work for me. The alligator didn't leave any trace of him behind.

But this...

Stephen is a bloody mess in a gallery in the middle of York. I hope to fuck there's not a camera in this office.

Probably not, since he won't have wanted a recording of what he was doing to Abigail.

My fists clench at my sides, and I wish I could kill him all over again.

I take a breath and force myself to think.

I'll have to leave Stephen here. I don't have a hope of dragging his body anywhere to dispose of it; there are too many tourists in the city for me to get him very far without someone screaming.

There will be an investigation once his body is found in the gallery, but there's nothing concrete to link me to the crime. I had reason to be in this building only yesterday. If I've left any small traces of myself behind, they can be easily explained away.

I inspect my hands. None of the blood is mine. My heavy

boots did most of the work until I squeezed the last of the life out of him.

I'll have to dispose of the boots. And my clothes. I'll drop them in the river later.

Luckily, I'm dressed in a black shirt and dark wash jeans. The blood that's splattered my clothes won't be easily visible when I step outside into the night.

I'm no forensic expert. I might be missing something, but if I get the hell out of the country as soon as possible, I won't be around for the police to question me.

I have to get Abigail back to the safety of the penthouse. As soon as she wakes up tomorrow, we'll leave. London is only a couple of hours away. We can be on a flight by tomorrow night.

I lift her limp body and cradle her close to my chest.

"You're safe," I promise. "Everything will be okay."

51

DANE

Abigail stirs in my arms with a groan. I shush her and pull her closer, stroking her silken hair to soothe her. Warm tears wet my chest, and she sobs softly.

"You're all right," I promise. "We're back at the penthouse. I've got you."

Her delicate body convulses in a violent shudder.

"He can't hurt you." I can't quite keep the growl from roughening my reassurance. "He'll never touch you again."

"What happened?" she asks, shaking against me. "We had one drink. I was so hot and dizzy. And then..."

My throat is too tight to speak. Her distress shreds me.

My failure to protect her twists my insides into painful knots.

"Did he..." She chokes on the question. "I don't remember..."

I force myself to say, "When I got to you, his hands were on you, but he was fully dressed."

She blinks up at me. "So you...got to me in time?"

I manage a jerky nod.

It hadn't been in time. Not at all.

He'd groped her and stripped off her shirt. He'd imprinted his taint onto her creamy skin.

She wraps her arms around me, clinging on to me like I'm her anchor in the storm.

I don't deserve it, but I'm selfish enough to cage her in my own embrace.

"I wanted you so desperately," she murmurs against my neck. "I wanted to leave."

The words should be a balm to my ravaged heart, but all I feel is shame searing my chest.

For an insane, agonized moment, I'd thought she was with him willingly. I'd assumed the worst because deep down, I've always known I'm not worthy of her.

I've craved her too much to care about my unworthiness.

I wanted her, so I took her. I made her mine, whether she consented or not.

She's still mine.

I can't let her go, no matter how undeserving I am.

"We're at the penthouse?" she asks, peering around to get her bearings. "Why?"

"Because it's the safest place for you. As soon as you feel ready to travel, we'll go back to Charleston. We can be in London in two hours for the flight."

"I mean..." She shakes her head as though to clear it. "Where are the police? Didn't you report Stephen for what he did to me?"

A shadow of my righteous rage tightens my muscles. "I'm sure the police are dealing with him now."

They'll have found his dead body this morning. He's in a body bag, already rotting.

"Is it okay for us to go back to Charleston now?" she presses. "Won't the police want to talk to me?"

I contemplate her for a moment, debating how much to tell her. She'll probably be upset if I tell her Stephen is dead, but I also don't want to lie to her.

"What is it that you're not saying, Dane?"

As always, she sees right through me.

"We need to leave the country because Stephen is dead," I say, flat and matter of fact.

"What?" Her eyes go wide, and she reels back.

My arms tighten around her, trapping her.

"He tried to rape you," I growl. "I saved you."

"And you..." She swallows hard. "You killed him?"

"Yes. He can never hurt you like that again."

"No." She tries to pull away again, but I don't allow it.

"It's done, Abigail."

The sooner we can move past this, the better.

"You killed someone, Dane!" she exclaims, as though she can't quite believe it.

"To protect you," I counter roughly.

I don't like the way she's looking at me. Like she doesn't know what I'm capable of.

She hasn't looked at me like that since the day we fucked in the ruined barn in the rain.

"That's worse!" she cries. "That means it's my fault."

"It's *his* fault," I snap. "That bastard drugged you. He was going to rape you. The world is a safer place without him in it. You're safer."

She threads her hands through her hair. "No, no, no."

"It's all right." I try to soothe her, but she cringes away from my tender touch.

My heart shreds into bloody ribbons.

"Let me go," she moans. "Let me go, Dane!"

I grasp her closer. "I can't."

A sharp knock on the penthouse door shatters the awful moment. I want to ignore it. I don't want to put an inch of space between my body and hers.

Another knock, harder this time. "North Yorkshire Police."

Fuck.

How are they here already? What clue did I leave behind that would so obviously lead to me?

I smooth my hair into a neater style and climb off the bed. I'm already dressed, ready to head to London the moment Abigail was prepared.

I can deal with the police. I just have to remember how to put on my charming mask.

They have nothing concrete connecting me to the crime. They can't.

Even if they did have forensic evidence that raised suspicion, there's no way it's been processed this quickly.

I take a breath, summon up an expression of confusion and mild concern, then open the door.

"What's this about?" I ask, affable but bewildered.

The uniformed woman peers past me, looking for something. Or someone.

"Is Abigail Foster here?" she asks, her voice clipped and official.

Abigail.

Why would they want to talk to her?

"I'm here," she says from behind me, and I bite back a curse. "What do you need?"

For a moment, fear swamps me. She's going to turn me in. She's going to tell them that I killed Stephen.

But she doesn't say anything else. She steps up beside me and takes my hand in hers, just like when she defended me in front of my family.

I stare down at her with open awe.

She's frightened of my murderous capabilities, but she's still standing by me. She's still choosing me.

"Abigail Foster, you are under arrest on suspicion of the murder of Stephen Lansing."

"No!" I bark, angling my body between the officer and Abigail.

There's another officer at the end of the hall. He fixes me with a grim stare and comes to join his partner.

"Step aside," he warns me.

Horror crashes down on me, heavy enough that my knees threaten to buckle.

Abigail was Stephen's last appointment yesterday. There will be a written record of it. The police might've already found some sort of drugs in his office. His time of death will align with the time she was in the gallery.

I killed Stephen to save her, but I condemned her.

"Sir, I need you to step aside. Now," the woman insists.

"I'm the one you want." My voice is cold, utterly unfeeling.

Both officers look at me, and they immediately recognize the face of a predator. I don't try to hide it. I let them see exactly what I am.

"Dane, no!"

Abigail's hand tightens around mine, but I yank free of her weaker hold.

Prison has always been my worst-case scenario, ever since the day I shoved Peter out of the window when I was eleven years old. I've spent my entire life since then avoiding this fate.

I wanted so badly to have Abigail, but I was never worthy of her.

I never will be.

"I killed Stephen Lansing," I announce without an ounce of remorse.

After everything I've done to Abigail, redemption isn't possible. I stalked her and violated her. I kidnapped her and caged her. The least I can do now is walk into a cage of my own to save her.

52

DANE

I stare at the mangled remains of Stephen Lansing, and I don't bother to prevent my lips from curving with vindictive pleasure.

The detective taps the photo. "You don't seem disturbed by the crime scene."

I blink, and my fleeting expression of cruel satisfaction drops away. I meet the detective squarely in the eye, and he flinches ever so slightly. He can sense that there's an unrepentant predator in this tiny gray room with him.

"Why did you do it?" he presses. "Stephen must've done something terrible to deserve this kind of beating."

I don't say anything. I simply skewer the man with an icy stare.

I'm supposed to be under questioning, but he will be the one to squirm, not me.

The detective shifts in his seat and tries a different angle. "Something happened between the two of you, and things got heated. Maybe it went too far. Maybe you didn't mean to kill him."

He makes the suggestions like he's extending a helping hand, offering me a scenario with a reduced sentence.

He thinks he can win some sort of battle of wills between us, but he doesn't understand yet that I'm not engaging.

I confessed to the arresting officer in order to save Abigail, but I'm not going to give this man one more incriminating word out of my mouth.

The prospect of spending a life sentence in a cage sends a chill shuddering down my spine, but I resolutely ignore it. I will not show fear.

If it means securing Abigail's freedom, I'll pay any price. I'll face the consequences for my actions, even if I don't feel a shred of remorse for what I did to the bastard who assaulted her.

I'd kill him again a thousand times over.

She's the only thing that matters to me.

A sharp knock on the door to the interrogation room cuts through the thick silence. The detective jolts with surprise, and he takes a moment to collect himself before standing to see who's interrupting us.

A middle-aged woman with a severely sharp gray bob haircut waits in the open doorway.

"I'm Madeline Taylor, Dr. Graham's solicitor," she introduces herself.

"No," I dismiss her before she can step foot in the room. "I've already waived my right to representation."

I've already confessed. There's no point trying to plead not guilty.

Ms. Taylor narrows her brown eyes on me. "I implore you to reconsider."

It sounds more like a command than a request, and I raise a brow at her.

"No."

"Lord Graham sent me," she insists. "I'm here to ensure—"

"Go away." I don't try to keep the snap from my tone. No fucking way am I accepting help from my father.

He's not actually concerned with helping me; he's trying to avoid a scandal.

I'm not even sure how he found out about my arrest so quickly, but I'm not surprised. He has connections in law enforcement and local government. Someone will have alerted him to the mess I've made.

"If Dr. Graham doesn't consent to your presence, I'm afraid I'll have to ask you to leave," the detective says.

He probably thinks that my refusal to cooperate will make his job easier. I plan to make this process as painfully frustrating for him as possible, and I don't need a solicitor for that.

"Daniel!" My mother's voice is shrill, echoing down the hallway just outside the interrogation room.

My stomach drops.

Fuck.

The last thing I want is to see my parents when I'm in such a vulnerable position.

Mum pushes Ms. Taylor aside and strides into the room, my father right behind her.

"You can't be in here." The detective's chest puffs with outrage.

My father flicks an imperious wave at him. "Leave us."

"I don't think—"

"This is Lord David Graham," Ms. Taylor cuts him off in

brittle tones. "If you want him to leave, complain to your superiors. See what they say to that."

The detective's cheeks turn red, and his shoulders stiffen. His jaw works as though he's chewing over a retort as he exits the room.

"I'd like a private word with my son," Dad tells the solicitor.

She quickly excuses herself with a deferential nod.

Her obsequiousness sets my teeth on edge. My father thinks he can buy anything he wants: her loyalty, the detective's compliance, and my freedom.

But I'm not going anywhere. Abigail will not face arrest because of my cowardice. I will not bend to my family's will.

"What have you done this time, Daniel?" My mother huffs, beady green eyes flashing with fury. "A murder charge? I thought we were clear when you were a child. You've always known what would happen if you didn't curb your violent nature."

"Do you know what you might've cost this family?" Dad thunders, face going almost purple with his own rage. "If the chief constable hadn't called me, this might've gone too far for damage control. As it is, you will be able to walk out of here within the hour, and this incident will be forgotten."

"And then you're coming home, where you belong," Mum insists. "No more wayward behavior or galivanting off to America."

"I gave up the fucking title, and I will not come home to accept it," I growl, hackles up like a cornered beast. "Now, get out."

My mother scoffs. "As if you would ever be allowed to inherit the title after what you've done. No, James remains the heir. You will come back to the estate where we can keep an eye on you."

All of my muscles tense with barely suppressed aggression: the primal urge to defend myself. She wants to lock me in a cage far smaller than prison, even if it would seem vaster. I'd rather be confined to a cell than that awful manor with my parents as my jailors.

"I've already confessed." I fling it at them like a grenade. "By the time the morning news comes out, your precious reputation will be in tatters."

Mum splutters, at an uncharacteristic loss for words.

"Damn you!" Dad barks. "I will not permit this! Retract your statement."

I lean back in my chair as though it's a throne, enjoying my power over them. I'm about to condemn myself to jail, but I'll take them down along with me.

"I hope this scandal ruins you. Just like you've deserved ever since you killed my sister. This punishment is thirty years overdue."

"That was an accident," he seethes. "You're acting like a little boy with a grudge. If you want to act like a child, you will be treated like one."

"Was it an accident to get behind the wheel of that Jeep when you were intoxicated?" I demand, my own decades-long rage bubbling to the fore. "Was it an accident to pay off the authorities to look the other way about your blood alcohol level when you were taken to hospital, and they saved your miserable life? You know what you did. You killed your own daughter. Admit it!"

"Fine!" he rails. "I was an irresponsible parent. And it's my greatest regret that *you* weren't the one to die that night. You have no idea the shame you've caused this family, do you?"

"Your father's right," Mum adds, voice sharp enough to rake me like claws. "You've been rotten since the day you were born. What did I do to deserve a child like you, Daniel?"

"You made me this way!" I thunder. "You want to know why your precious heir is a psychopath? Look in the fucking mirror."

"I won't tolerate this nonsense any longer," Dad growls. "Retract your statement, and then you're coming home."

I cross my arms over my chest and fix them with a heartless glower.

"You can't control me any longer. There's nothing you can do to stop this. In a few hours, the news will break that you raised a murderer, and the Graham name will be dragged through the mud. You deserve so much worse, but I'll do everything in my power to destroy your precious reputation. It's the only thing you've ever cared about, and I will make sure you never recover from this."

My mother buries her face in her hand, and my father's mouth opens and closes like a fish out of water.

My lips curve in my cruelest smile.

"You wanted me to be part of the family unit, didn't you?" I drawl. "You're finally getting your wish. We all go down together."

53

ABIGAIL

The man I love is a murderer.

Dane killed Stephen Lansing to save me. And now, he's turned himself in to the police in order to spare me from being arrested.

I should feel safer with him in handcuffs—he's the psychopath who stalked and kidnapped me, and he's a cold-blooded killer. I saw it in his icy stare when he told the cops that he's responsible for Stephen's death.

But now that he's been taken to the police station, cold settles over me. I hug my arms to my chest, as though I can hold myself together when I'm threatening to fall apart.

"Do you have tea?" the cop who arrested Dane asks.

Her partner is waiting in the corridor outside the penthouse, and two other officers have already left with Dane in cuffs. It took a while for them to call in backup to take him away, so it's probably been almost an hour since the awful scene started to unfold.

An hour since I discovered that Dane truly is capable of murder.

If I'm being honest with myself, I've suspected it before. Once he kidnapped me, I wasn't sure what he might do in order to possess me completely.

"There must be tea here," the woman, Officer Singh, says when I don't answer right away.

She's speaking to me in a calm, almost gentle tone. As though she actually cares about my mental well-being.

Before, she'd been abrupt and coolly professional.

That was when she thought I was the killer. Now, she's all warmth and concern.

I'm not convinced. She wants me to relax around her so that I'll give evidence against Dane.

My teeth worry at my lower lip as she steps into the open-plan kitchen and finds tea in the cupboard. This rented penthouse is well stocked, so I'm not surprised that she easily finds what she's looking for.

In the few minutes it takes her to boil the kettle, I take several deep breaths and struggle to untangle my thoughts.

"How do you take it?" she asks, as though she's my gracious host.

I don't drink tea unless it's iced and has heaps of sugar, but I'm chilled to the bone, so I decide that a hot drink is a good idea.

"Lots of milk and three sugars, please," I request.

She tries and fails to hide a grimace.

I shake my head slightly to clear it. If she wants to be friendly, I need to keep things cordial. An adversarial tone won't get me out of this.

Exchanging verbal barbs won't save Dane.

It's an automatic thought, and I try to ignore it. I'm not at all certain that Dane should be freed from police custody.

He's dangerous.

"Sorry," I apologize as Officer Singh approaches me with the cup of tea that she clearly finds offensively sweet. "I should've made a cup for you."

"It's not a problem," she replies, settling down on the plush cream armchair beside where I'm perched on the edge of a matching couch. "I'm sure this is very difficult for you."

I cut my gaze away from hers and look out at the view of York Minster and the distant countryside that's visible through the floor-to-ceiling windows. Only yesterday, I marveled at the perfection of this stunning place and the fact that I was sharing it with Dane, my dark god.

I take a sip of tea and don't reply in any way, not even to nod in agreement. The hot liquid is still too bitter on my tongue, even though it's sweetened with sugar and diluted with milk. I force myself to swallow it down, and I welcome the warmth that suffuses my chest. At least it chases the worst of the chill away.

"I'd like to get a clearer picture of what happened to Stephen Lansing," she continues, and her soft tone doesn't reach her sharp brown eyes. "You were the last person to meet with him, according to the schedule we found on his tablet. He took thorough notes of your meeting, and the last entry was timestamped around his estimated time of death. We'll know more as we process the scene, but now you have an opportunity to help us understand Dr. Graham's motives."

I press my lips together. I have no idea what to say, what I even *want* to say.

I could tell her the truth: that Stephen drugged me and tried to rape me.

Dane didn't have to kill him in order to save me, though. That doesn't excuse what he did.

When I think about the fact that Stephen is dead, I don't feel a shred of distress. If he wanted to violate me like that, he could do it to another woman. Maybe he already has.

The world is a safer place without him in it.

But Dane has implicated me in the murder. I didn't kill Stephen with my own hands, but in a way, I'm responsible.

"I don't know what happened," I say, skirting around the truth.

I don't remember anything about last night other than disjointed, hazy memories of fear and despair.

And Dane's fierce green eyes when he caressed my cheek and said, *Don't watch, Abigail. I'll take care of this. I'll take care of you.*

When I woke up in his arms an hour ago, I'd been shocked to learn of Stephen's death. It's not entirely a lie that I don't know the details of what happened to him.

Officer Singh's lips pinch to a thin line, the only sign that she's irritated with my reticent response. "Dr. Graham didn't say anything to you about Stephen Lansing before we arrived? Where was he last night between ten and midnight? Was he with you?"

"Yes. He was with me." Another true statement that doesn't fully answer her question.

I've always been a terrible liar, so sticking as close to the truth as possible is my best course of action for now. Until I can clear my head enough to sort out how I want to handle this nightmare.

The sound of the penthouse door opening makes me jolt, and I whirl to face the stranger.

A heavyset, balding man in a charcoal gray suit strides toward me with confident steps that border on arrogance.

"Who are you?" All the warmth has drained from Officer Singh's tone.

"I'm John Wells, Miss Foster's solicitor," he replies, his navy blue eyes fixing on me through his rectangular, black-rimmed glasses. "She's done talking to you."

The officer stiffens. "We're simply having a conversation. Miss Foster isn't under arrest."

John stares her down. "And your conversation is over." His gaze cuts to me. "Not another word, Miss Foster." He gives Officer Singh a dismissive wave. "I'd like to be alone with my client."

My head spins. I've never even heard of this man, and I have no idea how he knows about me.

But he's offering me a reprieve from police questioning, so I'll take it.

"Yes," I assert. "I need to talk to Mr. Wells, please."

"You are welcome to sit in and offer advice," Officer Singh begins. "But I want to—"

"What you want doesn't matter." He cuts her off in clipped tones. "Miss Foster has rights, and, as you said, she's not under arrest. Give us the room."

She scowls at him but stands. She stalks toward the penthouse door in stiff strides, visibly bristling at the dismissal.

Mr. Wells waits for her to exit into the corridor before he sits in her vacated seat and turns his attention on me once again.

"What did you tell her?" he demands with professional authority.

I straighten my shoulders and counter coolly, "I have a few

questions for you first. Who sent you to represent me? How do you even know about me?"

"Lord Graham keeps my firm on retainer," he explains. "My colleague should be arriving at the police station now to prevent Daniel from saying anything incriminating."

It's too late for that. Dane already admitted to the cops that he killed Stephen.

I choose not to tell the lawyer. That's a mess for his colleague to sort out.

"So, Dane's father sent you," I say. "How did you find out about this? I'm sure Dane didn't ask his family for help."

The last time he saw them, he'd shouted that he hated them. Of course, they wouldn't send help because they care about him; this is all about appearances and their family name.

Mr. Wells blinks, as though he's surprised that I'm not thanking him profusely for coming to my aid.

"Lord Graham has connections in law enforcement. The chief constable phoned him personally to tell him that his son had been arrested. I'm here to clear up the situation."

I press my lips together for a moment, considering.

"Everything I tell you is confidential?" I ask.

"Yes," he confirms.

"There's nothing to clear up," I confess. "Dane already admitted that he's guilty when the cops came to arrest me."

The lawyer sucks in a sharp breath. Then he clears his throat, professional mask back in place. "I'm sure my colleague can handle him. As long as you didn't say anything else incriminating to the police?"

"I don't think anyone can *handle* Dane," I reply. "Especially not anyone sent by his father."

Mr. Wells' bushy brows draw together. "Lord Graham

hired my firm to protect his family. Estranged or not, Daniel is a Graham."

My fingers knot in my lap. Dane will hate this.

But if the lawyers can spare him from prison, isn't that what I want?

"I didn't tell the police anything," I say quietly.

Even in my distress when I'd learned what he did for me, I'd known deep down that I wouldn't betray him.

I can't.

I love him, and I don't want to live without him.

"You were having tea with that officer," Mr. Wells presses. "What did you talk about before I arrived? I need details, Miss Foster."

"I told her that I was with Dane last night around the time of Stephen's death. And I told her I don't know what happened to him. That's true."

He doesn't quite succeed at suppressing a grimace. "So, let me get this straight. Daniel has admitted to killing Lansing. And you were with him at the time of death. You were at the scene of the crime, but you don't know what happened?"

I blow out a sigh and commit to telling the lawyer everything. If we're going to save Dane, he needs to know.

"Dane was protecting me," I assert. "Stephen pressured me to have one drink with him after our meeting concluded. The drink was drugged, and he assaulted me. Dane found us together and saved me."

Mr. Wells takes a moment to process what I've told him before speaking again.

"I've seen the crime scene photos. It could best be described as a crime of passion, not defense."

I suppress a shudder. I'm glad that I don't remember

anything about the murder. Knowing Dane and his protective rage, I can imagine that Stephen's death was brutal.

A spark of vindictive satisfaction flickers in my chest, a feeling that I'm reluctant to acknowledge.

Men have touched me without my consent so many times, but it will never happen again. Dane won't allow it.

I settle into my decision to protect my white knight, my dark god. I'll do everything in my power to save him.

"The police will find the mug Stephen gave me," I say quickly. "It'll probably have traces of the drug, won't it?"

If they find that piece of evidence, it won't be too difficult for them to paint a picture of what happened to Stephen.

Mr. Wells nods grimly. "I'm sure it's already been collected as evidence, but they won't have had time to test anything yet. I'll inform Lord Graham, and he will make it disappear before that happens."

I'm not shocked that Dane's father has the connections necessary to destroy evidence. Especially not now that I know he can muster a team of lawyers in less than an hour once he learns of a threat to his family.

"Dane won't like it," I inform Mr. Wells. "He won't want to accept anything from his father."

"Not even if it costs him his freedom?"

"Not even if it costs his life."

I know it deep in my bones. Dane loathes his family, and he truly would rather die than accept anything from them. Especially when they're only helping him to save their own reputation.

Some cruel part of him will probably be satisfied at ruining them with the scandal of his arrest and incarceration.

I can't allow that to happen.

I straighten my shoulders. "I need to talk to Dane's brother, James."

HALF AN HOUR LATER, James is sitting in the chair formerly occupied by Mr. Wells; the lawyer is waiting outside to give us privacy.

James' eyes—so like Dane's incisive green stare—skewer me. "So, my brother has already confessed to murdering Stephen Lansing."

I nod. "He did it to save me."

James' auburn brows draw together. "I understand that Lansing drugged you, but my brother didn't have to kill the man to save you."

"No," I agree. "But Dane is very protective. And that's not what I meant. He confessed because the police came to arrest me. They knew I was with Stephen at his time of death, so they thought I might be guilty."

James scoffs. "I saw the crime scene photos. Considering your stature, it's highly unlikely that you could be capable of inflicting that kind of damage."

I suppress a shudder. I hope no one ever shows me the photos. Knowing that Dane killed to save me is difficult enough, even if I'm not upset that Stephen is dead. I'd rather not see the evidence of his gory demise.

"Dane would do anything to protect me," I assert. "And I love him for it."

In this moment, I accept that I'm not responsible for Stephen's death by proxy; the blame lies with him for drugging and assaulting me. If he hadn't been a sexual predator, he'd still be alive.

James sighs. "I'm not sure if my brother deserves such loyalty if he's a murderer."

"He does," I declare.

Dane deserves to be loved. Especially because his family has never loved him. He needs someone in his corner, and I resolve that from now on, that person will be me.

"Well, you'll be relieved to know that everything will be fine," James says. "My father will make sure that Daniel—Dane—is released without any record of his arrest."

The fact that he's actively choosing to use Dane's preferred name makes me soften toward him. After their conflicts at the family manor, it's clear that Dane feels nothing but contempt for his younger brother.

But maybe James doesn't deserve his resentment.

I shake my head. "Dane won't accept anything from your father. It's far more likely that he'll double down on his confession in order to destroy your family's reputation."

James curses softly and rakes a hand through his hair. "You really think he's willing to face prison just to spite us?"

I fix him with a level stare. "You were there when he confronted your parents at the estate. What lengths do you think Dane would go to in order to punish them?"

He curses again. "This will destroy my mother."

"Maybe she deserves a bit of suffering," I say coldly.

Dane will strike where it hurts most: her reputation.

James narrows his eyes at me. "I know Dane had the luxury of leaving the family, but I don't. He made sure of that when he gave up the title and fucked off to America. I'm the heir now, and that means I have to deal with my parents, whether I want to or not. The family name will be my responsibility one day. That's all I have, Abigail. It's what I was raised for: to be the Earl of Ripley. Now, my brother is making sure

I'll be Lord of the Ashes. All because he thinks it's my fault that our parents replaced his twin sister with me."

The last is bitter with decades of resentment.

Dane might be in too much pain to see that his brother isn't at fault, but I'm not blinded by years of cruelty at the hands of his parents.

"It's not your fault that they did that," I say quietly. "Your parents chose to forget Katie. It's not right that Dane blames you for their actions. You were just a child yourself. I think he'll see that one day."

"*One day* will be too late," James counters. "I'll be ruined by morning when the news breaks that my brother is a murderer."

I press my lips together, searching for the right thing to say. Dane's parents deserve ruin, but James doesn't. In his own way, he's suffered as much as Dane, but he was never able to escape. If Dane goes away for Stephen's murder, James will have to deal with the fallout for the rest of his life.

And I will have to live my life without Dane by my side.

That's not an option.

An idea sparks.

"What are you thinking?" James asks.

"I think I know how to save Dane, but I'll need your help."

54

DANE

"I don't want to see you either," I sneer when my brother appears outside of my holding cell. "There's nothing you can say that will change my mind."

Years of resentment are etched into every taut line around his eyes and mouth. "I know. But maybe you'll listen to her."

He steps aside, and my stomach drops.

"You can't be here." My knuckles turn white as I clutch at the bars, as though I can tear them down so I can get to Abigail. The urge to throw her over my shoulder and drag her out of this place tenses all my muscles, but there's nothing I can do.

As long as I'm caged, I'm powerless.

Her chin tips back in that defiant posture that transforms her into an imperious queen.

"I'm here because your brother made sure I could get in to see you," she says, infuriatingly calm. "If you just listen to me, you can walk out of here."

I gnash my teeth. "I will not let you take the fall for what I did."

It's madness that she might even think of sacrificing herself for me after everything I've done to her. Maybe our time in my family home warped her mind. Maybe I've broken my little dove without realizing it.

"Neither of us has to go to jail," she reasons.

Her dainty fingers close around mine, so that we're both gripping the iron bars to my cell. I didn't realize how cold my hands were until she touched me.

"Your family can ensure—"

"No." I recoil as though she's thrown acid at my face. "I'm not accepting anything from my father."

She reaches through the bars, grabbing my forearm before I can fully retreat. "Not your father. James is going to help you."

My lips curl with contempt, and I glare daggers at my brother. He put her up to this. He's putting her at risk.

"Get her out of here," I seethe. "If I'm not guilty, they'll look at her again. They'll arrest her."

He scoffs. "She's physically incapable of inflicting that kind of damage on a man. The police have no evidence to hold her. Especially once I arrange for that drug-laced mug to disappear. There will be no motive or evidence to build a case against either of you."

"I've already admitted that I did it." I fling at him like the physical blow I so desperately want to deliver. "There's nothing you can do to save me now."

Abigail's fingernails bite into my forearm, commanding my attention.

"If you tell the police that you only said it to protect me

from arrest, your family's lawyers will get your admission omitted from the record."

My stomach sours with betrayal. "You of all people should understand that I won't accept my family's money and influence. I thought you knew me better than that."

Her lips twist in a disapproving frown, as though I'm being unreasonable.

And maybe I am, but I'll die before I accept a bail-out from my parents. If I do, they'll hold leverage over me for the rest of my life. I'll never submit to their control.

"I'm not asking you to accept anything from your parents," she insists. "I know you won't want to hear this, but James has done nothing wrong. It's not his fault that your mom and dad tried to replace your sister with him. He was a child, just like you were."

I scowl at him. "He's not a child anymore."

"No, I'm not," he snaps. "And I've accepted a man's responsibilities while you ran off to America. I have to be the heir now. You took that choice away from me. You've been free to live as you choose for years. You can be free again if you just listen to Abigail. Do you want to spend the rest of your life in prison?"

Abigail's hold on my arm gentles, and she laces her fingers through mine. My fist loosens to accept her.

"Choose us," she urges, her aquamarine eyes shining. "Be with me, Dane. I don't want to face a future without you."

Something twists painfully at the center of my chest. "I can't risk it," I rasp. "I won't let them arrest you."

She squeezes my hand in a pulse of comfort. "They won't. James won't let them."

That gets my hackles up again. "It's not his job to protect you."

She's *mine.*

Her shoulders straighten. "It's my job to protect *you*, and I won't let you face a life sentence. There's a way for both of us to walk out of here. Together."

I reach my free hand through the bars and cup her cheek, tracing the delicate line of her jaw with my thumb. She's so fragile, even in her defiance. If I'm not by her side, anything could happen to her. Some bastard might try to hurt her again, and I won't be there to kill him for her.

"I'm listening," I rumble.

I can swallow my pride and bend for her. I would sacrifice anything for Abigail, even if it means putting myself at my family's mercy.

THE SPACE outside my cell is more cramped than inside it. Mum, Dad, James, and Abigail are clustered together, all their attention fixed squarely on me.

"Has the American made you see reason, then?" Mum demands, not even bothering to use Abigail's name. "You'll retract your statement of guilt?"

I cross my arms over my chest and fix her with my fiercest scowl. "Yes."

"At least she has some influence over you," Dad sneers. "I suppose you'll want her to come live at the house with us. You might be easier to handle if she's around. I'll arrange her visa today."

"We're not going back to the manor." I drop the words like a bomb. "I have one condition to retract my statement: you will give up your title and retire to the villa in Spain."

Dad's mouth opens, then closes. His lips seal shut, as though he's holding in a tirade, and his face turns beet red.

"Daniel!" my mother squawks. "How dare you even suggest such a thing."

I lift a brow at her. "I dare. It's your choice. Face ruin or flee the country. Surrender your precious place in society, and you can at least keep your dignity intact. Whatever dignity you possess."

"Preposterous!" Dad thunders. "You have no right to ask such a thing."

"I'm not asking." The words are icy daggers. "Let me be clear: this is a threat. I'll give the press a full interview with my explicit confession about how I murdered Stephen Lansing with my bare hands, or you will pass on the title to your rightful heir."

"You... You think..." Mum splutters. "If you expect us to make you the heir again after this..."

"Not me. I'm going back to America with Abigail. James is the Earl of Ripley now. He's more than earned the right." I look at my younger brother. "The better man will get the title."

He blinks, and his jaw goes slack with shock.

I suppose it's the nicest thing I've ever said to him.

Possibly the only kind words I've ever spoken about him.

Abigail was right. It's not his fault that my parents replaced Katie with James. He had no control over their actions. I should've realized that years ago, but I was too wrapped up in my own loathing for my family name to see that he's innocent in all this.

"You can't do this," Dad blusters. "You want to go to jail? I hope they bring back the death penalty for you. You can hang for all I care."

A slow, cruel smile spreads over my face. "The only thing that will die is your reputation. I'll happily rot in a cell if it means your ruin."

"You're bluffing," Mum says shrilly. "Always these sick games, Daniel. We're not falling for it."

I fix her with a steady stare and allow her to see the depth of my vindictive loathing in my eyes. "It will be my greatest pleasure to see you brought low. I will relish your downfall. If I'm going away for life, guaranteeing your demise will be my sole purpose. Or..." I draw out several beats of tense silence, watching my parents squirm. "You can be content with my quiet return to America. You can disappear from high society, and James will do you proud. Only we will know your shame."

"You are my greatest shame," Dad seethes.

"Your greatest shame should be the fact that you killed your own daughter. But if I have to take up that mantle, I will. Gladly."

No one says anything for a full minute. I spend the first several seconds relishing my parents' anguish. But, as always, my attention is drawn to Abigail like a magnet. The cold satisfaction that pulsed through my veins warms to a gentle heat as I thaw in her rapt gaze. She looks at me like she's...proud of me. Those perfect lips are curved in a small smile, and her lovely eyes glow with pale blue fire.

I should've known she would never ask me to compromise myself. She wouldn't beg me to succumb to my family's control and place myself in their cruel hands.

My clever Abigail devised this plan to punish my parents for all the pain they've caused me. After decades evading justice, they will finally pay penance for what they did to Katie. What they did to me. And James.

At least he'll be free of them now too. He can live his own life as Lord Graham, and he will answer to no one.

He's almost a stranger to me, but maybe that's been to my detriment. I've always spurned my family, but I might not have to be entirely alone anymore.

I have a brother.

And I have Abigail.

"Give up the title, or your murderous son will be the first thing the British public sees on the morning news." I twist the knife, compelling my father's compliance.

He's almost purple now, but my mother's complexion has gone chalk white. Even her lips are pale; they're pressed together so hard that I wonder if she'll ever be able to unlock her jaw to speak a cruel word again.

"Damn you," Dad hisses. "Fine. James will have the title. We will go to Spain. Return to your American exile. I never want to see your face again."

"The feeling is mutual," I assure him. "I anticipate our renewed estrangement."

He braces a supportive arm around my mother before her knees can buckle, and he mostly drags her out of the cramped space.

Abigail is beaming at me, as though we've been engaged in a thrilling game, and we've just won. Her giddy energy is catching, and I grin right back at her like a fool.

James sighs, but I don't bother looking in his direction. I can't tear my gaze from her: my perfect Abigail, my miracle.

When she found out that I killed Stephen for her, I'd thought she would never be able to live with it. Some part of me preferred prison to the prospect of seeing her disgust at my murderous capabilities. A jail sentence would've been easier to bear than her rejection.

But she's not turning from me in horror. She's choosing me. She devised a way to make my parents pay for their sins and free me at the same time.

"Come on," she urges. "Let's get out of here."

I nod. "I'm ready to retract my statement."

Wherever she goes, I'll follow. I won't allow anyone to separate me from her ever again.

55

ABIGAIL

Dane is stunning in the mid-morning sunlight, even if his midnight hair is slightly disheveled from the sleepless night in the police station. Once he was released, I insisted that we go on a walk instead of returning to our rented penthouse to nap. After being trapped behind bars for hours, he needs fresh air and freedom.

His untrimmed beard is a shade darker than usual, but it only adds to his rugged perfection. Despite his fatigue from the ordeal, his forest green eyes are intent on mine as ever. He studies me like he's memorizing each of my features.

"I thought they might not let you out," I confess, my chest tight with residual anxiety. "James promised that he could handle everything, but I wasn't sure until we walked out of the station. It still doesn't quite feel real that we're walking around York."

The setting is lush: gardens surround the ruins of a centuries-old abbey, and the public space is quiet at this early hour. It feels as though we have the entire park to ourselves. I'm grateful for the intimate time with Dane.

His hand firms around mine. "I won't let anything separate us ever again," he promises. "Did the police give you a hard time while I was being questioned?"

"No," I reassure him. "The officers were nice to me once they arrested you. I think they expected me to talk if they treated me kindly. But I would never betray you," I swear. "And I wouldn't ask you to take anything from your parents that might come with strings attached. Thank you for accepting James' help."

His eyes pierce me straight to my heart. "I would do anything to be with you. Thank you for making me see reason. James doesn't deserve my hatred." His lips quirk in a cruelly satisfied smile. "You came up with the perfect solution. My parents will be utterly miserable spending the rest of their lives in their quiet slice of paradise, unable to return to England."

"They deserve worse," I assert, fiercely protective.

He drops a doting kiss on my forehead. "I've spent my entire life trying to make them suffer. Nothing will ever be adequate punishment for all of their sins, but you've ensured that they will finally face some consequences. It's more than I ever managed."

"You don't have to waste one more minute of your time or energy on them," I reply staunchly. "You're free, Dane."

"Thanks to you, my clever pet."

I flush at the endearment, not remotely irked by the diminutive term. I could never feel degraded by it when Dane says it with such reverence.

"I had several long hours to think last night," I say, considering my words carefully. "Before I was sure that they would release you, I thought I might be compelled to give evidence against you."

Dane's jaw firms. "If it ever comes down to that, you will do what you have to do in order to protect yourself. If that means telling the police the truth about what happened so that you won't be implicated, then you'll do it."

"No, I won't." I swallow hard, and then I say in a rush, "I think we should get married."

His eyes flash, and his hand tightens around mine.

"I mean..." I fumble, unsure how to read his fierce expression.

Is he angry at my suggestion?

"I don't want to have to testify against you," I reason quickly. "If we're married, they can't make me, right? I'm not sure what the law is here in England. But that would protect both of us, wouldn't it? If we're husband and wife, you'll be safe."

"No."

My heart stops at his flat refusal.

"What?" I ask on a puff of air, my chest constricting so tight that I can't breathe.

His dark brows draw together in forbidding slashes. "You won't marry me to protect me. You'll marry me because you're *mine*."

"Oh." My mind whirs. "Is that... Are you proposing?"

His lips pinch with distaste. "Of course not. You deserve a much better proposal than that. When I do propose, there will be no question of my intentions. And you will have only one answer for me."

"But I just said I want to marry you." His edgy mood is throwing me for a loop. I think I might've offended him with the way I worded things. "It's a *yes*."

His eyes turn stormy. "You want to for pragmatic reasons. That's not how our marriage will work."

He's talking about our marriage as if it's a foregone conclusion, but he still seems angry.

I study each sharp line of his tautly drawn features.

"It's not only for pragmatic reasons," I say quietly when I realize what he needs from me. "I wouldn't say I want to marry you if I didn't love you." I place my hand on his cheek, and his jaw ticks beneath my palm. "I love you, Dane."

His expression is almost feral with desire, but his eyes are cautious as they search mine. "After everything I've done to you?"

I think back to the dark day when I realized he was my stalker. He kidnapped me away to England. He held me in his family home against my will.

But he's changed somehow. He's still the man I fell for in Charleston, but I understand him more deeply now. Back in the studio he built for me in his manor, he dropped to his knees and apologized. He swore that he couldn't live without me.

Then I learned what happened to his sister. I saw how his family treated him, how they tormented and warped him.

I've known that I'm still in love with Dane ever since we arrived in York, but I haven't said it aloud yet.

"Even though I'm a murderer?" he rumbles in challenge. "You can love a killer?"

I trace the line of his cheekbone with my thumb, as though I can smooth away his tension.

"I made sure you got out of prison, didn't I? I couldn't bear the thought of spending the rest of my life without you. I love you, and I will marry you, Dane."

His fingers tangle in my hair, capturing me in a firm grip. "You're all I need in this life, Abigail."

My heart soars. It's not *I love you*, but I don't require that to pledge myself to him forever. Dane's affection for me is stronger than any words could express, and I feel the depth of his need for me in the way he tugs at my hair to pull me in for an almost savage kiss.

He consumes me, his tongue plundering my mouth without waiting for invitation. He knows that I belong to him. I sigh into him, demonstrating my utter devotion. I know now that there's nothing he could do that would make me stop loving him. Some part of me must be sick and twisted, but the fact that he's a murderer hasn't dulled my craving for him.

I meet his kiss with hungry lashes of my tongue against his, and I dare to graze his lips with my teeth in a primal demonstration of my own claim over him. His low growl rumbles into my mouth and rolls lower through my body. My core heats for him, and my pulse begins to race.

I wouldn't protest if he laid me down and fucked me right here in the ruins. When he's touching me like this, we're the only two people in the world. The tourists filtering into the gardens as the morning progresses don't register in my mind. I'm wanton for him, wet and needy.

A few hours ago, I thought I might have to spend the rest of my life without him.

But we overcame that challenge together. He leaned on me and accepted my help.

He's so much stronger than I will ever be, but my dark god respects and reveres me. In his restraining arms, I'm more powerful than I've ever been.

When I'm panting against his mouth, he finally breaks our kiss with a cruel smirk.

"Don't worry, little dove. I will fuck you senseless soon enough. Indulge me for a few more hours, and then I'll make you come so hard that you'll pass out from pleasure."

I huff, not bothering to hide my pout. "Hours? Why can't we go back to the penthouse now?"

He chuckles. "We have some shopping to do first."

I lick my lips with open desire. "I don't need to buy anything. All I need is you inside me."

His nostrils flare. "Now you're being a tease intentionally, naughty pet. Don't make me punish you later. I'd much rather give you orgasms."

My inner muscles contract with a pulse of lust, and my fingers curve into his broad shoulders. "If it means feeling your cock filling me up, I'll gladly take any punishment."

His low hum of consideration is downright predatory.

"It seems I'll have to behave for both of us," he rumbles. "I do love your desperation, but we'll work on your self-control later, greedy little thing."

I shiver and melt into him, my body ready for his sweet torment.

But he has other ideas. He laces his fingers through mine and urges me to follow him out of the garden. Within minutes, we're walking down one of my favorite medieval streets that has a view of the Minster at the end. My steps quicken in anticipation of another visit to the imposing cathedral, but, again, Dane tugs me in a different direction.

He stops at a shop with a green frontage and large windows that display a glittering array of antique jewelry.

"See anything you like?" He gestures at a ring with a massive, pale-yellow gemstone bracketed by two round cut white stones. "What about that one? It reminds me of your sunny smile."

I gawk at the price tag. "Dane! Those are *diamonds.*"

He quirks a brow at me. "Aren't engagement rings usually diamond? Do you prefer something different?"

My jaw drops, and he grins. He's so beautiful when he smiles like this—like a wickedly amused fallen angel.

"So..." I suck in a breath. "This is your proposal?"

He chuckles and shakes his head. "Hardly. I thought you'd like to select your ring. You'll be wearing it for the rest of your life."

The last is deeper, darker. Almost a threat.

I lean into him and brush a kiss over his stubbled cheek in reassurance. "Then I'd better pick out a good one."

His smile is dazzling, sharper and brighter than the diamonds that wink at us through the shop window. Looking up into his deep green eyes, I know exactly what gemstone I want to wear to declare our bond.

"I'd like an emerald."

His smile turns almost smug, but I don't mind his arrogant satisfaction one bit. After everything his family has put him through, he needs my love, and a symbol of my devotion will provide him with a sense of security he's never had before.

I'm going to be his family now. His wife.

And he'll be my family too.

He doesn't break our intense connection, holding me in his steady green stare as he presses the bell beside the shop door. It buzzes, and the lock clicks back to permit us entry.

Within minutes, I have a glass of champagne in my right hand, and I hold out my left to try on a small, princess cut emerald set in yellow gold.

Dane grasps my fingers and directs them away from the ring.

"No. The first time your ring goes on your finger will be when you say *yes* to me."

"I already said yes," I remind him.

He shakes his head, a disapproving but indulgent god. "This one isn't good enough," he declares, gesturing at the ring. "Something bigger. With diamonds."

"I don't need you to buy me an expensive ring to prove that I love you," I say.

His jaw firms. "I want every man to know that you're taken. This doesn't look like an engagement ring."

"So possessive." I sigh, but it's a happy jibe. "All right, what about that one?"

I indicate a large, oval emerald that's surrounded by a halo of diamonds set in platinum. The price is insane, but I know better than to put up a fuss about the expense. Dane wants a clearly visible marker of our commitment to one another, and I won't deny him.

I want it too.

I'm no longer worried that he'll try to use his money to control me. He sees me as an equal, and he wants to provide a comfortable life for both of us. One day, I'll contribute to our partnership, our home. Once we return to Charleston, I'll devote all of my time to my art, and I'm determined to finally open a gallery.

My whole future is opening up before me, and I choose to share it with Dane.

56

DANE

I'm relieved that the street "performer" on the purple bike isn't stationed beside the Minster this morning. Abigail seemed to find him amusing, but I don't want anything garish to distract from the moment I'm about to share with her.

She's practically glued to my side as we stroll toward the cathedral, and her face is upturned to drink in the imposing, ancient edifice with its intricate stone carvings.

I don't care about the church; I can't take my eyes off her. She's the most breathtaking thing I've ever seen, her porcelain complexion shining with ethereal light beneath the late morning sun. It illuminates her eyes, and they glow with otherworldly vibrancy. The soft, contented curve of her perfect lips makes me think about how she looks when she's cuddled up with me in bed, and their rosy hue is offset by the amethyst curl I love so much.

This miracle of a woman loves me despite everything I've done to her.

She wants to marry me.

I'll never be worthy of her, but I'm selfish enough to claim her anyway. The least I can do is give her the proposal she deserves.

I reach into my pocket to retrieve the jewelry box. It takes all my willpower to peel myself from her side so that I can take her hand in mine and drop to one knee before her.

Her lovely lips part on a soft gasp, and she turns to face me. Her eyes are alight with something between giddy excitement and wonder, and for a few long seconds, I simply stare up at her. I'm thoroughly under her spell, at a loss for words for the first time in my life.

I haven't said anything when she extends her left hand. Her fingers tremble slightly as she offers herself to me, a silent promise of forever.

"Abigail." Her name is a rasp, and I have to draw a breath so that I can speak clearly. "You've given my life meaning. I didn't think I was capable of feeling this..." I swallow hard against the strange constriction of my throat. "You've made me feel alive for the first time in my life. I can't live without you. I refuse to live without you. I know I'm not an easy man to love. I've wronged you in so many ways, but I plan to keep you anyway. Do me the honor of sharing the rest of your life with me."

It's not a question.

But she answers with a soft, "Yes. I want to be with you, Dane. I love you, and I want to marry you."

I take the emerald ring from the velvet box and slide it onto her slender finger, sealing her fate. It fits perfectly, securely. She'll never take it off.

I lift her hand and press a reverent kiss over the green

gemstone that marks her as mine. Now every man will clearly see my claim over her, and the ring is large enough that they'll know it's a warning.

No one touches what's mine.

57

ABIGAIL

"I have something for you," Dane says when we step into the bedroom at the penthouse.

"I don't need anything else today," I protest. "You already bought my ring. I just want to be together now."

He guides me to sit on the edge of the bed and reaches for a small, gold gift bag that waits on the nightstand.

"I arranged for this to be delivered while we were out," he explains.

"When did you possibly find the time for that?"

His smile is indulgent when he urges me to take the gold bag from him. "You were distracted by the antique art at the jewelry store."

"Sneaky," I huff, but I'm not really annoyed.

He lifts a dark brow. "I prefer *cunning.* I'll also accept *ruthless.*"

I giggle, and the bubbly sound suffuses my entire body in an effervescent wave. I feel incredibly light, carefree and happy in a way I've never known.

Nestled within layers of gilded tissue paper, I find a long, slim velvet box. I peek up at Dane, hesitating. He's already spent a small fortune on my engagement ring.

"Open it." This time, it's a stern command.

Whatever he's purchased for me, my acceptance is important to him.

I snap open the lid, and I'm momentarily dazzled by the multitude of diamonds that lay on the silken interior of the box. Dozens of small, marquis cut white diamonds are arranged in a pattern reminiscent of leaves on a vine. They come to a delicate point in the center, where a pear-shaped pink diamond drips like the bud of a small flower. If I put the necklace on, the pink stone would rest just between my collarbones, and there are enough marquis diamonds to encircle my neck.

"Dane..." I breathe, overwhelmed at the lavish gift.

"Don't say it's too much," he warns. "I want to give you everything you could ever desire. I'll give you the world, Abigail. Let me."

I brush my fingers over the pink diamond, and it winks at me from its delicate rose gold setting.

"It's beautiful," I murmur, entranced by the multifaceted beauty of the gemstones and the artistry of the craftsmanship.

"I thought the pink would complement your unicorn badge," he says. "If you still want to wear it without your apron, that is."

My eyes meet his, and I'm locked in his emerald gaze.

I remember our first date, when he mentioned that he'd noted my silly pins at the café. He said he knew I had a sweet tooth because of my lavender cupcake and smiling donut.

I'd been surprised and gratified at his attention to detail at the time, but now I know the depth of his obsession.

Dane had made sure to learn so much about me before that date.

And yet, I don't feel a flicker of horror or disgust at the thought. I don't think I ever want to hear the extent of his stalking, but I accept Dane for all that he is. That means I forgive what he did to me. I want a future with him, so I'll leave all that ugliness in the past.

"You don't like it," he surmises when I don't say anything in response. "I'll get you a different one. Whatever you want, name it, and it's yours."

I close the box and set it aside so that I can take both of his broad hands in mine.

"I love it," I assure him. "Thank you."

"You never need to thank me for anything," he says with the weight of a decree. "And don't mistake the gift for a sweet gesture. You should know by now how selfish I am. I want to see you wearing it."

I smile and kiss his lips, which are set in a warning slash.

"How do you always manage to make gifts sound like a threat?" I tease. "You can relax, Dane. I accept. I'll gladly wear something so beautiful, especially if it makes you happy to see me wearing it. That's what I really care about: I want you to be happy. The rest is just stuff. I only need you."

Abruptly, he picks up the slim jewelry box and tucks it into his pocket. Then he stands and strides across the bedroom, putting several feet of space between us.

"Show me." It's a dark command.

I'm reeling from his sudden distance after our intense conversation. "What?"

"Show me how much you need me." He points at the carpeted floor between his designer shoes. "Get on your knees and crawl to me."

My stomach flips, and I edge away from him. Lust fizzes through my system in a giddy rush—the fear-tinged desire only he can elicit.

"Dane..."

He fixes me with a challenging smirk. "I do love when you say my name in that breathy little whisper, but that's not how you address me when we're alone, is it? Crawl over here and beg your master for your pretty new collar."

I tip my chin back, meeting his cruelly amused energy with defiance. "You want me to debase myself for a few diamonds? My pride is worth more than that."

His savage grin is sharp enough to cut. "Everything about you is priceless, my precious pet. But you will yield. One way or another, you will end up on your knees with this collar around your throat."

I narrow my eyes at him. "I agreed to marry you, not obey you. That won't be part of our vows."

His low laugh is pure seduction, and I suppress the urge to shiver as it wraps around me like a palpable caress. I won't lose this battle of wills so easily. Because as much as I crave to do as he commands, I want him to earn my submission. He will have to force me to comply with his wicked demands.

"By the time I'm finished with you, you will sweetly crawl down the aisle and let me fuck you over the altar while you vow to obey me for the rest of our lives."

My core pulses, but I keep my words acerbic. "You're delusional."

He clicks his tongue at me. "Psychopathic," he corrects me. "I'm obsessive and ruthless, and I always get what I want. If I want you on a leash, worshipping at my feet, then you will oblige me. You chose me, Abigail. This is who I am. This is what I expect from you. What I will take from you."

"So many threats," I counter coolly, despite the maddening pulse in my clit. "But we both know that you can't make me do anything. You're *mine*, Dane."

His smile is pure, evil delight, and his dark green eyes dance. "Poor pet," he mocks. "You want to come to me so badly. I can see it in your pretty blush and the way you're pressing your thighs together. Only your pride is stopping you from getting what you really desire. You said it's worth more than a few diamonds, but I'm not trying to buy it. I plan to take it. I will shatter you."

I stand, shoulders squared so that I'm at my full height. I will not crawl.

Instead, I hold my head high and walk right past him—keeping a few feet of careful distance so that I'm not within easy reach. His low laugh follows me out into the open plan living room, and now that I'm out of sight, I allow myself a small shiver of anticipation.

He doesn't come after me right away. I know he must be planning something, drawing out my anxious anticipation. With every passing second, my body coils tighter, and my pussy throbs in time with my thudding heartbeat.

I busy myself in the kitchen, putting on the kettle for a cup of tea that I don't want to drink. My hands tremble slightly as I go about the menial task, just trying to give myself something mundane to occupy me.

I could flee the penthouse altogether, but I don't really want to evade him. And I'm not at all certain that would stop him from dragging me back here kicking and screaming, no matter how much of a scene that would cause.

He strolls into the kitchen, and I pointedly keep my attention on the kettle. It's taking ages to boil, and my fingers tap the marble countertop in a nervous, staccato rhythm.

"You don't like tea," he remarks.

I shrug. "Maybe it's not for me. Maybe I plan to toss it in your smug face."

He just laughs in response to my barbed threat. We both know I'd never actually do anything to hurt him, but he's loving our dance on the edge of consent.

"It's been too long since I tamed your sassy mouth," he remarks. "Your punishments are adding up, naughty pet. You teased me in the park, you refused a direct order, and now you're threatening violence against me. How shall I handle these infractions?"

"You won't *handle* me at all," I shoot back, reaching for the kettle.

It's an empty gesture, but before my fingers brush the handle, he's on me. Like a striking viper, he grabs me from behind, yanking me away from the potential weapon. His other big hand clamps over my nose and mouth, muffling my scream and my ability to draw breath.

I kick out at nothing as he lifts me off the floor and drags me out of the kitchen. Fear spikes through my system in a lightning strike, crackling and dancing from my core all the way to my fingers and toes. I surrender fully to our dark game, fighting him like a wild thing.

My nails sink into his restraining hand like claws, but with each passing second, it becomes more difficult to draw breath. My lungs begin to burn, and I jerk in his arms with erratic, desperate attempts to free myself. I'm consumed by primal survival responses, and I slip deeper into my thrilling, fear-drenched headspace.

Darkness creeps in at the edges of my vision as we enter the bedroom, and my struggles grow weaker. His low, cruel laugh winds around me like a subversive caress, so at odds with the violent way he's holding me. Even though I'm thoroughly restrained and helpless, he's careful not to harm me. I won't so much as bruise from the cage of his iron grip.

Dane would never hurt me.

But that doesn't mean I'm not going to put up one hell of a fight.

He wants me to crawl for him. He'll have to earn that privilege.

I won't surrender so easily.

58

ABIGAIL

Black spots dance at the edges of my vision, and my fingers soften on Dane's forearm, no longer clawing at him as my consciousness wavers.

"Are you done already?" he taunts. "Such a fragile little dove. Shall I treat you more gently? I don't want to break you."

His hand drops from my nose and mouth, and I drag in a deep, burning breath.

"Fuck you," I say on the exhale, voice hoarse.

The bedroom spins around me at the rush of oxygen back to my brain. I start to struggle again, but he easily wrestles me to the floor. A shriek tears from my throat when he grabs my wrists and pins them at the small of my back. I thrash, but I only succeed in stimulating my hard nipples against the plush carpet, even through the thin barrier of my dress.

The familiar feel of hemp rope encircling my wrists draws a sound of feral denial from my chest, and he hums in pure, masculine satisfaction. He makes quick work of binding me before grabbing my flailing ankles. He pulls my body taut into a stress position, tying my ankles to my wrists so that I can't do more than wriggle and curse at him.

His long fingers encircle my nape, and he presses my cheek into the carpet so that my shouts become garbled. His other hand caresses my jawline with reverence.

"Such a filthy mouth," he remarks. "I thought you were a pure, polite Southern belle. I'll have to teach you how to behave properly. You'll learn some respect and humility."

"Respect is earned," I seethe.

He cocks his head, considering me. "Is that what all of this is about? You want to make me work for your submission?" His slow grin is cruelly beautiful. "You're the one who will struggle and suffer. I get nothing but sadistic enjoyment out of degrading you, pet."

"Stop calling me that," I snap.

He traces the line of my cheekbone, lingering over my freckle. "Never."

His touch withdraws from my cheek, and then my collar dangles from his elegant fingers, swaying in front of my trapped face in a mocking rhythm.

"You'll have to earn your diamonds," he taunts. "You'll beg me for them before I'm finished with you."

"You can lock that collar around my throat, but it won't tame me," I hiss.

My body burns for him, rage-tinged desire coursing through my veins like fire. My indignation isn't fake—I will never meekly bend when he's taunting me like this. But my surging emotions are as powerful as the whitecapped waves on a stormy sea, drowning me in primal chemicals as my body struggles to defy his cruel control.

With Dane, I don't freeze; I fight back. I'm safe to use my claws because he will never truly hurt me in retaliation.

This exchange is fully consensual, and that means I can lose myself in the power struggle. I can indulge in the thrilling fear and intoxicating adrenaline, and they make the world come into sharp relief around me. My senses come alive, and every inch of my flesh crackles and dances, my bound body humming with sensual awareness.

"You think I've only planned to tie you up and collar you?" he asks, sounding almost disappointed. "You underestimate my capacity for sadism. I will strip you down and reduce you to a weeping, desperate mess. And then I'll torment you some more, just because it pleases me to hear you whimper and whine."

Before I can issue a terse retort, the collar encircles my throat, and he draws it tight enough to make me choke. He holds the tension for several long seconds, until my blood pounds in my ears. Only when my body begins to soften does he ease the bite of the supple leather. His fingers are gentle and tender as he buckles it into place and secures it with the small, rose gold padlock.

He traces the line of the collar around my neck. My nerves jump beneath his featherlight touch. The first traitorous shiver races over my body, and my cheeks flame.

Something silver glints in his hand: a pair of blunt-tipped shears.

"No knives for you today," he says, as though it's a kindness. "You're especially feisty, and I don't want to accidentally cut my pretty plaything. Every ounce of pain I deliver will be deliberate and by my design, not because of your pitiful struggles."

I jerk against the restraints and release a growl of pure frustration when the rope tightens around my wrists and ankles. I'm just as helpless as he said, but I'm not ready to surrender.

"Don't you dare," I warn. "I like this dress."

"I'll buy you another one. I'll buy you a dozen more."

"I don't want another one. I want this one."

He shakes his head. "You should've thought about that before you decided to be so willful and disrespectful."

Another rough, animal sound grates between my clenched teeth as he slips the shears beneath the hem of my dress. The thin cotton parts easily. The blades are sharp, but the blunted design ensures that he won't slip and cut my skin. I can't suppress another shiver as the cold blade slides up the length of my spine, slowly robbing me of any sense of dignity.

He snips the spaghetti straps, and the dress pools around me on the carpet. My back is completely bared to him, my pale pink thong a mockery of modesty. He cuts it away, depriving me of the small scrap of dignity.

He takes a few indulgent minutes to trail his fingers down my back, stroking me in a slow, tingling slide that's subversively calming.

I stiffen. I'm not his pet. I will not melt for this tender treatment.

His gentle fingers reach the base of my spine, and he takes a moment to tease me there, stimulating a sensitive patch of nerves I didn't know I had. With every slow circle, it feels as though he's circling my clit instead. The hard bud pulses madly, and I can't help wriggling in my bonds.

I'm not sure if I'm trying to evade his sensual torment or stimulate myself against the plush carpet.

"Do you want me to touch you?" he rumbles.

"No." My refusal is a husky groan, an obvious lie.

"No," he agrees. "You don't deserve such mercy."

His touch shifts suddenly, and his fingers sink into my ass to part my cheeks. I'm terribly exposed, and there's nothing I can do to stop him when he squeezes a drop of cool lubricant onto my asshole.

I can't help closing my eyes, as though I can hide from what he's about to do to me. He knows exactly how to devastate me, how to make me feel achingly vulnerable and small in his ruthless hands.

"Open your eyes," he commands. "I want you to see what I'm going to do to you."

I comply, and it takes me a moment to process what I'm looking at. Even when I take in the shape of the silver hook, I can't make sense of it. One end is round and blunt, and the metal is about an inch in circumference. The other end is shaped in a loop, and he's tied a length of rope through it. The whole thing is a bit bigger than his massive hand.

"What is that?" I ask, voice hitching slightly.

But I already know. I shake my head in wild refusal.

"Hush now, pet," he soothes. "You'll be much calmer in a few minutes."

"Dane, no," I whisper, and it's a plea.

"*Master*," he corrects me. "You'll love your new leash."

"You can't..." I lick my dry lips and try again. "I can't..."

His heartbreaking face settles into the cold, unfeeling planes that make me quiver. "I can do whatever I want, and you will take it all. You are powerless to stop me. Curse at me, plead with me, beg for mercy. I have none."

The cold tip of the hook presses against my tight asshole, and I yelp in alarm. He shushes me gently and stimulates my clit with his free hand. He rubs me in the exact way I like, and my inner muscles clench in a pulse of desperate desire before softening to welcome penetration.

Unyielding metal slips into my ass, entering me in a slow slide.

The toy is slender enough that there's no pain, but the degrading act floods my cheeks with hot shame. It churns through me, turning to white-hot lust. Wet arousal coats my labia, dripping onto his hand where he relentlessly stimulates my clit.

The cool curve of the hook presses between my spread ass cheeks, extending up to my tailbone.

I tremble, unable to make a voluntary movement when he has my most vulnerable area harnessed in a perverted way I never could've imagined.

"Please," I whisper. "I'll be good. You don't have to do this."

The humiliation of my predicament is almost too much to bear, and he revels in my complete subjugation.

"But I want to do this to you," he counters calmly. "I already warned you: I always get what I want. I know you'll be good for me. You'll be much better behaved now."

He's not finished with my torment. He has a seemingly endless supply of cruel implements waiting to subdue me. I never should've gone into the kitchen and allowed him time to plan all of this.

But it's too late for regrets now. I'm trapped and thoroughly humbled.

An animal whimper eases from my chest when he holds up a black, egg-shaped vibrator on a thin silicone loop. His wicked grin cuts into me, and he presses a button on the small remote in his other hand. The egg buzzes to life, vibrating in an irregular pattern that I already feel in my aching pussy.

"Don't..." I choke on the plea, even as I know it's useless.

The power he holds over me makes my insides quake, but I'm molten for him.

There's nothing I can do to stop him as he slowly presses the egg into my tight channel. My slick desire makes it slide into my swollen folds with embarrassing ease. It settles deep inside me, and the vibration is echoed by the unyielding hook that penetrates my ass.

A soft sob convulses my chest at the cruel hit of ecstasy.

"That's it," he encourages. "Weep for me. You're so pretty when you cry."

The vibrator stimulates my g-spot directly, and my entire body tenses as my orgasm builds like an oncoming tidal wave.

Then it stops, and I cry out at the denial.

Dane's dark green eyes glint with a cold, cruel light as he considers me like I'm a particularly intriguing new toy.

"No orgasms for you just yet," he chides. "You teased me in the park, remember? If you don't have any self-control, I'll have to control your impulses for you."

"I'm sorry," I babble. "I didn't mean to. I just wanted you so badly. Please, Dane. Please. Master," I correct myself when his expression darkens. "Mercy."

He cocks his head at me. "And what sort of mercy do you want, little dove? Do you want me to release you? Or do you want to come?"

I squirm in my restraints, at a loss. My entire body throbs with the painful need to orgasm, but my pride is on the verge of shattering entirely if I remain in this predicament much longer.

His smirk is downright demonic: a prince of hell reveling in tormenting his damned captive. "That's what I thought."

He presses a button on the small remote again, and the

egg vibrates gently inside me, enough to keep me on edge but not push me to completion.

"No..." I moan.

He doesn't deign to reply this time. He doesn't have to. My refusal means nothing, and I have no hope of denying him.

In the back of my mind, I know I could stop this with a single safe word, but I'm just as deeply lost in this dark game as he is.

He slips the remote into his pocket so that he can slowly free the knots that secure my wrists and ankles. As the tension releases, he tenderly rubs my arms and legs, chasing away the pins and needles that were beginning to prickle at my flesh. He'll never damage his precious pet.

The thought doesn't stir so much as a shadow of resentment. I crave this cruel caretaking. I want to be his: degraded and adored, defiled and cherished.

Once he's satisfied that my blood flow to my fingers and toes hasn't been restricted for too long, he picks up the loose length of rope that's tied to the end of the hook. The smooth metal rod shifts inside me ever so slightly as he tugs at the back of my collar and loops the rope beneath it. I can't do more than quiver and pant, my fingers clawing at the carpet.

Then he tugs on the rope, and my strangled shout echoes through the bedroom. The hook presses deeper into my ass, and my collar pulls tight against the front of my throat at the same time, restricting my airflow. The sense of utter helplessness is crushing, and something deep inside me yields.

I'm a being of pure, primal sensation. My master has taken control of my body, and my soul sings for him. This is exactly where I want to be: on his perverted leash, at his feet.

I'm *his*, and being utterly owned by him is the sweetest bliss I've ever known.

Nothing bad can touch me when I'm with my dark god. No one can hurt me.

No one but him.

And I will welcome any pain he deigns to inflict. Each touch is a cruel blessing, a carnal indulgence.

"There she is." His smile is warm and indulgent, and his attention is fixed on me like I'm the only thing that matters in the world. He strokes my hair back from my sweat-dampened brow. "My sweet pet."

He gives the rope leash a gentle tug, and another garbled sound babbles from my lips at the hit of ruthless pleasure.

"Are you ready to crawl for me?"

I turn my burning face into the carpet. "I can't…" I wheeze. "It's too much."

I'm too shaky to get to my hands and knees. All I can do is sprawl on the floor beneath him and tremble.

He hums softly. "Still so defiant. No more protests or excuses, little dove."

Yet another object for my subjugation appears in his deft hand. The pink ball gag is fixed into a complex white harness that I can't quite make sense of in my befuddled state. My mind reels, and my thoughts are too scattered to put up any form of resistance. The rubber gag presses against my lips, and it only takes the gentlest pressure of his fingers on my jaw to coax my mouth open.

"Good girl."

I shudder as the praise draws a fresh wash of pleasure from my core that's so much more visceral than physical sensation.

He makes quick work of buckling the straps into place. One secures at the back of my head, drawing the pink ball deep into my mouth. Another fastens beneath my chin to keep my teeth locked around the rubber, and more straps crisscross my face to extend over my brow.

There's a small metal loop at the back of the harness. He ties a thin length of black cord through it and applies steady pressure. My head draws back inexorably, and the gag sinks deeper into my mouth. He secures the loose end of the cord through the loop at the end of the metal hook that still penetrates my ass.

Tears slip down my cheeks, and all I can do is whimper around the gag. I never could've conceived of such a wicked predicament, and my brain struggles to process my complete, abject vulnerability.

He cups my jaw, guiding my chin to tip back a fraction farther.

"My proud pet," he praises. "You wanted to hold your head high, didn't you?"

I mumble around the gag, an unintelligible plea for the mercy I know he doesn't possess.

He strokes my hair in a tender display of affection. "Time to crawl for me. You don't have to make the choice. I'm in control now."

He straightens from where he was crouched beside me. He looms over me, and I cower in his imposing shadow.

I can't, I try to say, but it's nothing more than a high whine.

He can't possibly expect me to move when I'm completely overwhelmed by carnal sensation. He can't—

He pulls on the rope leash, an inexorable pressure that causes the hook to penetrate me more deeply. At the same time, the pressure of the rope looped through the back of my collar draws the leather tight around my throat, and I choke on my wordless mewl of protest.

My vision flashes white with a vicious strike of dark

ecstasy, and when it clears, I'm somehow on my hands and knees.

He takes a ruthless step forward, and I'm dragged along in his wake. My movements are jerky as my trembling limbs fumble to keep up with his slow, steady pace out of the bedroom.

I want to hang my head in shame, but the cord securing my gag to the hook forces me to hold it high. My back arches at the warring pressures of the hook pressing deep and my collar tugging tight, putting my dripping pussy on lewd display as my hips sway. My master has me leashed, body and soul.

I've been so consumed by my predicament that I didn't notice the crop that he holds like a casual extension of his hand. The supple leather tongue snaps against my ass, a quick, sharp bite that commands my attention.

"Keep your focus on me, pet," he chides. "I know it's difficult, but you want to please me, don't you? I know," he says in soothing reply to my pitiful whimper. "You're my good girl now. We're just getting started."

He chuckles in response to my wide-eyed shock, and he snaps the crop against my other ass cheek.

"That's it. Eyes on me."

He becomes the center of my universe, and I'm only dimly aware of our surroundings as the world falls away. He's all that exists: his powerful body looming over me, his elegant hand gripping the rope, his glinting emerald eyes.

My core contracts around the vibrating egg, riding the painful edge of the orgasm that he denies me. I sink into the sweet pain, allowing it to purify me until I don't have any thoughts left in my mind. There's only *him*. Nothing else matters. Nothing else exists.

I watch him intently as he pours himself a splash of his favorite whisky into a crystal glass. Then he opens the freezer and finds a large ice sphere. He considers it for a moment, then finally blesses me with his full attention.

"I don't usually take ice in my whisky," he remarks, utterly cool and casual. "I'll have to melt this down a bit. You can help me, my sweet pet."

I try to nod in eager agreement. I'll do anything to please him. But the minute movement of my head is restricted by the twine tied to my gag, and my small sign of assent morphs into a full-body shudder.

His low laugh caresses my soul like dark velvet as he drops to his knees beside me.

"This will hurt, but you'll take it for me. You do suffer so beautifully."

I cry out at the first icy kiss of the sphere against my lips. He rubs it over them where they're forced apart around the gag. I never knew my lips could be so sensitive, and the sensation of the ice is almost cold enough to sear them.

Hot tears spill down my cheeks, and he captures them on the sphere, further melting it for his drink.

"I can't wait to taste your tears," he rumbles, licking at the salty wetness on the ice.

An ecstatic wave shudders through me at the pleasure he finds in my subjugation. His happiness is all that matters to me. Even in his torment, he's wringing bliss from every throbbing inch of my most intimate areas. I will do anything to please him in return.

His cock is a hard, thick rod straining against his jeans, but he makes no move to free it. He's enjoying himself, taking his sadistic time with me.

The ice touches just beneath my chin, then rolls down the

column of my throat. My skin sparks everywhere it caresses my heated flesh. My mind begins to float, all lingering thoughts melting away with the ice as he rubs the sphere along the underside of my breasts.

A high-pitched whine echoes off the tiles, and I don't recognize that I'm making the animal sound.

Cold sears my nipple, and I scream into the gag. Hot, wet arousal soaks my inner thighs as my core contracts madly around the vibrator. It stimulates the hook in my ass, and my inner muscles undulate around the intrusion.

He keeps me on the edge of a vicious orgasm as he deftly rolls the sphere around my nipples, torturing my breasts.

When tears blur my vision, I blink hard to keep his perfect face in focus. The handsome lines of his features are drawn sharp with carnal hunger, and he studies my body with clinical precision. He rolls the sphere down my belly, pausing just above my clit.

My scream resounds through the penthouse when the ice hits my sensitive bundle of nerves. The pain sears my consciousness, and my entire body goes rigid. As my muscles lock up tight, they squeeze around the vibrator and the hook, and my elusive orgasm finally rushes through me with the force of a riptide.

My lashes flutter, my eyes threatening to roll back in my head, but I resolutely keep my gaze locked on my dark god. His eyes are still fixed on my pussy, watching my body intently through my orgasm.

"Perfect," he growls, his own lust riding him hard.

He swirls the remnants of the ice sphere through the desire that wets my thighs and teases the small ball through my aching labia.

"I'll taste your delicious cunt with every sip." He drops the ice into his whisky and takes a moment to inhale the perverted scent.

His eyes finally lock on mine, and he takes a slow draw of the amber alcohol.

A visceral aftershock of pleasure sizzles through me at the sight of his twisted pleasure in tasting me. He lowers the glass slowly, swirling it slightly so that the ice clinks against the crystal in a mocking song.

He clicks the button on the remote, and the vibrations inside me increase to a ruthless intensity. My pleasure crests again, but it doesn't abate this time. It goes on and on, and all I can do is moan and shake as cruel ecstasy consumes me.

He holds his glass in the same hand that grips the rope leash, and with every sip, he tugs on the hook, stimulating me to the point of madness. Idle snaps of the crop against my ass make fresh licks of pain stoke my lust, and I don't know the difference between pleasure and pain. There's only erotic sensation and my master's control.

He takes his time, savoring his drink while he keeps me pinned in his imperious stare. My dark god's attention is a divine mercy. I don't have meaning without his rapt focus. If he looks away from me, I won't exist. I'm his, completely and irrevocably.

When he finally finishes his drink, he sets the glass down on the counter and retrieves the slim jewelry box from his pocket.

"I think you've more than earned your diamonds," he rumbles. "Are you ready to accept your new collar? Once it's on, you will never take it off." He says the sweet promise like a warning. "You'll wear it every minute of every day, and you'll know that you're mine."

He drops the crop so that he can unbuckle the gag. It falls

from my mouth, and I immediately begin to babble my devotion.

"Yours, Master," I vow. "I'm all yours. I love you."

His slow grin appears almost drunken, as though my words of devotion grant him the most intoxicating high he's ever experienced.

"Sweet pet," he praises. "My Abigail."

The diamonds settle around my neck, draping just above my collarbones. The delicate clasp closes at my nape, more permanent than the rose gold padlock on my leather collar. A sense of security and peace bathes me in a warm glow, and I bask in the perfection of being his.

"Hold on to me," he commands, his voice dropping to a deeper register as he loses himself in our connection too.

My hands fly to his hips, and I cling to him like he's the only solid thing in my world. His powerful muscles flex as he quickly frees his thick, hard cock from the confines of his jeans.

He doesn't have to order me to open my mouth to accept him. I greedily part my lips in wanton invitation, and his precum wets my tongue as he enters me in a slow slide. He doesn't stop when he hits the back of my throat, and I struggle to suppress my gag reflex so that I can take all of him. When he's deep inside me, he stills for a moment, fixing me in his emerald stare.

Then he tugs on my leash, and I cry out around his cock.

He curses and withdraws, allowing me to draw the breath I so desperately need. His fingers tangle in my hair, and he starts to fuck my mouth in a steady rhythm. With each ruthless thrust, he toys with the leash, so that the hook gently fucks my ass in time with his cock in my throat.

I lose count of my orgasms, each peak crashing into the

next. All I can do is cling to him and breathe when he deigns to allow me oxygen. The ecstasy is vicious and all-consuming, burning me up inside.

My desperate, blissful tears stream down my face, and I taste the salt on his cock as it slides between my lips.

"One more," he snarls. "Come for me, Abigail."

My final orgasm claims me in a violent crescendo, and I scream around his dick. He roars out his own completion, and his hot cum spills onto my tongue. I greedily swallow everything he gives me.

I'm his, and he's mine.

My beautiful, cruel, perfect master's knees buckle, and he sinks to the tiles before me. His strong arms close around me, pulling me into a careful embrace as though I'm made of glass. I'm his precious pet, his most treasured possession. He'll never let me go.

And I'll never release him either.

59

ABIGAIL

Terror grips my mind in a vise, and all of my muscles tense with the survival instinct to flee from an encroaching threat. A shadow in the shape of a man looms at the bedroom door, a dangerous silhouette against the moonlight at his back. A copper tang coats my tongue, and I open my mouth to scream.

No sound comes out. I try to scramble away, but my bones are made of lead. I can't so much as twitch my limbs in an effort to fight him off.

I can't move. I can't speak.

Fear climbs up my throat in a choking vine, cutting off my ability to breathe.

The shadow draws closer, flickering toward me like a malevolent apparition.

Sweat beads on every inch of my skin, but I'm frozen. My skin burns, but my flesh is icy, and the dichotomy makes nausea churn in my gut.

The shadow flickers again, and the man is a foot closer now.

He's going to touch me, and there's nothing I can do to stop him.

Another shadow stirs at the foot of the bed. Only my eyes move in my paralyzed body, and I watch in pure horror as the shadow coalesces into a small child. She can't be more than five years old, but her haunted expression makes her even more horrifying than the encroaching man. Tears stream from her aqua eyes, and she begins to crawl up the length of my legs, reaching out a beseeching hand for my help.

The man is coming for both of us, but I'm even more petrified of the little girl. If she touches my face with that tiny, trembling hand…

My eyes snap open, but the nightmare doesn't disappear. The shadowy man still looms over the bed, and the sobbing child fills my vision as she crawls onto my chest, seeking comfort.

My vocal cords finally loosen, and a strangled, sharp cry tears from my throat.

"Abigail!"

The man and the child dissipate as though they're made of smoke.

Strong hands grasp my shoulders, and I twist away from the restraining hold with a defiant shriek.

The night-darkened world swirls around me, and I fall. I hit the carpeted floor, and my head spins. I'm not sure what's real anymore. I search the shadows frantically for the little girl, torn between an aching yearning to save her and stomach-turning dread that I'll have to face her again.

Light sears my eyes, and my lashes flutter. I'm scared to

close my eyes again. The man might get me if I let my focus waver for even a second.

My heart races like I've been sprinting for miles, and my hair sticks to my sweat-slicked brow and nape. I gasp for breath, and my lungs burn in protest when I force them to expand.

A man looms over me, solid and all too real.

I cover my head with my hands and curl into a tight, protective ball.

"It's me. Abigail, you're safe. I won't hurt you."

It takes several seconds for me to register the familiar, accented voice.

"Dane?" His name is a ragged whisper.

"I'm right here." His promise is a touch shaky. "Look at me."

Cautiously, I unlock my arms so that I can peek up at him. His eyes are tight with worry, and his lips are set in a tight slash.

"Dane!" I fling myself at him, and his strong arms close around me.

He draws me close and holds me to his chest, cradling my shaking body. My fingernails bite into the back of his neck, but he doesn't flinch in my desperate grip.

"I've got you," he says. "It was just a nightmare. You're safe."

I don't feel safe. My skin prickles with residual awareness of danger, and I barely resist the urge to claw away the maddening sensation. Instead, I cling to Dane more tightly and resolutely inhale his scent.

"That's it," he encourages. "Breathe. Just keep breathing. Stay here with me."

I can't deny him anything. He's my anchor to sanity, to reality.

I sink into him, memorizing the feel of his corded muscles bulging and flexing around me, as though he's preparing to fight off my monsters. The fine hairs that dust his sculpted chest tickle my cheek, and I turn my face into him to meld our bodies even more closely.

He strokes my chilled body with the elegant, dexterous hands that I love so much, and slowly, he imbues me with his warmth. As I thaw beneath his tender touch, the lingering terror begins to dissipate, leaving me wrung out and limp in his arms.

He lifts me up and carefully sets me on the soft mattress, immediately climbing into bed with me so that he can shape his body around mine.

My brain finally accepts that I'm with my white knight, and I'm safe.

Nothing can hurt me as long as I'm under his protection.

I cast a fearful glance toward the open bedroom door, and I release a shuddering sigh when I find it empty.

The shadowy man is gone.

And so is the distressed little girl.

"Talk to me," Dane urges. "Tell me about it."

I shudder and snuggle deeper into his embrace.

He strokes my hair in a soothing rhythm. "You'll feel better once you say it out loud," he urges. "It won't have power over you anymore."

"There was..." My stomach lurches at the thought of the shadowy man, and I swallow against the sudden urge to vomit.

I shake my head. "I can't talk about it," I say, my voice small. "I just need you to hold me. Please?"

"Always," he reassures me. "I'll be right here whenever you're ready."

I shake my head again and shove the terrible memory of the nightmare from my mind. I don't want to think about it ever again, much less talk about it.

"All right," he soothes. "It's all right."

"Thank you," I whisper, pressing closer to him.

"Never thank me for taking care of you," he says, but there's no bite to the admonishment. "It's my job to protect you. I won't allow anyone to harm you ever again."

I think about Stephen Lansing.

Don't watch, Abigail. Close your eyes for me. I'll take care of this. I'll take care of you.

Dane's form of caretaking can be lethal, but I barely experience a twinge of disquiet over his murderous capabilities.

"I don't want you to kill for me," I say softly.

He tenses slightly, but his fingers remain gentle in my hair. "I will do what's necessary to keep you safe."

"I know." I have complete faith in him.

"If you think that you're somehow responsible for my actions, you're mistaken," he declares. "Stephen is dead because he was a fucking rapist. You bear no responsibility."

I turn into Dane so that I can meet his fierce gaze. "At first, I felt like he was dead because of me, but I can see now that I was wrong. I've already accepted that he faced the consequences of his own actions, and that's not my fault."

I try to brush away the furrow in Dane's brow.

"If you're asking me not to kill out of some sense of morality, that argument won't sway me. You should know by now that I don't possess a moral compass, and I feel nothing but satisfaction when I think about the fact that Stephen paid for what he did to you. My only regret is that he should've suffered so much more."

He breathes a soft curse, and his body relaxes around mine. "I'm scaring you. I'm sorry, little dove. I don't want that."

"I'm not scared," I reassure him. "The only thing that scares me is the prospect of being separated from you. I can't bear it if you go to jail. No more killing, Dane."

He shakes his head. "I won't make that promise. I can't. Not if you're in danger."

I blow out a sigh, exhaustion sapping my bones. In the wake of my nightmare, I don't have the energy to continue with this argument.

He presses a kiss to my forehead. "No one will separate us," he vows. "No one will take you from me."

I lean into him and allow my heavy eyelids to droop. His scent enfolds me, more comforting than the softest blanket. The hands that are holding me so tenderly are capable of brutal violence, but they will never touch me with anything but reverence.

With that reassuring thought, my body finally relaxes, and I drift into a deep, dreamless sleep.

60

ABIGAIL

"Abby! You're back!" Franklin hugs me in a quick but warm embrace. My friend has always been respectful of my physical boundaries—it's one of the reasons I'm so grateful to have him in my life.

He steps into my shabby little apartment with the ease of familiarity, and I welcome him in with a broad smile. Stacy is right behind him, bottle of red wine in hand.

I've only been back in Charleston for a few hours, but my friends have already descended on my apartment to welcome me home. In the warmth of their presence, the lingering chill from my nightmare in York yesterday fades away completely.

"You were gone for ages." Stacy pouts her berry-painted lips and pulls me into a hug too. "The café isn't the same without you. Don't get me wrong," she says quickly. "I'm not trying to guilt you into coming back. I'm so happy that you're going to pursue your art fulltime."

"Do you have an English accent now?" Franklin teases

before I can respond. "I bet you sound more like your hot boyfriend than a Carolina girl."

I scoff. "I was only away for a few weeks."

Stacy blows out a dreamy sigh. "I wish I could go on vacation to Europe with a sexy man for weeks. You're living the dream, girl."

I wave her off, but before I can say something dismissive, Franklin grabs my left hand with a gasp.

"Excuse me, what is this *rock* on your ring finger?" He stares at the glittering emerald with open-mouthed shock.

"That's Abigail's engagement ring," Dane rumbles from behind me, emerging from my bedroom with a packed suitcase in one hand.

We only stopped by my old place to grab my clothes. I'll be all moved out within a few days, and then Dane and I can start to make a home together in his house in Harleston Village.

We haven't spoken about the powder blue house across the street. I don't think either of us is eager to revisit the painful day when I found his secret shrine to me.

The momentary darkness of that thought immediately dissipates when his arm drapes over my shoulders, and he drops a kiss on the top of my head. Warmth suffuses my chest, and a happy grin nearly splits my features.

"Oh my god, you're glowing!" Stacy exclaims, glossy black curls bouncing as she does a little shimmy of excitement on my behalf. "Are you really engaged?"

"We are," Dane declares, his accented voice deep with pride.

"Dane proposed in York," I say.

"So romantic," Franklin gushes. "You have to tell us all about it. When did this happen?"

"Two days ago," I say, still smiling. "It was deeply romantic and absolutely perfect."

Dane beams at me. "I'm glad you think so."

"Could you two be more stunning together?" Franklin enthuses. "Abby, you found your prince!"

I giggle, and my cheeks flush with a touch of embarrassment. I've secretly thought of Dane as my dashing prince, but I've never told him that.

His long fingers brush over my cheek, testing the warmth of my blush. His lips curve in that cocky smirk that makes my knees weak.

"I'm opening this bottle," Stacy announces. "We're celebrating."

I peek up at Dane. "I don't know..." I say slowly. "We were going to move my stuff to Dane's house."

"*Our* house," he corrects me. "And don't worry about that. Spend time with your friends. I should go to the office and meet with Meadows. He's texted me five times since we landed. I'll finish moving your things over the weekend."

"Perfect," Franklin says, as though it's settled. "Then we're going out for karaoke and dancing."

Stacy claps her hands. "Yes! A bachelorette party!"

A giddy laugh bubbles from my chest. "I don't even have a date set yet for the wedding. It's too soon for a bachelorette party."

"We'll have another one," Stacy insists.

"At least three," Franklin agrees.

"You'd better plan those quickly," Dane says. "I'm marrying you as soon as possible."

His tone lightens the fierce declaration, but I hear the dark warning beneath the words. He told me that we were returning to South Carolina to get married because it's faster than the process in England. If Dane has his way, I'll be his wife within a few days.

I go up onto my toes and press a quick kiss to his lips, a silent promise of my acceptance and eagerness to be married to him.

"Text me when you're ready for me to pick you up," he says, a subtle command. "I don't care how late it is. Enjoy your celebration."

My heart lifts. Until this moment, some part of me had still worried that Dane might be an overbearing husband. After what happened with Stephen, I know it will be difficult for him to let me out of his sight. We've agreed to share our locations on our phones, and I think that puts both of our minds at ease; we can find each other at any time.

Dane isn't a mindless, possessive beast. He knows I value my autonomy, and he won't stop me from spending time with my friends.

"Thank you," I say, imbuing my gratitude with so much more than just simple thanks for the celebratory night out.

He's trusting that I can handle myself.

"I'll call you if I need anything," I promise.

He drops a quick, fierce kiss on my lips.

"Abby, you'd better put wine glasses on your registry because I'm tired of drinking out of these juice glasses," Stacy teases, breaking into our private moment before I can get lost in our potent chemistry.

"I don't need any wedding gifts," I reply with a laugh. "Just celebrating with y'all tonight is enough."

"Well, you're not buying a single drink tonight," Franklin declares. "The bride doesn't pay for her drinks."

The moment seems surreal. I can hardly believe that I'm going to be Dane's bride.

He'd said our wedding day was coming soon like it's a threat, but I can hardly wait.

"I'll see you tonight," Dane promises.

Then he's out the door, and I'm alone with my two closest friends.

"I'm texting the girls," Stacy declares. "We're getting tacos before karaoke."

Franklin places a juice cup filled with red wine into my hand.

"We've seen the ring, but are we going to talk about that necklace?" he teases, gesturing at my throat. "Those can't be real diamonds. Is any of this real? Are we in some sort of crazy dream world where you ended up with the hottest man on the planet, *and* he's rich?"

I touch my collar with a dreamy smile. "I know, it's crazy."

"It's so fast," Stacy says, her voice dropping to a more serious tone now that Dane is gone. "Are you sure he's not too good to be true?"

I think about how he stalked and kidnapped me. Nothing about that was *good.*

"Dane has his flaws," I assure her. "But I love him anyway."

"Abby is in love!" Franklin declares, my romantic friend practically buzzing for me. "You deserve it."

"Just make sure he treats you right," Stacy says sternly. "The diamonds are a good start, but he'd better cherish the fuck out of you, or he'll have to answer to us."

"He does," I assure her. "No need to go on the attack. But I appreciate you so much for being in my corner."

"Well, if you're sure about him, I'm thrilled for you," she says earnestly. "Cheers to Abby and Dane!"

Franklin clinks his glass against each of ours and joins in

the toast. I beam at my friends and take my first sip of wine. I don't intend to get drunk, but I'm more than happy to get a little tipsy. It's my first bachelorette party, after all.

61

DANE

Two weeks later

"We're going to The Magnolia?" Abigail's delicately arched brows draw together as I guide her toward the boutique hotel where we had our first date. "I thought you said we're going to the beach. I'm not dressed for the rooftop bar."

She gestures at her casual sundress. The straps of her dark purple bikini are visible at her neckline, a tantalizing suggestion of what she'll look like in the skimpy swimsuit.

I blink the wolfish glint from my eyes and offer her a teasing smile. "We are going to the beach, just not right now. We're stopping at The Magnolia first."

"Dane!" she protests, even as she allows me to lead her into the entry hall that's set up as a small art gallery.

None of the work on display compares to her masterpieces, but her gaze instantly strays to the paintings. Her lovely eyes shine with an awestruck light as she drinks in the art like it's the most breathtaking thing she's ever seen.

All qualms about her outfit are forgotten as soon as she loses herself in her artistic nature.

She's so distracted that she doesn't notice Stacy practically bounding down the corridor, Franklin hot on her heels. His cheeks are a bit rosy above his neat black moustache—he must've started partaking of the champagne I ordered for them already. And, judging by her giddy energy, Stacy might be a bit tipsy too.

"Abby!" she squeals, "You're here!"

"Stacy?" She blinks as the exuberant woman barrels into her. "Hey, y'all. What are you doing here?"

She's baffled but clearly pleased to see her two friends.

A quick, jealous impulse tightens my hand around hers for a moment, but I force myself to remain calm and collected. I can share her attention for a short while. In a few hours, she'll be mine forever. I can allow her this time with them to make the day special for her.

"Dane got a room for us," Franklin gushes, then adds in a conspiratorial whisper, "With champagne."

"What? Why?"

I curl two fingers beneath her chin, drawing her gaze to mine. I want her looking into my eyes when I say, "Your friends are going to help you get ready for our wedding."

Her lips part on a soft gasp. "Now?"

"Now."

My grin is probably sharper than it should be, but I can't bring myself to soften it in this moment of triumph.

"But...I'm not even wearing makeup. You told me we're going to the beach, so I only put on sunscreen."

I cup her cheek. "You are stunning just as you are."

Franklin lets out a long sigh, and Stacy says, "I brought makeup if you want it. Dane asked if we wanted to help you get ready, and we're so thrilled to be part of your Big Day!"

"A private ceremony on the beach at sunset, so romantic," Franklin says with approval. "But we get to spend the afternoon with you. I have our favorite musicals ready for a singalong while you get glammed up. Dane didn't give us much notice, but luckily, I already have a thirteen-hour-long playlist ready for emergencies like this."

Abigail's eyes are still fixed on mine, wide and guileless as ever. "I get to be your wife today?" she breathes.

I stroke her purple curl. "Today and every day for the rest of our lives." I press a quick, fierce kiss to her parted lips. "I'll meet you on the beach, little dove."

I force myself to walk away from her before I lose my tenuous control. The craving to throw her over my shoulder and carry her to the ceremony right now is nearly overwhelming.

I grit my teeth against the grating sound of her friends' excited screeching behind me and remind myself that Abigail enjoys their company. They're important to her, so from now on, they're important to me.

Every aspect of this day will be absolutely perfect for Abigail, even if that means I have to be parted from her for a few hours.

The next time I see her, my bride will be walking toward me dressed in white, ready to pledge herself to me forever.

~

The private stretch of beach owned by Meadows' family is serene and quiet—not a tourist in sight. My partner was all too happy to allow me use of their property for the weekend, even if he did seem a bit disappointed that he isn't invited to my wedding.

But this moment is only for Abigail and me. We aren't performing for the sake of others; they won't take little pieces of our happiness for themselves.

By now, she's had several hours to celebrate the day with her close friends. That will have to be enough, because I'm not capable of sharing more of her today.

The officiant waits with me, the surf lapping closer to his shoes with every passing minute as the tide comes in. I refuse to budge. Abigail will have her wedding by her beloved ocean, and I don't care if the man gets wet. I paid him enough that he's not complaining.

Or maybe it's my warning glower that's keeping his mouth shut. I'm not interested in idle small talk while I wait for my bride.

My genial mask has fallen away entirely, and I intend to be my true, ruthless, cruelly possessive self when we make our vows.

"If the storm draws much closer, we'll have to move this inside," the violinist dares to say, gesturing in the direction of Meadows' grand beach house.

I look out at the dark clouds churning on the horizon and smile. Everything will be perfect for my Abigail.

"We're getting married right here," I announce. "Start playing."

She should be arriving any minute now. I stare at the boardwalk, my intense anticipation for my bride setting my teeth on edge. It's a discomfiting sensation, but thanks to

Abigail, the *feeling* is a revelation I've only known since meeting her. She's my miracle, my everything.

The wind is just starting to pick up when she appears like an angel blessing me with her presence. She practically floats down the worn wooden steps of the boardwalk, and her bare feet sink into the soft sand as she slowly glides toward me.

The rose petals that I laid out as an aisle for her are whipped up by the oncoming storm, and they whirl around her. Ivory lace appears to have been painted onto her porcelain skin, perfectly fitted to her bodice. Her full white skirt swirls as though she's dancing, and her gossamer veil seems to be lifted by an invisible, benevolent spirit behind her. Loose, sable curls float around her delicate face, my favorite purple one winking through the undulating locks.

She's like an enchanted princess out of one of her favorite movies.

Or maybe I'm the one who's under a spell, because I can't tear my eyes off her.

Then she's in front of me, lifting her hands so that I can take them in mine. Her aquamarine eyes glimmer and glow like jewels, and her rosebud lips are petal pink. I can't help brushing my thumb over them to test their soft texture. Then I trace the line of her fragile cheekbone, lingering on her unique freckle.

The violinist stops playing, and the officiant is speaking. I'm barely aware of a word he says; Abigail has harnessed my full attention. She's the only person who matters, the only thing that exists in my world.

The wind starts to blow off the ocean with more force, and a light spray from the crashing waves mists around us. The moisture makes her cheeks glisten like a dew kissed flower.

"Dane." My name in her breathy voice goes straight to my

head in a rush of power and desire. "I promise to be with you always." I realize that she's repeating the officiant's words, saying the vows I chose for us. "I promise to honor and sustain you, and I will be true to you in all things forever."

There will be no "until death do us part" in our ceremony. Nothing will take my Abigail from me. Nothing.

"Abigail." I savor the shape of her name on my tongue. "I promise to cherish you always. I promise to protect, honor, and sustain you, and I will be true to you in all things forever."

A single tear rolls down her cheek, brighter and more precious than the diamond collar around her throat.

"With this ring, I, Abigail Foster, take you, Dane Graham, to be no other than yourself. I will have faith in our bond, through all our years, and in all that life might bring us."

The ring burns like a brand when it slides onto my finger, searing her claim into my flesh, into my soul.

"With this ring, I, Dane Graham, take you, Abigail Foster, to be no other than yourself. I will have faith in your love for me, through all our years, and in all that life might bring us."

She already wears the emerald engagement ring and the diamond collar, but now I adorn her slender finger with another mark of my ownership.

Abigail is my wife.

I don't wait for the officiant to finish pronouncing us husband and wife before I sweep her up in a savage kiss. My tongue plunders her mouth, and she shivers in sweet delight at my feverish onslaught. Her arms twine around my shoulders, pulling me closer, as though she can't get enough of me either.

The officiant and the violinist flee the storm, but I'm too caught up in her to relent.

Thunder rumbles around us, and warm, fat drops of rain slide down our faces to wet our lips. I don't stop claiming her mouth until lightning forks over the whitecapped waves. Her safety is more important than my desire to fuck her in the sand while the storm rages around us.

I scoop her up in my arms and take off toward the house at a run. Her delighted laugh is the sweetest melody I've ever heard.

I climb the boardwalk stairs and stride along the aged wooden planks toward the beachfront mansion. It's all I can do to get her to the shelter of the porch before I shove her up against the wall and wrap her amethyst curl around my fist. I crush my lips to hers, and she meets me with equal fervor.

Lust burns in my veins, pulsing hot enough to cause me pain. I revel in it, sinking into the feelings that only Abigail can give me.

I drop to my knees so I can worship her.

My fingers tangle in her voluminous skirt, tearing at the delicate material as I shove it out of my way. I find her bare thighs, and my fingers sink into her soft, creamy flesh.

She grabs at my hair, and my scalp tingles with carnal awareness when she tugs my head up so that I'll meet her flame blue gaze.

"I want you," she pants, trying to pull me up to kiss her again.

I shoot her a wicked smile and graze her clit with my teeth through the thin barrier of her white lace panties. She cries out, and I firm my hold on her before her knees buckle.

"Watch the storm," I command. "You will remember every detail about this day."

She shivers, and her gaze locks on the horizon.

I keep my eyes on her gorgeous face as I hook my thumbs

beneath her panties and drag them down her legs. The scent of her arousal mingles with the smell of freshly fallen rain and salty ocean spray, intoxicating. I take a long moment to simply breathe her in as I watch her study the storm.

Her eyes flash brighter than the lightning, and her sharp cry wars with a clap of thunder when I press a tender kiss to her clit.

Her cunt is hot and wet on my tongue, and I never want to stop tasting her. I'm a man obsessed, devouring her pussy like I'm starved for her. Soft whimpers give way to deep, guttural moans as she begins to grind her hips into my face. Her fingers firm in my hair, and I allow her to direct me where she wants me.

I promised to give her the world. The least I can do is satisfy her every erotic desire.

"Dane, Dane, Dane…" She whispers my name like a litany, and I'm drunk on her desire for me.

With every flick of my tongue over her clit, she winds tighter and tighter, until she's quivering in my hands.

I slide two fingers into her tight sheath. "Come for me."

She shatters on a scream, and I nip at her clit while I rub her g-spot. Her willowy body shakes, and she rotates her hips, wantonly drawing out the last aftershocks of her orgasm as she stimulates herself on my tongue.

I'm done waiting to claim my bride.

I surge to my feet and unbuckle my belt.

"Yes," she urges. "Please fuck me. I need you."

I free my cock and find her slick opening. She locks one leg around my hip, opening herself to me.

I pause, making both of us suffer.

But I want something from her first.

"You love me. Say it."

She blinks, and her eyes soften. "I love you, Dane."

I enter her in one brutal thrust, and she releases a guttural cry. I'm going to fuck her to the edge of pain, and she will feel this vicious union with every step tomorrow.

My fingers sink into her ass, and I lift her so that I can fill her more deeply. Her hands fly to my shoulders for support, her eyes going wide.

"I've got you," I promise through gritted teeth. "Now, say it again."

"I love you!" she cries as I rut into her. "My Dane, my Master."

Pleasure builds, hot and fast, swelling inside me with ruthless force. I snarl and hold back my release. She'll come again before we're finished.

With each brutal thrust, she starts up a new litany: "I love you, I love you, I love you..."

I can't hold back any longer. Her cunt grips my cock, and I come with a roar. As I brand her with my cum, she finds her own completion. Her fingernails bite into my shoulders as she screams my name louder than the booming thunder.

We're joined in perfect, savage pleasure.

Husband and wife.

Forever.

62

ABIGAIL

The shadowy man hovers at the end of my bed, close enough that he could reach out and grab my ankles.

Terror thrums through me, but I'm frozen in place. There's nothing I can do to evade him.

Dane. I need Dane.

I open my mouth to scream for him, but no sound comes out.

He can't save me if he doesn't know I'm in danger.

Another shadow appears at the man's side. The little girl's lips are parted on a wail that's as silent as my own. Tears stream from her aqua eyes, and she reaches for me, seeking help that I can't give.

The man's silhouette wraps around her, dragging her into darkness. An echo of the shadow's touch clings to my skin like toxic sludge, and I shudder in pure revulsion.

There's nothing I can do. I'm powerless to stop him. I can't save the little girl.

I can't save myself.

My vocal cords are raw from my silent screams, and I swear I can hear the anguished sound locked inside my own head.

"Abigail!"

My eyes snap open, but I'm not fully free of the nightmare. The crying child is enfolded by the shadow, dragged deeper into the man's sick embrace until she disappears entirely.

I sit bolt upright, my hand shooting out to grab at nothing. There's no small hand to clutch. She's gone.

A primal wail fills the bedroom, and hot tears sear my cheeks.

"You're safe. Abigail, look at me."

Dane's voice. Dane's hands on my shoulders, holding me as though I'm made of porcelain. Dane's piercing green eyes, dark with worry.

I blink away my tears, and the shadows dissipate entirely. The bedroom is illuminated by the bedside lamp, the light chasing away the looming threat of the man's silhouette.

Dane cups my chilled cheek with aching care. "Look at me."

It's a low command this time, even if the words are rough with desperation.

A sob tears from my chest, and I throw myself into his arms. He catches me, holding me gently. His big hand strokes my hair, playing through the sable strands in the way that always calms me. I shake against him, and he murmurs reassurances.

Slowly, the fog of terror ebbs, and my rational brain comes back online.

"I've got you," he promises over and over again. "I won't let anyone hurt you."

I nod against his chest, and the flow of my tears slows.

His hand curves around the back of my head, tenderly holding me close as he presses a kiss to my brow.

"I need you to talk to me," he beseeches. "I know you didn't want to tell me about your nightmare last time, but I have to know."

My stomach lurches with a surge of nausea, and I squeeze my eyes shut. The shadowy man lurks in the darkness of my mind, so I open them again and focus on Dane.

"Please, Abigail. Tell me about it. I'll make it better."

The words to describe the full horror of the nightmare stick my throat.

"He'll never breathe the same air as you again," Dane vows darkly. "You'll be safe, and you won't be troubled by another nightmare about a man threatening you."

He thinks my night terrors are about Stephen.

I shake my head.

"There was a man," I confess. "He was just a shadow, but I know it wasn't Stephen."

Dane's arms tense around me, but his hold remains gentle. "What did this shadow do to you?"

I draw in a shuddering breath. "Nothing. He just scared me. And there was..."

My stomach twists violently at the thought of the anguished child.

Dane strokes my hair and waits for me to continue.

After several sickening seconds, I manage, "There was a little girl. She was desperate for my help, but I couldn't move. I couldn't save her." Then I force myself to admit, "She scares me more than the man."

Dane freezes, his hand stilling in my hair.

When he finally speaks, the words are so gravelly that they're barely intelligible. "What did she look like?"

"Me," I say, voice small. "She looked like me."

Dane remains unnervingly still, and although his jaw works, he doesn't make a sound.

His distress shreds me. I reach out and trace the taut line of his anvil-hard jaw.

"It was just a nightmare," I reassure him. "I'm safe with you."

He draws in a deep breath and resumes stroking my hair, but his eyes are still dark with an emotion I can't name.

"You are," he swears. "Go back to sleep. I'll be right here for the rest of the night."

"Are you okay?" I ask, brushing my fingertips over his furrowed brow.

He turns his face into me and captures my hand so that he can kiss my palm. "I'm fine, my sweet Abigail. Don't worry about me. Sleep, little dove."

Exhaustion saps me all the way to my bones, and his tender touch soothes me like nothing else. I close my eyes and am dragged back down into sleep in a matter of minutes, completely wrung out from the night terror.

As long as Dane is holding me, nothing bad can touch me.

63

ABIGAIL

I spin around the empty room, arms outstretched to encompass the space. "It's perfect!"

"I'm glad you're satisfied with it," Dane says, voice rumbling with mirth at my shenanigans.

I shake my new set of keys so that they jangle, making a happy song to go with the little dance I can't resist.

"*Satisfied*?" I repeat. "This is my dream come true! My own gallery. I can't believe it."

"You deserve it," he says, tone dropping to something deeper and more serious. "The world needs your art."

I beam at him and bound into his arms. He catches me, and then we're both spinning. My delighted laugh echoes through the empty space, bouncing off the blank walls that will soon display my paintings.

It's surreal. This seemed impossible only a few months ago.

But Dane believes in me. No one has ever believed in my art like he does.

Not even me.

But now, when I see him studying my paintings like they're altering his entire worldview, I dare to think that I can actually succeed at this.

"I'll pay you back as soon as I can," I say breathlessly when I finally stop laughing.

He kisses my brow and sets me down on my feet, but his hands remain firmly on my waist, trapping me in his possessive hold.

"I'm not concerned about it," he reassures me. "You'll be able to cover the rent yourself in no time. Then you can look at buying a more permanent space."

He'd offered to buy a property for my gallery, but I want to earn this for myself. Rental was a compromise until I can generate enough revenue to buy a place for myself.

It's a small miracle that we were able to secure this place so quickly. It's only been three weeks since we returned to Charleston, but Dane was single-minded in his determination to make my dream come true.

His eyes glimmer with almost feral anticipation. "How shall we celebrate, my queen?"

My breath catches. He's never called me that before.

"I have a few ideas," he says in a wicked rumble that makes my core quiver.

I lick my lips, catching on to his carnal mood. "Like what?"

He tips his head in the direction of the back room. "We could find out how soundproof the office is."

My cheeks heat even as my core flutters. "Dane!" I scold. "I don't want to scandalize the neighboring businesses on my first day in the building."

He grins. "Then you'll have to be very quiet, pet. I'm sure I can figure out a way to gag you if you'll be more comfortable that way."

I scoff. "That's not helping."

"On the contrary," he teases. "If you don't want to bother your neighbors, I think a gag will be very helpful. Your panties will do nicely. Are they already wet for me?"

"Dane!"

"Abigail."

I release a huff of exasperation, but I'm not really annoyed.

A bell rings, shattering the intimate moment. We both look toward the glass door in confusion. No one should be interested in entering an empty shop on a Saturday morning.

My stomach drops to the floor.

My mother strides into my new gallery like she owns the place, my father trailing after her with a bored expression on his weathered face. And—oh, god—even Uncle Jeffrey is with them.

Dane angles his powerful body in front of mine, instantly protective in the face of my relatives.

I gather my courage and step up beside him. I can't cower behind my husband.

"What are you doing here?" My voice is clear and calm, and Dane threads his fingers through mine in a show of solidarity and pride.

His support bolsters me like nothing else. I'm able to square my shoulders and meet my mother's ice blue gaze without flinching.

Her Botox-frozen features give nothing away, her expression unnervingly enigmatic. But her voice is all honeyed warmth when she says, "We came to see your gallery, darling."

Confusion knits my brow. "How did you even know I'd be here?"

Her affable smile doesn't reach her sharp, calculating eyes. "A member of my bridge club owns this building. She was so excited to tell me that you've rented the space for your little art project."

Dane tenses beside me, and I quickly place a restraining hand on his corded forearm.

"We just had to come see it for ourselves," she continues. "It's been ages since Meadows' wedding, and we barely had a chance to speak to you before you two ran off." She makes a sound like a conspiratorial giggle, but it's too sharp to be genial. "You'd think we scared you away."

"I took Abigail home," Dane says, ice cold. He's not bothering to put on a show for my family. "We found the company distasteful, and I didn't feel like putting up with the farce any longer."

Mama draws back slightly in the face of his emotionless, clinical stare. Even my spine tingles with unease at the primal recognition of a predator at my side.

I edge closer to my dark protector.

"Now, wait just a minute," my dad blusters. "You can't speak to my wife like that."

"You are not welcome here," Dane says, each word a sharp, icy dagger. "Leave."

"Oh my gosh, Abby!" Mama says, as though she hasn't heard a word he's said. "What is that ring on your finger? Surely, you didn't elope without telling your mother."

Uncle Jeffrey beams at me like it's the best news he's ever heard. "Our little Abby is married? We'll have to throw you two a party at the house. A belated wedding reception at home would be perfect."

"I'm not going back there," I announce, holding my head high despite the nausea rolling through me. "Elysium isn't my home. Not anymore."

Just the thought of the grand plantation with its vile history makes cold sweat break out on the back of my neck. I will never return there.

"Aw, don't be like that," Uncle Jeffrey cajoles.

Shock punches me when he brashly closes the distance between us and slings an arm over my shoulder like we're best friends.

"It's time to put all unpleasantness behind us." He's still talking, but there's a high-pitched ringing in my ears. "You belong with your family. Blood is everything."

His familiar tobacco and amber scent permeates my senses. My vision tunnels, and my entire body locks up tight.

The empty gallery flickers around me, and a nauseating image flashes across my mind: Uncle Jeffrey is looming over me, his broad smile filling my world. His pupils are dilated, darkening his pale blue eyes with sick excitement. Massive, masculine hands are on my shoulders, so much stronger than me. His weight crushes me, and something hard presses into my belly.

The flash is gone as quickly as it came, and I'm in the gallery again. The ringing sound is deafening, blocking out my mother's voice. She's right in front of me, but I can't hear her speaking. Everything blurs around me, as though I'm underwater. I can't breathe.

Uncle Jeffrey's body is heavy and hot, and I smell the tobacco of his beloved pipe. His face is so close to mine. Every part of him is close.

My stomach twists, and I lurch away from him, stumbling as I desperately free myself from his restraining arm.

I don't understand what's happening. All I know is that I'm about to be sick.

The ringing in my ears pierces my brain, making it throb and ache. I rush to the bathroom and barely manage to slam the door behind me before I fall to my knees and vomit.

Then Dane is with me, holding my hair and stroking my back.

"I'm sorry," I gasp before I gag again. "I don't know what's wrong."

He grunts, but he doesn't say anything else. His tension heightens the anxiety that rakes my tight chest like razorblades on my burning lungs.

He shushes me gently, his hands tender and careful with me, as always.

When I don't have anything left inside me, I'm shaking and wrung out. My head aches, and my empty stomach is still in knots.

"Let's get you home," Dane says. His voice is rough, like he's angry about something.

"I'm sorry I'm sick. You don't have to stay with me."

"I'm not leaving your side," he growls. "I'm taking you home. Now."

I'm feeling too weak to argue, so I allow myself to lean on him as he helps me to my feet and guides me out of my gallery.

Fifteen minutes later, we're back home. I quickly brush my teeth to wash the lingering acidity out of my mouth, but it barely dulls my persistent nausea.

Dane doesn't bother to remove our clothes before tucking us both under the duvet. I shiver despite the warm blanket, and his arms wrap around me, as though he can shield me from all the bad things in the world.

"What happened?" he asks, his voice still rougher than usual.

I peek up at him. "Are you angry with me?"

He cups my cheek. "No, Abigail. I'm not angry with you." His tone gentles slightly. "I need you to tell me what happened that made you sick."

I blink. "I… I don't know. I guess I was more stressed out by my family than I realized." My cheeks flush with shame. "That's so stupid of me. I'm sorry."

"No more apologies," he says curtly. "You are not stupid."

He studies my face intently, analyzing each of my features as though he's searching for something.

"What happened when your uncle put his arm around you?"

I flinch.

His thumb hooks beneath my jaw, gently holding my face so that I'm trapped in his tender hand.

"I understand if you don't want to remember," he says quietly.

The flashes from the gallery flicker over my mind again, and I shudder in pure revulsion.

"I don't know," I whisper. "I just felt…trapped."

"By your uncle?" That rough, gravelly tone again.

I look up at him, beseeching. "I don't understand what's happening."

"Don't you?" Dane prompts, gentler this time.

My heart gives a painful twist, as though it might tear asunder.

"Your nightmares," he says. "You said there was a man who scared you. And there was a frightened child: you."

"What are you saying?" I ask raggedly, even though I already know.

But I don't want the knowledge. I want to forget.

Just like I've managed to forget for all these years.

But now, the memories are bubbling just beneath the surface of my conscious thoughts, threatening to spill over and taint the happy new life I'm building with Dane.

"You had a flashback," he tells me. "Has that ever happened before?"

"No!" Alarm bursts through me. I don't want this to be real.

Because if it is, all the horrors of my adult life are starting to make some sort of terrible sense. I can't face it.

I thread my fingers through my hair, tugging at the delicate strands as though I can tear the memories from my brain.

Dane's long fingers encircle my wrists and direct my hands away from my head before I can hurt myself.

"No." This time, my refusal is a low groan.

His face is drawn in lines of anguish, as though my pain is his own. I can't bear the sight of his suffering. My determination to spare him pain gives me the strength I need to draw in a ragged breath.

"Why do you think…" I swallow against another surge of nausea. "Have you always suspected?"

I can't bring myself to put the crime against me into words. If I say it aloud, I'll never be able to take it back. It'll be irrevocably true, and I'm not ready to face that.

He shakes his head. "Only since you described your nightmare. But from what you told me about your debutante date and how you reacted to Ron's assault, I drew a likely conclusion based on your freeze response. I just didn't know who it was."

His eyes glint with a lethal light, but I'm too bogged down in my trauma to think about my uncle's potential murder.

"If you suspected, why didn't you talk to me about it?"

"I didn't want to force you to remember if you didn't want to. I'd hoped you never would." His thumb traces the taut slash of my lips. "I never wanted to cause you this pain."

"If this is true..." I swallow hard. "You said you drew your conclusion because I freeze when I'm threatened. Because I was...conditioned not to fight back." My gut twists. "Part of me was conditioned to like it. Some of what he did to me felt good physically."

Agonized lines draw deep around Dane's stunning eyes, but he doesn't say anything in response.

My horrific revelations issue from my numb lips like someone else is speaking. "I orgasm when I'm violated. It feels good because my brain was wired this way from the beginning. Men look at me, and they know I'm prey. I was designed to be raped. And I like it."

If my stomach weren't empty, I'd vomit again.

"No," Dane snarls. "Never say that about yourself."

His perfect face blurs as my eyes fill with tears. "But it's true. I get off on being overpowered and violated. I let it happen. I always let it happen."

"None of this is your fault," he insists.

A sense of powerlessness hollows out my chest. Everything I've built with Dane, all of the dark desires I've learned to accept, are rooted in something disgusting. In this moment, I'm robbed of all agency. There's nothing empowering about embracing my sexual nature with my master. Because it's never been my choice. I'm like this because of what a sick man did to me when I was a child.

My soul shreds, and an animal wail fills the bedroom.

Dane's arms wrap around me as though he can hold the remnants of me together.

But even my dark god doesn't have the power to fix me. I've been broken for my whole life. Now I finally understand why.

64

ABIGAIL

My eyelids are sandpaper, and my tear ducts are dry from crying all night. Dane held me through it, stoic and silent. I know he must be wrestling with his own reaction to the revelations about Uncle Jeffrey, but he's bottling up whatever he's feeling for my sake.

I was surprised and almost disappointed when he allowed me to leave the house without him. I'm desperate to keep my husband close, but I can't lean on him all the time. And he deserves some space to sort through his feelings too.

I take a deep breath and kick off my sandals at the end of the boardwalk. My mother waits for me on the beach, lounging in her chair with her face tipped back to catch the sun.

This is an exclusive, members only stretch of beach, so we'll have relative privacy for this awful discussion. There are a few couples with children splashing in the surf, but they're several yards away. No one will hear this conversation over the sound of crashing waves.

I straighten my large sunglasses, ensuring my red-rimmed eyes are covered. The last thing I need right now is a cutting comment from my mom about my appearance.

"Abby!" She smiles when I approach her, and she almost sounds genuinely happy to see me. "I'm so glad you called. I was worried about you when you got sick. That husband of yours is very cold. He was downright rude when he told us to leave your gallery."

"Hi, Mama." I greet her instead of responding to her pointed comments.

I settle down into the chair next to her and attempt to lean back in a casual posture. But I'm far too stiff to pull it off, and her eyes rake over me, noting my vulnerable state.

"Marital troubles?" she guesses piteously. "That's what you get when you don't ask for your mother's advice in choosing a husband."

I decide to cut the bullshit. I'm too exhausted to dance around this difficult subject.

I have to know for sure.

"I was sick yesterday because I had a flashback when Uncle Jeffrey touched me," I say, keeping myself carefully detached from my emotions. After my anguished night, they're dulled enough that I'm able to talk about this in a calm, rational tone.

"I think he might've..." I stumble over the words, but I force myself to continue. "I think he abused me when I was little."

My mother waves a dismissive hand. "No need to be so dramatic. Your father was hard on you sometimes. I acknowledge that. But children these days don't understand discipline and respect." She shakes her head. "In any case, Jeffrey doted on you. Don't you remember how often he used to babysit you? He loved it."

I suppress the worst of my shudder.

"Be honest with me, Mama. I'm not talking about being beaten."

Her icy blue eyes flare for half a heartbeat, and then her face becomes impassive. She takes a sip of her wine.

I won't allow her to evade me.

"I think Uncle Jeffrey molested me as a child." I force the declaration past the lump in my throat. "I have to know if it's true."

She stares out at the ocean, her expression disturbingly serene.

I scarcely breathe while I wait for her reply, my chest drawing tighter with each passing second.

"You might want to pretend that we're not even related, but we have a lot in common," she finally says, voice eerily soft and flat.

Dread pools in my belly. "What is that supposed to mean?"

"My father was a complicated man." She takes another sip of wine. "I have a very clear memory from when I was twelve. He took me out to the ranch in Montana, just the two of us. My older sister was so jealous. Daddy always spent time alone with her, but they'd grown apart in that last year or so."

She drinks her Sauvignon blanc and continues to stare out at the horizon. "I was so excited to go on a trip with him. And then I remember..." She pauses, and I'm not sure if she's going to say anything else for several agonizing heartbeats. "My sister was so jealous when I told her what happened."

If my stomach weren't empty, I'd be sick again. My throat burns, but there's nothing in me to purge.

"Jeffrey takes after him." The horror isn't over. "He always had a sick interest in me when we were children. You know he's eight years older than I am, right?" She says it in an offhand tone, as though she's reminding me of a forgotten, distantly related aunt. "He was so cruel when we would play together."

The waves crash, and gulls screech overhead, but the world feels silent in the wake of her horrific revelations—as though an atomic bomb has gone off, and there's nothing left but a toxic wasteland.

"You knew?" I finally ask, my hands shaking as much as my voice. "And you left me alone with him?"

My mother blinks, and she finally turns to look at me. Her usually incisive eyes are dull, her tone still soft and detached, when she says the most disturbing thing I've ever heard in my life.

"I didn't explicitly know it was happening, and I'm sorry that it did. But I can't say that I'm surprised. These things run in the family."

She sips at her beloved wine, almost serene while I'm utterly devastated.

Some part of me recognizes that she's endured more trauma than I ever realized, and she's probably disassociating right now.

But she's my mother. She's supposed to protect me.

She's supposed to love me.

My battered heart takes another beating, and I press a hand to the center of my chest in an attempt to dull the pain.

She doesn't say anything else. No words of comfort. No promise to make her brother suffer for what he did to me.

What he did to both of us.

I get to my feet and walk toward the boardwalk on leaden legs. I feel like I've aged a decade over the last twenty-four hours, and my entire body aches.

Dane.

I need Dane.

He can't fix what happened to me, but as long as I'm in his arms, I'm safe.

65

DANE

I've almost finished packing when Abigail enters our bedroom. Pure panic threatens to rise up and choke off my ability to breathe, but I ruthlessly shove it down.

I'm cold, unfeeling. A monster in human skin.

This is my natural state, the way I'm meant to be.

But nothing feels natural about being coldly calculating with Abigail.

Not anymore.

She notes the large leather duffel bag in my hand, and her brows knit above her red-rimmed eyes. Her cheeks are chalk white, and her sable hair is disheveled, as though she's been running her hands through it repeatedly. The perfect purple curl is broken and snarled. My fingers itch with the desire to smooth it.

I tighten my fist around the strap of the bag.

"Are we going somewhere?" Her melodic voice is heavy with exhaustion, but her eyes are clear and trusting.

"No." The refusal is cold and terse.

She edges back slightly, as though my tone is cutting into her delicate skin.

"Then why are you packing?"

"I'm leaving," I explain, icy and unperturbed. "My lawyer is drawing up the paperwork now. You'll have the house and enough money to live comfortably. The rent for your gallery will be paid."

She looks as though I've punched her in the gut. She hugs her arms around her middle, clutching at the invisible damage I'm inflicting.

I force myself to blink away the anguish that threatens to tighten my stony expression.

For Abigail, I'll curb my most selfish impulses. I covet and crave the feelings she brings out in me, but I can't allow myself to indulge in them any longer.

I can't indulge myself in *her.*

"What are you talking about?" she asks in a horrified whisper.

"I'm divorcing you. The paperwork will be straightforward enough. All you have to do is sign when it arrives, and then a courier will deliver it to me to countersign."

Her eyes shine. "Why are you saying these awful things? Stop it right now, Dane."

I won't stop. I can't.

My gut twists in agony, but I manage to shrug and stride for the bedroom door.

Her dainty hand closes around my forearm, so weak and fragile. But I can't quite manage to wrench my arm free from her grip. Her touch burns me like a brand, but I don't allow so much as a flicker of pain to cross my face.

"Where are you going?" she demands.

"To England. I'm going home."

The word is ashes on my tongue. The manor where I was raised isn't my home. But I'll walk into the cage my parents have built for me. It's my penance, even though no amount of suffering will be enough after my crimes against her.

"What? No!" Her fingernails dig into my arm. "I won't let you go back there. You only just got free of your family. I won't let them hurt you."

I draw on long years of practice to force my lip to curl in a sneer. "As though you could do anything to protect me. You're weak, Abigail. Stop posturing. It's pathetic."

Her soft gasp knifes through my heart.

"You don't mean that," she whispers. "Why are you being like this? Talk to me."

I scoff. "All you ever want to do is talk. I'm sick of hearing your whining. I'm leaving, and there's nothing you can do to stop me."

I wrench my arm free from her grip, and her grasping nails seem to score my flesh to the bone.

"No!" she insists, stumbling after me as I walk out of the bedroom.

I can't turn to look at her. I can't bear to face her, or I'll break. Her tears will shatter me.

I've always vowed to protect her. At first, it was a sadistic game designed to lure her in and gain her trust. But over time, it became my entire reason for being. She is my only reason for existence. My heart beats for her, and I don't know if I'll be capable of breathing once I leave her sweet scent behind.

The prospect of spending the rest of my life without her makes whatever I have of a soul scream in agony.

The pain is far less than I deserve.

"Don't you dare leave me," she seethes, following me down the stairs. "I won't let you do this."

I'm beyond words now. I've said every cruel thing I could muster. She'll have to stew in it. She'll learn to hate me in time.

"You promised!" she shouts raggedly. "You promised yourself to me. You're mine, Dane Graham."

I can't stop my body from reeling like she's landed a physical blow. My sweet Abigail is every bit as fiercely possessive of me as I am of her. She's my perfect match, my everything.

My fingers tremble slightly as I reach for the handle on our front door.

"Look at you," she accuses. "You're shaking. I don't know why you're doing this, but I know you don't want to."

I turn the knob.

"I love you!" She flings it at me like a dagger.

The blade hits its mark deep in my chest, and I can't suppress a pained grunt.

She wedges herself between me and the exit, pressing her back against the door to prevent me from opening it. Her small hand rests directly on my heart, and I can practically feel her looping a cord over it, tethering me to her.

"I can't stay." The admission is gruff.

I'm wavering. I can't waver.

"Step aside." There's no force in the breathless order. "You have to let me leave."

I'm not commanding; I'm begging.

Her other hand comes up to cup my cheek, grounding me to her. "No." Her stunning eyes search mine. "Tell me why you're doing this."

"I'm saving you!" I thunder. "I promised to always protect you. I'm the most dangerous person you've ever met. I'm sadistic and selfish, and I've wronged you in ways you can't even imagine. I've hurt you, Abigail. Just like all the other men who've hurt you. I have to protect you from *me*."

Her petal pink lips part, but she doesn't have an opportunity to speak before I barrel on.

"You said men see you as prey. Well, I'm the worst predator you've ever encountered. Do you know how much pleasure I derived from hunting you? Trapping you? I bound you to me in every way I could, and I never intended to let you go. You were right: you never had a choice."

Her brows draw together in determined slashes. "You're wrong. I chose you. You know how stubborn I am. I could've fought you for the rest of my life, but I married you instead."

"Abigail—"

"No. It's my turn to speak. Do you know what my plan was back in England, when I first woke up in your family home? I was going to prove to you that I didn't love you. I was convinced that you would tire of me if I showed you how much I reviled you.

"But I failed miserably, because even when I was terrified and enraged, I never stopped loving you. I'm not capable of it."

"That's because I warped you," I growl. "You don't love me. You can't. Because you don't know the real me. You've never wanted to truly see me for what I am."

She tips her chin back. "And what is that?"

"Your worst nightmare. All the terrible things other men have done to you when they've violated you is nothing compared to how I've treated you. I wanted you, so I took you. Like you're a toy I could play with."

"Stop it," she seethes. "You're trying to be cruel and push me away again. I won't allow you to do that. I know you care for me. Possibly more deeply than you understand. I'm not a fool. I know you're obsessed with me, and our connection is twisted. That doesn't make it any less real. It doesn't change how I feel about you."

"I'm your stalker!" I lash out in a final, desperate attempt to force her to see reason. "I'm the masked man who attacked you in your own home and violated you in the worst way. We've never talked about what happened that day when you discovered the truth of what I am. I was violent with you. I choked you out and restrained you so that you couldn't run away from me. I drugged you and held you captive."

She flinches, and her eyes tighten with an echo of horror at the memory.

"And even as I broke you piece by piece, I claimed to be your protector. I deluded us both. I won't cause you another ounce of pain. The only way I can guarantee that is to extricate myself from your life. You'll be better off without me. You'll be free."

Her delicate jaw firms. "You have freed me. Before you came into my life, I hated myself. I was disgusted by my dark urges. After what happened with Tom, I was in survival mode, just making it through every day through sheer force of will. But that was all a cheery, pretty lie." Her voice becomes more ragged. "I was alone. I've been alone all my life. Now I have you. We belong to each other. We're supposed to be together.

"You say you can't live without me. I refuse to live without you. If you go to England, I'll follow. I'll move into that awful manor, and we will suffer through every day of it together. There's nothing you can do to stop me."

My voice drops to a more dangerous register. "Can't I?"

She shakes her head in staunch refusal. "No, you can't. You can manhandle me. You can tie me up if you want to. But you won't. Not if I don't consent. I hold all the power here, Dane."

"You can't forgive what I've done to you," I insist, even though my chest tightens with longing.

"You don't get to tell me what to do. I'm your queen, aren't I? I demand that you stay. You will accept my forgiveness. You're the one who doesn't have a choice. Because I'm not letting you go."

My knees fold, and I'm kneeling before her. I grasp her hands in mine and press reverent kisses to her knuckles, paying fealty to my queen. My goddess.

"We're equals, even if I do hold all the power," she insists, grabbing my shoulders in an effort to pull me to my feet.

"No, we're not," I declare. "You are so much more than I will ever be. I will spend the rest of my life striving to be worthy of you. I'll prove it to you every day. I..."

My heart swells to the point of pain, and strange words I can't quite formulate tease at the tip of my tongue.

I swallow down the bizarre urge.

I can't say them, because I won't lie to my wife.

I'll never be fully capable of that feeling, no matter how deep and depraved my obsession is.

She grabs the handle on the duffel bag that I dropped.

"Come on," she urges, tugging at my hand. "We're putting your things back where they belong."

I take the bag from her. My queen won't strain herself to carry out a menial task ever again. That's my job.

I lace our fingers together. My hand is a careful cage around hers, but she has my heart on a chain. With one delicate tug, I'll follow wherever she leads.

66

DANE

"I'd still prefer it if you would let me kill your uncle," I say darkly. "Are you sure I can't change your mind? He more than deserves it."

If I had my way, I'd take the bastard apart piece by piece.

She gives my hand a gentle squeeze and presses herself closer to my side. We're sitting on the couch in our living room, waiting.

"You need to keep those thoughts to yourself," she says firmly. "The officer will be here soon to take my statement, and I can't have you talking about murder in front of the police."

I grind my teeth. "You don't have to tell them anything. I can handle this."

She places her hand on my tense jaw. "We talked about this last night," she reminds me. "*I'm* going to handle it. I'm taking my power back. You have to respect that, Dane."

I turn my head so I can kiss her palm. "I do respect you. You're so much stronger than I am, little dove."

I crave to surrender to my most primal, vicious impulses, but my stubborn wife is determined to take her uncle down on her own. All she will allow me to do is sit by her side in solidarity.

The inaction sets me on edge, and I resist the urge to flex my fingers with unspent aggression.

It's a miracle that she's allowing me to sit by her at all. After the cruel things I said to her yesterday, she has every right to punish me, even if I was trying to protect her.

But my sweet, gentle Abigail has practically been wrapped around me for nearly twenty-four hours, as though she can't bear to put an inch of distance between us.

If she wants to cling to me, I'll gladly oblige her. I'll never reject her touch again.

The doorbell rings, and she draws in a shuddering breath. Then she squares her shoulders and stands to answer the door.

I accompany her, my hand glued to hers.

A police officer stands at the threshold, her bearing bold and official. Her rich umber skin is slightly creased with years of experience, and her stance conveys confidence and authority. Her brown eyes flick from Abigail to me.

I carefully summon up my genial mask, fixing my features in a polite but concerned expression.

The officer seems to buy it, and her attention returns to Abigail. "I'm Officer Johnson. You're Abigail Graham?"

She nods. "Yes, I'm the one who called to make a report. Please, come in."

I note that her partner has remained in the car that's parked at the curb—a man. Given the nature of Abigail's report, I'm grateful for the officer's tact. A strange man's presence might make this too difficult for her.

Officer Johnson follows us into the living room, and Abigail motions for her to sit in the armchair across from the couch.

"Can I get you anything to drink?" she asks, a gracious hostess. "We have tea or lemonade."

The officer shakes her head and pulls out a notepad. "No, thank you. Please, take a seat."

Abigail and I sit down on the couch, her hand still firmly in mine. I brush my thumb over her palm in a silent promise of support, and her stiff posture relaxes slightly.

"You want to make a report about your uncle, Jeffrey Zillman," the officer begins, making a quick note. "Is that correct?"

"Yes," Abigail confirms.

"Do you think there are any children at immediate risk of harm?"

Abigail falters. "I...I'm not sure. There are other children who live on the same property; there are houses for the groundskeepers and their families."

Officer Johnson makes another note. "Where is the property you're referring to?"

Abigail swallows hard, as though bracing herself to talk about the nightmarish place where she was raised.

"Elysium. It's a plantation about an hour's drive from here."

"So, it's within the state of South Carolina?"

"Yes. I think there are about half a dozen families living there. It's isolated and completely closed to the public." Her cheeks have gone pale. "I'm not sure how many children might be at risk."

The officer makes another note. "There's no statute of limitations for child sexual abuse in South Carolina, so if you're able to provide enough evidence yourself, we'll have cause to investigate. We can obtain a warrant and search the property. If we're able to press charges, you'll be included. Are you prepared for that?"

"I am," my brave wife replies staunchly. "I'll do everything in my power to get my uncle locked away."

The officer fixes her with a level stare, but her voice is gentle. "The process will be very difficult for you. If this goes to trial, you'll have to give evidence in court. Your credibility will be questioned. The evidence has to support your story, or he won't be convicted. Even then, there's a chance of a not-guilty verdict. You can always take civil action, but you need to prepare yourself for the potential outcomes."

Abigail's palm begins to sweat, but I keep my careful hold on her.

I'm barely maintaining my human mask. The prospect of Abigail going through all that pain just for her uncle to walk free is enough to make me see red. That motherfucker is going to pay for what he did to her.

I'll make sure of it if the law fails her.

"I'm doing this," Abigail asserts, delicate chin tipped back in the imperious posture that I admire so much. "I won't let my uncle hurt anyone else."

Officer Johnson nods. "To get a warrant to search his property, I'll need details from you. When did the abuse take place?"

Abigail's mouth opens, then closes. Her fingers have gone cold, and I rub them to imbue her with my warmth.

"I'm not sure," she admits. "I don't have clear memories."

"Tell me what you can. Why did you call to make a statement? Why now?"

"I forgot until a few days ago," Abigail admits, cheeks coloring with something like shame.

The red flush sets my teeth on edge. She has nothing to be ashamed of.

"There was an altercation with her family two days ago." This is her story to tell, but I'll back her up. "Her uncle touched her, and she had a flashback. She's been having nightmares about him."

The officer's brows knit. "Nightmares. So, these are just dreams?"

"No," I growl. "Listen to my wife. She's telling the truth."

"I'm not calling her integrity into question," the woman replies, placating. "But I need details: specific incidents and the dates when they occurred."

"My mother confirmed it," Abigail says, voice thin.

She's forcing herself to continue, but I know her well enough to recognize the fear that darkens her eyes. She's scared that the investigation will come to nothing, and she won't be able to save the other children. She won't get justice for herself.

"Mama said she knows my uncle is a sexual predator. She said he abused her too."

Another note scribbled down. "And your mother is willing to give a statement? That would strengthen our request for a warrant."

Abigail's shoulders dip. "No, she won't do that. But it's true, I swear."

Officer Johnson blows out a short sigh, and her lips twist with regret as she puts her notepad away. "I'm sorry, but that's not enough evidence to move forward with an investigation. You can try civil action."

"Sit down," I snap when she shifts her weight to get to her feet. "My wife isn't finished. She will have justice."

The officer focuses on Abigail, whose features are drawn with devastation.

"I'm sorry, Mrs. Graham, but there's nothing more I can do. If you remember anything more clearly, please contact me."

"You must care about protecting the children who live on that property," Abigail says, desperation roughening her tone. "You have to help me."

"It's not about whether or not I care. This is about the law, and my realistic assessment is that this will go nowhere if you try to press charges." Her voice deepens with compassion, but her firm countenance doesn't waver. "You'll put yourself through hell for nothing, and he will win."

Abigail wilts beside me, and I wrap my arm around her shoulders.

"Get out," I bark at the useless officer.

If she doesn't leave right now, I won't be able to restrain my cruelest impulses. The woman has hurt my wife with her callousness, and it's all I can do to remain by her side instead of forcing the officer to give her the justice she deserves.

"I really am sorry," Officer Johnson says.

Then she's gone, and Abigail sags against me. She buries her face in her hands, pressing her palms to her eyes as though forcibly containing her tears.

"It's all right." I soothe her. "You can cry."

"I'm sick of crying." Her hands drop away, and her eyes shine with a vicious light, not tears. "I won't let him get away with this."

I won't suggest my murderous plans again. Yet.

"I'll call a lawyer today," I promise. "We can start putting a civil case together."

"But that won't send him to jail." She shakes her head. "It's not good enough. They might seal the record. There could be a gag order. And you heard Officer Johnson. I don't have enough concrete evidence to move forward."

I rub her back. "We're not giving up."

Her eyes flash. "Take out your phone. I need you to record something for me."

"What are you planning?" Whatever it is, she has my complete support.

My phone is already in my hand, and she's retrieved her own phone from her pocket.

"I'm going to call my mother."

Her eyes glow with a fierce light, like a vengeful goddess seeking retribution.

"I've never told you this, but my ancestor was Andrew Zillman. My mother and her siblings are his last living descendants. Well, other than me, but I'm not part of that family anymore. I want nothing to do with them after today."

I search my mind. The name is vaguely familiar. "Zillman?"

Her nostrils flare with righteous anger. "Yes, one of the infamous American robber barons. My mother always prefers to call him a *captain of industry*. But he built his fortune on other's misery, and he left a rotten legacy behind."

She waves a hand, directing us back to the present. "The family name is recognizable. There will be a certain level of local interest in a scandal, at the very least."

"So, you intend to cause one?"

She gives me a savage nod. "I'm going to record my mother's confession, and then I'll leak it to the press. They will be ruined. Uncle Jeffrey will face intense public scrutiny for the rest of his life. He won't dare harm another child."

It's similar to how I threatened my parents with ruin, but Abigail's family doesn't deserve the option of a reprieve. There will be no posturing about going to the press. She will destroy them without warning.

I press a kiss to her forehead. "My clever, ruthless queen."

She looks deep into my soul and says, "I love you. Thank you for letting me handle this my way."

I tuck a stray lock of hair behind her ear. "You're handling it far better than I would have. If I had my way, he would've died too quickly. You're ensuring a lifetime of pain. It's still less than he deserves, but he will suffer."

She nods. "I'll need you to record the entire call, but we'll cut out anything that suggests that my mom was also abused. It's not right for me to tell what happened to her, but I can take control of my own story."

"Whatever you need," I reassure her.

She finds her mother's contact details and connects the call.

"Abby." The greeting is frosty. "What do you want now?"

"I want you to tell me the same thing you told me on the beach yesterday. I want confirmation of how you failed to protect your own daughter from a sexual predator."

As she exacts her vengeance, my muscles flex with the need to throttle someone. My own mother is a piece of work, but even she hasn't done something so heinous.

"You're being dramatic," her mom replies tersely. "You're an adult now, Abby. Grow up."

"I wasn't an adult when you left me alone with Uncle Jeffrey," she seethes. "You knew he was capable of molesting me, and you let him babysit me anyway. You knew that he had a history of abusing children."

Her voice hitches on the last. I can't even imagine the pain of her mother's betrayal.

The woman is a monster.

"You revealed a pattern of generational abuse," Abigail continues, jaw flexing with barely restrained rage. "You told me *these things run in the family.*"

My stomach turns at the horrific words. It's unfathomable that a mother could say such a thing to her daughter.

"Yes, they do," her mom shoots back. "What did you expect me to do about it? I can't control Jeffrey. What he did to you isn't my fault."

"It was your job to protect me!" Abigail accuses. "But you were too wrapped up in yourself to care that your daughter was being abused."

"I can't believe you would say such things to me. You will speak to me with respect. I am your mother." She says it like an edict, a threat. As though the fact that she gave birth gives her the right to treat Abigail in whatever cruel way she chooses.

"Like it or not, we're family, Abby. Blood is everything."

Abigail swells with fury. "All my life, you've said that. It might as well be the family motto. You all say it, just to keep each other close enough to inflict pain where it hurts most—over and over again. It's a nest of vipers, and I got out of it."

"You're being a nasty little bitch. How dare—"

My hand shoots out, and I end the call.

Abigail blinks and looks up at me in surprise.

My hands shake slightly when I cup her cheeks. "I couldn't listen to that for one more second," I rumble. "Back in England, I made a promise not to kill any of your family members. If I'm going to keep that promise, I can't hear another narcissistic word from your mother."

She places her hands over mine, urging me to hold her. "I got what I needed. Thank you for hanging up on her. I didn't need to hear any more either."

She presses a sweet kiss to my taut lips, and slowly, I soften at her tender treatment.

When I first met Abigail, I thought she was soft. Weak. Easy prey.

I've never been more wrong about anything in my entire life.

67

ABIGAIL

My teeth worry at my lower lip. "Do you think this was a mistake? Should I have waited for everything to settle down a bit before opening?"

Dane steps in front of me, his bulky body blocking the anxiety-inducing view of the small crowd outside. Through the glass frontage of my gallery, I can see at least three dozen people gathered on the sidewalk.

Two long fingers curl beneath my chin, lifting my gaze to his. "The caterers are almost finished setting up," he informs me calmly. "But I can send them away if you want me to. I can go out there and tell people that the event is postponed. Whatever you need from me, say the word."

I search his deep green eyes for signs of worry, but I'm the only one feeling anxious.

"What if they're all here because of the article?" I ask, strained. "I want tonight to be about my art, not about my trauma."

I'd anticipated some local interest in my story when I

leaked the recording of my mother's confession to a journalist, but for the last two days, I've been dodging calls from national news networks requesting interviews. My mother's shocking callousness coupled with my uncle's heinous abuse seems to have hit a nerve with people online, and the original article is going viral. Add in the rotten entitlement and privilege of a dying American dynasty, and the scandal is attracting more attention than I was prepared to deal with.

"The why doesn't matter," Dane insists. "Maybe they're curious because of the article, but they will see your brilliance, and your art will become the focal point. And if anyone wants to ask you an inappropriate question, I'll be right by your side all night to make sure they don't dare."

I swallow hard. "I don't want the success of my gallery opening to be because of *him*."

Dane's eyes flash. "Your success belongs to *you*, Abigail, not your uncle. Those people are here because of your bravery."

I take a deep breath, finding calm in his staunch support. Then I nod. "I can do this. But I have one thing I need to do before we unlock the door."

I take his hand in mine and lead him toward the center of the gallery, where I have a large painting covered with a cloth.

He cocks his head at me. "Don't you want to wait to unveil this one? You can build some anticipation for the end of the night."

"No. This one is for you."

I tug the cloth free, revealing the scene I captured for him. For us.

Lighting forks over white capped waves, and the horizon darkens in blue gradients to a rich navy shade at the horizon. Red rose petals float in the foreground, whipped up by the incoming tempest. The hint of a gossamer veil flits at the right edge of the canvas, and the elegant curve of a violin peeks above the frame at the bottom left corner.

His jaw goes slack for a long moment, then tightens with unmistakable hunger. His fingers clamp around mine, dragging me closer to his side. He's staring at my art as though it's the most fascinating thing he's ever seen, and I drink in the perfection of his covetous stare.

"It's not for sale," I tell him. "But I wanted to show everyone how much I love you."

My love for him is fiercely beautiful, as powerful and awe-inspiring as the storm. Maybe a little terrifying in its intensity. Definitely dangerous.

But Dane will always shield me from harm. The only danger he poses is to anyone who might try to separate us.

I'll do anything to keep and defend him, too, even if I'm not as strong as he is physically.

My love for him has made me a little more vicious, but I'm becoming more comfortable with my newfound ferocity. I'm powerful in my own right. I don't have to wear false smiles or bend over backward to please others.

My happiness is genuine, even if that means it's a little sharper than the fake cheer I used to present to the rest of the world.

Dane finally tears his gaze from the painting so that his eyes meet mine. His handsome features split in a wild, silly grin, and he brushes his thumb over my unicorn badge in an offhand display of affection.

He's helped me find my strength, but I've softened something in him.

Well, only for me. I don't think my fierce, psychopathic husband will ever be soft for anyone else.

The knowledge only makes me that much more enamored with him.

"We should probably let everyone in," I breathe, even though all I want is to linger in this moment with him.

He drops a quick kiss on my lips. "We'll celebrate your success properly later."

It's a dark, sensual promise, and my pulse quickens.

"Don't do that to me right now!" I protest with a giggle. "I don't want to be a flustered mess when I'm greeting people."

His grin sharpens, unrepentant. "I like when you're flustered for me. But I'll make you a mess when we're alone at home."

"Dane!" I scold, but I loop my arm through his.

He escorts me through the gallery, toward the glass door and the waiting crowd.

He just chuckles, a slightly cruel promise.

I hold my head high, and his low laugh morphs into a satisfied hum. "There's my queen," he praises. "I'm so proud of you."

I flush with pleasure, but before I can reply, he unlocks the door.

The next hour flies by in a haze of compliments and champagne toasts. The entire night seems surreal: a dream I never dared to indulge before meeting Dane.

A few people mention the article, but they keep it to brief, respectful comments of solidarity and support. Dane's warning glower ensures that no one discusses my trauma in detail.

A commotion at the door pierces my happy bubble. I recognize my mother's haughty voice, slurring slightly from indulging in too much wine.

"You can't stop me from seeing Abby," she insists. "I am her mother."

She says it like that gives her the authority to do anything she wants to me, as though she holds power over me by some sort of divine right.

"I'll handle this," Dane promises, voice dropping to that flat, cold register that makes my spine tingle in primal warning.

I push past him. "No. I will."

As I near the door, I note that one of the catering staff is blocking my mother's entrance. He's considerably bulkier than the other servers, and I realize that Dane probably hired him as discreet security. The man is acting as a bouncer, physically preventing my mom from stepping into the gallery.

"What are you doing here, Mama?" I ask, my own voice cold and carefully controlled.

Her cheeks are red, and I'm not sure if she's flushed from alcohol or rage. Probably both.

"You won't answer my calls," she seethes. "How else am I supposed to talk to my daughter?"

"I haven't answered because I blocked your number," I reply coolly. "I don't want any further contact from you."

"You little bitch!" she seethes, going almost purple. Her ice blue eyes flash in her fury-darkened face, even though her features are eerily frozen. "How dare you speak to me that way? We're family."

"Not anymore." I straighten my shoulders. "We are related by blood, and I can't change that. But you are not my family. You gave up that right when you failed me as a mother."

"You have ruined us!" she shrieks. "You ruined the family name."

My fists furl at my sides. "*The family name.* That's all

you've ever cared about. But I didn't ruin anything. Uncle Jeffrey did that. You did that when you didn't protect me from him."

"You betrayed your blood," she thunders. "Blood is everything."

I narrow my eyes at her. "That's bullshit, and I'm not buying into it anymore. I've chosen my family, and you are not part of it."

Her eyes blaze as they fix on Dane, who stands behind me. He's allowing me to deal with this confrontation while still supporting me with his menacing presence.

"You've done this." She hurls the accusation at him. "You turned my daughter against me."

"You alienated me all on your own," I say coldly. "I cut you off two years before Dane came into my life, remember? You might've pretended that we weren't estranged for the sake of appearances, but I chose to live without your toxicity. I chose to be completely alone rather than suffering through a relationship with you."

I lace my fingers through Dane's. I'm not alone anymore. And I never will be again.

"You're making a scene," I inform my mother. She's been too incensed and inebriated to notice that several phones are pointed in her direction, recording her narcissistic outburst.

Her gaze darts around the room, noting dozens of eyes fixed squarely on her with clear disapproval.

Her shoulders dip, and her eyes shine.

For a moment, my heart gives a painful beat, and some of my righteous rage ebbs.

Despite everything she's done to me, she was a victim too. That doesn't change the fact that she failed me in the worst way. It doesn't change the lifetime of abuse.

But I have to acknowledge that her cruelty and narcissism comes from a place of pain.

"You should go now, Mama," I say, tone gentler.

"Go where?" she asks raggedly. "No one will take my calls. I've lost all my friends. I have no one left. They've turned their backs on me, Abby. You're my daughter, my flesh and blood. You can't abandon me too."

"I'm sorry for what you've been through," I say truthfully. "But I can't have you in my life. I choose me. You have properties all over the country. You can leave South Carolina and start fresh somewhere else."

"This is my home!" she almost wails. "I can't leave Elysium."

"That's your choice," I reply evenly. "What you do now is not my responsibility."

"Leave," Dane commands. "This conversation is over. Never contact my wife again."

Mama casts a panicked gaze around the room, as though searching for an ally.

No one steps forward to defend her.

Her reputation is in tatters, and she will not find welcome in Charleston society ever again. Especially not after this public outburst.

I search my heart and find that I don't feel a shred of vindictive pleasure at her utter devastation. All I feel for her is compassion and more than a little pity.

Dane's arm loops around my waist, and I lean into him as my mother turns and flees.

I'm with my family now, and the woman disappearing into the humid night will never bother me again.

68

ABIGAIL

I unlock the door to enter my gallery, already missing Dane. He left to run an errand only half an hour ago, but I feel his absence like a missing limb.

My addiction to my husband is definitely unhealthy, so I'm resolved to manage my Sunday on my own.

The catering crew did a good job cleaning up the gallery after the grand opening last night, but I still want to check the space for myself. I could wait until Monday, but I'm excited to spend more time building my new business. I sold eighteen paintings after my confrontation with my mother. I have some bookkeeping and delivery logistics to manage before I can devote a day to my art again.

I smile to myself. It's a wonderful problem to have.

I can still hardly believe that people want to buy my art. I'll gladly deal with paperwork as a result.

I step into my office at the back of the gallery, but I don't quite manage to turn on the light. Rough hands grab me from behind, one clamping over my mouth to smother my shocked cry. Something sharp pierces my neck, and the horribly familiar sensation of soporific drugs oozing into my system makes panic spike through my heart.

"We need to talk, little Abby."

Uncle Jeffrey's low growl follows me down into darkness.

THE DARKNESS PERSISTS when I open my eyes. I blink hard, struggling to process the fact that I'm conscious. I lift my hand in front of my face, but all I see is inky blackness.

Then the dank smell registers, stirring a scent memory.

I'm nine years old again, and I'm trapped. My older cousins' laughter echoes through my ears. I stretch out my arms, and my fingers connect with the cold, thick metal door.

"No!" I moan, shoving against it. The lock on the outside rattles, and the door doesn't budge.

My cousins shoved me in here and secured the aged lock. They told me that ghosts of Yankee soldiers haunt these cells beneath Elysium. An icy finger trails down my spine, one of those ghosts brushing against me. Their malevolent aura surrounds me, and my chest tightens to choke off my scream of abject terror.

I scramble wildly in the confined space, my nails breaking against rough bricks that surround me on three sides, squeezing me into a tiny box. There's not enough oxygen in here. I can't breathe.

My fists slam into the door, and a metallic boom resounds through my haunted cell.

"Let me out!" My voice is high and thin. "Let me out!"

The grate on the door screeches as it slides open, and a small square of yellow light sears my eyes.

"You're not getting out of there until you see sense."

Uncle Jeffrey's voice. Not my cousins.

My mind reels, and I struggle to ground myself in the present. I'm not that frightened child anymore.

But I'm as helplessly trapped as she was when they locked me in here and left me to scream in the dark for hours.

"What do you think you're doing?" I manage to wheeze. "You can't keep me in here."

All I can see of my uncle is a pair of icy blue eyes and the tops of his rage-flushed cheekbones.

"Oh yes, I can. You're going to stay in there and think about what you've done to this family."

I shake my head to clear away the ghostly hands that clutch at my face, trying to draw me back into darkness and mind-numbing panic.

"I haven't done anything wrong," I hiss. "If you're facing the consequences of your sick actions, that's on you."

His eyes flash. "You're going to recant the vile story you told that reporter," he insists. "Then I'll consider letting you out of there when you learn to be better behaved."

My fists slam into the door in a pulse of pure rage, and he reels back a step.

"Did Mama put you up to this?" I demand. "Let me out, or you will all regret it."

"Your mama and daddy left this morning for the ranch in Montana. They're not coming back unless you sort out the mess you made. I'm going to make sure you fall in line."

I bare my teeth at him in primal defiance. "You will never touch me again. I'll kill you before I let you hurt me."

He scoffs. "I'm not going to lay a hand on you. I never hurt you, Abby."

My fists boom against the door, and I launch myself at him as though I can tear him apart.

"You violated me!" I shriek. "I was a child. Your own niece. You're a sick piece of shit, Uncle Jeffrey, and now everyone knows it. You will never harm another child. I won't let you."

"Damn you!" he thunders. "You're trying to ruin me, but I will not permit it. You'll take back what you said."

"Never," I seethe. "You should be the one rotting in a cell. If I ever manage to get the evidence I need to put you away for the rest of your life, I will. If you think you're suffering now, just wait until I make you pay for kidnapping me and locking me up in here."

"You'll sit in the dark and think about what you've done," he says with twisted, paternal disapproval. "I'll come back when you're more agreeable."

The grate slams closed, cutting off my only source of light. Darkness presses in on me with crushing weight.

I scream out my rage and terror, punching the door again and again.

But all I manage is to split my knuckles against the unyielding metal. The stinging pain doesn't stop me. I'm reduced to my most feral self, ruled by survival instincts. I can't stop fighting. I can't stop trying to escape.

The icy fingers of my ghostly cellmate clutch at my hair, scoring frigid lines down the back of my neck. I shudder and scream as I throw all of my weight against the door to no avail.

"Abigail!" Dane's voice is muffled by the heavy door, but I instantly recognize my dark god.

"I'm in here!"

He came for me.

I'm grateful for the fact that we agreed to track each

other's locations. No one will ever be able to take me from him.

"I found a key," he calls back. "I'm getting you out."

The aged key scrapes in the lock, and then fresh oxygen floods the cell along with blessed light. I throw myself into Dane's waiting arms. He wraps me up in a fierce embrace, cradling the back of my head to press my face close to his chest. He's breathing hard, as though he ran all the way from Charleston to get to me.

"I've got you," he promises. "You're okay. You're safe."

"I want to leave," I say in a rush, grabbing his hand so that I can drag him toward the exit. "I can't stand to be in this house for another minute."

He doesn't budge. All of his powerful muscles practically vibrate with some unseen strain.

"Who put you in there?" he growls.

"Uncle Jeffrey. He wanted to convince me to tell the press that I made everything up."

"Did he touch you?" The question is barely intelligible.

"No. He just tried to scare me." I can't suppress a shudder. "He knows I don't like it down here."

It's a massive understatement, but I don't want to waste time going over that particular trauma inflicted by my sadistic older cousins. I just want to go home with Dane.

"Where is he now?"

"I don't know, and I don't care." I tug on Dane's hand. "Please. I need to leave."

I want to crawl out of my own skin. Every passing second in this nightmarish house makes me itch, as though the toxicity of my past is a palpable irritant on my flesh.

"All right, little dove," he says, voice smoothing to the gentler cadence that soothes me. "We're going home."

He finally allows me to lead him out of the awful basement. "This way."

We climb the brick stairs, the dank scent clearing from my senses as the air becomes fresher above ground.

Fear clings to my psyche, and my footsteps are quick as I rush into the armory. Antique weapons from every era over the last several centuries line the wood paneled walls, and a pool table dominates the center of the room. An illuminated stocked whiskey cabinet is to the right of the massive fireplace, and the cigar humidor on the other side of the mantle is open.

I register that Uncle Jeffrey must be close in the moment that I hear the sickening *crack*.

Dane jerks at my side, then drops. A green pool ball rolls away from his still form, a smear of crimson marking the white band around its middle. Blood begins to spread out on the cream rug beneath my husband's head.

I cry out his name and drop to my knees, but before I can reach for him, cruel hands grab me from behind.

"I'm putting you back where you belong," Uncle Jeffrey snarls, dragging me away from Dane.

He isn't moving.

My wail fills the armory, and I thrash in my uncle's restraining hold.

"Calm down," he admonishes. "I'll make sure he lives if you just do as I say."

We're almost at the stairs. He's going to throw me back into that cell. Horror churns in my gut, but I force myself to stop fighting. Dane needs help. My uncle could do anything to him while he's unconscious. There's nothing to stop him from killing my husband.

Nothing except me.

"I'll cooperate," I say desperately. "I'll do whatever you want."

The darkened stairwell yawns before me, and a furious roar echoes off the brick passageway.

My uncle's hands are ripped from my arms, and I whirl to find Dane grappling with the older man. He's bigger than my uncle and so much stronger, but the right side of his face is covered in blood, and his green eyes are slightly out of focus.

Uncle Jeffrey throws his full weight against my husband, tackling him to the floor. His fist slams into Dane's jaw.

Dane goes still again, and Uncle Jeffrey shoves to his feet. For a moment, I think he's going to come after me again, but he lunges toward the fireplace, reaching for one of the swords that serves as perverse decoration above the mantle.

I don't pause to think. I grab an antique, Civil War era rifle from the wall. It will never fire a shot again, but the bayonet is still sharp.

My defiant scream is a battle cry, and I lunge at the man who has caused me so much misery. He whirls to face me, pale blue eyes wide with shock. The sword is in his upraised hand, but I'm faster.

The bayonet slams into his stomach, shredding flesh and vital organs. He roars in agony and tries to stumble away from my attack.

But he's still holding the sword. He's still a threat to Dane.

I yank the blade free and jab again, plunging it straight into my uncle's chest. He falls to his knees, jaw slack as he stares up at me.

My lips peel back from my teeth in a vicious snarl. "You will not hurt my husband. You won't hurt anyone ever again."

I twist the rifle, and the blade shreds his black heart.

His body goes rigid for a moment, and then he slumps

over the rifle. My fingers are locked around the weapon, and I'm dragged down to my knees from his dead weight on the bayonet.

"You can let go now, Abigail."

Dane's steady, elegant fingers tug at mine, urging me to release the rifle.

I instantly drop it and wrap my arms around him with a sharp cry of relief.

He shushes me gently. "You're all right. He's not a threat anymore."

I pull back so that I can cup his cheeks in both hands. His blood wets my palm. It flows from a gash at his brow in a sluggish stream.

"You're hurt!" I exclaim. "Where's your phone? I'll call an ambulance."

His fingers thread through my hair, grounding me to him. "I'm fine," he promises. "It looks worse than it is. Head wounds bleed a lot."

"But you were unconscious," I protest.

"For a few seconds," he reassures me. "We can't call an ambulance, or the authorities will come to the property. I need to clean up this mess."

My gaze finds my dead uncle. I simply stare at his body for several seconds, and I realize that I don't feel a shred of distress or remorse.

He was going to hurt Dane, and I stopped him.

He hurt me, and I made him pay for it.

No one will ever suffer at his perverted hands ever again.

I turn back to Dane. "What do we do now?"

He traces the shape of my purple curl with reverence. "My brave Abigail," he praises. "I need to get patched up. Then I'll destroy the evidence. You can wait outside in my car. I'll handle this."

I shake my head. "I'm not leaving your side. You're the medical professional, but you're injured. I'll be right here if you need me."

His lips twist in a lopsided smile. "My wife is so fierce. Whatever you say, my queen."

Ten minutes later, Dane's head wound is bandaged, and his face is no longer covered in blood. He made quick work of treating the gash with a first aid kit that we found in the downstairs bathroom. I'm calmer now that his eyes are fully focused, and he's able to walk in a straight line without wavering.

We return to the armory. Uncle Jeffrey looks smaller in death, diminished. The shadowy figure that haunted my nightmares has been vanquished: he's flesh and blood. Fallible.

I've slain my own personal monster.

Dane moves with unhurried steps, his posture relaxed and utterly unbothered by the dead man. He crosses to the humidor and selects a cigar. Then he grabs a bottle of whiskey from the cabinet.

I lift a brow at him. "Are we celebrating?"

"We'll celebrate later," he reassures me. "I'm destroying the evidence."

He drags Uncle Jeffrey's body into one of the green leather armchairs beside the drinks cabinet.

He pours two fingers of whiskey into a crystal glass before tipping it so that the alcohol spills onto my uncle's ruined chest. A discarded newspaper sits on the small table beside the armchair, and Dane sets the empty glass atop it. His fingers loosen around the bottle, and it smashes on the floor.

I jolt slightly at the sound of shattering glass, but I don't say a word of protest. I simply watch while he lights the cigar and places it on the newspaper. The paper curls as it begins to burn. Dane waits for flames to lick the antique wooden table before kicking it over. The spilled whiskey acts as an accelerant, and fire races to the alcohol-soaked cream rug.

"Let's go," he rumbles, picking up the bloody bayonet. "We'll drop this in the river on our way back to Charleston. Where's the fuse box?"

"This way."

His hand wraps around mine, and we both walk out of the armory.

In less than two minutes, we've cut the power and made it out of the house. Dane is leading me toward his waiting car, but I pause and turn.

"Wait," I request.

He seems to know what I need. His arm drapes over my shoulder, holding me close as we watch the orange glow in the armory grow brighter. It takes several, long minutes for the fire to spread across the first floor. With the power off, there will be no alert to the authorities that the place is burning. And the families who lived on the plantation left in disgust when my story went viral.

There's no one around to stop the destruction of the historic mansion where centuries of evil have taken place.

Flames gradually engulf the nightmarish house that I used to call home. The fire is cleansing, searing the toxicity of my past from my soul. I watch it all burn, imprinting the scene on my memory so that I can paint it later as a reminder that I'm free. I survived.

When the house is nothing more than a glowing skeleton of its former self, I finally turn to Dane.

"It's over. I'm ready to go home."

The flames are reflected in my dark god's eyes. Night has fallen, but the raging fire throws his heartbreaking features into fierce relief.

"I love you, Abigail."

My breath catches, and my heart squeezes to the point of pain.

"You don't have to say that," I protest, even as longing tugs at my chest.

His hands frame my face, so that I'm trapped in his reverent hold. "I love you."

"Dane..."

His fiery eyes flash. "I mean it. I've never meant anything more in my life. I didn't think I was capable of feeling this way, but I do love you. I was a coward not to say it before. Maybe it's obsession to the point of madness, but I choose to call this love."

My heart swells, my love every bit as obsessive as his. "If this is madness, then I don't want sanity," I declare in a feverish whisper. "I love you, too, Dane."

He crushes his lips to mine in a hungry, savage kiss, as though he wants to devour my declaration of devotion.

As my painful past burns to ash behind us, I'm swept up in the man who is my future. My family. My everything.

69

DANE

The warm water grows cloudy as I carefully wash the soot from Abigail's hair and face. She does the same for me, her slender fingers gentle on my scalp. My head aches slightly from the blows her uncle managed to inflict, but the pain is nothing when she's blessing me with her tender touch.

We linger in the shower until the water starts to go cold, simply holding one another. The feel of her safely in my arms calms me like nothing else, and panic has ridden me hard for hours.

Earlier this afternoon, I'd checked her location and realized that she was at Elysium. I'd known that she wouldn't go there of her own volition, and every second it'd taken me to get to her had been an agonizing eternity.

Her uncle tried to inflict yet another psychological wound when he locked her in the darkness of that cell. He tried to scare her into cooperating with his demands to retract her statement about his crimes against her.

Now, he's paid the ultimate price.

No one touches my wife.

I turn off the cool water in our shower and wrap her in a fluffy white towel. She leans into me, allowing me to take care of her.

Her trust in me is a miracle, and I'll never take it for granted.

"You were so brave back there," I praise as I run a brush through her damp hair.

She turns to face me, and her glowing eyes illuminate my soul. "I did it for you. He was going to kill you." Before I can reply, she admits more quietly. "And I did it for myself."

I cradle her delicate jaw in my hand. "Never feel guilty for killing that bastard. The world is a safer place without him in it. What you did was justice. He deserved far worse."

She blinks up at me. "I don't feel guilty. I'd do it again if I had to."

"Good," I say with savage approval. I don't want her to lose so much as a moment of sleep over that motherfucker's death.

"All I want is to be with you," she declares. "I want a future with you, just like we promised on our wedding day. Nothing will stop us from having that."

I grin. "I promised you the world, Abigail. You will have everything you desire."

"I desire *you*." Her voice takes on the breathy quality that goes straight to my cock.

I hum in consideration. "I think you deserve more than that. I never did give you a proper honeymoon. How does Whitby sound?"

Her eyes spark with excitement. "Really? I've always wanted to go there."

I chuckle. "I remember your fascination with *Dracula*. I remember everything you tell me."

I'm still greedy to know everything about her. I don't think my maddening craving for this woman will ever abate, and I wouldn't have it any other way.

She leans into me with a happy sigh. "I'd love to go to Whitby, but I know you need to focus on work. And I have my gallery now. We can't just leave Charleston for a honeymoon."

I fix her with a stern stare. "We're leaving tomorrow. Your gallery will wait for a week."

"But Meadows—"

"Will make do without me," I cut her off. "We're partners. He can't tell me what to do, and he can't run that practice without me. I went private so that I have the freedom to set my own schedule. I choose to make time for my wife. No one can tell me *no*."

She giggles. "I can."

"But you won't."

Her chin tips back. "Won't I?"

Fuck, that challenging stance and impertinent tone stir my darkest urges.

But my hand is gentle when I stroke her hair. "Don't goad me, little dove."

"Why not?"

I trace the shape of her pretty pout. "Because you're not ready to face the consequences. You've been through enough."

Those aquamarine eyes flash. "That's not solely your decision to make. When I remembered what Uncle Jeffrey did to me, I felt robbed of all agency. Well, I'm not going to let him take one more thing from me, much less my intimacy with my husband."

I search her expression and find nothing but determination and defiance in every sharp line of her stunning features.

"I don't want to do anything that will hurt you," I confess.

"I like the pain," she reminds me. "And I trust you completely. I want you, Dane. All of you. Even the dark parts. They match my own perfectly."

"Abigail..." Her name is a warning. I'm clinging to my control by my fingernails.

"Dane," she replies evenly. "I want to be with you. I need to feel you inside me."

I bite out a curse, and my control snaps.

I scoop her up in my arms and promise, "I'll be gentle with you."

Her eyes flare. "I don't want gentle. I want *you*. My dark god."

The reverent endearment goes straight to my head, and I capture her lips in a desperate kiss. I set her down on our bed and immediately cover her naked body with my own. I grab her slender wrists and pin them above her head with one hand.

She mewls into my mouth and tugs against the shackle of my firm grip, but I show no mercy. I pinch and tug at her nipples, tormenting them in the way she likes best. She grinds her hips against me, wantonly seeking stimulation against my thigh. I wedge it between her legs, welcoming her to rub against me.

My tongue plunders her hot mouth, savoring every desperate whimper and low, sensual moan. With each cruel pinch on her nipples, her body coils tighter beneath me. She presses her clit against my thigh and cries out.

I don't rebuke her for the orgasm. I love how greedy she is, and seeing her embrace her sexual nature after everything she's been through is the greatest satisfaction I've ever known. This strong, brave woman has chosen to give herself to me. And that makes me the most powerful, luckiest man in the world.

"Please," she pants against my lips. "I need you. Fuck me."

"How can I deny you anything?" I rumble, dropping tender kisses down the column of her throat.

"You can't," she says in a smug, breathy whisper. "You're mine, Dane Graham."

"Oh yes," I agree, lining my hard cock up with her slick opening. She's already wet and more than ready for me. "All yours, little dove."

As I declare her ownership of me, my fingers wrap around her neck, squeezing gently. She sucks in a soft, erotic gasp, and her eyes shine with devotion as she looks up at me.

"I love you." I seal my promise with a harsh thrust, spearing her to the hilt.

My love for her makes my heart ache with a throbbing beat. It's so strong that the vital organ threatens to burst, but I would gladly ruin every part of myself just to be with her.

"I love you," she promises in return.

I increase the pressure on her arteries, restricting her blood flow to grant her the ecstatic high she craves. She begins to soften beneath me, and I claim her pliant body in ruthless, deep strokes. Her legs lock around my hips, her heels digging into my ass to spur me on.

I release her throat, and she flies apart on a blissful scream. Her cunt contracts around my cock, and I surrender to the torrent of my own pleasure. My rough shout fills our bedroom as I pump my cum deep inside her, marking her.

Before I met Abigail, I didn't think I possessed a soul. But now I know that mine belongs to her. It might be black—selfish and more than a little cruel—but it's hers.

And she's offered me all of herself in return.

My miracle. My wife.

My Abigail.

70

ABIGAIL

Two days later

"I can't believe we're in Whitby!" I exclaim, twirling on the spot so that I can take in a full view of my surroundings.

The ruins of the famous abbey on the clifftop are every bit as gothic and atmospheric as I always imagined. It's overcast, but it's not raining. Beneath the gray sky, the grass is such a vibrant green that it's almost otherworldly. There's an eerie quality to the midmorning light that glows through the dense clouds, and I can't wait to try to capture it at my easel.

"Sorry about the weather," Dane apologizes. "It's England."

I stare out at the heavy fog that completely obscures the beach and North Sea, and I let out a happy sigh.

"I don't want to be anywhere else," I declare.

Back in Charleston, Uncle Jeffrey's death is all over the news. There's wild speculation that he either drank himself into a stupor or started the fire on purpose.

No one has suggested murder, so it seems Dane did a thorough job of covering up what I did.

In any case, I'm more than happy to be out of town until it all blows over.

"The weather is perfect," I say. "Everything about this place is perfect."

He shakes his head. "It's...soupy."

"I want to walk in it."

I've never seen such thick fog. It almost looks velvety, and the prospect of feeling it on my skin calls to me like a siren's song.

He gestures out at the beach, incredulous. "In the fog? At least we can see three feet ahead of us up here on the cliff. Don't you want to explore the abbey?"

I grab his hand and lead him toward the steps down into town. "We can come back to the abbey. We're here for the whole week, right?"

His eyes glint with mischievous light. "Oh yes, we have time to come back up here."

"Good," I declare. "Then you can stop questioning me and join me on the foggy beach."

He barks a laugh. "I don't know how you make this dreary place so beautiful."

I beam at him. "That's because it is beautiful." My tone drops to a more serious register, and I squeeze his hand in a pulse of understanding. "I know you spent time here when you were growing up. I understand if you don't have the best memories of this place. Thank you for coming here with me."

He lifts my hand and brushes a kiss over my knuckles.

"I'm making new memories with you. The past has no power over me anymore." He shakes his head ruefully. "Although, I can't say I enjoy the weather."

I continue our progress toward the beach, steadfast in my goal. "We'll see how you feel when we get onto the beach. If you hate it, we can walk back into town and get fish and chips."

He doesn't protest again; he seems content to follow me anywhere.

The thought elicits a warm glow at the center of my chest, and I flush despite the slight chill in the air.

We make our way through town and then descend a steep hill. As we near the beach, we walk into the fog. It starts to lap at our ankles, then reaches our torsos, before it closes over our heads. We're engulfed in a pale gray cloud, and the rest of the world disappears. There's only Dane and me and the damp sand beneath our feet. Even the gentle waves sound muffled, but we make our way toward the surf.

In the distance, a dog barks, and a child laughs. But they're so far removed from us that we might as well be on our own planet.

I kick off my shoes, and my toes sink into cool sand. The salt water is icy when it rushes over my bare feet, and I laugh in shocked delight.

"Abigail," Dane admonishes. "It's too cold."

I shake my head and dance out of his reach, wading in to my calves.

"I have to touch the sea," I insist. "I'm making a memory of this moment."

His expression darkens to something forbidding. "Not without me."

He kicks off his shoes and strides into the cold surf with

grim determination. I giggle when he grabs me in a fierce embrace, pulling me in for an almost punishing kiss.

"You're *mine*," he growls. "Every moment of every day for the rest of your life."

I trace the harsh slash of his lips and tease. "Such romantic threats."

I love his possessiveness. Mine is every bit as intense.

I killed for my husband, and I'd do it again a thousand times over. Anything to keep and protect him.

I thread my fingers through his midnight hair and pull him in for a soul-searing kiss, imprinting my claim on his mouth.

Dane is all mine. Always.

71

ABIGAIL

A gloved hand clamps over my mouth, and I snap awake as pure terror spikes through me.

"Don't scream, or I'll have to gag that pretty mouth of yours."

The worst of my fear abates when I register Dane's rumbling voice, but the aftershocks of my initial burst of terror crackle through me. Adrenaline floods my system, making my fingers and toes tingle with the primal imperative to escape.

I thrash, but rope tightens around my wrists and ankles. The bindings were loose enough not to wake me, but now that I'm struggling, the rough fibers abrade my delicate skin.

I scream into his hand, and his low hum of cold consideration rolls over my sensitized flesh.

"I warned you not to scream. You chose this," he informs me just before his fingers dig into my jaw.

I cry out at the flare of pain, and my lips part. The shocked sound is immediately muffled when he shoves something into my mouth. I recognize the lacy texture on my tongue: my panties.

I shake my head, trying to force them out of my mouth.

But he's prepared. A length of black cloth draws tight between my teeth, forcing the underwear deeper into my mouth. He secures the perverted gag with a firm knot at the back of my head.

My growled curse is garbled, and he simply laughs at my predicament.

More rope loops through the cuff around my wrists, securing them to the bindings around my ankles so that I'm forced to bend at the waist. Even if I could get to my feet, it would be impossible to run away.

That doesn't stop me from trying to fight.

I ball my hands into fists and swing wildly, throwing my entire body into the attack.

He reels back, easily evading my clumsy attempt to resist him.

He clicks his tongue in reprimand, and that's the last thing I hear before a thick black cloth hood drops over my head. His strong arms close around me, cradling my bound body to his chest. I twist and writhe, but he holds me firmly.

Several racing heartbeats later, he places me down on my side on padded leather.

The back seat of a car?

My fingers grope at my surroundings, and I feel the familiar shape of a buckle.

Yes, I'm in a car. I barely hear the engine rev through the thick hood, and then we're moving. I'm completely disoriented, and despite the fact that I know I'm completely safe with Dane, fear sparkles through me.

I allow myself to sink into it, loving our dark game.

I'm not sure how long we drive before the car comes to a stop. My heart hammers against the inside of my ribcage, and my fingers shake with the force of my unspent adrenaline. My clit pulses in time with my racing heartbeat, and my nipples are tease against my pink silk nightgown.

His hands are on me again. There's tension on the ropes, then a sudden release of pressure. He's severed the one that connects my hands to my feet. Then the binding around my ankles falls away. I'm free, other than my tied wrists.

He helps me out of the car, and I feel cool, damp grass beneath my bare feet.

He must think that my bound wrists and the hood will keep me subdued while he leads me wherever he wants me to go, but he's mistaken.

I extend my elbow and throw my body in the direction of his torso, driving it deep into his stomach. He releases a low grunt, and his hands fall away.

I reach up and tear the hood from my head as I lurch in the opposite direction. It takes a moment for the night to coalesce around me, but I don't stop running in the time it takes my vision to focus.

I'm several paces away from him when he growls my name.

Giddy fear thrills down my spine, and my maddened laugh is muffled by the gag. My hands are still tied in front of me, so I can't waste time fumbling at the knot behind my head. Instead, I devote my full focus to putting as much distance between me and my assailant as possible.

My feet pound the soft earth, and my breath begins to saw in and out of my lungs as I sprint toward the ruined abbey. There's no shelter up here on the clifftop, nowhere to hide.

The museum and café will be locked, and if I tried to break in, an alarm would probably go off.

I don't want anyone to interrupt my twisted game with my husband.

I'll take refuge in the shadows of the abbey. If I can evade him and then circle back to the car, I might be able to drive off without him. That would be disappointing, but the shock on his smug, handsome face would almost be worth it.

"Abigail!"

He's coming after me. Whatever damage I managed to inflict has barely slowed him down.

I slip into the abbey, running beneath the skeletal arch of the ruined building. The moon is full overhead, far too large and bright on the cloudless night. The only advantage is the long shadows cast by the ancient stone pillars.

I duck into one of them and press my back against the pillar. Damp seeps through my thin nightgown, and I shiver at the chill. It's a shocking contrast to my flushed skin, and the dueling sensations only heighten my physical awareness of an encroaching threat.

He's almost completely silent, appearing like an otherworldly being in the moonlight. He isn't even bothering to run after me; his confidence in my helplessness sets my teeth on edge.

I hold my breath and wait for him to stroll past me. When he's twenty paces away, I sneak out of my shadow and try to duck into the adjacent section of the ruin.

"There you are." He says it with warm indulgence, but my heart leaps into my throat.

I start running again.

But he's always been faster than I am, his long strides

eating up the distance between us. My toes sink into the turf, and I put on a desperate burst of speed.

His weight slams into me from behind, and he tackles me to the ground, turning our bodies at the last moment so that he bears the brunt of the impact. I thrash out of his grasping arms, but he quickly rolls, pinning me with his weight.

Something silver glints in the moonlight, and I go still before my brain fully registers the wickedly sharp hunting knife. The cold blade kisses my throat, the lightest scrape that makes my skin crackle and spark.

"You're going to be my good little plaything now." He smirks, his perfect face demonically handsome.

"Fuck you!" My insult is ruined by the gag, but he seems to understand.

A slow smile sharpens his features. "My pretty captive is so proud and defiant. I will relish stripping you down to nothing. By dawn, you'll do anything to please me. You'll beg for my cock, and if you're good for me, I might fuck your sweet cunt instead of your mouth." He lowers his face to mine and brushes a kiss over the gag. "If you're bad, I'll claim your tight little ass."

I try to curse at him again, but all that elicits is a soft, delighted laugh. His eyes glint in the moonlight, cruelly beautiful.

My bound hands shove at his chest, but he easily grabs them and pins them above my head. His other hand holds the knife steady at my throat.

He cocks his head at me. "You don't seem to fully grasp your predicament. You still think you have a hope of fighting me off. But there's nothing you can do against me. You're so fragile. I could crush you without a second thought." His hands tighten around my wrists to the point of pain before releasing the pressure. "I won't damage you, but I will punish you if you don't behave."

The tip of the knife drags along the column of my throat, between my collarbones, and down to the lace neckline of my nightgown.

"Don't you dare," I try to warn him through the gag.

He shakes his head at me as though he's disappointed in me. "No growling, pet. I'd much rather hear you purring for me."

The knife hooks beneath the lace, nicking the delicate material. I go utterly still, primal survival instincts freezing my muscles as the blade nears my heart. My nightgown parts at the slightest pressure of the knife. He takes his time destroying it, watching me intently as he tears the silk in two. With each passing second, I fall deeper into his dark green eyes, as though I'm under some sort of spell.

Erotic tension crackles between us, heating the chilly, damp night air.

With one final tug, the hem of my nightgown tears. He makes quick work of severing the two thin straps at my shoulders, and the garment pools around my naked body.

"What shall I do with my pretty captive now?" he muses.

The knife drags along my collarbones, the lightest scrape without breaking my skin. He traces the line of my sternum, his glittering gaze fixing on my tight nipples.

"You like this," he observes. "My kinky little plaything. Are you wet for me?"

I shake my head in wild denial, even as I can feel the wetness of my arousal coating my inner thighs.

"Don't lie to me," he warns.

I shake my head again, this time in protest as he directs

the knife toward my pussy. I stop breathing when the cold flat of the blade kisses my clit.

"Even in the moonlight, I can see your cunt glistening for me," he admonishes.

He releases my wrists so that he can tweak my nipples, and pleasure arcs straight from the abused buds to my vulnerable clit. A garbled sound of carnal fear catches behind the gag, and he shushes me gently.

"I promised not to damage you," he soothes me. "But you have to learn to behave. Now, be very still for me when you come."

He says it as though my orgasm is a foregone conclusion, something he can command with a single word.

And he's earned every ounce of that arrogance.

With every sharp twist of my nipples, my body winds tighter for him. My clit pulses madly against the cold blade, a frigid reminder of his order for me to remain still. His control pushes me over the edge, and I whimper out my rigid orgasm.

"Good girl," he praises. "You like my knife?"

The blade finally, mercifully, leaves my clit, and he flips it in his gloved hand. The rounded hilt presses against my wet pussy, and I shake my head in denial. My pride can't bear it.

But I don't have any pride. Not when we're together like this. Dane strips away all barriers between us, and there's nothing that can keep me from him. He owns every part of me, and I love the fact that he will do absolutely anything to possess me completely, no matter how depraved or ruthless he has to be to get what he wants.

What we both want.

As the cold steel handle slides through my slick folds, tears gather at the corners of my eyes. I blink hard, releasing the last of my pride along with them. I part my legs, dropping them wider in invitation.

His white grin is dazzling in the moonlight.

"That's it. Submit."

The handle pumps in and out of me in short, shallow thrusts. The metal is cold and unyielding, and he's careful not to use bruising force. Slowly, he pushes it deep and tilts it, and I cry out when he finds the sensitive spot inside me.

"So beautiful," he says, rubbing my clit with his other hand. "I want another one. Come for me, Abigail. Come all over my knife."

The gag muffles my ecstatic scream, and my entire body shudders as pleasure rips through me, every bit as ruthless as he is. I ride the wave of ecstasy, greedily chasing every last drop of bliss.

When I go limp beneath him and gasp for breath, he finally withdraws the knife from my pussy. His eyes lock on mine as he lifts it to his mouth and licks the handle clean.

My inner muscles clench in an aftershock of my orgasm, and I shudder at the erotic sight of my husband tasting me on his knife.

"Did you get a chance to see where we are when you darted in here?" he asks, voice deep and rough with his own pleasure. He tips his head to the right. "I'm going to fuck you over that altar."

I can't tear my eyes from his to look in the direction he's indicating. I simply nod in eager agreement.

Yes.

His fingers tangle in my hair, and he uses it as a leash to guide me onto my hands and knees.

He doesn't have to command me to crawl for him. With

the knife still held loosely in his other hand, I'll remain obedient.

Even though I just came, my core clenches. I need him inside me, joining us in the most intimate way possible.

When I feel a cold stone slab beneath my hands, he tugs my hair.

"Wait."

He releases me, but I don't move an inch. He reaches into his back pocket and retrieves a coil of rope.

I lick my lips in anticipation, ready to be bound and at his mercy.

"I'm going to hurt you now," he warns, voice cool and unconcerned.

He revels in my suffering, just as I do.

He crouches beside me and grasps my ankle, applying pressure so that I have to roll onto my back. The rope winds around my calf before drawing tight enough to dig into muscle. Pain flares as he imprints a deep bruise on my flesh, but he doesn't hesitate; he simply continues to torment me with smooth, controlled movements. He wraps the length around my leg, and when it crisscrosses over my shin, I cry out.

The pain sparkles through me, and I surrender to it on a low groan. My body is tense from enduring it, and my ragged breaths hiss through my clenched teeth. But primal chemicals swirl through my system. I welcome everything he wants to do to me, craving more of this sweet, mind-numbing torment. I float on the pain even as my leg kicks out in wild rebellion.

"You can take it," he says. "Suffer for me."

He ties off the rope at my ankle and grabs my bound calf.

His fingers sink into my pillowed flesh, drawing a shout from my chest. My back arches, and I writhe on the altar beneath him.

He holds me fast, and his free hand presses down on my sternum to pin me to the cold stone.

He toys with me for a while, relishing my whimpers and muffled pleas.

When tears blur my vision, he releases me, only to repeat the sadistic binding on my opposite calf. My legs are free, but the thought of running away doesn't even cross my mind. I'm immobilized by the pain, and I revel in enduring it for him.

With each of my harsh cries, I bask in his praise.

"Good girl. You scream so beautifully."

His hands close around my waist, and he drags me upright.

"Kneel for me."

My shins rest on the stone altar, and the pressure on the crisscrossed ropes is almost unbearable. I throw my head back on a garbled shriek, but he has no mercy.

He gently grasps my shoulders, pushing me down so that my knees fold more sharply. A fresh wave of agony ripples through me as the rough hemp digs into my muscle.

"You will kneel," he says, stern and ruthless.

I heave in shuddering breaths and force my body to soften. I sink down until my butt touches my heels, and I can't suppress a high whine.

Two fingers curl beneath my chin, tipping my head back so that I stare up at him. He looms over me, dark and imposing. The moon frames him from behind, rendering him a shadowy silhouette.

My demon prince, my fallen angel.

"Stay," he commands.

I watch him with covetous eyes as he strips off his shirt and jeans, so that he's gloriously naked. The moonlight illuminates his corded, rippling muscles, and I'm in awe of his powerful perfection.

His hand trails down the length of my spine.

"Such a beautiful sacrifice to your dark god."

Pleasure shudders through me, and I arch into his touch.

He grasps my hips and gently directs me onto my back. The remains of the ancient altar are cool and damp beneath my bare skin, a delicious contrast to my desire-heated flesh.

His weight settles over me, and I part my thighs for him. His thick cock enters me in one brutal thrust, jarring my entire body to the edge of pain. I welcome its sweet sharpness. It makes this moment keen enough to cut, our twisted bond the most visceral thing I've ever experienced.

He drives into me in deep, demanding strokes, staking his claim over me. I loop my bound wrists over the back of his neck, pulling him closer. He nips at my lower lip where it pouts around the gag, heightening my pleasure with another little flare of pain.

My core tightens around him, and he grits his teeth in a feral snarl as he holds back his release.

He reaches between us and torments my nipples in the way I like best, dragging me to the edge with him.

"Abigail!" he roars out my name, and his hot seed pumps into me.

My own release claims me with vicious force, crashing through me in relentless waves. All I can do is moan and shake beneath him, clinging on as though he's my anchor to reality.

As we both come down from our high, he frees the

knotted cloth at the back of my head and tugs the gag free so that he can claim my lips in a branding kiss. I tip my head back and welcome him to ravage me.

I'll gladly allow Dane to ruin me again and again.

For the rest of our lives.

EPILOGUE

ABIGAIL

Six Months Later

"I have a surprise for you," Dane announces as soon as he comes home from work.

I bound up to him, throwing myself into his waiting arms. He doesn't admonish me for bruising the bouquet of flowers he's holding; my husband will never fail to embrace me.

"You didn't have to get me flowers."

He touches two fingers beneath my chin. "How many times do I have to say it, my sweet pet? I know I didn't have to. I wanted to. You will indulge me."

"So bossy." I brush a kiss over his lips, loving the little warning growl that vibrates into my mouth.

"The flowers aren't even your surprise," he rumbles,

placing the bouquet on the table in our entry hall. "I can do much better than that."

He reaches in his pocket and withdraws his wallet. I watch him in puzzlement when he pulls out a business card.

"This is for you."

Baffled, I take the card from him. The familiar logo of his plastic surgery practice is emblazoned on the front.

"Turn it over," he instructs.

On the back, there are three names: Dr. Dane Graham, Dr. Meadows Coatesworth, and Dr. Rachel Emory.

"Who's Dr. Emory?" I ask, even more confused.

"She's the new addition to our team. She starts next month."

My brow furrows. "You took on a new business partner? Why?"

Dane hasn't seemed stressed with his workload, but maybe he's been hiding some professional strain from me.

I don't like the idea of my husband hiding anything from me. We're supposed to lean on each other for support.

He smooths the tension from my jaw. "I'm taking two days a week away from the practice. I'm going to do pro bono work at the hospital."

My heart tugs toward his. "Really?"

He grins. "Really. I know you've never liked the nature of my career. I'll never be a good man, but I can do some good for you, Abigail. You're earning plenty from your gallery. I can take a step back at work and do something more meaningful with my life."

I bracket his beautiful face with both hands. "You're doing this for me?" I ask with awe.

He traces the outline of my parted lips. "Anything for you."

Then he blows out a soft sigh. "But it's for me too. Do you remember what you said to me on the night I first told you about my sister, Katie? You asked if her death is why I became a doctor—so I would have the power to fix people." He shakes his head. "I've never been that altruistic, but you make me want to be the man you see when you look at me. I will do everything in my power to be even half the man you deserve."

My eyes sting. "You do deserve me, Dane. I choose you. I will choose you every day for the rest of our lives because you've proven your love for me. But this..." I swallow down the lump forming in my throat. "I never expected this. I never would've asked it of you."

"I know you wouldn't. You accept me for all that I am, but I think it's time for me to adopt a little of your compassion too. Well, maybe not compassion. I don't know if I'm capable of truly feeling that. But I can at least help people."

I hold the business card to my heart like it's my most precious treasure. "Thank you. I love it. I love you."

He pulls me in for a deep, hungry kiss and carries me up the stairs to our bedroom. I stake my claim with my teeth, and he groans against me. He doesn't rebuke me for my ferocity; he seems to revel in it.

We tear at each other's clothes. Within a few frenzied minutes, I'm naked, and he's shirtless. Before I can remove his pants, he places his hands on my shoulders and breaks our kiss with a firm shove. My shocked gasp turns into a delighted giggle when my back hits the soft mattress.

I reach for him, but he shakes his head with a small, regretful smile. "Patience, little dove. I don't want to fight you today."

"I don't want that either." I relax, waiting for his next move.

After the touching revelations about his career changes, I want to be intimate with my husband. I don't feel like engaging in a power struggle with him right now. All I want is to hold him and have him hold me, but he has other, more wicked ideas.

He ducks into the closet for a moment, and when he comes back to me, he's holding a thick, black wand with a cord attached. At first, I think it's a vibrator, but it doesn't have a rubber head. Instead, he inserts a narrow, rounded plug into it that's attached to a long cable that ends in a metallic silver plate.

"What's that?" I ask, curious but also slightly anxious.

The little thrill of fear fizzes through me, fueling my mounting lust. I'm already wet and ready for him, and my inner muscles contract in anticipation of his cock.

"It's a violet wand," he replies, as though that explains everything.

"That doesn't answer my question."

"You'll see, my curious pet."

He tucks the metal plate beneath his waistband, so that it's secured against his hip.

I watch his strange actions, puzzled.

He drops a quick kiss on my forehead. "Trust me."

"I do."

His smug smile is a touch triumphant, and I grin at him in return.

Then he plugs the wand into the power socket beside the bed and sets it down on the nightstand.

His flashing eyes pin me like I'm a butterfly. "Are you ready?"

I lick my lips. "Ready for what?"

His smile turns cruel. "For whatever I want to do to you."

I lift my chin and open myself to him, allowing him to look straight into my soul. “Yes, Master.”

“Stay very still for me,” he commands, slowly lowering his hand toward my forearm.

My brows knit together in the long seconds it takes for him to bridge the gap between us. My entire body coils tight with anticipation, and every inch of my flesh comes alive for him. My skin seems to crackle and dance, but in the moment his fingers near my arm, real sparks fly.

I shout more in shock than pain when electricity arcs between us in a sizzling, tiny lighting strike. He closes the small space that separates us, and the moment his skin makes contact with mine, the spark disappears.

“What...” I gasp for breath. “I don’t understand.”

“As long as I’m touching you, we’re grounded to one another,” he explains. “But if there’s a small gap...”

He withdraws, and another sharp spark dances between us. It tingles and burns, and this time, he allows it to linger for several seconds. He splays his hand, and each finger becomes electric, stroking my arm with sizzling pleasure that rides the edge of pain.

I wriggle for a moment, overwhelmed by the strange, novel sensation.

His touch trails up my arm, raking hot lines along my sensitized skin.

“I feel it too,” he rumbles.

He pulls back, breaking the connection. I’m not sure if my short cry is one of relief or loss. His low chuckle rolls over me, and I arch into him like a cat seeking more attention.

“Greedy little thing,” he says, voice deep and indulgent. “Tell me you want more. Beg me to torment you.”

I pause. “But you said you feel it too. Does it hurt?”

"We'll suffer equally today, my queen."

He keeps me fixed in his burning stare as he slowly lowers his hand toward my breast, giving me time to refuse him.

I don't move a muscle; I simply keep my back arched for him and wait for the sparks. I'm his wife, his equal. Dane thrives on control, but he's willing to suffer for me.

His long fingers splay around the curve of my breast, and I'm quivering by the time the sparks jump. I shriek at the prickling burn on one of the most tender areas of my body, but I know Dane's fingertips are packed with sensitive nerve endings too. He'll experience the same sharp, sweet pain that's tormenting me.

The knowledge goes straight to my head, and I release a low moan of raw need and desire for him. The power I hold over this formidable man is like nothing I've ever known, and I crave more.

He toys with my other breast, circling my nipple but not quite making contact. It throbs in time with my heartbeat, an ache that's echoed in my pussy.

"Breathe, Abigail," he reminds me as I shudder beneath his cruelly erotic, electric touch.

I obey, drawing in a deep breath. When I exhale, he flicks only his forefinger, concentrating the sparks to a single, sizzling point that burns hotter than all five combined. The lightning dances directly over my nipple, and I scream at the shock of pain.

My core contracts, and an orgasm bursts through me with sudden, ruthless force.

His low laugh mingles with my ecstatic cry, and he flicks over my other nipple, prolonging my release.

"You are so perfect for me," he praises. "My beautiful wife."

He finally withdraws, severing the painfully sweet connection. I go limp, and all I can do is draw in panting breaths and stare up at my husband, taking in the hard planes of his muscular chest and his rippling abs. He looms over me, impossibly imposing, and I feel deliciously small in his shadow.

He grabs my hips, grounding us as he rolls onto his back. He easily arranges my body so that I'm straddling his face, my pussy only inches from his mouth.

"I'm going to release your hips, and then you're going to ride my face," he commands. "You control the current. You decide when and how I hurt you."

My core clenches, and my heart soars. He's still my dark god, my master, but he's handing over control. With each deviant order, he's proving to me how much he values and respects me.

I keep my gaze locked on his as I slowly lower my pussy toward his waiting mouth. He extends his tongue, creating a point for the spark to jump between us. My thighs begin to shake in anticipation of the spike of hot pain, but I boldly offer my pulsing clit.

I shriek at the lick of searing pain to my most sensitive spot, and I quickly press myself fully against his tongue to ground us again. The brief pain disappears entirely, without even a shadow of the burning sensation that'd shocked me. Now there's only the decadent pleasure of his mouth on me, his tongue toying with me in the way I like best.

My head drops back on a low moan, and I brace myself for another hit as I lift my hips. The sparks drag along my labia, crackling and dancing over my tender flesh. I begin to roll my hips, alternating between pressing my pussy into his face and pulling back for his cruel, clever tongue to torment me.

I don't know where the pain ends and pleasure begins. I want it all, and Dane gives me everything I demand of him. He takes his time feasting on me, and although I know he must be hurting, too, his low grunts are clear sounds of desire rather than pain.

When I can't take any more of the carnal onslaught, I finally ease back just enough for him to flick my clit one last time. I come apart on a scream, and he licks away the shock as I ride him through my orgasm.

My legs start shaking too violently to hold me upright, so he finally grabs my hips and lifts me off him.

I lay in a puddle on the bed while he quickly turns off the wand and strips out of his pants. His cock is thick and hard, ready to claim me after long denial.

I'm already soaked for him, but he grabs a bottle of lube from the nightstand and rubs a generous amount over his length.

"Get on your hands and knees." His voice is guttural, almost inhuman with the intensity of his lust for me.

I summon the last of my strength to get into position. He grabs my hips and settles behind me.

"I'm going to claim your tight little asshole, wife," he growls. "Every part of you belongs to me."

"Yes," I moan. "Take me."

His cockhead presses against my tight bud, and I try my best to relax for him.

"Push back against me," he rumbles, stroking his hand down my spine in a soothing motion as the pain begins to build.

I whimper but obey, breathing through the discomfort as his massive cock slowly penetrates me. A burning sensation sears my pleasure, but I crave more. I want to give myself to him in every way, and I'm determined to accept him.

One broad hand grasps my hip, anchoring me in place. His free hand snakes around me, and his clever fingers find my clit. It's still overly sensitive from my powerful, electrified orgasm, and another layer of stinging pain enhances my dark pleasure. He rubs me in sure, steady circles, coaxing my body to relax with his masterful touch.

Finally, his cockhead slips past my tight ring, and the worst of the discomfort eases. He continues to stimulate my clit as he pushes deeper, entering me in a slow slide.

A strangled cry tears from my chest. I'm almost unbearably full, my virgin asshole stretched around his massive cock.

"Good girl," he praises. "You're doing so well, my brave pet."

I press my face into the pillow and bite down for purchase. He starts to gently thrust into me in slow, short strokes. Forbidden ecstasy I've never known crackles through my body, made all the sweeter by the lingering pain and intense vulnerability of being claimed in every way.

Blissful tears stream down my cheeks, and I whimper with each of his careful thrusts.

"Does it hurt?" He grinds out the words, his control over his release tenuous.

"Yes, Master," I say, voice small. "But it feels so good. More."

"Beg." One harsh thrust. "Beg me to fuck your tight little ass."

"Please fuck me, Master," I pant. "Please."

Another punishing thrust. "Not good enough. Tell me what you want."

"Fuck my ass, Master. Claim me. Make me yours."

His only response is a primal snarl, and he increases the pressure on my clit as he drives deep inside me. Pain knifes through me as pleasure assails me. The dueling sensations push me over the edge.

"Dane!"

His name in my garbled shout is a trigger for him, and he bellows as he pumps into me. With one final thrust, he spills his seed inside me, marking me as his.

I'm owned, revered, and cherished. I'm his pet, his wife, and his queen.

And I intend to keep my dark god forever.

Thank you for reading Favorite Malady!
I hope you loved Dane and Abigail's dark romance.

Want more dark stalker romance from Julia Sykes?
Check out DUPLICITOUS!

She's on the run from the horrors of her past, but she doesn't know that she's being stalked by the most dangerous predator yet...

I've been obsessed with Karolina for years.

I've watched her. Waited for her. Protected her from the shadows.

Any man who dared to try to touch what's mine has been eliminated.

Now, I've finally become the man she'll want, not the monster I've hidden from her.

She only knows me as "Bones", her masked online confidante.

But it's time for the mask to come off, even if I can never reveal who I really am.

I'll insert myself into her life, and she'll finally be mine in every way.

I crave to torment and cherish her.

If she ever tries to run away, there's nowhere on Earth she can hide from me.

Because I know her darkest, most depraved secret: Karolina wants to be hunted.

ALSO BY JULIA SYKES

Stalker Romance

Favorite Malady: A Dark Stalker Romance

Duplicitous: A Dark Stalker Romance

The Captive Series

Sweet Captivity

Claiming My Sweet Captive

Stealing Beauty

Captive Ever After

Pretty Hostage

Wicked King

Ruthless Savior

Eternally His

Their Captive Bride

In Their Hands

In Their Power

In Their Hearts

The Impossible Series

Impossible

Savior

Rogue

Knight

Mentor

Master

King

A Decadent Christmas (An Impossible Series Christmas Special)

Czar

Crusader

Prey (An Impossible Series Short Story)

Highlander

Decadent Knights (An Impossible Series Short Story)

Centurion

Dex

Hero

Wedding Knight (An Impossible Series Short Story)

Valentines at Dusk (An Impossible Series Short Story)

Nice & Naughty (An Impossible Series Christmas Special)

Dark Lessons

Her Mafia Protectors Trilogy

Mafia Captive

The Daddy and The Dom

Theirs to Protect

Theirs Forever

Fallen Mafia Prince Trilogy

Fallen Prince

Stolen Princess

Fractured Kingdom

Made in the USA
Middletown, DE
03 March 2026